STARSTRUCK

JAY TROTT

Copyright © 2024 Jay Trott

All rights reserved.

ISBN: 979-8-3304-1580-9

TRUE NORTH

ACKNOWLEDGMENTS

Many thanks to Beth Trott for her invaluable assistance with preparing the manuscript.

The story and characters depicted in this book are fictitious. Any resemblance to real persons, living or dead, is purely coincidental.

I

The scene

SOME PEOPLE THINK Providence puts couples together for their own good. Other people think Providence is just a town in Rhode Island. Poor Jim didn't have an opinion.

It was a warm spring Friday night in June, 1998, and Jim and Bob were ambling out of the bar and down among the silent hulking cars of the parking lot, singing snatches of "A Wandering Minstrel, I" and other such incomparable nonsense, and enjoying themselves as only young men with few cares can do, when they spotted her sprawling in the driver's seat of an open yellow Jeep.

And we do mean sprawling. She was mostly in but not all the way in. Her body did not seem to know what all the way in was. Clearly she was incapacitated. This was almost as interesting as the fact that she appeared to be rather well put-together.

"Do you see what I see?" Bob said.

"'A star, a star, shining in the sky,'" Jim sang beerily.

"No, over there, you idiot. The Jeep."

"I'm not sure what I see. Is it real?"

"What are you, Bishop Berkeley? Of course it's real. The real question is what are we going to do about it."

"I don't see why we have to do anything about it. She appears to be having a nice nap."

"I guess your cold, hard heart is not moved by the sight of a damsel in distress. I'm going over there and see if she's all right."

"Help yourself," Jim said in the full bloom of ambivalence, since he doubted that his friend's intentions were entirely pure.

Bob meandered in the general direction of the Jeep but stopped when the mystery maiden raised herself up with a mighty effort and promptly slid out onto the pavement, whacking her head with a soft crack.

They looked at each other in amazement. She was lying on her side with her face flat on the still-warm blacktop, as if it were comforting somehow.

Bob went to her, bent over, and touched her tentatively with his fingertips. "Are you alright?"

"Bug off!" she barked in a disconcertingly commanding tone, waving him away with her free arm, or attempting to. A moment later she was sobbing. Then she mumbled something.

"I'm sorry, I didn't hear you."

"I said take me home!" she shouted blue-faced.

"Uhh, we'd be happy to. But we don't know where 'home' is."

"*Your* home, then," she said, waving her free hand again with a dramatic flourish. She tried to raise herself up. She collapsed with a moan. She passed out cold.

Bob looked at Jim with wide eyes. He shook his head no.

"Come on," he wheedled. "She told us to."

"We are not taking her home. That's kidnapping."

"No jury would convict you. At least not a jury of your peers. Besides, we have to do *something*. We can't just leave her lying here."

"Why not? We found her lying here."

"Are you crazy? A woman alone at night?"

"Oh yes, it's very dangerous here in the middle of Westport. She'll be lucky if Frederick and his band of merry rogues don't come along and abduct her. Oh—wait."

"Come on; be serious. She can't spend the night passed out on the bloody pavement."

"Okay, then why don't we put her back in the Jeep."

"You can see what that leads to. Or worse, what if she tries to drive? She could kill somebody."

"Then that's their fault for going out at night."

"Oh, come on. We have to do *something*."

"What did you have in mind, other than calling the police?"

"The police! A fair maiden asks you for help and you send her to jail. It will go on her record."

"Okay—an ambulance then."

"They'll charge her a thousand bucks for the ride. Look, why are you being so dense about this? She told us what she wanted us to do. She can have my room."

"That's crazy. She doesn't even know what she's saying." But then he had a brilliant idea. "All right, let's do it. Help me get her into my car."

"Really?"

"I thought that's what you wanted."

"It's not what *I* want. It's what *she* wants."

"Yeah, yeah; right. Let's just do it."

They could not get her to stand up. She was completely out. Finally Jim picked her up and carried her to his Acura coupe. Maneuvering a completely limp body into the back seat was trickier than he realized. They accidentally whacked her head on the door.

"Oww!" she groaned before returning to the shadowlands.

"Oops!" Bob said.

Jim looked at the completely limp body in the back seat of his car and suddenly had a very bad feeling. But it was too late. He couldn't drag her out and put her back on the pavement. Besides, he had a plan. He was going to drop her off at his parents' house. They were on the Cape for the weekend with his sister.

Somehow he managed to get a seatbelt around her. It was not easy—he had to reach under her, and she was not helping. Then he gave Bob his house key. "Go get the door unlocked so we can carry her in. I'm going over to that Coke machine for a bottle of water. She may need it."

"Oh—good idea," Bob said, feeling remarkably cooperative now that he had prevailed. "See you there."

Jim laughed inside. This was just what he wanted. The plan was to let Bob go on ahead and then whisk the fair maiden out of sight on the back roads. He took his time getting to the vending machine and making his choice. A wide grin spread over his face when he heard the black Porsche roar to a start and saw it zipping toward the exit. Then things got complicated. Bob stopped. Apparently he was waiting for him. Now what was he going to do?

He got into his car and drove up behind him reluctantly and blinked his lights. To his relief, Bob took off. He did not want to be in the lead. Now he just had to figure out a way to disengage himself. It wasn't going to be easy. He knew he couldn't outrun the Porsche. He tried the opposite strategy and slowed down to the speed limit, figuring this would be too much for the Impatient One to bear, but Bob must have had his eyes glued to the rear-view mirror because he slowed right down with him.

They crept northward for almost an hour. It was unbearable. What was he going to do? Finally they reached the road to

Bridgewater. Jim waited until Bob was already half-way through the intersection—and then peeled off abruptly toward the bridge. The Porsche zoomed on into the dark night.

"Yes!" he said with a fist pump. But then jubilation gave way to other feelings as he heard moaning from the back seat indicative of gyroscopic dislocation, probably caused by going too fast on winding country roads. Sure enough—there was the tell-tale sound. A few moments later there was the tell-tale smell.

He opened his window as he made his way to his old house, thinking how happy he was to see the familiar forsythia bushes. In fact he had never been quite so happy to see them. He drove up to the back door and commenced the formidable task of extracting the limp form from the back seat.

It was exhausting. He was trying to be polite, which precluded a surprising number of useful holds. He carried her to the porch and put her in a chair while he searched for the key under the flower pot. It wasn't there! He panicked. What was he going to do? Then he remembered. They put it under the bird-bath bowl now.

He unlocked the house, picked her up again and carried her upstairs to Grace's room (his sister). He did not know why he didn't take her to his own room. It just seemed like the right thing to do. He pulled back the covers and laid her on the bed. He slipped off her shoes and pulled up the sheet. It was hot—no need for a blanket.

Now for the first time Jim looked at her in the moonlight. He gulped. She was beautiful. There was a sweetness to her resting countenance that made it surprisingly hard to tear himself away.

It may not quite be accurate to say he was smitten. The circumstances were too strange. Besides, she had just thrown up in his car. But he was definitely affected. He made it halfway down the stairs but stopped and went back for another peek. Next time he made it all the way down before he went back. He wasn't sure why. She wasn't going anywhere. Not for a while anyway. Finally he had to throw himself out of the house.

He drove home with the sweetness of that face filling his soul. It was all he could think about. It was still foremost in his mind when he opened the door and greeted his friend with a blank look.

"Where is she?" Bob demanded.

"I took her to Bridgewater."

"You did *what*? I thought she was staying here. I was planning to sleep on the couch."

"Good idea. Then when she wakes up she can have us both arrested. This is better, believe me. She has her own space. She can take her time. There's nothing to accuse us of—or at least not *that*. You'll thank me when you sober up."

"I doubt it. I wanted to see her in the daylight. Didn't you think she looked a little like—oh, never mind. Like that would ever happen. In any case it will be fun to see how she reacts to waking up in a strange house with no one there and no idea of how she got there and no cell phone."

To tell the truth, Jim had not fully considered this. His parents' house was home to him, but not to the comatose girl. "She'll be fine," he said with more confidence than he actually felt. "She's in a safe place. There's a landline she can use."

They had a nightcap or two and chatted for a while and listened to music and eventually wandered off into irrelevance. Jim went to his room and fell into bed and thought he was about to fall asleep when all of a sudden he was wide awake. Wide, wide awake. It was two in the morning and it was two things. First it was that face in the moonlight. He thought he might be in love. But it was also Bob's comment. It was true. He had deposited a complete stranger at his parents' house. Hopefully she wouldn't burn the place down.

Okay, so that didn't seem very likely. But there were other possibilities. Bob was right. She would have absolutely no idea of how she got there. She was thirty miles upstate, as the crow flies. If she happened to walk outside she would find herself in the middle of nowhere with a lot of stars overhead and no neighbors in sight.

She did not have a car. She did not have a phone. He and Bob checked the Jeep, but they didn't see one or a purse or anything else of a personal nature. Even the glove compartment was clean. Would she panic if she woke up in a strange place and realized she didn't have any way of getting in touch with anyone? There was a landline in the kitchen, as he said, but would she even think to look for such an anachronism?

He did not know how she was going to react. The more he thought about it the more it rattled him. She seemed to have a bit of a temper from their little interaction in the parking lot. What if she decided to trash the house? His parents would love that. He would have a grand time trying to explain it.

But no, he would not believe it. She wouldn't do any such thing.

He had seen her sweet face in the moonlight. She looked like an angel. A dark-haired angel, but still. He went over the train of events again and again—finding her, Bob's transparency, falling out of the Jeep, getting her into the car, carrying her up to Grace's bed.

Carrying her to Grace's bed! His own little epithalamium. What ancient love poet ever had such an adventure? They wrote about other people's adventures. Most of it was bald-faced lies. She was no figment of someone's imagination, however. Jim could still feel the impression of her limp body in his arms.

He did not know whether to be afraid of what might happen or excited. He was a little bit of both. He lay there almost all night thinking about it before finally drifting off to sleep…

II

Face to face

Only to be awakened about an hour later by an obstreperous wren outside his window. The sun had not yet managed to raise its shaggy head above the wooded hills, but there was no way he could go back to sleep. He did not feel like sleeping. He wanted to go over there. He wanted to see what the heck was going on.

He threw on some clothes and crept out to the kitchen. Bob was snoring like a madman behind closed doors, which made him smile. It was a good time to make his escape. He wanted to go by himself for a variety of reasons and did not feel up to attempting any awkward explanations.

He rushed out to the car, forgetting about the little—accident—and was promptly greeted with a blast of frank pukery. Fortunately the spillage was largely contained to the right floor mat, which he removed and tossed onto the dewy grass. He found it necessary to wipe his fingertips on the grass as well. The smell did not go away, either on his fingers or in the car.

Jim was remarkably impatient to get to his destination. They say lovers are impatient. Was he a lover? Perhaps, but he was also nervous about the house. Nobody was on the road at that hour, so he opened up the throttle and went screaming recklessly around corners. There was a sigh of relief when he reached the house and saw that it was still standing. She hadn't burned it down after all.

He sat there for a few moments gazing at it in the early morning light. An angel was inside. Was she still asleep? He wanted to go in and see but he also did not want to go in. He was under such a wonderful spell at the moment just thinking about her being in the house that he did not want to risk having it broken. He knew it was foolish to entertain any romantic thoughts about his guest. He had never seen her before and knew nothing about her—except that she was light in his arms. Well, she was pretty light.

But this was a bond between them, this carrying her into the house, wasn't it? Of course the bond was all in his own mind. The chance of her remembering seemed rather small. On the other hand, maybe it was better if she did *not* remember. He did not know how she would feel about having been carried into the house and laid upon his sister's bed. She might not be inclined to thank him for such presumed gallantry.

They had rescued the fair maiden at her own request. They were perfectly justified from that point of view. But from another point of view their actions might not seem so pure. This was not just any maiden. She was highly attractive. Frankly, it would have been better for them if she had been highly plain. Also she had been highly incapacitated. There were rules about those sorts of things. He did not want to wind on the cover of the *Rolling Stone*.

He had not done anything untoward, except perhaps to violate the sanctity of the unconscious Diana with his eyes. But the amorous emotions he was now experiencing made him feel somewhat compromised. What was he going to say if she accused him? Was he going to try to pretend he didn't find her attractive and wasn't wondering if he was in love with her? Not "in love" like Marcel and Albertine but really in love? He didn't want to pretend. He really did want to be in love.

He sat there in his car gazing at the house with all these thoughts washing over him like the Bay of Fundi riptide. Finally he managed to rouse himself from his reverie and go in. He crept up the creaky stairs to Grace's room and felt a little jolt when he saw the exquisite stranger lying there on the bed with her back to him. Yes, she really was there. He hadn't just imagined it.

He stared. He couldn't help himself. He was looking at her back under a sheet and still he stared. It was like he couldn't move. Then he regained his composure and slinked down the carpeted stairs to the living room. He grabbed *As You Like It* off the shelf and lay down on the couch and managed to get to the "time hurries withal" scene before falling into a deep sleep, full of strange dreams in which the Forest of Arden was somehow mixed up with the familiar Connecticut woods.

A couple of hours later he was jolted awake by sunlight pouring in the porch windows. He remembered the girl in his sister's room. Was she still sleeping? He glanced at the clock on the mantle—it was almost nine. What should he do? He thought about tip-toeing upstairs for another bed check, but this seemed excessive. She was still there. Where else would she be?

Now he started to become anxious about the time. He had a guest at home and had to get the apparition back to Westport somehow. He couldn't see himself trying to wake her. He didn't know how she would react. Then he had an idea. Why not make some breakfast? He wasn't just thinking about being a good host, although he was mostly thinking about this; he was also hoping the smell of bacon and coffee would rouse her from her slumbers.

Besides, he felt at peace in the kitchen. He liked to cook and was pretty good at it. He started a pot of coffee and put some bacon in a frying pan and whipped up some frozen orange juice into a colorful froth and fetched some watermelon from the refrigerator. It was calming to have things to do. He was enjoying himself, almost, or pretending to. But then the bacon was done and the coffee was perked and the toast toasted and the watermelon sliced—and still there was no sign of his supernal guest.

Oh, well. He decided he might as well make himself some eggs. He was concentrating on not breaking the yolks as he dropped them into the cast iron pan, humming *misterioso* to himself from *La Traviata*, when suddenly he became aware of a Presence in the doorway. He did not dare to look at her but he knew she was there.

"Hello?" she said, sounding puzzled and a little strained.

"Oh! Good morning!" he replied in his sunniest faux manner. "Didn't see you there."

It was true in a literal sense anyway.

"I guess this sounds a little strange, but do I know you?" she said in a tone that was more puzzled than accusative.

"Sort of. I mean, no—not really. We met last night. Not 'met,' exactly. That's probably not the right word. You were—well—you don't remember?" He was nudging the eggs around in the pan and glaring at them while he babbled.

"I don't remember a thing. But you are—?"

"My name happens to be Jim Wilmot. Well, not 'happens.' It *is* Jim Wilmot. If that makes any sense. Which it doesn't. Obviously."

"Jim Wilmot. Okay. Doesn't ring a bell. But you certainly seem harmless. By the way, where am I?"

"This is my parents' house. I also have my own house," he added, although it occurred to him that this didn't necessarily convey the particular form reassurance he was trying to give without more explanation.

"I'm glad to hear it," she said, still looking puzzled. "By the way, my head really hurts. I don't suppose you have any aspirin."

"I don't, but I think my mother does," he said, scrounging the cabinets for the universal cure. He waited while she sat down tentatively in the breakfast nook and then handed her the bottle and a glass of ice water.

"Thanks," she said, opening the bottle and washing down some white pills. She sat for a moment with her eyes closed and the cold glass pushed against the center of her forehead. Then she opened one of them and squinted sideways at him. "So I hate to be so dense, but how did I get here? Was there a party or something?"

Jim gulped. "Not really. To tell you the truth, I—uhh—brought you here. But don't worry. I stayed at my own house with my friend. I just figured you would probably appreciate the privacy."

"Oh—right. Privacy. Good thinking. But how did we meet? I don't remember it at all."

"Well, we didn't really meet. We sort of—found you."

"*Found* me?"

"Yes. We happened to see you in the parking lot. You know, at the restaurant. You were—let's just say not in the best condition for driving. You were *trying* to drive. But it wasn't working out. In fact you fell out of your Jeep."

He wasn't trying to be funny. It just came out that way. She wasn't laughing.

"So is that how I got this?" she said, touching the glass to the painful-looking bump on her exquisitely-shaped head.

"Yes. You sort of landed on the pavement."

"Yikes! Unfortunately this is starting to sound familiar. I do remember the smell of pavement. It doesn't go well with scotch. But I don't quite get how I wound up here. Wherever 'here' is."

"'Here' is Bridgewater. It's a town. In Connecticut. Mia Farrow lives here. Diane Sawyer. Also, my parents. In fact this is their house. But I already told you that. Anyway, you told us to take you home. So this is where I brought you."

"I think I probably meant *my* home."

"We didn't know where that was. So then you said 'take me to your home.' You were quite definite about it. We figured it was better than calling the police." (He played his trump card.)

"The police! Why would you call them?"

"Well, you were—uhh—incapacitated. We didn't know what

else to do. We couldn't leave you lying on the pavement in the middle of the night. Not that the night actually has a middle. That's just a figure of speech. Anyway, it occurred to me that you could stay here, since my parents are away. It seemed like a good idea at the time. Maybe not."

"It's better than calling the police, that's for sure. I guess I should thank you," she said, softening a little.

"Not at all. Happy to do it. How about some breakfast?"

"Oh God, I couldn't. Maybe just a piece of dry toast."

Which was dutifully supplied. He sat down across from her. Now for the first time he really looked at her in the daylight. He had never seen anything so beautiful in his life. She had a light complexion and very dark, curly hair. But it was the shining dark eyes that made perhaps the most impact. He kept his own eyes to himself for fear of being upended. He felt like he was being swallowed up by her beauty, sucked into her aura.

There was an awkward silence, except for the occasional "crunch." He couldn't think of anything brilliant to say. And he was determined not to say anything that wasn't brilliant. On the other hand maybe it was better not to say anything at all. He seemed to have mollified her with his explanation, which was the thing he was worried about the most. Why risk making trouble for himself by saying more when nothing more needed to be said?

She nibbled her toast and drank some more water. She really drank it. She was not dainty, in spite of her elfin looks. Then she seemed to be thinking about something. She looked up at him with a wry smile of unknown significance.

"So—what's your story? Why are you such a nice guy to take me here and let me have your parents' house all to myself?"

"I don't know that I have a story. I mean, everybody has a story, I suppose. It would be silly to say they don't." He didn't know what he was saying. He was disoriented. Every time he looked at her his mind went blank.

"Oh come now. You must have some kind of story. You don't run into many Good Samaritans these days, that's for sure."

Then he realized what this line of questioning was all about and the reason for the sly smile. She was accusing him of finding her attractive. But what an accusation! Anybody would. She was the most ridiculously attractive thing he had ever seen in his life. It was like a force field dragging him over the table. But of course he had no idea whether she found *him* attractive. And in that case it seemed better to pretend not to understand her.

"It wasn't a big deal. It's on the way home. I just took a little detour to drop you off. Anybody would have done it."

"'Anybody.' I see what you mean," she said with a teasing laugh. "Anyone from my very large fan base would have been glad to do the same thing you did."

Now it was his turn to laugh, although he didn't know why. "We didn't think we could just leave you there. I mean in the—well—condition you were in. And to tell you the truth, I did feel a little apprehensive about how you would react to being kidnapped by a couple of strange guys. I know how it looks. But I promise you we were just trying to help."

"No—you don't have to promise. I believe you. I know you were trying to help. By the way, I'm Karen McNamera," she said, looking at him intently as she offered him an icy hand.

"Pleased to meet you. I'm—oh, I already told you that."

"So are you in the habit of bringing complete strangers to your parents' house and putting them to bed, or am I an exception?"

"There's a first time for everything. We did try to find out who you were, but there was no purse or wallet or even a cell phone that we could see. We do have your keys, which are in my car. But we weren't particularly worried. You didn't seem dangerous."

"You'd be surprised. Or maybe you wouldn't. By the way—speaking of keys—where is my Jeep?"

"It's still in the parking lot at the restaurant."

"The parking lot. And how far away is that?"

"Oh, it's about an hour from here, if there's not too much traffic."

"An hour! Oh my God. I have an eleven o'clock appointment."

"I'd be happy to drive you down there."

"Really? Are you sure?"

"Not a problem. I make that drive all the time. Every day in fact. It's the least I can do to make up for dragging you all the way up here against your will. Well, not really against your will—but you know what I mean. Or at least I hope you do."

"I think I do. And if you don't mind, that would be very much appreciated. And I mean *very* much."

"Of course. I was planning on it. Obviously you don't have any other way to get there."

She had a puzzled look on her face, but he was dead serious. He was planning to do it all along and didn't mind doing it. In fact he was glad to do it if it made her misgivings go away. She was starting to make him nervous with all her strange questions. He wanted to demonstrate good faith, even if it required a heroic sacrifice of an hour or two. Besides, who wouldn't want to do something for her?

She sat there for a moment pondering him. What was she thinking? Could she possibly be interested in him? She seemed amazed by his willingness to go out of his way—twice—although to him it wasn't much. He wasn't lying when he said he would have done it for anyone. Okay, so maybe he was doing it a little more gladly in this instance, but he liked helping people. And he liked to drive on sunny summer mornings.

Once again he couldn't think of anything to say. The silence went on until it became uncomfortable. Was she expecting *him* to say something? What could he say? This was one case where he wished he were more like Bob. He could not bring himself to banter with her, as much as he wanted to. He did not know if she had any interest in bantering. He was afraid to find out that she didn't. All he could do was keep his eyes on his rapidly diminishing eggs and try not to make a fool of himself.

Finally she spoke up.

"So, not to be pushy, but do you mind if I take you up on that kind offer of yours?"

He blinked. "Of course not. You mean now?"

"Actually, yes. Sorry. I absolutely cannot be late for that meeting. That would not be good, believe me."

"No problem. I need to get back to my house guest anyway."

Jim laughed at himself. What an idiot. She wasn't gazing at him; she was waiting for him to get moving. He thought he detected a little of the imperious tone from the night before, almost a sense of entitlement. To tell the truth he was inclined to be offended. It wasn't like he needed to be nudged to do the right thing—he was ready and willing to do it. On the other hand he was the cause of the delay. He was sitting there eating his eggs and thinking dreamy thoughts while she was expecting something else entirely.

A wall had gone up, it seemed from her tone, and he tried to convince himself he was glad. He couldn't deny he wanted her to smile on him. She *was* smiling, but it was a different kind of smile from the one he wanted. Oh, well. It was probably better in the end. The best outcome of the morning was for him to take her back to Westport and put the whole debacle behind him.

She made a trip to the bathroom and they headed out to the car. It was starting to warm up. The big June sun was beating down on the poor little Acura. For a moment he thought about opening the door for her, like his father did for his mother, but then he laughed at himself. People don't do that anymore. Chivalry is dead, and it was people like her who killed it, he thought to himself, without actually asking her opinion. He climbed in and then she climbed in.

"Do you mind closing the windows and turning on the AC?" she said in the same semi-commanding tone, her sweetness not fully covering the steel.

"Sure," he said with raised eyebrows.

It didn't take long.

"What is that smell?" she said.

"Well, let's just say there was a little contretemps in the back seat last night on the way here."

"Contra-what?" She looked at him. He had a very slight smile on his face that he was trying to conceal. "On second thought, don't tell me. I guess it's okay to have the windows open."

Jim reveled in this triumph, small as it was. What was the big deal about the windows? But then he didn't want to revel. He had the upper hand but didn't really want it. He didn't *want* her to feel embarrassed about him having incriminating evidence against her in his car. He wanted her to feel completely comfortable with him.

In short, he wanted her to be his friend. It didn't seem to be in the cards, however. There they were on the road together for a long drive, completely alone, but Orlando's weights were hanging on his tongue. It wasn't that his mind was blank. Oh, no; he was full of entertaining things to say. But he was not sure if he *should* say them—or if they were sufficiently entertaining for the goddess at his side. One must be careful when making an oblation to Athena. *She* wasn't saying anything either. She was as silent as the proverbial stone as they tooled along green country roads. Had he embarrassed her? Would embarrassment turn into anger?

Now he regretted his little triumphant smile. He didn't mean to smile. He wasn't laughing at her. He was trying to be polite, show restraint. To tell the truth he didn't care if she had thrown up in his car. She could throw up again if it made her feel better. He was fine with it. Throw up all you want! Should he try to apologize? He felt an urge to. He wanted to do anything to make her happy. But would an apology have that effect? Or would it make it worse by bringing up the very thing that was causing her pain?

After all, he didn't know what to apologize for. To begin with, what he said was true. It's silly to apologize for telling the truth, like those English people who are always going around saying "sorry." Second, he couldn't apologize for the little smile he'd had on his face because that would imply he was laughing at her, which was exactly what he did not want her to think. No, it seemed better to say nothing at all in that awkward moment than to make things worse by awkwardly trying to smooth them over.

They reached the highway, heading south into the sun, and she broke the unpleasant silence to ask him if he happened to have any sunglasses. Her headache was killing her in the glare. He offered her a pair from the glove compartment. They were his sister's. She put them on, and then she looked even more unapproachable.

The silence was becoming unbearable for him, so he flicked on the classical station. It was a Mozart piano concerto.

"You like this sort of thing?" she said with a smile, but still looking straight ahead.

"I must confess I do."

"Interesting."

Interesting! Well, that was something. It could have been worse. He wanted to try to get her to expand on this word, but modesty and caution prevailed. He was constitutionally incapable of fishing for compliments with someone like her. He was afraid of catching something he didn't want. After all, the word *interesting* can have many connotations, although in this case he thought he noticed something in her tone. She seemed impressed.

But this impression could be misleading. He could not read her. He was usually fairly good at reading people, but in this case it was like they were having conversations on two different planes that did not intersect. She seemed to be reading deep significance into everything he said, much more than he intended. Was it because she suspected him of liking her? He didn't mind being suspected if such liking was welcome. In fact at that moment there was nothing he wanted more than for her to welcome a little liking on his side. But he didn't have the courage to try to find out.

While he was pondering these things, she spoke up again. "So don't just sit there. Tell me something about yourself."

"What would you like me to tell?"

"Well, like what do you do?"

"I'm a copywriter. No, I don't do copyrights. I'm a writer who writes something called 'copy.' Whatever that is."

"I know exactly what it is. I'm sort of in that business myself. So did you go to school for that?"

"Well, I went to Yale. I don't remember them having a copywriting department."

"You went to Yale! I'm impressed. So what did you study there, if not copywriting?"

"English lit, believe it or not."

"I do believe it. I noticed *As You Like It* on your coffee table. That's not something you see every day."

"'I can suck melancholy out of a song as a weasel sucks eggs,'" Jim recited with as much flourish as he could muster.

"Ha! Jaques. I know it well. In fact you'd be surprised how well. Or maybe you wouldn't."

She seemed to expect him to say something. He didn't know what to say. He could have raved about the play, which was his favorite Shakespeare comedy, along with *Midsummer Night's Dream*, if he thought raving was what she wanted; but he didn't know what she wanted.

"How about you? Where did you go to school?"

"Iowa State," she said forthrightly. "Theater program. But you probably guessed that."

"That would be quite a guess," he said with a laugh. "Although you do look like someone who could be in the theater."

He blushed when he realized how this probably sounded. She didn't seem to mind.

"Thank you. But not anymore, unfortunately. I loved doing plays, but things change."

"Indeed they do," he said wisely.

Now for the first time she actually looked at him through Grace's sunglasses. There was that puzzling smile again, this time accompanied by, it seemed to him, a puzzled look, or perhaps an inquiring look. He tried to follow up his sage comment with something even sager, and failed. It was the kind of comment that tags a conversation. To speak before spoken to was to descend from the heights.

Jim was determined not to descend. For the first time since she had appeared in his mother's kitchen he felt they had reached a rapprochement. There was a connection between them of some kind over Shakespeare and theater and a new comfort level in the car in spite of the redolence, at least for him. He had opened up and so had she. It didn't seem like she was mad at him for bringing up last night. She was quite friendly. Inscrutable, but friendly.

Apparently he had scored with the Yale thing. Personally, he had his doubts about the prickly campus environment there and the quality of the education and the fact that everyone seemed to get A's no matter how insufferably boring or sycophantic they were or how many seminars they ruined with their interminable droning. But he did not bother to share these feelings with her. *She* thought it was impressive, and that was certainly good enough for him.

As much as he found her attractive, he was almost content to let things end on that high note. The ice had been broken. She was impressed by his education and had said so. Apparently they agreed in a love of Shakespeare. If she was angry with him and Bob for kidnapping her, she didn't let on. And that was the thing he feared the most. They'd had a pleasant conversation. Jim decided not to spoil it by overtrying. Plus he lacked the courage.

In any case there was no time to try to do anything more because they were almost at their destination. A few minutes later they were turning into the parking lot. Jim drove over to the Jeep and pulled in beside it. He was relieved to see that there did not seem to be any damage from having been left open overnight.

Karen surprised him by not getting out right away. "So I guess this is it," she said cryptically.

"I guess so. Oh! You mean the keys." He pulled them out of the console for her.

"Actually that wasn't what I had in mind. I was wondering if was there something you wanted to say to me."

Jim's mind was racing. "I guess I really should apologize for making you late for your meeting."

She laughed. "No, that isn't it. And in any case I'm right on time. Besides, you have nothing to apologize for. You've been a perfect gentleman. Actually you probably saved my life, now that I think about it."

"I don't know about that. I'm sure someone else would have come along eventually."

"Not someone like you. Well, anyway, thanks for not calling the police. That would have been a complete disaster. You have no idea. Or do you?" She looked at him again through his sister's sunglasses, almost challenging him, he thought.

"Of course. Nobody wants a run-in with the police. Fortunately I haven't had any—yet."

She looked at him for a moment with that indecipherable smile. "I'm not quite sure what to make of you. I can't tell if you're pretending to be the most gallant guy in the world or if this is what you really are like. But I guess it doesn't matter. This has been almost fun, in a weird way. A little break from the usual routine and the usual people. Even my headache went away."

"I'm glad. It must be the wonder drug."

"Or something. Well—goodbye," she said, offering him her dainty hand. "Thanks for everything."

"I didn't really do anything, but you are very welcome."

As she turned to get out of the car she bumped the visor, causing a few of his business cards to come fluttering down. She picked one up.

"Mind if I keep this?"

"Not at all."

"Maybe we'll see each other again some time."

"Maybe," he said, although he couldn't imagine how.

She got out and headed for her Jeep, apparently forgetting about Grace's sunglasses. He didn't bother to remind her. He drove off with his head spinning, trying not to look in the rear-view mirror, like Lot's wife. All in all, he felt pretty good about the morning. Sure, he was wasting two hours of a perfect summer day in the car, but he didn't mind. She made the burden seem light.

Why did she seem so interested in taking one of his cards? This was a tantalizing question. But of course he didn't have any idea. Maybe she was just curious. Maybe she was thinking about trying to do something to thank him. He didn't want to be thanked in any tangible way. It would diminish his heroic disinterestedness.

Or…was she *possibly* thinking of something else? Was she perhaps interested in him? For a moment his spirits rose. Then he tumbled back down to earth. It was highly unlikely. First of all, he knew things about her that she probably very much wanted to forget—like the way they found her and throwing up in his car. People don't like to be reminded of things like that. And besides, who was he kidding? He was no match for someone like her.

She was like the storied red rose in the walled garden—enticing and entirely unapproachable to a would-be poetic soul like himself. It was extremely unlikely that he would ever hear from her again.

III

More hilarity than was called for

WELL, THAT WAS strange. Jim went back to Bridgewater and covered his tracks by cleaning up the kitchen and making Grace's bed with fresh linen. He tossed the soiled sheets in the empty washer and thought about doing the wash, but he knew he had to get home.

"Where have *you* been?" Bob demanded as he eased through the screen door with a couple cups of coffee and a bag of doughnuts he had picked up as a peace offering.

"Westport," Jim confessed.

"Westport! You dog. You didn't."

"She had to get back for an important meeting."

"Yeah, right—'important meeting.' She sure didn't seem to be worried about any important meeting last night."

"All I know is what she told me. She became kind of agitated when she realized what time it was. I figured I might as well drive her down there and get it over with. You were still asleep."

"You could have woken me up. That would have been the decent thing to do."

"This from the guy who refuses to get up before noon. Besides, you were snoring so peacefully."

"Well, it's too bad. I really wanted to see what she looked like in the daylight."

"I bet you did."

"No, not that. Didn't you think she sort of looked like—oh, forget about it. That's crazy."

"Look at it this way. We got her back down there without further incident, which is far better than we deserved. You're really not supposed to take advantage of girls who are incapacitated. It's frowned upon these days."

"I suppose you're right. No way of knowing how someone like that might react. Still, I would have liked to see her again."

"Well, maybe you'll get your chance when she sues us."

"That's not going to happen. But what are we doing today, now that 'today' is already half over?"

"Whatever you want," Jim said, feeling even more obliging than usual. "You're the guest. What do you want to do?"

"How about some tennis? That is, of course, if you don't mind having your butt kicked. Which, by the way, you deserve."

"Tennis it is. Let's hope the courts aren't too crowded."

"Is Erin coming over?"

"Not that I know of."

"What! I need my dose of Erin, especially since you deprived me of the other one. Let's see if she wants to go out to dinner."

"Well, to tell you the truth I haven't heard from her in a while."

"What are you talking about? Give me the stupid phone."

Jim felt trapped. He wanted to do something to make up for his trickery, but there was a *reason* why he had not heard from Erin. They'd had "a bit of a falling out," as Indy would say.

Jim and Erin had known each other for three years. Everyone thought they were going to get married when Erin finished school. Everyone except Jim. He was of two minds. On one hand, a little voice told him they might be made for each other, as the hackneyed phrase goes. In fact this was the strange message he thought he received the very first time he saw her at the restaurant in Kent where she was waitressing for the summer. He remembered his mind going into something like a wormhole. It was as if reality were being physically altered in order to single her out in the crowd, which experience was striking because nothing like it had ever happened to him before.

Jim did not attempt to deny the strange phenomenon. How could he? It was too overpowering. It left a definite mark on his psyche. But he was skeptical about the implications. Was there really such a thing as love at first sight? It didn't make much sense from a scientific point of view. How could he know that this stranger was the right girl for him when he didn't even know who she was and had never seen her before? There did not seem to be any rational explanation for the strange thing that had happened, other than her attractiveness and an overactive imagination.

Then he saw her again at a concert on the green about a month later. He was surprised to learn that his parents and her parents had recently become friends. It seems the O'Connells had moved to town about a year ago and found themselves in the same church.

The two couples were very compatible and at this point were well on their way to becoming almost inseparable, with dinner parties and cookouts at each other's houses at decreasing intervals.

It was clear she remembered him from the restaurant. She was also clearly interested in him. After that they just seemed to drift together. Sometimes Jim would ask her to go to a play or a concert or a movie when she was home from school. Sometimes she would engineer things so she could see him. She was abetted in these efforts by Jim's mother, who adored her and was almost as eager to see them get married as Erin was herself.

In short, something told Jim she was the one, but something also told him to resist her steady charms. He was looking for a high-spirited heroine of the type you see in Ariosto or Shakespeare. That was not Erin. She was certainly pretty. She was earnest and affectionate. She clearly loved him. But there were no sparks between them like Beatrice and Benedict. It all seemed too easy. He could be very dull with Erin and she did not care one bit.

Three "Fs" were important to her: faith, family, and friends. She made no attempt to pretend otherwise. This sincerity was certainly admirable to anyone with moral taste, of which Jim was not completely incapable, but it was not exactly intoxicating. Also Erin did not try to hide how she felt about him. It was not in her nature to be coy. The more she made herself available, the more he pushed her away. He was aware of the irony, of the ridiculous psychological quirk, probably of ignoble origins, but there did not seem to be anything he could do about it.

Three years went by in this smoldering way without ever breaking out into open flame. It was a strange romance with no kisses. Sometimes they would hold hands when they were ice skating or taking a walk in the woods, but they seemed more like brother and sister than lovers. Or at least that's what they were to Jim. He knew his own ambivalence, even if she didn't seem to have any. He respected and liked her too much to take advantage of her good nature when he himself was not sure how he felt.

The thing was he enjoyed being with Erin. He was comfortable with her—probably more comfortable than he was with any other female in the world, including Grace. He knew she was a good person with a good heart. This did not have to be explained or demonstrated to him. Somehow he just knew it. In fact he knew she was a better person than he was, which he was not ashamed to admit to himself, or to anyone else for that matter. He was quite sure she would make a wonderful wife and mother, which was important to him, as he acknowledged to himself in his occasional thoughtful moments; which were very occasional. He just did not know if she was the right person for him.

Sometimes he dated other girls when she was away for long periods at school. He did not feel he was being unfaithful to her because, after all, they did not have that kind of relationship. By the way, those other girls were not exactly Rosalinds or Elizabeth Bennets either. If such amazing creatures actually existed—witty, vivacious, pretty, as well as trustworthy and tenderhearted and virtuous and kind—they did not seem to be very easy to find.

Then came the blow-up on the night of her graduation party. The salient problem, from Jim's point of view, was the unfair burden of expectations. It seemed like in everyone's mind he and Erin were an item. This included not only their families but also all of their friends. They had been "together" for three years. The consensus was that they would get married as soon as she finished school. Jim did not have to guess this was what people were thinking. He overheard it in various conversations usually involving his mother or sister, but even friends like Bob and Arthur.

But the thing was that no one, in all of this time, had consulted him about this almighty consensus. What if he did not think of Erin that way? What if they were just friends? Did he really have to be in love with her just to spend some time with her? They had never done the kinds of things lovers do. He was very careful about that. He avoided anything that would lead to entanglement. So why did everyone assume they were going to get married?

There was a party at her house, and he went with a giant chip on his shoulder, a Sequoia-sized chip. It seemed like everyone was just waiting for the graduation for them to get married. Well, the graduation was over—and what was he supposed to do now? Propose? What if he wasn't ready to propose? What if he needed more time to think about it? He didn't know what he wanted, to be honest. He loved Erin and he did not love her. He wanted to lose himself in her forever and he also wanted to run away and never see her again, because seeing her made him feel indentured.

Anyway, there they were at the party, Erin and himself and their families and a lot of their friends, and he happened to catch his mother and Erin's mother smiling at him at one point in a certain suggestive way. This made him angry. They were trying to push him into something. They had no right to push him. It was his happiness that was involved, not theirs. There was just enough Yankee blood in him to rebel at the tyranny of such expectations. Don't tread on me! In his mind he was looking out for Erin's best interests as well as his own. How happy could she be being married to someone who did not know if he loved her in *that way*? It would only make her miserable, with her tender heart.

Then the interminable party was over and everyone had gone home and Erin and Jim were sitting on the porch swing under the stars. It was the first time they had been alone, and Jim was feeling extremely self-conscious. He perceived it as a moment when he might be expected to say something to the point. Unfortunately this caused him to do the opposite.

"So it looks like you're going to be a nurse."

"I guess so," she said with a sigh.

"You could have been a doctor."

"True, except for a little thing called organic chemistry. Plus I didn't really want to go into debt."

"I'm sure your father would have helped you."

"Probably, but I can't do that to them. They're going to need their money for retirement. Besides, I don't know if I would want to be a doctor. They're on call 24/7 and have a lot of pressures people don't know about. Most of the doctors we work with seem pretty unhappy about the way things are going right now."

"They're compensated rather well," he said sardonically.

"I don't know. It depends on your point of view. They have huge liability fees. The insurance companies tell them who they can see and what they can and can't do. They're constantly afraid of being sued, which is one reason for all the tests they order, and then they feel guilty about it because so many patients can't afford them. And they have to be businessmen and administrators in addition to being doctors. No, you would have to really *want* to be a doctor to put up with all that. It would have to be your calling."

"Wait a minute. Are you saying doctors don't make good money?" he scoffed.

"No, I'm saying money isn't everything."

Jim did not mean to imply that money was everything. He was stung by this comment. He overreacted. "But don't you think being a nurse is kind of degrading?"

"*Degrading*? Why?"

"Bedpans and soiled sheets and silly uniforms and all that."

"Nurses help people. That's what I like about it."

"I thought they sat around the nursing station reading romance novels."

"I guess some do. But most of the nurses I've worked with are very dedicated and take it seriously. Like my aunt."

"I don't see how they could. You'd almost have to be not very bright to take that sort of thing seriously."

He did not mean this the way it came out. Not surprisingly, Erin was offended.

"So now you're saying I'm not very bright. I guess all the 'bright' people become copywriters."

"Well, you have to admit it's a little more interesting than wiping people's bottoms all day long."

"I don't have to admit any such thing," she said, turning on him with a fury he had never seen before. "Besides, what are you doing for the world that gives you the right to be so condescending? Encouraging people to buy things they don't need and can't afford? Well, good for you. I hope it gets you into a country club and a nice sports car. And by the way—thanks for ruining my party."

With that she got up and stormed into the house, slamming the screen door behind her. Jim was absolutely mortified. He hoped her parents hadn't overheard this outburst. They were still in the kitchen cleaning up. He slinked off to his car feeling like dirt—no, lower than dirt. It was the first time Erin had ever spoken sharply to him. Literally. It was shocking.

Then again, he deserved it. What was he thinking? He could not believe what he had just said. He wanted to blame it on the beer, but it was more. It seems he had been harboring certain reservations about Erin and her profession which had chosen this particular moment to make their way out into the open. For the first time he realized that nursing was not something he held in high esteem. It was not on the top of the totem pole of things people like him might want to do with their lives. In fact he realized he was kind of a snob when it came to nurses.

He knew Erin must absolutely hate him after what he had said. He would hate himself if he were she. He didn't exactly mean it in the way it sounded. He was trying to say that people who could find contentment in changing bed pans could not be very bright in the sense of taking delight in the intellectual side of life. To him, at least, the act itself was not something that was capable of engaging the mind. But it *sounded* like he was saying that nurses themselves weren't very bright. And he couldn't blame Erin for being angry about that. He felt terrible. He thought about calling her right away and apologizing profusely. But he didn't. Why? Because in another sense it was a manifestation of the ambivalence he was feeling about the whole marriage thing. He did not look down on nurses, necessarily, but he wasn't sure he wanted to marry one.

Jim hated the thought of Erin being angry with him. He coveted her good opinion. Besides, he did have feelings of some kind for her. He was very much aware of it. But the thought crossed his mind that maybe it was *better* for her to be angry, as bad as it made him feel; better in the long run—for her. He still wasn't sure about marrying her. And in that case maybe it was better to allow her to *stay* angry with him so she could make a clean break in her mind and get on with her undoubtedly happy life.

He let a day go by without calling her. Then another went by, and then another. Before he knew it, there was a whole armada of negligent days standing between him and making a call. And the longer he put it off, the easier it became not to call.

This had happened over a month ago. There had not been any word from Erin since then. She must *really* be angry. He felt terrible about it—but was it a good thing after all? Was it for the best for both of them? He certainly did not want to string her along. He thought too much of her for that. If he could not make up his mind, then maybe it was better for her to be released from whatever bond there seemed to be between them in the view of their friends and relations, if not his own.

Unfortunately Bob was not aware of any of this. And Jim was surprised to find out how hard it was to tell him. For some reason he did not want Bob to know they had broken up—if indeed they *had* broken up, since in his mind they had never been together. He knew all his friends adored Erin, as reflected in Bob's insistence on seeing her. He now realized that he enjoyed the idea of being associated with her in their minds. It made him look good. But it seemed this pleasant dream was about to come to an end.

Jim tossed Bob his phone, as requested. Bob tapped Erin's number with his agile thumb. It rang several times.

"Hello?" she said an uncertain voice.

"Hello! It's not who you think it is. It's your old friend Bob."
"Oh—hi."

Jim could tell she was surprised, and not in a good way.

"So anyway, I'm here with you-know-who, and we were just wondering what time we should pick you up for dinner."

"I didn't know I was being picked up for dinner."

"Are you on a hunger strike?"

"Not that I know of."

"Then how about six?"

Erin was too good-natured to say no. Jim didn't expect her to. But his hair was on fire. It seemed they were getting together for the first time since he had ruthlessly insulted her. And it was Bob who was bringing them together—her least favorite of his friends. The whole thing was extremely awkward, to say the least.

The afternoon dragged on in a state of heightened alarm. They went to the town park and played some desultory hangover tennis under a blazing sun. Then they went for a swim and lolled about on Jim's dock for a couple of hours. For his part, Jim was just pretending to loll. He carried on conversation as if everything were perfectly normal, about Beethoven or Byron or the usual thing, but inside he was full of apprehension about the night ahead.

It was a beautiful June evening, bright and blue and clear, and Bob wanted to use the Porsche with the top down, which gave Jim an excuse to hop into the jump seat when they picked up Erin. He flashed her a crooked smile and then sank down into his pit. Bob teased her all the way to the restaurant. He had no idea how she felt about him. She was a good sport about it.

They got to their table. It was all very strange. Erin seemed determined not look at him or even acknowledge his miserable existence—the same Erin who for three years had been—well, let's just admit it—probably his best friend, or at least the most loyal. Bob didn't seem to notice, which was a relief. He ordered a pitcher of beer and began working on it with great enthusiasm, becoming more and more loquacious by the swig. In fact he was talking so much that Jim started to relax a little, not being in the spotlight, and was therefore unprepared for the following assault.

"Oh!" Bob said to Erin after they had ordered their dinners. "I almost forgot to tell you about last night. Turns out our friend here is a regular Sir Galahad."

"He is?" she said, glancing at Jim.

"Definitely. He rescued a damsel in distress. Down in Westport. You probably didn't even know they had any of those. Anyway, there she was, passed out cold on the pavement in the moonlight. It was obvious that she was in need of some serious help. So what did our hero do? He lifted the fair maiden in his arms and whisked her away to his castle."

"Did you say 'passed out'?"

"Oh yes; she was definitely passed out. You can't get much more passed out than she was. And he insisted on helping her. He refused to leave the poor girl there by herself."

"Wait a minute," Jim said, becoming alarmed. "You were the one who insisted on 'rescuing' her, not me."

"Ah, but you were the one who stole off with her to your parents' house when I wasn't looking." And with that he proceeded to tell the whole parking lot story in excruciating detail, naturally doing everything in his lawerly power to embarrass Jim, whom he still had not forgiven.

"It's not quite as exciting as he's trying to make it sound," Jim said, without exactly looking at Erin or her shocked face. "All I did was take her to Bridgewater and drop her off. My parents are on the Cape this weekend with Grace."

"Yes, and that's the most fascinating detail of all. There was *no one home* to witness such heroism. Not a single soul. Completely alone with this drop-dead gorgeous female in his parents' empty house—did I happen to mention she was gorgeous? So what does he do? He carries her up to Gracie's room and lays her on the bed. It's true! Scout's honor! He told me so himself."

"She was *unconscious*," Jim said. "It wasn't like she was going to walk up the stairs by herself."

"Exactly. But what I want to know is—what happens next? What does he do with this unconscious girl lying there in front of him on his sister's bed? There's no one there to see him. Even she was oblivious. Does he turn and walk away? Or does he linger for a moment, gazing upon her cherry-red lips gently parted with sleep?"

"Her lips weren't all that appealing. She threw up in the car."

"But she didn't throw up in the bed. So did it occur to our Sir Galahad to steal a chaste kiss from those comatose lips as a reward for his exertions? After all, who would know if he did? Certainly not his faithful Sancho Panza, who at that moment was ten miles away, wondering where in the heck he could be. Not even the girl herself, since she was, as he so cheerfully reminds us, *unconscious*."

Bob was having a grand old time. He was getting his revenge on Jim for the trick he had played. And his raillery was quite effective. Jim felt utterly and completely humiliated. It was like being roasted on a slow charcoal fire. But Bob was not aware of the pain he was inflicting on Erin. He thought she would find the story amusing. He did not know there was a rift between them, which he was making considerably worse.

Finally it dawned on him that something was not quite right. Erin was not responding with her usual smiles and sunniness. In fact a palpable gloom seemed to have descended on the table. He realized that he had somehow managed to ruin the evening, not intentionally but nonetheless. He was unhappy with himself. He liked Erin. The last thing he wanted to do was upset her. But he did not realize he was touching a raw nerve with his uproarious probes. And now it was too late to do anything about it.

They ate mostly in silence, and then they drove her home. She ran off with the barest of goodbyes. Jim wanted to kill his so-called friend. But then he calmed down and began to think about it in a different way. As horrible as it was, it achieved his goal. He had already made up his mind to put some distance between himself and Erin. Bob's monologue would certainly do the trick. He knew exactly how it affected her. He could see the disgust on her face.

Jim did not want Erin to think badly of him. He did not want her thinking that there were ulterior motives when he took Karen to Bridgewater or that he had taken advantage of her in any way. He did not want to look like a blackguard in her eyes. But if this was the price he had to pay in order to sprinkle some cold water on her overly affectionate attachment—in short, to push her away from him—then he was willing.

He did not want her to hate him. But he did want her to stop thinking he had to marry her.

IV

Erin in her own words

THE FOLLOWING MORNING, Erin's parents ambled off to church. She went out to the porch swing and sat there gently rocking as sunlight flooded the wooded hills. It was soothing to her to breathe in the hemlock-scented air and admire the deep verdure. She was still sitting in the same place, staring into the woods, when they came home two hours later. She gave them a perfunctory greeting that worried them.

Erin's mom (Amy) made her favorite sandwich without asking her—thin-sliced pepper turkey and Boston lettuce on fresh white bread—and carried it out to her with a glass of sun-made iced tea.

"I brought you some lunch," she said cheerily.

"Thanks. Just put it down," Erin replied without looking up.

"Honey, what is it? Is something wrong? You seem unhappy."

Erin found herself fighting off tears. "I'm not going to see him anymore," she blurted. "I'm done with him."

Amy was shocked. She didn't have to ask who. "I'm so sorry. Are you sure that's what you want?"

"It's a waste of time. He's not interested in me and never really was interested in me to begin with."

"Oh, I don't believe that for a moment. Of course he's interested in you—who wouldn't be? You are beautiful in every way. He's just a little—confused."

"You don't know what he said to me. It was so mean. And then he didn't call me. He was willing to let me go. So—fine. I'll go. I don't know why I bothered in the first place."

Amy wasn't sure she was following this, but she also wasn't sure she wanted clarification. She longed to comfort her daughter but did not know how. Her first instinct was to try to reassure her—make her think Jim was serious about her and whatever might have happened between them was just a glitch that would work itself out in the end, when he came to his senses.

But when exactly was that? She was starting to lose patience with him. Her husband had lost patience long ago. They saw the way he treated their daughter and were not happy about it. He wasn't abusive, at least as far as they knew; he was just, well, emotionally remote. They knew how much she loved him. He did not give them enough evidence of loving her in return.

Amy believed Jim was a good person who would do the right thing by her daughter. She truly believed he had a good heart, in spite of all appearances. He was a young man and exhibited some of a young man's immaturity and unwillingness to grow up, but she thought he would come around in the end. She thought he would realize what a treasure Erin was.

At this point she was starting to have her doubts, however. She did not want to think ill of her good friends' son, but his behavior was, well, strange. They had been seeing each other for three years. Erin was out of school now. There was nothing keeping them apart, nothing to wait for. So why was she sitting on the porch swing crying?

Amy wanted them to get together. It was her fondest hope, as was also true of Jim's mother. But maybe it was better if they didn't. She did not want Erin to be hurt. Part of her wanted to say "Oh my" when her daughter delivered the stunning news—but another part simply said "Good." It was over. If he wanted her, he would have to make up his mind and stop fooling around.

Meanwhile Erin was trying to talk herself into not loving someone she loved, in which effort she was not entirely successful. Jim had been the one for her ever since she first saw him. She did everything she could to bring them together. Mostly it was just a matter of inviting him to her house or making sure she was invited to his house. But typically, she was the instigator. He called sometimes, but not as often as she would have liked.

She was able to excuse all this—because of love. She knew he liked her. She could sense it. He liked spending time with her and her family, although he was a little intimidated by her father. He was never unkind to her, always seemed happy to see her. But he did not act like a lover. There was the time he kissed her after having a little too much wine at his mother's fiftieth birthday party. But the kiss was never repeated.

Erin had mixed feelings about this. She hated the "dating conventions" of the day, if that was the right word for the campus hook-up culture. She did not believe in sex before marriage, not because she was a prude, but because she didn't think it was a good idea—especially for women. She did not believe two could become one in a casual way without offending whatever was true and noble in their own nature, or break apart without unseen damage.

So in one sense she was glad she didn't have to fend off any amorous attacks from Jim. But she worried that he was not attracted to her. She did not want him to try to sleep with her, necessarily, but she did want him to hold her. She wanted him to kiss her. He didn't, and this did not seem like a good sign. Did he just see her as a friend? She wanted to be much more than that.

This thing about them waiting until she finished school—that wasn't her idea. Their respective parents cooked it up as a rationale for his behavior. She was ready to get married anytime. She didn't care about college. She went because it seemed like the thing to do. She chose the nursing program because her favorite aunt was a nurse and it was a career where she might be able to do some good.

Their parents thought they were waiting, but the real reason Jim did not allow the relationship to go to a deeper level and did not ask her to marry him or even talk about marriage was because he did not know if he wanted it. She had been trying to ignore this inconvenient fact. For three long years she had tried to ignore it. But now he had thrown it in her face.

He said some things that were frankly unforgivable. Her chosen profession was "degrading." Nurses weren't very "bright." She knew she wasn't as bright as he was. She didn't pretend to be. She didn't go to Yale. She couldn't always keep up when he was talking about cultural things with his friends or his brilliant sister. But being bright wasn't all there was in the world, in her opinion.

Besides, Jim was not necessarily as "bright" as he thought he was. He was bright about books and that sort of thing, but he had thrown away someone who loved him and was devoted to him. In her opinion he could be rather dim when it came to the things that really mattered. What good does it do to have your eyes on the stars if you walk into a ditch?

In any case it was a long, long day for Erin. There was crying and anger but most of all there was self-recrimination for being so blind and stupid and allowing it to go on for so long. He was taking her for granted—and she let him. She was not going to let him anymore. She was not going to make excuses for him like she usually did. She didn't even want to try.

After all, what excuses could she make? He had been downright nasty. She wondered if it was how he had felt about her all along. Funny, he had never said anything about it before. He always knew she was going to be a nurse. Did he really have to wait until her graduation party to humiliate her?

She thought about her aunt. Was he embarrassed to be connected to her? Was that the reason for the outburst? How arrogant. So what if nurses aren't doctors? That doesn't mean they're not important. Try spending some time in a hospital without them. You would soon find out if they are needed.

What galled her the most, however, was the assumptions he was making about her. She wasn't trying to pretend her career choice was something more than it was, and yet he seemed to think she needed to be put in her place. She became a nurse because she wanted to make herself useful. That was all. She was pretty good in science. Biology was just a matter of memorization. She wanted to help people. Nursing seemed like a natural choice.

The only other career that remotely interested her was teaching, but she could not quite picture herself as a teacher. She didn't think she would be able to control a classroom. At one time she thought she might want to become a vet, but the training was almost as formidable as med school.

Nursing was something she *knew* she could do. She cared about people. She was not afraid of hard work. She believed in her role and had a sense of mission. So nurses wore "silly uniforms." There was a reason for that. Personally she liked the idea of everyone being pretty much the same. The egalitarian spirit was strong in her. She saw the way they dressed as a sign of both service and comradery, of unity in purpose, of dedication.

Besides, what kinds of work were not "degrading," in his view? Business? She had no interest. The law, like his good friend Bob? He himself said he went into it to make money. Nothing wrong with that, of course, but no one could pretend there was anything noble about it. Advertising, like Jim? Please. She didn't see herself as part of the cult of smugness and empty wit that was on display at all times on all media.

She was sorry to have such feelings about Jim, but she couldn't help it. She was hurt and frustrated over wasting three years of her life. She thought about the strange way he acted at the restaurant. He would not even look at her. He made no attempt to engage her in conversation. Forget about an apology—how about a simple "how are you"? Apparently even that was too "degrading" for him.

Then she thought about Bob's story. Jim did not try to deny it, so apparently it was true. What they had done was very wrong. There was no way to justify it. If a couple of guys happen to stumble across a drunk woman passed out on the street at night, they should either call 911 or try to call her family. They definitely should not throw her in the back of the car and take her home.

First of all there was the health issue. How did they know she didn't have alcohol poisoning? She could have died. Also Bob said she cracked her head on the ground. She could have had a concussion—or a fractured skull. But more than that, it was just so wrong. There was no consent. Apparently she was too drunk to know what she was doing. They were stupid to take advantage of "the situation," as Bob called it. His hilarity horrified her.

The last part of the story, in which Bob had taken such delight, was especially traumatic for Erin. Apparently Jim took this strange woman to his parents' house and put her in Grace's bed. She knew Bob was teasing her, but it did not feel like teasing. Did Jim really do it out of the goodness of his heart—or did he have something else in mind?

Erin wanted to think the best of him, but she was jealous. He had never carried her into any house. He had never laid her down on any bed, gently or otherwise. Was he attracted to this drunken woman? Was that the reason why he dumped Bob and whisked her away? They had been completely alone. It was hard not to obsess over these discomfiting details. She couldn't help it.

He did not say a word to her through the rest of the meal. He talked to Bob, but never to her. He hardly even said goodbye from the back of the Porsche when they dropped her off. He just waved at her. What did it mean? Why did they invite her out? Was he trying to humiliate her all over again? Was their plan to have Bob tell his devastating story and see what effect it had on her?

Erin had a warm heart, but she also had a bit of a temper. She had strong feelings that she was not always able to control. Right now she was mad at Bob for the way he told his stupid story and even madder at Jim for letting him get away with it. So one went to Yale and the other to Dartmouth. Good for them. It wasn't nice to make fun of people. It was childish, to her mind.

Jim had not called in a month. Clearly he did not want to talk to her. There had been times in the past when he didn't call. She was always the one to jump in and call. But this time it was different. She was not going to jump in. She still had *some* pride and dignity left after chasing him for three years. If he wanted to see her, he would have to call her, and he would have to apologize.

But what a struggle it was for her to come to this point! What agony and sorrow she felt as she sat there in the love seat where she had often sat with him and tried to get herself to accept the fact that she would never sit there with him again! All she knew was she did not want to feel this way—desolate, worthless, alone. If it meant giving up Jim, then that was what she had to do.

She thought about becoming a missionary and disappearing into deepest Africa never to be seen or heard from again. She thought about becoming the "lupine lady" in that wonderful children's book her mother used to read to her and finding a house on her beloved Maine coast where she could live by herself and tend her garden.

Then she thought about reality. Her aunt had told her many times that she could get her a starting job on the night shift. She had been putting her off because she was thinking about a wedding. But now she went into the house and called her. She needed a job. She needed something to keep her occupied. She wanted to start as soon as possible.

V

The fellowship of the ring

Jim went to work on Monday morning pondering his freakish weekend. The thing with the mysterious female was strange enough, but what happened with Bob and Erin was even stranger. He didn't know what to think about it. Part of him was glad if Erin was mad at him. He *wanted* to push her away. But at the same time part of him was sad. He was not sure he wanted to let her go. He didn't really know what he wanted.

He was completely aware of Erin's good qualities and how she felt about him. He was also aware of the possibility that his best chance for happiness was to give up his resistance and return her love. But his resistance came from her lack of resistance, and there didn't seem to be anything he could do about that.

It was already warm when he left the house and forecast for another hot day. He got to work in the same fog as most corporate drones on a Monday morning and smiled wanly when someone said "another day in paradise" on the elevator. He got himself some hot coffee and went to his office and was surfing tedious news sites when Dave Rodriguez came bombing in.

It was not Monday for Dave. It was never Monday. He was a high-powered, hard-charging operator on the marketing side who for some reason had singled out Jim in his struggle against Henry Booth, the old-salt advertising director who had lost his saltiness and needed to be thrown out, as Dave saw it.

Jim was ambivalent about this attention. On one hand, it was flattering. Dave was clearly an up-and-coming force at Prometheus Corporation. He had gravitas and a theatrically gravelly voice to go with it. People listened to him in meetings, even though he was barely thirty and most of what he said was corporate boilerplate, at least as far as Jim could determine, and that's the polite word for it.

Jim wasn't sure how he had managed to catch Dave's eye, but he suspected it had something to do with the degree he had from a certain institution up the coast. The degree wasn't necessarily all that impressive to *him*, knowing how much partying had come with it and how little studying, but it seemed to be impressive to other people, and he was not modest enough to try to disabuse them.

Also Jim kind of liked Henry Booth, who had hired and mentored him. He did not see very much of him—Henry was the ultimate hands-off manager—but there was an integrity about him. He was smart, in a street-savvy kind of way. He had a good mind for creating promotional campaigns that sold the product, or at least for finding the right people to help him.

"The guy has his cachet," Dave conceded while Jim smiled and attempted to pay attention. "I'm not disputing that. He has a reputation as one of the best small-market guys in the business. But that's the problem. At some point you have to realize you're not a small-market company anymore. It's not about the niche. You need to start acting like the big boys if you want to be one of them. You need to start putting the systems and the processes in place to support that. And you need the messaging to go with it."

Jim reached down deep for some energy, not readily available on a Monday morning. "I guess he is a little old-fashioned, but he works hard. He treats me well, anyway."

"Yeah, but that's no reason to put him in charge of advertising. Marketing is a science. You need marketing people running things who know how it's done and not just creative guys, who let's admit it, can be kind of flaky at times."

There was a pause while Jim, one of the referenced "creative guys," was trying to think of something trenchant to say. Then his phone rang. It was an outside call, possibly the agency, so he decided to risk offending his high-powered friend and picked it up.

"Hello there," purred an unfamiliar voice on the other end. "I bet you're surprised to hear from me."

"I certainly am," he said, although he didn't have the slightest idea who it was.

She laughed. "It's Karen. The parking lot girl. Remember?"

"As a matter of fact I do," he replied, zooming into the ether as he looked up at Dave from under raised eyebrows.

"So how have you been?"

"Good, good."

"Great! I'm glad. You were so nice. I really did appreciate it. But you probably know why I'm calling."

"I do?"

"You didn't find anything that might belong to me?"

"Umm—not that I can think of."

"Oh, dear. That's not good. The problem is I seem to have lost something, and I think I may have lost it at your house—your parents' house—whatever. It's sort of a ring. A pretty nice one, actually. The thing is I'm in bit of a bind and I was hoping you could help me out. I'm meeting someone and I really have to have that ring. I mean I really, really have to have that ring. It's a long story. I would be happy to go up there and look for it myself if you would just tell me the address and how to get in."

"Probably not a good idea," Jim said, his parents being scheduled to arrive sometime that afternoon. "I can stop by on my way home and see if I can find it."

"That would be so sweet of you."

"Not a problem. Happy to do it."

There was a little pause. "You're probably going to hate me for this, but is there any chance you could do it now?"

"You mean *right* now?"

"I know. It's terrible. I feel bad. But if I don't have that ring this afternoon I'm going to be in a lot of trouble."

Jim's mind was racing. "Well, okay, I think maybe I can do that. Let me see what I can arrange."

"You've got someone with you, right? Don't worry. I'll let you go. Do you have my cell number?"

"I'm looking at it right now."

"Great. So we're good then?"

"Yes. I will take care of that as soon as I can."

"Thank you so much. I can't tell you how much I appreciate it."

And with that she was gone.

"Problem?" Dave said smiling.

"Oh, just the usual code red," Jim replied with a stone face.

It took another twenty minutes to maneuver the talkative one out of his office. Those twenty minutes were pure hell for Jim, who was bursting with chivalrous enthusiasm. The fair maiden, as Bob called her, had tasked him with an aventura. The conversation kept playing on a loop in his mind, making it hard to concentrate while Dave went on and on about his usual hobbyhorses.

But even Dave had to do some real work eventually. Or at least he had to go to a meeting. As soon as he left, Jim went into clandestine mode. He wanted to get out as fast as possible and do the fair maiden's bidding, but there was no reason for him to be leaving the office. Also there was an evil admin named Donna who insisted on knowing where the entire team was at all times.

"Off to a meeting," he said, breezing past her cube. He didn't bother to glance back to see if she had the usual look on her face.

He was out of the building in a flash and in his car and on the highway and racing to his parents' house. He couldn't believe what was happening. The goddess had actually called him! Okay, so it was because she wanted him to do something for her. It was not a social call. But he was happy to be doing something for her. Very happy. He also told himself it was fun to get out the office on a tedious Monday morning.

He raced up there. Fortunately there were no police on the roads. He wanted to impress her, and he had already lost twenty minutes to that idiot Dave. Okay, maybe not "idiot." But he certainly could be annoying at times. Also the house did not seem likely to cooperate with his desire for speed. Picture a rambling old New England colonial, and a little tiny ring, and you will see why.

There was no sign of anything in Grace's room. He ran to the hall bathroom, the master bathroom, downstairs to the kitchen and the breakfast nook—nothing. He went back to Grace's room and got down on his knees and felt around under the bed. He even stripped it and shook out the sheets and the mattress cover. Then he pulled off the mattress itself. No sign of any blasted ring.

By this time he was sweating profusely and also profusely frustrated. What made her think the ring was even there? Wouldn't she know where it was if it was such an important ring? He pulled the mattress back up and collapsed onto it. A crow cackled from the open window. He agreed with its assessment. Then he looked over and happened to notice a glint under the floorboard register.

Jim got down on his hands and knees again and felt around with the dust kittens and coins and bobby pins and whatever else his sister had under there and finally managed to pull it out. He immediately realized what all the fuss was about. It was the biggest diamond he had ever seen in his life. It was obscenely big.

"Wow," he said, as he sat down on the bare mattress and gazed at it in dismay. He did not know much about rings, but this one had to be worth at least a nice car, maybe even a yacht. It wasn't a fool's mission after all. She really did leave something at the house.

He pulled out his phone and tapped her number, which looked very nice at the top of the list.

"Hello?" she said, sounding different from before.

"I think I may have found something for you."

"Really? Oh, thank God. You are my savior."

"Well, I don't know about that. How can I get it to you?"

"Can you meet me at the Westport Library?"

"I think I can. It will take me at least an hour to get there."

"That's perfect! And thank you SO much!"

Jim put his sister's room back together and then headed down to the coast with the same disregard for life and limb as before. There was no sign of the yellow Jeep when he arrived, so he plopped himself on a bench facing the river, where there was the hint of a refreshing summer breeze.

He was just getting settled when all of a sudden she appeared at his side, like a theophany. It startled him. He looked up at her and realized he was wrong. She was way more beautiful than he remembered behind a pair of enormous sunglasses.

"Hi there!" she said with sweetness and sunshine in her voice and promptly sat down next to him.

"Hi," he said through a strangled larynx.

"Been here long?"

"Nope—just arrived."

"Me too. Funny that you came here. This is my favorite spot. People tend to leave you alone, which is nice."

"So you vant to be alone."

"That's the worst Garbo I've ever heard," she said laughing. "But I wouldn't put it quite like that. I'm not some kind of recluse. I just don't like to be hassled all the time. You know?"

"I do know," he said, although he didn't really have any idea. He didn't have much experience with being hassled. Of course he was not as beautiful as this girl. He could imagine her being hassled quite a bit. "Well, I have something for you."

He reached into his pocket and pulled out the ring and held it for her in the palm of his hand. She looked at it for a moment with joy and relief on her face and then reached out and daintily plucked it with her exquisitely slender fingers. It was not a surgical operation by any means. Her soft skin touched his. He managed to control himself. Barely.

"Ah yes—kind of nice, don't you think?"

"You don't see something like that every day," he averred.

"No, you don't. And after today, I hope I won't ever see it

again. I suppose that sounds strange, but you wouldn't believe how much grief this ring has caused me. In any case you can probably see why I was so anxious about it."

"Absolutely. I would have been anxious too."

"So you forgive me, then? I mean for dragging you out of work in the middle of the day?"

"Of course. It was nice to get away for a while, to tell you the truth. Not a lot going on right now. Summer lull."

"Well, that's good at least. I'm glad I didn't interrupt anything. I can't imagine how I lost it. I must have taken it off in the middle of the night and forgotten about it."

Jim did not reply. He was thinking about where he found it. How did it get all the way under the register? Was she trying to throw it out the window? This thought was mind-boggling, considering the magnitude of the ring in question.

"Oh! I almost forgot," she said. "I have something for you, too." She reached into her purse and pulled out Grace's sunglasses. "These really came in handy. Thanks!"

"No problem. You didn't need to return them."

"They're your sister's! I wouldn't keep something like that. In fact I think it's kind of sweet that you have her sunglasses in your glove compartment."

He was touched by this—although she didn't know Grace.

"Thanks. Not that she ever wears them. She probably forgot they were in there. She has quite a collection."

"Fashion hound, eh?"

"Not really. More like the absent-minded professor. Not from any lack of intelligence. Think of that other Gracie."

"I believe I know the one you mean. What a talent."

They had shared another moment! He was tingling. His love of late-night TV paid off. Now he struggled to think of something else to say. He saw her looking at him through those sunglasses with a strange little smile on her face. It was unnerving.

She spoke up. "So I have to ask you—again. How is it that you happen to be so accommodating? I don't think I've ever met anyone quite like you."

"I was just trying to help. You sounded like it was important—and I can certainly see why."

"Okay, but that's all? Really? Are you being honest with me?"

Now his mind was racing. What was she looking for? "I guess

maybe I felt partly responsible. It wasn't your fault that we kidnapped you and left you in a strange house out in the middle of nowhere. You were a good sport about it."

"Oh, yes. I was definitely a 'good sport.' I barked at you and forced you to drive me down here. I don't know what to make of you—if you're quite real. I guess the easiest thing would be to just believe you. Should I just believe you, Jim Wilmot?"

He looked at her blankly. Really, really blankly. Was she talking about his apparent willingness to go on the ring-finding mission with no expectation of reward? Was that what she couldn't believe? If so, he certainly didn't want to disappoint her. He was perfectly willing to be the disinterested "savior" and leave it at that. Maybe not for everyone, but definitely for her. Or did she possibly have something else in mind? Naturally he hoped she did, but he wasn't bold enough to try and find out. Not in the absolute glare of her almost unbelievably beautiful face.

"Either I'm real, or you're hallucinating," he replied.

"Ha! Good one. I don't do that in the middle of the day. Anyway, I'm more of a champagne girl. Friday night I was drinking something else. I told you scotch, but on second thought it might have been tequila. I can't remember. Isn't that bad? I blame it on the salt. Hopefully I learned my lesson this time."

"Champagne's for the classy girls," he managed to tease.

"I love it. It makes me think of Fred Astaire and Ginger Rogers. Fortunately I don't have to worry about the cost. But you probably know all about that," she said, looking at him intently again.

"You don't strike me as the worrying type," he said, completely clueless as to what in the world she might be fishing for, although she was obviously fishing for something.

"There you go again," she said laughing. "Mr. Deflection. I still think you know more than you're letting on. I mean, who picks up a total stranger and lets them stay in his parents' house?"

"To be perfectly honest, my friend Bob was the one who insisted on it. And it's not as strange as it seems, based on your—ahh—appearance. He was very, shall we say, taken with you."

She laughed again, much to his relief. "Aha! So the truth finally comes out. I guess I'll have to meet this Bob person sometime."

"He would like that. He would like that very much. Let's just say he was not happy with me for taking you back to Westport."

"And how about you? How did *you* feel about taking me back to

Westport? It was a lot to ask."

"Not a problem. The drive was nice. The company was good." The company was *very* good.

"You know, you're really something. I guess I'll just have to make up my mind to believe you."

"Is it really that hard?" he said.

"A lot harder than you realize." She sat there looking at him for a moment. The moment went on and on. "So listen, how can I repay you? I want to do something."

"I don't want you to do anything. I wasn't expecting it."

"I know that. But I want to."

"Do you always get what you want?"

"Well, as a matter of fact—yes," she said giggling. "Do you like the ocean?"

"I do. It's big."

"So why don't you come and have dinner with me on the beach tonight? You could meet me at Sherwood Isle, since it's so close."

"Isn't that kind of a madhouse?"

"Only on the weekends. I like to go in the evening. It's pretty quiet. No sunbathers. I walk on the beach or sometimes I just sit there and watch the waves. Nobody ever bothers me, which I like. What do you think?"

"Sounds interesting. I could come after work."

"Excellent. I will see you then."

VI

Beach party

TIM WENT BACK to the office in a state of modified ecstasy. This girl was absolutely stunning, especially in a cloud-like blue dress that did little to obscure her well-crafted thighs. On top of that she was interesting. It was not your normal chit-chat. It was like a Humphrey Bogart movie with dialogue by Faulkner. She was full of gnomic proclamations. She seemed intelligent in addition to her other, er, attributes. She was even funny.

He couldn't believe the invitation. True, she said she wanted to repay him. It did not necessarily mean she was interested in him. But what about all of those strange questions? Obviously she had *something* on her mind. He just wasn't sure what.

Her inquisitiveness was very puzzling. She seemed to want him to admit that he was trying to impress her with his ring-searching activities. Was she just wondering if he really was as charitable as he seemed—or was it a manifestation of partiality of some kind? Either way, vanity was against him. If all she wanted was for him to be a disinterested doer of good deeds, then he was willing to oblige. He liked the idea of being seen as someone who would go out of his way to help people. It was a cherished part of his self-image.

But if all this coy testing was perhaps indicative of a desire for him to be in love with her—well, he was beginning to wonder if maybe he *was* in love with her. She certainly discombobulated him. She was constantly on his mind. True, he might have done those things for anyone, but he probably would not have done them so willingly or with such alacrity. He would not have been so willing to rush out of the office and potentially risk his position on the career ladder and reputation if his only incentive was to be helpful.

The signals she was sending seemed to favor the happier interpretation. She touched his hand when she fetched the ring. She spent a lot of time gazing at him—or studying him—he wasn't sure which. She said flattering things about him, in spite of the fact that she barely knew him. She wanted to share the beach with him. Beaches are romantic. If all she wanted to do was thank him, then why would she invite him to the beach?

There were a couple of things that dampened his enthusiasm, however. Like the way they found her. Who gets so drunk that they pass out in a parking lot? It was one thing for some college guy to do it—college guys are crazy—but it seemed unseemly somehow in someone like her. Not that he was trying to be sexist or anything. But the image of her falling out of her Jeep was still fresh in his mind. And it was not a good image, to be honest. Not to mention the lingering tart reminder of her comatose ride in his car.

Then there was the occasional display of imperiousness. She had pretty much commanded him (or them) to take her to their home. Then she commanded him to drive her to Westport. Then she commanded him to look for the ring and come to the beach. In romantic tales of yore, which he loved, the knight proved his worth through a commission from his fair lady. Jim was happy to prove his worth to such a worthy maiden, but he did not necessarily like being bossed around, even with a perfectly dazzling smile.

But these were just quibbles. The truth was he could not wait to see her again, to be alone with her, to see what might happen next. He knew what he wanted to happen. He couldn't help wishing it would happen. But of course he had very little reason to expect such happiness from a picnic on the beach. He did some work on a project he had been putting off, but it was lackluster at best. All he could think about was Karen. He imagined greeting her. He would smile and she would smile and he would gently touch her hand, just like in the movies. Right, like that would ever happen! Then he pictured them wading in the surf together, smiling and laughing. Unfortunately he was not dressed for the occasion.

All sorts of pleasant *mental pictures* came to mind as he sat there dawdling away a summer afternoon and were promptly pushed away again with a vigorous shake of the head. He laughed at himself for entertaining such wildly romantic thoughts—but that didn't stop him from thinking them. The rest of the workday dragged on literally forever. By the time it was over he was worn out. He shot out of the office like water through a fire hose. And then he was almost running to his car.

He drove to the park wondering how he was going to find her in the massive lots. Fortunately it wasn't difficult. The bright yellow Jeep was sitting all by itself near the picnic tables under the trees. She was right; the picnic area was quiet at that time of the day. There was a hirsute middle-aged wifebeater guy in a lawn chair with his *Daily News* and a nasty-looking cigar, but that was about it.

Jim saw her on the beach. He got out of the car and started

stumbling in her direction. He had never felt so self-conscious in his life. His feet had suddenly gone klutzy in his hard-soled wingtips and twice he almost tripped over a protruding pine tree root. Good thing she was looking at the water.

"Hello!" he barked out awkwardly, coming up behind her.

She turned slowly and smiled. "You're here! I'm so glad. How are you?"

"You mean in the six long hours since we parted? Pretty good, I guess."

"You guess?" she teased from behind her sunglasses. "You're not sure?"

"I'm not sure about anything anymore," he said, surprising himself.

"I know exactly what you mean," she retorted.

That's good, because he *didn't* know. He had no idea what he meant. It was all he could do to keep his wits about him. She was wearing a different outfit and was absolutely stunning in the late afternoon light. She was looking at him and he found himself having to look at her because he didn't want to be rude. But the experience was traumatizing. Once again he had that feeling of being sucked into her aura. He had never experienced anything like it in his life.

"I was thinking about going in the water. You want to?"

"Sure," he blurted, although he felt very awkward in his slacks and dress shoes.

He followed her to the surf. It was tending toward low tide with the attendant odors. She walked directly in, dodging seaweed, and a floating diaper, almost up to her waist. "What are you waiting for?" she teased. He smiled.

Wait—did she really expect him to come in? Sad to say, he considered it. At that moment he wanted to do anything to please her. But he remained frozen to his spot with saltwater occasionally lapping at his $200 shoes. And then he realized that she didn't really expect it and was grateful.

She splashed around a little and slowly returned to him with her eyes eastward down the beach. "Whew! Water's cold."

"Yes, it's too early. It will warm up considerably in July."

"Good to know! I just started coming here. Still not quite used to the routine."

"You probably don't have too many beaches in Iowa."

"No, but we do have a lot of cows."

This was said deadpan, and he was pretty sure she was making a joke, but he was afraid to laugh just in case she wasn't.

"Come on. Don't be so serious," she said. "You must know all the Iowa jokes."

"I wasn't aware that was a genre," he replied, regaining some of his composure.

"It is where I come from. In any case, you can see I don't live there anymore."

"By the way, where *do* you live?" Jim said.

"Oh, here and there," she replied with the same adorable smile.

"So you're saying you travel a lot."

"I do. I do. I have to for my job." Now she seemed to give him another one of her curious glances. Or maybe he was imagining it, with the sunglasses and all.

"And what is it that you do, exactly?"

"Exactly what I want," she said laughing again. "Well, that's not really true. I guess you could say I'm in sales."

"Sales?"

She nodded. "They definitely expect me to sell something. That's what they're always telling me, anyway. The producers, the publicists, the whole ungodly lot of them. But I love them all. I really, really love them."

"And what is the product, if I may ask?"

She paused for a moment. "Dreams," she said at last.

"Dreams? Are you a pillow salesman?"

"I've been called worse," she said laughing. She looked at him again with that smile, almost as if challenging him. If she was trying to pique his interest with all this obfuscation, she was succeeding. Here was a delicious mystery. She was not opening up to him and he wondered why. Did she have a job that required secrecy? Government job, maybe? Something like the CIA? His impressions of such things were formed entirely from movies. But he could easily see her in one of those movies. She had the mystique. He wanted to probe further, as it were, but felt maybe he had already probed too much. She was clearly reluctant to be forthcoming. And he figured she must have a good reason.

"So, are you hungry?" she said.

"I'm always hungry," he replied wittily.

"Then let's eat!"

They walked back to the table without talking. At this point Jim was just following her cues. He could not think of anything to say because he didn't really know her and did not know what she liked or disliked. He wished *she* would talk. He wished she were more like Grace—or Erin. He felt self-conscious as Erin's name popped into his head. He never felt this clueless around her.

The "picnic" was a surprise. He was figuring fried chicken and a baguette and maybe some cheese. She started unpacking and he could not believe what he was looking at. OK, so there *was* a plate of fried chicken and there was cheese—a brie and a Gloucester. But there was also a stunning lobster salad. There were roasted peppers. There was an elaborate pasta salad. There was freshly cooked asparagus in vinaigrette. There was foie gras. There were raspberries and grapes and watermelon pieces. There were *two* delicious-looking baked desserts.

Jim was overwhelmed. It seemed like there was no end to the wonders she was capable of pulling from those baskets. He thought of the monster diamond. What in the world was he dealing with here? No one shows up at a picnic with a spread like this unless there is some serious money involved. Mere mortals would not even dream it was possible. For one thing you'd have to spend a month with Martha Stewart just to figure it out.

"No hot dogs?" he joked.

"Hot dogs! Yuck. You don't like it?"

"I love it. I'm amazed. I'm sure the other twenty guests will feel the same way."

"All for you, my friend. All for you. No, seriously, I wanted to do something to show my appreciation. You rescued me. Twice. I don't know what I would have done if you hadn't found that stupid ring. That would have been a major disaster."

"Which is much worse than a minor disaster," he quipped. "But I really wasn't expecting anything like this."

"Are you surprised?" she said, pulling her sunglasses down a bit to reveal her twinkling eyes.

"Totally. All this time I thought I knew what a picnic was."

"What do you think of the lobster salad?"

"Very colorful. Fills out the color palette nicely. Note to self: if you don't have beets, you must have lobster. I have a personal relationship with lobster. Goes back to my grandparents' house on the Cape where I spent many happy summers. I ate so much they had to change the name of their deck to the Nutcracker Suite. It wasn't the best name, but it was butter than most."

He was pushing hard.

"I hear the Cape is great. Haven't been there yet."

"You would love it."

"How do *you* know what I love?" she teased.

"Everybody loves the Cape. Real beaches, not like this pale imitation. Real ocean. Quaint little towns. Quaint little people. Summer traffic Armageddon on weekends."

"Sounds wonderful. Except for the Armageddon part. I have heard about that, actually. One bridge, right? But I'm glad you're surprised. Very glad, actually."

"Anybody would be surprised at a spread like this."

She shook her head. "I still don't know quite what to make of you. But if you're pulling my leg, I must say you're doing a very good job."

The thought of pulling her leg made him pause for a moment. "No, I really am surprised by all this. Shocked, in fact. I wasn't expecting it. I really didn't expect anything."

"I know you didn't. That's what makes it so much fun."

As a final touch, she reached into a small but elegant wood-panelled cooler and pulled out a bottle of champagne. And not just any champagne. Dom Perignon.

"Whoa! You sure you want to waste that on me?"

"Waste? What do you mean?"

"I'm not exactly a wine connoisseur."

"But you know what this is. So clearly you don't know anything about it. But don't worry. This is the only thing I drink these days. Well, except for Friday night. But let's not go there."

"You can't go there. If it were tomorrow night you could go there, eventually. Time is funny that way."

"You're the one who's funny. I love guys with a sense of humor. Would you open this for me?"

Alcohol was, strictly speaking, verboten in the state park, but Jim did not feel he was in a position to say no. He took the bottle and carefully squeezed off the cork. It was the first time he had ever held a bottle of that particular precious potable in his plebian hands. It made him a little nervous.

She produced two sparkling champagne glasses from a velvet-lined box. Real crystal flutes, right there on the beach. Went well with the decaying picnic table. He poured the effervescence for her.

"To my knight in shining armor," she said with a mischievous smile, and they clinked.

The champagne was cold and bubbly and, on an empty stomach, frosted his brain like the touch of the white witch.

"Thank you," he said. "But I was glad to help out. Besides, you never would have found it by yourself. Not in a million years."

"Really? Where was it?"

"Under the register, believe it or not. You know—the heater. All the way back against the wall."

"I know what a register is. But how in the world did it get under there?"

"No idea. Maybe you put it on the end table and knocked it off somehow?"

"I guess. I don't remember. I do remember waking up. I definitely remember that, because I didn't know where I was. But I wasn't really scared. More like puzzled. I remember smelling the coffee and the bacon. That was so nice of you. And of course I remember you standing there in the kitchen. You were so funny."

"I was a little nervous," he admitted. "Not sure how you would react to the—um—situation. And by the way, that was my sister's room. The sunglasses maven." For some reason he felt the need to add this.

"So you took me to your sister's room and put me to bed. The sister-bride. That's nice. Will she be mad at you?"

"Not at all. I put everything back together. She won't even know. Hopefully. I wish you could meet her. You'd like her."

"Sounds like you're fond of her."

"Well, she is my sister."

"It doesn't always work that way, unfortunately. I have a sister, and I wouldn't say I'm fond of her. In fact I wish she would just get a real job and leave me alone. I guess that sounds cold."

Jim did not know what to say. It did sound a little cold. They filled their plates and sat down to eat facing the water, side-by-side.

"This is absolutely delicious," he said. He wasn't exaggerating one bit. The food was amazing.

"I made it myself," she replied with a laugh.

"You're quite the cook."

"Oh, yes. Quite the cook. Cooking all the time. Cooking, cooking, cooking. If you don't like the heat, get out of the kitchen.

How about you? Do you like to cook?"

"I do. Nothing like this, of course. Not gourmet."

"Of course you do. And I bet you do it very well. I could sense that you felt comfortable in the kitchen and weren't just making it up as you went along. And the breakfast looked delicious, even if I was unable to eat any."

"You are kind."

"Yes, that's the problem. I'm inclined to be kind. Something tells me I shouldn't be, but here I am," she said with a sigh. And then she was silent as this thunderous proclamation rattled around in Jim's brain. "To be perfectly honest with you, I almost didn't come. Even after all the food was made and packed. I almost called you and told you I couldn't make it."

"Really? Why?"

"I guess I'm just suspicious by nature. Part of me wants to believe you really are just a nice guy who likes to do really nice things for people, whether they deserve it or not. But another part of me says you could be just like all the rest of the guys in my life who try to do 'nice' things for me."

Well! He didn't quite know what to say about that. He was afraid to say anything at all because he wasn't sure what she was talking about. He didn't want to seem stupid. They finished their meals in silence. He noticed that she hardly ate a thing. Some white meat scratched from a skinless chicken breast. A few spindly asparagus spears. Four raspberries. Exactly four. She counted them out meticulously. She did finish her champagne, however. Then she had another. Maybe fifteen minutes went by in complete silence. At least it felt that long to him in his highly self-conscious state.

Then she spoke up. "Okay—I guess maybe I went a little too far there. I don't really feel that way about you. Not at all. It's just that I've had some bad experiences with men, especially lately. Not that you're like them. You're not like them at all. But anyway, that's why I'm here. You're different. Or at least you seem to be."

"I'm really not here to get anything from you, you know. I don't have any expectations. And I don't consider myself any kind of hero. The whole thing was just a coincidence. We happened to be walking out of the bar at the moment when you happened to be falling out of your car. If you don't mind my saying so. It wasn't anything more than that."

"No—I get it. It wasn't like you were stalking me. And I

definitely wasn't accusing you of anything." She paused and stared out at the waves for a moment. "So I guess I should ask you what happened that night, in case something comes up down the road."

"Well, we were at the bar, doing the usual Friday night thing, which isn't really much of anything, except drinking beer and shooting the breeze. Bob met me there on his way up from New York. We were headed out to our cars, and that's when we saw you. And again, to be perfectly honest, my friend was the one who insisted on seeing if there was anything we could do to help. He was also the one who insisted on taking you home—that is, after you sort of insisted yourself."

"No, I get it. I told you to. You're worrying too much about that. I've done worse. But I was just lying there? Literally? In the middle of the parking lot?"

"Yes. That's why we felt we had to do something. Personally I thought we should call the police or an ambulance. But he talked me out of it. Maybe he's the one who should be here," Jim said with a self-effacing laugh.

"So you wanted to turn me over to the police!" she said with an arch smile.

"No, not really. I didn't know what to do. I didn't think it was right to take you home under those circumstances. Maybe that seems strange."

"It doesn't seem *strange* at all. I can perfectly understand why you would be reluctant to take me home, even if I ordered you to. I'm sorry I was so demanding. I put you in an impossible position."

"I'm not saying I resent it. In fact I'm rapidly beginning to think of it as one of the most fun things that has ever happened to me."

"Really? Are you having fun?"

"I am. Although I'm having a hard time believing this is real. Or that you're real. But it's definitely fun."

"I'm glad. I really am. I'm having fun too. I'm grateful that you took me to your parents' house and didn't call the police. That was very kind. And the ring thing—that was way above and beyond the call of duty. Honestly. I figured you would just tell me to get lost. But I really did need it. I wasn't kidding about that. At all. Things could have gotten pretty ugly if I didn't have that ring."

"So was it an engagement ring or something?"

"I guess you could call it that. That's how I thought of it, anyway. I'm not sure *he* ever did. But why am I telling you this?"

"The champagne," he suggested.

"Yes, the champagne. Horrible stuff. Give me some more. But seriously, I can't tell you how much I needed that ring. I am so grateful to you for getting it for me. I'm happy to do this for you and would be happy to do a lot more. You literally saved my life."

Hmmm. What could he say to this? On one hand, what did she mean by "happy to do a lot more"? A lot more of what? Gourmet cooking? The thought of doing a lot more, whatever it was, made his mind shimmer under the influence of the bubbly. But then a less-cheering thought came to him on the downdraught. It could be that she was sending him a definite message. It was all about the ring—the beach, the crazy spread, everything. It wasn't about him at all. Or not him personally, anyway.

They talked until the park closed, mostly about cultural stuff. A lot about plays, building on their previous conversation about *As You Like It*. She was definitely quite knowledgeable on the subject, which was not surprising for a theater major. And this led to a conversation about movies and the differences from stage plays. They agreed about some things and disagreed about others, but *c'est la vie*! You can't agree on everything.

At that point he wasn't worried about offending her. It seemed increasingly likely that this was a thank-you party and not the other thing he was thinking of. She made a couple of statements that could be interpreted either way, but the overall message seemed clear. This was his bounty for recovering the ring.

They parted cordially. He offered to help her with the baskets. She laughed and said "okay." He didn't know why she laughed. Even with two of them it took two trips.

She surprised him with a quick little hug as she hopped in the Jeep and drove off. In his excitement he did not notice the black Escalade idling at the other end of the lot.

VII

Tangled up at Tanglewood

ANYWAY, WHAT DID it matter? He would never see her again. She had done her thing and shown her gratitude but given no decipherable sign of any interest in him. There was no more than parting in their parting, no sweet sorrow, except for that one little hug. His mother also gave him hugs. It didn't mean she was attracted to him.

One thing was different. He had her number on his cell phone now. But he knew he would never have the courage to call. There was no reason to think she wanted him to. There was nothing even remotely romantic about her behavior, certainly not flirtatious. Nor was he expecting there to be. As far as he was concerned, she was way out of his league. If sheer beauty did not reveal this to him, then the fabulous diamond definitely did. He read about people who had diamonds like that and may even have met one or two at school. But he wasn't on a first-name basis with them. His social circuits were of a distinctly lower wattage.

Apparently she thought of him as her disinterested savior, her knight in shining armor, as she put it. He definitely liked having her think of him this way. It didn't mean he expected her to love him, however. The fair maiden was to be put on a pedestal; chaste, not chased. All this agonizing over whether or not he was "real"—well, he wanted his chivalry to be real, even if it was partly an illusion. But he knew that if he used his advantage to call her, the *illusion* would be shattered. He would cease to be her sacrificing savior and become something very different. Or worse, attempting to be.

Jim just could not see himself as her suitor. For one thing, she was stunning. This was not your normal human beauty. It impaled the eyes. He could barely force himself not to stare. She could have her pick of any guy, so why him? He could not think of a good reason. He knew his station. He was in no position to acquire a trophy wife. Things might be different if she had shown any unambiguous interest in him. But virtually everything she said was ambiguous. The only thing that did not seem ambiguous was her skepticism regarding his motives. And this skepticism certainly seemed justified in someone who was as pretty and apparently rich as she was. There are a lot of shady characters out there!

Jim consoled himself with the thought that he seemed to have come through the strange encounter with his halo intact. True, he was in danger on more than one occasion, sitting next to her in the twilight—let's just say there were a couple of moments when he could feel his hand inching over towards hers in his mind, if not on the actual table. He couldn't help thinking about it, but he refused to contemplate it. Everything was perfect. Why risk disaster by introducing an element in which she had showed no interest? He felt like he was practically on fire, or could be if she wanted him to be, but this inclination toward conflagration was not reciprocated, or she did a pretty good job of concealing it if it was.

No, sadly, it was better to let her go and not try to do anything foolish. It was better (he felt) to preserve the pristine image he had apparently obtained in her mind and not ruin it by revealing himself to be just another one of "them," presumably referring to the gaggle of would-be suitors hanging all over her and hassling her for a date. Jim had no doubt there was such a gaggle. There would have to be. He didn't particularly want to be goosed into it by his own foolishness. So he decided to let the evening be an unspoiled memory and an amusing story to tell his family and friends.

In fact he called Bob in the car on the way home. "You're not going to believe what just happened."

"Don't tell me—the parking lot girl."

"Boy, you're good. Somehow she managed to lose a ring in Grace's room. By the way, you should have seen this ring. The Bolshoi Ballet could stage the *Firebird* on it."

"I assume we're talking about a diamond."

"Of course. I've never seen anything like it. Anyway, as a reward I got invited to Sherwood Isle for an unbelievable picnic. Lobster salad and Dom Perignon."

"I'm impressed. Then what happened?"

"Nothing happened. That was it."

"Nothing? That's the whole story? You got invited to a picnic?"

"Okay, so maybe it's not all that exciting. I just thought you might be amused."

"No, it sounds incredibly amusing. Girl with giant diamond ring serves lobster salad. More to come on *Entertainment Tonight*."

"Now I'm sorry I called."

"Don't be. In fact I was going to call you. I have first dibs on some Tanglewood tickets for Saturday. You interested?"

"Of course. How much are they?"

"Let me worry about that. Here's the thing. I feel terrible about what happened Saturday night with Erin. You think she would feel like going with us?"

"You mean you want to make it up to her?"

"That's kind of what I had in mind. Is it stupid?"

"I don't know if I would call it *stupid*. I'm just not sure how she would feel about it."

"Can you call her and ask?"

"Well, no; not really. To tell you the truth we're not exactly an item anymore. Had a little argument at her graduation party, I'm afraid."

"About what?"

"About getting married. Everybody seems to think we have to. I'm not ready for that."

"What if you decide you *are* ready later on? You can't just assume she'll be waiting around for you."

"I'm not assuming anything."

"But where are you going to find someone like Erin? Women like that don't just grow on trees."

"Maybe *you* should marry her."

"Oh, right. That's really what I'm talking about. But do you mind if I invite her to come with us anyway?"

"I guess so. There's no reason why we can't hang out together. But I hope it's not a double-date."

"Not at all. I already called Arthur, and he's coming. It will be just the four of us."

"Okay, that sounds safe."

That's what he said, but in reality Jim felt very mixed up by this conversation. He was always happy to go to Tanglewood, but he felt ambivalent about Erin. His spirits rose as it occurred to him that she might decline the invitation, based on how she felt about Bob. But they sank again when he realized he was not really sure he *wanted* her to decline. Part of him did not want to see her, the part that was trying to run away from her, but part of him longed to see her. These two feelings were the flip side of the same coin, but he couldn't see it.

He was surprised by Bob's reaction to the break-up. It was clear that he was not happy about it; and not for any self-serving reason, but apparently because he was concerned about Jim and his well-being. Really! It was almost as if Erin was the only person in the world who could make Jim happy, in Bob's mind. Or at least that was the way it came across. This was the opinion of a friend who seemed to have his best interests in mind. Jim would be lying if he said he wasn't affected by it.

It was almost enough to push him in a certain direction—*almost*. But the influence of friends was the very thing he was trying to resist at that point in his life. There were plenty of people in his inner circle who wanted him to marry Erin, starting with his mother and sister, and probably his father, although he would never openly say so. And now Bob, the confirmed bachelor. They all seemed to think they knew what was best for him. He was inclined to think he knew better himself. Now he decided he did *not* want Erin to come. Bob's forcefulness backfired. There was no reason why he should succumb to his matchmaking efforts any more than to those of his own family. In fact there was less reason, because in Jim's mind Bob was a very poor judge of women and a dubious philosopher of happiness, and specifically of relationships.

No, he decided he definitely did not want her to come. He did not want to risk breathing new life into the beast he was trying to kill. He called Bob and told him. But it was too late. The deed had already been done. Erin was coming. Bob wasn't sure how *happy* she was about coming from her tone, but it was understandable after Saturday night. Anyway, that was his plan—to try to make it up to her when they got there.

Bob had never been aware of Erin's true feelings towards him. She didn't exactly hate him—she didn't hate anyone—but it would be fair to say that she couldn't stand him and had little or no desire to be in his company. He was too arrogant for her and too self-absorbed. It didn't seem fair to Jim to try to enlighten his friend about these feelings without her permission. So he decided not to say anything. Besides, he didn't know if Bob would believe him. He had a self-esteem that seemed almost invincible.

He was surprised that Erin actually agreed to go. All he could think was that Bob must have caught her off guard like when he invited her to the restaurant. As far as he knew, these were the only two times his friend had ever called her, and the other time he had used Jim's phone. Or maybe she did try to say no and he coaxed her into it. Bob was a very good browbeater. He was a lawyer, after all. If he had his mind set on something, it was hard to resist him. And in this case what he had his mind set on was doing what he thought was a favor to Erin, which in fact was the reason for the entire trip.

It was going to be very awkward in any case. But fortunately it wasn't just the three of them. Arthur was coming too, their good friend from prep school and a fellow classical music nut. This was comforting. A fourth would definitely make a big difference. Jim couldn't imagine what it would be like to spend an afternoon alone with Bob and Erin after what had just happened at the restaurant.

Saturday came, and it was a cloudy summer day, no real rain but occasional drizzle. Jim drove instead of Bob, since his car could accommodate four comfortably. They cruised up Route 7 along the mighty Housatonic, admiring the ghostly mist in the Connecticut highlands. Bob and Arthur were quite chatty in the back, catching up. Jim and Erin were awkward and silent in the front.

They had planned on a picnic before the concert—it was dry enough for the hopeful—and found a nice spot with a view of the Berkshires to spread out a blanket. Bob had brought along a couple of pricey bottles of Malbec in an attempt to make the occasion extra-special, not realizing that this was probably the last way in the world to impress Erin, who didn't drink and had no idea of their monetary or aspirational value.

Oh, well! The boys enjoyed it, and their tongues soon loosened in the usual way.

"So what are you going to do with yourself, now that you have your degree?" Bob said to Erin, eager to pour the balm of his famous charm into the still-raw wound.

"I'm not sure," she said with an embarrassed laugh. "Well, no, that's not exactly true. What am I saying? I'm a nurse. In fact I just started at the hospital."

"It sounds like you know what you're doing, but you're not quite sure why you're doing it."

"That's an interesting way of putting it. It's a good profession. I definitely feel fortunate to have a job. And the money is certainly good, with the shortage of nurses. In any case it's time to start working on those college loans."

"At least until you get married and have five kids."

"Five! Does Jim know about that?" Arthur teased.

"I don't know what Jim knows. You'll have to ask him."

"She can have as many as she wants," Jim said defensively.

"Wonders never cease. This from the guy who swore he would never have more than one. Bad for the planet and all that."

"Jim won't have to worry about it. We aren't seeing each other anymore." Erin wanted to say this. She wanted to get in a little dig in front of his friends.

"Oh! Really?" Arthur said, trying to catch up.

"He can't see himself being married to a nurse. Too degrading. You know, bedpans and all that."

"So what does he want you to do—become a capitalist?"

"Oh right—like I'm some sort of capitalist," Jim sputtered.

"Wait a minute. Aren't you the guy who writes ad copy?" Bob said laughing.

"Look, I have nothing against nurses. That's ridiculous. Some of my best friends are nurses."

"Name one," Erin said with a smile. "Anyway, you should have heard him at my graduation party. He basically told me I didn't have a real degree."

"Interesting," Arthur said. "People in glass houses."

"I can't believe you actually said that at her graduation party," Bob piled on. "What were you thinking?"

"I didn't say it, exactly. In fact I don't remember saying it at all. All I said was I thought she would make a great doctor."

"Maybe I should tell you what he *really* said. You wouldn't believe it."

"Please don't. Sometimes I say stupid things."

"Word," Bob said, siding with Erin, since he was still peeved at his friend for apparently breaking up with her.

Jim was annoyed but decided to keep his mouth shut. Which was probably a good idea since there was absolutely nothing he could say. Erin's openness took him by surprise. There was no way he could defend himself, with both of his friends so adamantly in her corner. After all, what happened at the party was completely indefensible. There was nothing he could say to exculpate himself. All he could do was stew silently and hope they didn't wheedle it out of her, because she had kept the worst part to herself.

But was this really the time for her to bring up what happened? Did she have to embarrass him in front of his friends? He was peeved with her, while acknowledging that she had every right to say what she said. He was peeved with the day, dreary and gray.

Then they went into the Shed and heard a crappy concert, and he was peeved about that too. Well okay, it wasn't really crappy. But Jim was still stewing over his discomfiture and could not settle down and enjoy it.

When they got to the car somehow Bob wound up in the front with him with Erin and Arthur in the back. It started to rain harder, and they found themselves sitting in traffic in the muddy parking lot. All three men were on the downslope from their wine-induced giddiness. The silence was awkward. Jim pulled out an old CD that he had found in his mother's collection and popped it in the player.

"Ah!—*Tout le Matins de Monde*," Arthur chirped up from the back seat. "Have you seen the movie?"

"No, not really. My mother likes it."

"As she should. It's wonderful. It's about art versus popularity, integrity versus selling out; very unusual in every way. The hero is a viol player who is a true artist, deeply soulful, and an outcast of his own making from the fashionable world and its shallowness. Meanwhile Gerard Depardieu is his young student who becomes successful by catering to the crowd. Quite profound, really, which isn't something you can say about too many movies these days."

"Love Gerard Depardieu," Jim said. "Love his Cyrano."

Now Bob chimed in. "Speaking of actors, you remember that girl we told you about, Erin—the one in the parking lot?"

"Yes," came the clenched-tooth reply.

"Well, it seems our hero saw her again. She invited him to the beach, believe it or not. Something about a ring."

"She lost a ring at my parents' house and I found it for her. That's all there is to it," Jim said testily.

"Right. Whatever. Anyway, what I didn't tell you is she looks just like Kerry Morgan. I'm not kidding. She's a dead ringer."

"Oh sure, like we'd find someone like Kerry Morgan passed out in a parking lot. People like that have an entire entourage."

"Do you even know who she is?"

"Of course! Who doesn't?"

"Okay, what movies was she in?"

"She was in—" Jim stopped there. He didn't really know what movies Kerry Morgan was in. He just knew she was in the movies and was one of the top stars. The very fact that she was one of the top stars was incentive enough to ignore her, since in his view movie stardom was highly overrated.

Bob laughed at him. "I was right. You've never seen any of her films. You probably couldn't pick her out of a police lineup."

"He thinks any movie not made in black and white is garbage," Arthur explained confidentially to Erin.

"I know."

"You really should Google her," Bob said. "You're not going to believe it. In fact I thought it *was* her."

"So that's why you were so intent on bringing her home."

"This is getting interesting," Arthur said.

"No it isn't," Erin replied, which immediately shut him up.

Then they all shut up. There were some pretty strong emotions in the car at that point. Jim was perplexed. He was trying to understand his feelings toward Erin. When she said "I know," he melted. She knew all about him. But when she said "No it isn't," she closed the door. It hurt to have her close the door in front of his friends. He was a little upset with her for that.

But *why* was he upset? She had every right to despise him after what he had done at her party. There was nothing she could say or would ever think of saying that was even remotely as hurtful as what he said to her on that horrible night. Besides, wasn't he the one that wanted to move on? Shouldn't he be glad if there was no longer a link of familiarity between them?

Also there was the matter of Karen. This thing about Kerry Morgan seemed ridiculous. She was one of the biggest movie stars on the planet. Still, he could not get it out of his head. Bob was right. He had no idea of what Kerry Morgan looked like. Then he thought of the ridiculous diamond ring. It might explain some things. He thought of the elaborate picnic and all the strange questions she asked him. But no—it wasn't possible. It couldn't be.

Jim was not the only one in the car with rioting emotions. Erin was completely fagged, and she hadn't even had anything to drink. She was worn out emotionally. She had had her great and shining moment of revenge during the picnic, but there was no satisfaction for her in it. In cutting Jim she also cut herself. It wasn't her choice to break it off; it was his. This still hurt.

Then there was all the talk about that girl again. They seemed to think it was a big joke. It was not a joke to her. Now on top of everything else Jim had gone to the beach with her. Erin did not want to be hurt by this, but she couldn't help it. She had made up her mind to get over Jim. Apparently her mind and her heart were not in full communication.

Meanwhile Bob was kicking himself for having blown it...*again*. The whole point of the excursion was to make it up to Erin. He also had a vague idea about helping Jim and Erin to get back together. He wanted them to be together. He wanted it enough to shell out $300 for the tickets alone—Arthur paid for his own. Things were going fine until the end, and then he just couldn't help teasing Jim about the Kerry Morgan look-alike. Now Erin was mad at him again. He wanted to apologize, but the dynamics in the car were wrong. He was afraid of making her even madder.

Arthur's cogitations were of a different kind altogether. He did not know how he wound up in the back seat with Erin, but he was not unhappy about it. He had feelings for her and had for some time. Was it true she and Jim were no longer involved? He couldn't believe it. If she was not entangled with Jim, then he did not feel obligated to keep the distance he had been studiously maintaining ever since he met her. Jim's loss was his gain.

He was sitting next to her in the back of a small car. They were almost close enough to touch. Could she possibly have any interest in him? He wondered what she was thinking. It was dark. They were together. Like Bob, he wanted to talk to her; and also like Bob he did not know what to say. He was afraid to say anything at all with the two of them listening in the front.

It was not mere outward beauty that drew Arthur to Erin; it was the beauty within. Truly—we kid you not. There are men like that out there, and Arthur happened to be one of them. In his mind, Erin would make an ideal wife. She was just the sort of person he felt he needed in order to be happy. She was sweet-tempered. She was rational. She was affectionate and kind. Okay—so she was also very pretty. He could not deny it. He didn't want to.

It seemed Jim and Erin were no longer attached. This was big. It made Arthur happy, although he knew he should be sad for their sake. But the fact is it made him very happy indeed.

VIII

Time out in the rocking chair

WHEN ERIN GOT HOME she went up to her room and sat down in her favorite rocking chair, the one she had painted so carefully, white with the red and gold trim, thinking about rocking chairs, and about the future, when she was an innocent girl of thirteen and full of dreams. She sat there rocking for quite a long time. Most of the night, truth be told.

That chair, that beloved chair, was her purgatory. So many summer nights she had sat there and dreamed about her life with Jim and the happiness they were going to have. She made a family in that chair, and a home, and friends, and many rituals of their own devising; she even managed to get him into the choir with her, because she knew he had a nice voice, and because she pictured them doing things together for as long as they both might live.

She had built a lovely dream world in that chair, but now she knew she had to let it go. She wondered if she was being punished for her dream world. It was selfish to put someone in your dream without their consent. Maybe God had better plans for her. Maybe happiness was something different from what she imagined. Maybe she was going to have to find out what happiness really was, instead of forcing it into a certain mold in her mind.

She did not know. Oh! she did not know. And that was the problem. The tears came and rolled down her cheeks but they did not leave her with any more knowledge. They left her with etched cheeks. The one thing she did know was it was over for her and Jim. Three long years had been spent waiting for him to come to her. He did not come. He lingered; he gave every appearance of having an inclination to come. But in the end he stayed away.

She deliberately provoked him by saying they weren't seeing each other anymore. She wanted to put him on the spot and see how he would react. Be careful what you wish for, because the reaction was not what she wanted. She thought—she hoped—he would protest her brash statement. She hoped he would leap in and contradict her, tell his friends she was wrong, chase away her own unwanted conclusion.

Which isn't what happened. He did not react at all. There was not even a change in his expression. She knew because she glanced at him. Apparently he agreed. They were not seeing each other anymore. That's why he didn't chase her when she got up and walked away at the graduation party. That's why he didn't apologize. That's why he had not called in over a month.

He did not protest or seem surprised or regretful in the slightest degree. As far as he was concerned, it was over. She was very clear on this. She had to be. Clarity was indispensable for what she had to do now, the thing so long overdue, which was to let him go, really let him go this time. She needed to be very clear and she was very clear. Jim was not going to be a part of her life.

Could she have kept on chasing him and caused him to change his mind? Maybe. But she had been chasing him for over three years. It was time to stop making a fool of herself. You can't make someone love you. Well, perhaps you can, but it won't be real and it won't work out in the end. There has to be a willingness on both sides in order for a marriage to survive and thrive. It can't just be one person working.

Also that was not what she wanted. She had no desire for marriage without love. Since Jim did not seem to love her, she could not marry him. Her parents loved each other. This is what she wanted for herself. She had no desire to get married just for the sake of getting married. She wanted to love and be loved in return.

Once again Jim's behavior toward her had been cold. This was twice now. Was she going to act like she didn't get the message? Of course she got it. Loud and clear. The thing that threw her was being invited out again by Bob. She could not think of any reason for it except perhaps having been put up to it by Jim. Was this his way of getting together with her without directly approaching her? Was he still interested?

These were the foolish thoughts and false hopes she had taken with her on the trip. Otherwise she never would have gone. She did not like Bob and did not want to spend her summer afternoon with him. But if Jim was there and there was any chance—well, she knew how foolish she had been. There was no chance.

Erin thought and cried and was in agony all over again as she had been for a month now as she drew near to a very hard conclusion. She was in love with Jim but Jim was not in love with her. It was so hard to reach this point, to really reach it. She had to give up so much to reach it. And mostly what she was giving up was her own tender love and its natural optimism. It was a hope killing, the hardest kind.

She sat there and cried and thought and cried some more. If she could not have Jim, what did the future hold for her? What did it mean, this momentous change in her life? Did she have to give up her dream of a loving home and family? She could not even imagine it. Arthur was right. It was the thing she really wanted.

She did not believe in the things so many people seemed to believe in. She did not believe they could make her happy. She lived in a big house and her parents had nice cars and nice clothes and she was appreciative of these material blessings—but they did not make her happy. They were just things. There is no point in loving things. They cannot love you back.

At that very dark moment in her life, when it was hard to think rationally and the light seemed very far away, a terrible idea entered her head. Either she would have to change her dream or let it die. She could not see giving it up, her mental picture of the future. All the joy would go out of her life if she did, in which case she might as well be dead. But it was also quite certain that she could not go on banking on Jim.

The problem was she really was in love with him. Even after everything he had done to her, she still loved him. She saw things in him that he did not seem to see himself. She saw, or felt, that they were soul mates. This is a very deep thing to feel, and it is what she felt. She saw Jim as a good person. His heart was in the right place, she was sure. He would make a good husband and father, if he could just give up whatever it was that was keeping him away from her.

But what was this something? She had no idea. In the past she had managed to convince herself it was a passing thing. She liked to think he was going through a phase and would eventually come to see that they were meant to be together. But she could not trust herself to think this comforting thought anymore. She could not keep putting herself through this kind of pain. She did not think she could survive it.

Erin made a momentous decision that night. She could not have Jim, but she was not going to let him ruin her life. Just sitting there in her hand-painted rocking chair made it hard to give up her dream because—well, because it was her dream. But maybe it was time to compromise a little in her ideas about relationships. She may have to give up on the kind of love she felt for Jim.

She decided to try to think about love a little differently. She would take a more rational approach to love and begin to look for someone who would make a good husband and treat her well. If she did not love him the way she loved Jim, then maybe that was a good thing. Maybe the love she thought she had for Jim wasn't real love anyway. She would find someone who could really love her and reward him with her real love.

After all, it was not like she was lacking in admirers. There were quite a few guys who had let their interest be known. She had some friends from school that she still saw occasionally—one of them an old flame. She could sort of see herself rekindling something with him. He was a nice enough guy. A couple of doctors at her new job had done more than their share of smiling at her, although one of them was married with children and three times her age.

And then there was Arthur. She thought it was sweet the way he came to her defense. Arthur was good-looking, intelligent, respectful, kind, had a good job. What else could a girl want?

What else indeed?

IX

Lots to ponder

MEANWHILE JIM COULD not sleep. He went to bed, he closed his eyes, he fluffed up his pillow—but he could not sleep. He couldn't get this darned Kerry Morgan thing out of his head. It was ridiculous. Bob was crazy. But he couldn't stop thinking about it.

He got up and went to the kitchen table and opened his laptop and Googled her. A multitude of results came up. He couldn't focus on them. That was because of the thumbnails. It definitely looked like Karen. He clicked on some of them and *that face* filled his screen. There were casual pictures. There were posed pictures. There were stills from her movies.

And all those pictures looked just like Karen. There could be no doubt. Or could there? It was possible that she had a doppelganger. He knew someone at work who looked just like Russell Crowe. You could put him in *L.A. Confidential* and most people would probably not know the difference, except for the talent.

Why couldn't there be someone who looked just like Kerry Morgan? Well, first of all, it was not just a resemblance. It was much stronger than that. There were the expressions. There were the smiles. He knew them all so well. Also she had such a unique and distinctive face. He could see why she was a movie star. Even in photos you could not stop looking at her.

Then there were all the mysteries surrounding "Karen." He thought about the diamond. He thought about the Dom Perignon. Who drinks that stuff? He thought about the outfits. He knew a lot of women who wore attractive outfits, but these were different somehow. They definitely didn't come from Macy's.

He thought about the "important meeting" she had on a Saturday. Now it made sense. A meeting that a movie star was involved in could happen on any day of the week. He thought about the sunglasses she always seemed to have on, even after the sun went down. They were huge. Hiding something?

Most of all he thought about the conversations. If she was Kerry Morgan, then there was a perfectly good reason for her to be suspicious, and it had nothing to do with whether or not he was attempting to woo her. It was about knowing who she was. It was about being a gold-digger. Many of the things she said that made no sense before suddenly made a lot of sense now. She was "too inclined to be kind." She wasn't referring to the picnic spread, as he thought at the time. She meant she was giving him too much leeway and trusting him too much.

But the joke was he really did not know who she was. Well, he knew who she was, but not what she looked like. He didn't pay any attention to the star-making machinery. As far as movies go, he was perfectly happy to watch Katherine Hepburn in *Philadelphia Story* or Margaret Sullavan in *Shop Around the Corner*, but he thought modern movies were generally overblown and confected, especially anything involving a comic book hero, which seemed to be the only kind of movie Hollywood was making after *Star Wars*.

He remembered their conversations about movies and plays and had to laugh. Many of the things she said meant something completely different if she was Kerry Morgan. But that was a big if! He still could not bring himself to believe it. After all, they found her passed out in a parking lot. It seemed inconceivable that someone with her star magnitude would be out alone and not protected by a beefy crew. She was too precious a commodity.

He had seen stars in Westport, occasionally, without security, but this was different. This was a woman passed out in a parking lot at night. He had carried her in his arms. Was it possible that he had carried Kerry Morgan in his arms? The thought made him a little dizzy. But no, he could not believe it.

He looked at the pictures again and wondered. Either he'd had a close encounter with a movie star or with someone who looked so much like her that it was downright scary. He put the second thought first without quite letting go of the other.

Because of course he was rather thrilled by the idea of having had an adventure with Kerry Morgan. He wanted to dwell on the thought, revel in it, take a warm bath in it. But it was foolish to think so highly of himself if she really was Karen and not Kerry.

On Monday morning he went to work and was just getting himself settled in when Dave Rodriguez came bounding into his office, as he often did, since they were the only ones in at the ungodly hour of eight. He seemed juiced.

"So I guess you heard the news."

"Not really," Jim said, barely able to keep his chin off the desk.

"Re-org coming. We're going to a more traditional model,

separation of powers, marketing and advertising. And they're bringing in a real marketing guy to run things—Paul Davidson."

"Sounds exciting."

"Yeah, I knew it all along. They couldn't keep going the way they were. Starlan's becoming too big. I mean, it's fine to have the entrepreneurial model when you're an entrepreneurial company, but at some point you just have to change."

"Rivers doesn't strike me as someone who would like that kind of change."

"Oh, I don't think this was Rivers. I think it was the board. Yeah, it's his company—but it's their money he's playing with. They took the risk, and now they expect him to step up to the plate and reward them by taking this thing to the next level. Davidson's title is VP marketing. That should tell you something right there."

"Okay. I'll bite."

"It means he's technically Henry's boss. It hasn't really been spelled out, but I think that's just their way of saving Henry's pride. Davidson will control the purse strings. Davidson will choose the agency and direct the campaigns."

"So you're saying Henry's not in charge anymore?"

"I think the sun's setting on that scenario. And it's about time. Let's face it. Henry is a bit of a dinosaur. The suspenders, the bowties, those eyebrows—come on. When you reach the two hundred million mark you start becoming a big company, and then you have to act and look like a big company."

Jim did not know how to feel about this news. He was torn between wanting to support Dave in his obvious enthusiasm for the change and his loyalty to Henry. He wanted to stay on Dave's good side, but he was also grateful to Henry for hiring him and putting him in a responsible position fresh out of college and leaving him alone. Apparently things were about to change.

Before he could respond, however, his phone rang. It was "déjà vu all over again," as the dream catcher would say. He saw Karen's number and sat there staring at it in shock.

"You need to get that?" said the Dynamic One.

"Family thing," Jim fibbed, reaching for the receiver.

"No problem. Catch you later. Just thought you'd want to know." And out he bounded like Tigger.

Jim rushed to pick up the phone and almost bobbled it.

"Hello?"

"Hello again!" said that same purring voice. "How are you?"

"I'm...good. Nice to hear from you."

"Nice to hear you, too. So what did you think of my little picnic the other day?"

"I thought it was incredible. I've never seen anything like it."

"Did you enjoy yourself?"

"I didn't have to. I was enjoying the picnic."

"Ha! I don't know what to think about you. Anyway, I was wondering if you felt like doing it again."

Five hundred years or perhaps a thousand intervened while Jim was trying to absorb this tantalizing question. It was definitely not what he was expecting. He remembered his computer screen with all the perfect pictures of Kerry Morgan. Was this Kerry Morgan that he was talking to? The real Kerry Morgan? He wasn't sure he wanted it to be. He almost felt up to negotiating Karen McNamera. Almost. Kerry Morgan was another matter entirely.

"I would love to," he said after a pause. "Why don't you let me bring the food this time?"

"Don't be silly. I like doing it. How about tonight? It's supposed to be beautiful."

"Okay. Sounds good. I don't see any reason why not."

"You don't sound too sure."

"Oh, no. I'm just surprised to hear from you," he confessed.

"Good surprised or bad surprised?"

"Definitely good. I figured you had already thanked me and—"

"And what?"

"I don't know. Just 'and.'"

"You are so funny. Come to think of it, there is something you can do. You can bring *As You Like It*. I was thinking it would be fun to read through some scenes with you, since you love the play so much."

"I would be happy to." There was the commanding thing again. It wasn't like he kept a copy in his back pocket. He would have to make a stop at the library. But he didn't mind. He wanted to please her. In fact he had never felt more motivated to please someone in his entire life.

"Same time? Six or so?"

"Works for me."

"See you then!"

Jim sat there stunned, trying to understand what just happened.

The first time she invited him it could have been construed as pure gratitude, but this definitely seemed like something else. It wasn't just the fact that she invited him *again*. It was the tone. There was a smile in her voice. An affectionate smile he had not heard before.

Then other thoughts came crowding in on these very pleasant ones. She wanted to be the one to bring the food again. It was his turn, but she insisted. He did not know whether to be flattered by this or somewhat offended. It was flattering to have someone want to treat you, but guys like to treat too. Otherwise it's hard for them to feel like guys. He wanted to feel like her equal.

Then again he wasn't really her equal, was he? Not if by some weird chance she turned out to be the person Bob said she was. Compared to Karen McNamera he felt a little small, maybe, but compared to Kerry Morgan he felt like literally nothing. It was the first time he had thought about this. What if she really was Kerry Morgan? The idea was thrilling and terrifying at the same time.

What could he possibly bring to the table? Apparently nothing. Literally. She wouldn't let him. Also he had seen the diamond. He knew he could not compete with it. He could make some poor jokes. She seemed to like it when he did. She laughed at them, anyway. She said she loved guys with a good sense of humor. But if she really did turn out to be Kerry Morgan, he wasn't even sure he could do that. It would be like joking with the Queen.

What was it all about, anyway? Did she want to be his friend? Was he someone to spend time with, someone perhaps to entertain her? It seemed plausible, given her planned activity for the evening. He just could not get his head around any other explanation. Of course you can't actually get your head "around" something. That's just another one of those silly expressions.

He thought of Queen Bess and Essex, living in the drapefolds of history. It always seemed to him that they must have had a strange relationship, whether intimate or not. There can be no parity between a queen and her subject. She can never really be free with him because she has too much to protect—and he can never be free with her because it is too darned dangerous.

Jim felt a little like Essex at that moment—assuming, of course, that Karen really was Kerry. He wanted to go to her and he wanted to run away. He wanted her to smile on him and he was afraid of not being found worthy. In any case it was all speculation. He did not know if she was Kerry Morgan. He had every reason to doubt it—including this new invitation.

There was no need to be anxious about it, even if she was. He was going to a picnic. He knew how to do that. She wanted to read Shakespeare. This also was something he could do. He was pretty good at reading Shakespeare, or so he had been told. When he read it out loud he got lost in the masterful writing and psychology of the roles and the beautiful flow of the verse. It gave him a chance to prove himself.

He had discovered how to communicate with her. You just had to let her lead. She wanted the conversation to go where she wanted it to go. In a sense this made things very easy for him. All he had to do was watch for the cues. He had done it before. He could do it again. He was not the domineering type. He had plenty of strong women in his life, beginning with his mother and sister.

Besides, it was easy to defer to her. Kerry Morgan or not, she was gorgeous. Men are foolish creatures, as easily awed by beauty as a housemaid by the President. The best they can do is try to act calm in its presence, but even then they are faking it. If there is such a thing as an evolutionary imperative, then Karen/Kerry was issuing the orders. He could not countermand them. He was not Rhett Butler. He had no choice but to give in.

These were the kinds of thoughts that occupied him all day long. And what a long, long day it was! At least he had something to keep him busy. He was a procrastinator, especially when it came to the "b" products, and was up against a hard deadline for a "b" brochure. It was dreadfully boring, but it made the time pass. He was just wrapping it up when five o'clock rolled around.

Then he was off to Sherwood Isle for the *second* time. It was very much like the first time. She was parked in almost the same spot. There were more people on a hot night, but the park was not crowded. The food was different—buttery tenderloin sandwiches on baguettes—of which she took only about two miniscule bites—but the champagne was the same and so was the conversation.

They talked more, which made him happy. There were no long awkward silences. But it was still all on the surface, as if they were tacitly avoiding any warmth or intimacy. This was frustrating, first because it got boring after a while, but also because he kept hoping she would let her guard down. He wanted her to show some true friendliness, some connection, and she was not cooperating.

It was partly his own fault. All he could think about was the

Kerry Morgan thing. He was dying to ask her about it but afraid of jeopardizing any progress he might have made. What if she was not Kerry Morgan? Or what if she did not want him to *know* she was Kerry Morgan? If she was, there had to be a reason why she wasn't telling him. And he would look like an idiot if she wasn't.

He was not complaining, however. He was having a picnic on the beach on a summer night with a beautiful woman who may or may not have been Kerry Morgan. This was an omnibus of fun in itself. The sandwiches were fantastic. He was getting used to the champagne. And this time she sat quite close to him. So close he thought he could feel her body heat.

Actually he was generating some pretty serious body heat of his own. Every time he looked at her it was like he was seeing her for the first time. It took all of his advanced Jedi mind powers to resist the temptation to stare. His eyes were devouring her. He didn't know what they were feeding, but it was certainly very insistent.

After dessert—he had a piece of delicious strawberry rhubarb pie, she took a piece but appeared to push it around on her plate carefully without actually sampling it—came the reading. She knew exactly what she wanted. She directed him to Act 3, Scene 2. She wanted to play Rosalind…and she wanted him to play Orlando.

Well! This was interesting. On many levels. There was the hidden identity thing. Also he adored Rosalind. He thought he might be on the verge of adoring Karen as well. Let's just say it was not difficult for him to act his part. He wasn't really acting at all. "I am he that is so love-shaked: I pray you tell me your remedy." He wasn't kidding; at that point he was literally shaking with love.

Partly it was because of her reading. Maybe "reading" isn't the right word. She seemed to know the lines by heart. Her diction was perfect. Every word was clearly distinguishable and could have been understood without effort in a large theater. But most of all the *expression* was perfect. Absolutely perfect. She understood what was intended, how to deliver the lines. And that is rare. And a little overwhelming for someone with his mad love of the Bard.

"Wow," he said when they were done. "You are amazing."

"You think so?" she said with a smile.

"Absolutely. That is the best Rosalind I've ever heard. Did you play that part in school?"

"As a matter of fact I did. It was a lot of fun. I didn't know very much about Shakespeare before that. I didn't realize how fun it was to do his comedies. My professor taught me all that."

"Yes, but what you just did can't really be taught. Or at least I don't think so. You can't teach someone to feel the lines the way you feel them. That's just something you're born with, like Mozart at the piano, or Tony Gwynn with a fastball. And you can't teach someone to read them like poetry. That requires an ear for poetry."

"Well, thank you very much. You are sweet. As I said, I enjoy doing it. I thought you might enjoy it too, Mr. English major, Mr. Yale graduate. By the way, you read very well."

"Not like you," he said, and for once he didn't have to pretend.

She beamed at him. Jim was dying in this pause. He so much wanted to ask the question that was hanging on his lips. He so much wanted to know if this adorable actress sitting next to him was Kerry Morgan. But then it didn't seem right. Kerry Morgan was a movie star. To him there was a huge difference between what screen actors do and what happens on the stage. He couldn't imagine a movie star delivering those lines the way she had just read them. Or maybe he was just being prejudiced.

Either way, the burning desire faded and he shrank back into his unheroic self. After all, it was sheer madness to think she could be Kerry Morgan. Would someone like that come to a state park and spend time with a commoner like him? It was inconceivable. And yes, he *did* know what that word means.

The evening ended very cordially, much more so than the last time. They had a bond now—Shakespeare. She was looking at him differently; he could feel it, treating him differently. For the first time she showed something like affection and warmth. Her sharp lines softened considerably. She was not so much on guard, prickly.

He still wasn't entirely sure that he would ever see her again. But he did see her. She invited him for another picnic the following week. This time it was a Wednesday. They read another scene from the play. Then two weeks after that. She wanted to try something from *A Midsummer's Night Dream*, his other favorite. He thought she was hilarious. She was a very good comedienne. More Carole Lombard than Claudette Colbert, in spite of the hair color.

It was always the same routine. She would call him at work in the morning and issue the invitation. She always wanted to meet at the same place and parked in the same spot. There was always a tantalizing spread with champagne, although not as elaborate as the first time. And she refused to let him bring anything. He offered, but she refused. She laughed at him when he offered, which made him feel strange, and, well, to be honest, kind of small.

They always wound up sitting on the same picnic table looking at the Sound and chatting. If there was one thing Jim could do, it was talk. In fact he wondered if his willingness to entertain her was the thing that kept getting him invited back. There didn't seem to be any other reason. But in another sense it was all very, very weird. What were they doing? Was he supposed to be her friend? He had no idea what was going on in her head.

These were definitely command performances. She dictated the time and place and everything else for that matter, including what he did and did not talk about. They did not seem to be friends in the sense that he was friends with Bob or Arthur or—well—Erin. He still did not feel really comfortable with her, except when they were reading scenes from the plays; and not even then, because he was acutely aware of her superiority.

Still, for some reason she kept calling. He was happy to be called, singled out as it were. Nor was he a complete mendicant with his hat in his hands. He had a curious mind, knew something about music and philosophy and art in addition to literature, at least enough to fake it, which was the most important thing. She enjoyed listening to him talk about such things. She liked "intellectual conversation," as she called it.

This went on all summer. It wasn't every week, to be sure, but there was never more than two weeks between dates, or whatever the heck they were. Finally there was a change in the routine. It was the end of August and there was a bit of a chill in the air, a harbinger of fall. She had a fleece on. All he had was his pinstripe Oxford. The usual chatter stopped as dusk fell, and then he was chattering in another way.

"So when do I get to see this famous cottage of yours?" she said out of the blue.

"I didn't know you wanted to see it."

"Of course I do! Don't be silly. Why wouldn't I want to see it?"

"I don't know. There's not much to see."

"So that's why you're always raving about it. It will have to be soon, though. I'm going away next week. On business. Could be gone for a while, unfortunately."

"Okay. How about Saturday?"

"Sounds good! I'm free on Saturday. Can't wait to see it."

Jim did not know what to say. The polite response would have been something like "looking forward to having you there," but it occurred to him that this didn't sound right. He didn't know what to say because he didn't know why she wanted to come. Was it just idle curiosity? What was it?

It was very flattering, but by this time a strong impression had been established in his mind of the difference between them in terms of wealth. She could not spend money the way she did unless she had a lot of it. The champagne alone must have cost her a thousand dollars over the summer. Her picnics were like going to five-star restaurants. And her outfits and jewelry were like a bloody fashion show.

His humble two-bedroom man cave on the lake…not so much. He liked it; his friends liked it; but he felt some trepidation about exposing it to someone like her. Oh well, it was too late to worry about that now. She was coming and there was no denying her. "You can't stop a tidal wave."

They were quiet for a moment. Then she said, "Also, how come you never tried to kiss me?"

What? An electrical charge went through him. But once again he did not know how to respond. Did it mean she *wanted* him to try to kiss her? This thought made his head spin. Lord knows he was willing, if that was the case. But was it? Or was she testing him somehow? Was she trying to find out if his intentions were as pure as he was making them out to be? Her tone was not exactly playful. It was almost like she was challenging him.

"I guess I didn't know if I should," he said carefully.

She chuckled. "No, maybe you shouldn't. You're a strange one. Just when I think I have you figured out, you surprise me. But that's what I love about you."

Did she really say *love*? Now he wished he'd given a different answer. He didn't know what answer he might have given, but he definitely did want to kiss her. She was sitting right next to him. He wanted to touch her. He was cold. He wanted to put his arm around her and pull her to him. And oh yes, he wanted to kiss her.

He did none of those things. He could not see himself trying to kiss her when she had just said she loved him for not trying to kiss her. They had a perfect moment together and his instincts told him to leave it alone. Even though he was freezing and would have enjoyed a little kiss, two being better than one.

She gave him the now-customary hug when they parted at her car. But this time it was a little firmer and lasted a little longer.

X

The lake cottage

SHE WANTED TO COME to his *house*? Really? He was stunned and flattered at the same time. But what did it mean? Her behavior up to that point could best be described as—well, formal. She warmed up a bit when they were reading Shakespeare but otherwise seemed determined to keep a polite if friendly distance. She sat next to him on every date, but physical proximity was not matched by emotional proximity. She struck him as a barrier girl. He never felt any real warmth coming from her of the type that might be expected between prospective lovers.

Now of course this was explicable just on the basis of her beauty. She probably had to be on her guard at all times against all kinds of adventurism, all kinds of lies and posturing. And of course it was doubly true if she really was Kerry Morgan, which he was beginning to strongly suspect. People like that have to be very careful about whom they trust.

But he *wanted* her to let down her guard. He wanted to know where he stood. Why did she keep inviting him to these crazy picnics? Was it friendship or was it something else? If it was friendship, it was strange. She didn't really let him feel like her friend. But if it was something else it was even stranger. She was playful with him at times but not exactly amorous. More like cat and mouse.

And now she wanted to see his house. The whole thing seemed bizarre. *His* adoration was plain, or at least he thought it was, but she seemed unapproachable. And he respected that. He wasn't even trying to approach her. He wasn't the one doing the calling. She was calling him. But he did not know why. He had no idea of what she was looking for or what it was all about even after several interesting encounters.

He practically melted when she said she "loved" him for being unpredictable. But there were two problems with that. First of all, it was like saying "I love the way you fold those towels." It didn't mean she loved *him*. Second, he didn't necessarily want to be unpredictable. What he wanted was to love and be loved, the most predictable thing of all.

Besides, he didn't know how deep the well of unpredictability ran. She seemed to think he was playing four-dimensional chess when the truth is he wasn't playing anything at all. He quite literally did not know if he should try to kiss her. He was happy to be misunderstood if it endeared him to her, but it made him feel that his claim on her affections was a little tenuous, or even specious.

Also he did not *want* to play four-dimensional chess. It wasn't his idea of being in love. He wanted her to be Amelia, but sometimes she seemed a little more like Becky Sharp. It reminded him of his relationship with his sister. There was always too much going on in that pretty little head of hers.

And yet he could not deny that she was captivating. It wasn't just the beauty thing. No, she was interesting on her own merits. She was a good conversationalist on topics he enjoyed, like art and culture, if occasionally obscure. She played Shakespeare's heroines beautifully. This in itself was enough to make him adore her. She was literally his Rosalind, or had been for a few blissful moments.

She was also impossibly desirable. He was, after all, male. To be in her presence was to be in a perpetual state of, well, excitement. But it was the seeming impossibility that made it so exciting. And in that case what about the question she asked him? Did she want him to try to kiss her? It almost lowered her from the firmament. On the other hand, he was willing, if the call should come.

Friday night was a sleepless night under a nearly full moon, and Saturday was spent mowing and gardening and shopping and doing several months' worth of cleaning, all dulled by lack of sleep; but at last the much anticipated moment arrived, and he heard a knock and went to the front door and opened it, and sure enough, there she was, actually standing there, beaming at him.

She entered his lowly cottage like a goddess. It was late afternoon and no lights were on, but they were not needed. Everything was transformed by her presence. Her graces covered all that was drab and unsatisfactory, all afternoon shadows, but whether this was the coming of Venus or Diana he did not know.

In any case she appeared to be in a very good mood. He had never seen her like this before. There was none of the usual coyness or reserve, no challenging edge in her tone. She was almost human, full of good cheer and compliments, as if coming to his house was the most wonderful thing in the world. He was amazed.

"Can I get you a drink?" he said.

"Don't you think it's a little early for that?" she replied with a good-natured smile.

"Oh—right. Sorry. How about a swim, then?"

"That would be great. It's hot. Where can I change?"

He showed her to the guest bedroom and went to his own to put on a pair of trunks, deliberating over his collection, then getting confused, and finally just grabbing one. As he undressed, the thought occurred to him that she was doing the same thing in a nearby room. He felt a little faint.

In a couple of minutes she emerged from Bob's room (that's how he thought of it) in a very attractive one-piece swimsuit. He was momentarily paralyzed and had to steady himself. The curves were, well, curvy. He resisted the temptation to say "wow." He did not know her that well.

Somehow he managed to lead her down the long boardwalk and steps to the dock without falling flat on his face. He was carrying towels and did not know what to do with his hands. She actually laughed at him, but it was an affectionate laugh. From that point on he felt he would be in her debt forever.

He was still afraid to look at her. The one-piece bathing suit was not in the show-all style of the ubiquitous bikini, much less the vanishing thong, but on her it was ten times more alluring. It gave her an elegant look that perfectly matched her unmatched dark beauty. She was like something out of a dream.

Was this godlike personage with the annihilating smile really at his house and was she really walking with him on his dock? He prayed she didn't get a splinter in her delicate bare feet. He'd gotten one earlier that week. Dear God, don't let her get a splinter!

She did not. But then again it was not entirely clear that her adorable feet were touching the wood. He didn't see them touch.

"Oh—it's so beautiful!" she said. And indeed, it was beautiful, a perfect summer afternoon at a calm lake in the Litchfield Hills.

"Well, there's only one way to do this," she proclaimed. And with that she dove boldly into the water. A few moments later she came up screaming, pushing away a long strand of milfoil from her left shoulder.

"What is that?"

"Seaweed. Perfectly harmless," he called out, and then heroically plunged himself into the waters to succor her.

"There certainly is a lot of it," she said, playfully pushing him away.

"Yes, they have a major problem with it on the lake. Not sure who 'they' are, exactly, but they seem perturbed."

"It's yucky."

"It does tend to cling to you." He blushed when he realized what he had said. "Let's swim out a little farther. It goes away."

This was the first time he had given *her* an order. It felt kind of good. They swam out into paradise. The water was cool, the sky was blue, the high sunlit green hills rimmed the lake. She rolled over and floated on her back. He admired the maneuver exceedingly. But then there was a roar in the distance and smoke on the water.

"Okay, maybe we should go back in."

"Now what?"

"Well, technically we have the right of way, but we probably don't want to get run over. You can never tell how much drinking has been going on in these speed boats on a Saturday afternoon."

"Oh, great."

They swam in and climbed out of the water and sat on the edge of the dock, enjoying the warm sun.

"It really is beautiful here," she said. "You must love it."

"I do. The combination of the lake and the hills is very attractive. Not quite as spectacular as Lake George, obviously, but still wonderful."

"*I* think it's spectacular, anyway. If I lived here, I'd be out on this dock every single day, just soaking it all in."

"No you wouldn't."

"What!"

"You wouldn't. Trust me. I kayak all around the lake, and one thing that always amazes me is the empty docks. I think if you actually live here you forget how beautiful it is. You see it all the time, so you're not so excited about it."

"Not me," she insisted. "I'd be down here every day. Eating my breakfast, my lunch, having my cocktail before dinner."

"Jeeves could bring them to you," he suggested.

"Jeeves?"

"The butler."

"Oh—right. She would do that."

So she had a butler! Interesting. They sat in the sun for a while, happily padding their feet on the soft water. Then a couple of intense-looking gentlemen came floating into view on a bass boat.

"Who is that?" she whispered.

"Just some random strangers. They like to come by from time to time and share our lake experience with us, gaily chatting or tossing lures at our heads."

"I think I'll take that drink now," she said, suddenly rising and heading for the steps.

What was this all about? Was she afraid of fishermen for some reason? He hopped up and followed her to the house. He was not completely able to keep his eyes to himself. The one-piece suit did not cover her back, in fact dipped in a fashion that could only be called dramatic, which was a source of some fascination.

They changed into dry clothes and went to the kitchen and Jim made them drinks. Gin and diet tonic. He took his first sip. He had not had anything to eat or drink all day. It went directly to his head and floated there like a silvery cloud.

Jim felt safe and secure in his kitchen. She could not shake him from that tree. He did prep work while they chatted about the lake and the house. She was full of compliments, which surprised him. But why was he surprised? He scolded himself. He shouldn't be making assumptions about her.

He started the rice in stock and corn on the cob and green beans and melted the butter and swirled some garlic cloves around and threw in some fresh tarragon and finally the shrimp, which he gently sautéed until pink.

"Wow! You can do all this?" she said, seeming impressed.

"Are you kidding? This is nothing compared to your picnics."

"Oh—I had help," she said laughing. "Actually I'm a complete disaster in the kitchen. Just not something I'm interested in at this point in my life."

Jim pondered this information. It occurred to him that he had learned more about her in the past hour than in all their multitudinous evenings on the beach. She seemed to be in a revelatory mood. He was happy about that. Maybe his burning curiosity about the Karen/Kerry thing would finally be satisfied.

She had a butler and a cook working for her, apparently. This information seemed to tilt the scales in a certain direction. Still, he couldn't be sure—and he was afraid to ask. At this point he *couldn't* ask. He had been playing dumb ever since Bob pointed out the possibility. He didn't want to expose himself.

Also she must have a good reason for not wanting him to know—that is, if she was Kerry Morgan. He felt bound to respect that reason. But honestly, he was dying to know. It was almost all he could think about. It wasn't just idle curiosity. It was about them. He could not have a relationship with someone who was pretending to be someone else.

Suddenly he felt shy in his own house. Was this really Kerry Morgan sitting on his barstool? The thought was daunting. Still, he was able to carry on a fairly decent conversation. It helped that he was cooking. The simple ritual soothed him. He could keep two thoughts in his head at one time but not three. With cooking and conversing, the Kerry question was pushed to the side.

It came roaring back when all the cooking was done and they sat down together at the dinner table. He fetched the nice bottle of pinot blanc he had picked up that afternoon and uncorked it and filled their glasses. Now he almost regretted not getting the wine she liked so much. The price tag dissuaded him. He was feeling amorous, not insane.

She helped him with the serving dishes, which charmed him, and then they sat down. All of a sudden he felt very self-conscious and rather nervous. His cooking was on review.

"It looks fantastic!" she enthused. "Where did you learn how to cook like this?"

"Oh, I don't know. My mother is a very good cook. Lots and lots of entertaining. I guess I caught the bug from her. I enjoy it, so I think that's what makes the difference."

"I don't enjoy it, and I couldn't even imagine putting something like this together. But you are just full of surprises. What else don't I know about you?"

"At this point I think you know everything about me. But I still don't know very much about you."

"Of course you do! I told you everything. I'm from Iowa. I studied theater."

"That's 'everything'?" he teased.

"Pretty much. The interesting things, anyway. I don't really like talking about myself. It's much more fun to talk about you."

"You told me you sold dreams, but you didn't tell me what that really means."

"You still remember that?" she said laughing.

"I remember every word you ever said to me."

"You are such a tease. But are you sure you want to know?"

"It's a very interesting thing to say. Could mean a lot of things. All salesman are sellers of dreams, I suppose."

"A very wise man once told me that we are all salesman. We are selling ourselves all the time. I don't mean selling out—I mean trying to impress people for one reason or another. That was one of the best insights anyone ever gave me. It helped me get to where I wanted to go, because up to that point I was not thinking about the idea of selling myself, of who I wanted to be perceived to be."

"And where did you want to go?"

"Oh, you know—places," she said with an adorable smile. "Let's just say I had certain goals and didn't know how to get there at the time. But all that changed when I realized I had to sell myself, when I actually got this concept in my head. I was always good at what I did, but you need more than that to get to the next level. It's about so much more than that, I can't even tell you."

This was all very interesting. Should he push a little more? He decided not to. She was in such a good mood, so relaxed, smiling on him in a way she had never smiled before. And sans sunglasses.

"That's supposed to be a pretty good wine," he said apologetically. "I know it's not your favorite."

"Oh, stop. I didn't expect you to get me that. And yes, it is delicious. Very good with the shrimp. You have good taste."

"Well, I guess I'm like everybody else. I ask the guy at the store what's good with seafood and pretend to trust him. Kind of hard to tell with thousands of bottles to choose from."

"I know some people who really do know. Not me personally, I just have the same thing all the time. But I do know some real wine connoisseurs who can go on and on about this sort of thing."

"Ah yes, the fruity palate with a hint of citron that leaves a bright finish."

"Exactly! It can get out of hand sometimes. But they do seem to know what they're talking about."

"I don't know. Sort of a beer man myself. I do like wine occasionally, but good wine is so expensive."

"It can be. I was at a restaurant with some people a couple of weeks ago and the bill was two thousand dollars. And most of that was the wine. Fortunately I wasn't paying."

"Wow! Does that happen often?"

"Oh—that's nothing, believe me. I've seen it go way higher. People get kind of competitive in those situations. Certain people, anyway. I just sit back and enjoy the show. I really do like good wine, but I don't know much about it. Plus I have to be careful. Red wine goes right to my head."

"'You go to my head, like a sip of sparkling burgundy brew.'"

"Something like that," she said with a smile.

He surprised himself into silence with this burst of lyric verse. And then he felt too self-conscious to say anything else or even look at her. So they sat there eating quietly with Sting murmuring something about fields of gold in the background. She ate more than he had ever seen her eat. It was flattering. She seemed to like it. She said it was delicious. He felt like he was starting to relax with her for the first time, really relax. She seemed so relaxed herself and so uncharacteristically open.

Then he relaxed a little *too* much. He pulled his feet back in a casual way and immediately felt a white-hot dagger creeping up his right thigh. He was having a cramp. It was the morning gardening and the dehydration.

But how embarrassing! There was no way to hide it. He sat there in complete agony for a couple of seconds but then was forced to jump up and hop around like a madman. He managed to knock over his wine glass in the process.

"Sorry," he gasped.

"What is it? What's wrong?" she said in alarm.

"Leg cramp. Sat the wrong way." He walked around on his toes, which usually worked, but this was a cramp of Godzillian proportions. It kept coming and coming and coming. He didn't know what he was going to do. Meanwhile he was in agony twice over because he felt like he was making a complete ass of himself.

After what seemed like an eternity, but was probably only a couple of minutes, it stopped getting worse. It wasn't getting better, not yet, but at least he felt like he had a chance of surviving.

"Well, this is embarrassing," he managed to sputter.

"Embarrassing! Why? You have a cramp. It's not your fault. Is it going away?"

"Not really."

"Let me see if I can help." She came to him and knelt down and started massaging his leg. No—we're not kidding. Her warm little hands were on the back of his right thigh. He was caught somewhere between the agony and the ecstasy. Finally the cramp began to recede as other tidal forces took hold.

"Wow. That's great. Thank you," he said. And he wasn't kidding. She really did seem to be a skilled rubber of legs.

"I learned that in yoga class. You have quite a knot there."

"Yes, I'm very knotty." He realized what he said and looked at her. They both burst out laughing.

"So the reason you have a bad cramp is you're so muscular. Lie down on your stomach," she commanded, leading him to the couch. He felt compelled to obey. She kneeled between his legs and began to massage the tight hamstring muscle again.

"That's better," she said. "I can feel it loosening up."

"Must have been the gardening," he said, feeling very foolish or not really knowing what he was feeling.

"You garden, too?" she said with a laugh.

"A little. You're very good at that, by the way. Very soothing."

He wasn't kidding. Her warm touch was like magic. But as the physical pain subsided a certain mental anguish rushed in to take its place. What was he going to do now? He was starting to feel much better. He couldn't lie there pretending to have a cramp forever. But he also did not want her to stop whatever it was she was doing. He was enjoying the touch of her hands a little too much.

"Turn over," she commanded. He did, and much to his surprise she crept up on him and kissed him. The kiss was a little tentative at first but then not so much, and her lips were warm with wine. Jim was shocked. Was this really happening?

She stopped and looked at him with a little smile. "You look surprised. Were you expecting that?"

"I wasn't *expecting* anything," he said truthfully.

"But do you like it?"

Instead of answering he pulled her to him and kissed her again. Her kisses were soft and sweet. His pain was forgotten.

XI

Crickets

MUCH LATER, lying together dreamily on the couch, quite dark outside except for the bright moon over the lake.

"What is that racket?" she said.

"Oh, that's just the katydids and crickets. They get kind of feisty this time of year."

"It's spooky."

"I don't know, I kind of like it. Joyous cacophony."

He could feel her smile against his chest. A few minutes of bliss went by. Then something changed.

"So I need to talk to you," she said.

"Uh-oh."

"No, it's not bad. Remember I told you I had to go away?"

"I do remember something about that."

"Well, it's tomorrow. And it could be a while, unfortunately."

"How long?"

"Depends. If I get lucky, it'll just be a few weeks. That's what they're telling me, but that's what they always tell me. One time it was almost six months. It was ridiculous."

"I hope it isn't that long," he surprised himself by saying. She looked at him with an almost indescribable expression. "Did I say something wrong?"

"No, you didn't say anything wrong. You made me happy."

"But what?"

She paused. She stroked his chest. "I guess the question is will you still be here if it is? I mean, what if it really is six months? Oh—what am I saying? That is so selfish."

"Of course I'll be here. This is my house."

"No, that isn't what I mean. You're making fun of me."

"You mean will I wait for you."

"I don't know. I guess so." She looked up at him. "Will you?"

"I can do that. I'm pretty patient. Six months isn't very long."

She smiled and for the first time looked deeply into his eyes. "Thank you for saying that. It means a lot to me. I really don't think it will be that long. I just wish we could stay the way we are right now. I wish I didn't have to go away at all."

"By the way, where are you going? You never told me."

The smile faded. She looked away. "No, I didn't." She looked back at him. "Are you really sure you want to know?"

"Why wouldn't I want to know?"

"I don't know. I'm afraid. I've had so much fun with you. This has been so great. I can't even tell you. I needed this so much."

"But what are you afraid of? I don't understand."

For a moment she looked almost like she was going to cry. Then she looked a little cross. "What are you doing tomorrow?"

"Nothing that I know of. Why?"

"How would you like to come down and see me off? At my house, I mean."

"Of course. I'd be happy to."

"Good. Then I'll answer all of your questions. I promise."

They had a late dessert, homemade cheesecake, which she surprised him by eating. He made her a cup of coffee and she was off. Jim was overwhelmed. There was just too much for him to process. There were the kisses. He felt a certain soul-sickness about that. There was the nice time they'd had together, the first time he had really felt comfortable with her, ever. And then there was the hammer blow. She was going away!

She would not tell him where. It was a big secret, apparently. Also she did not seem to know how long. These things pointed to a certain conclusion. It sounded for all the world like a movie shoot. The timing depended on how things went.

He still could not be sure that she was Kerry Morgan. But now he had been invited to her house. She actually had a house, it seemed, and was not just some wood nymph who appeared from time to time to spread good cheer among mortals. She gave him an address. He would be going tomorrow.

He was surprised by her changing moods. What did they mean? He knew what he wanted them to mean, but he could not be sure. It seemed like he had made her happy by indicating a willingness to wait for her. She smiled on him. It wasn't the usual hard smile, either; it made him melt. But then the clouds rolled in when he wanted to know where she was going. He was not expecting such a strong reaction. He did not know what to make of it.

Was it possible that she was in love with him? The signs seemed to point in that direction, in addition to the most obvious one. This thought made him dangerously happy. But the mitigating factor was those changing moods, like cloud shadows on the face of a mountain. What was going on in that pretty head of hers? Did he really want to know?

He felt like he was very much in love with her. But her feelings toward him seemed a good deal more complicated. She had come closer to tenderness than ever before—closer to true intimacy—but then a moment later the old barrier seemed to go up and the tenderness fled.

It was his fault. He should not have pushed the issue and insisted on knowing where she was going. But it was natural for him to want to know, wasn't it? If they were in love, wouldn't he want to know where she was going? Wouldn't she be eager to tell him? Her reticence made him feel uncertain. He did not know where he really stood with her.

But still—he was going to her house! It was momentous. It seemed like a sign of…something. He just wasn't sure what. At the very least it seemed like she was beginning to trust him. She could have invited him to her house anytime. It would have been easier than inviting him to the beach. But she clearly had trust issues—had admitted as much. This seemed to have changed.

He was exhausted from his long day. He needed to sleep. It was hard to sleep with the full moon pouring in the windows. He loved the moon, but the pragmatist prevailed in the end and he got up and closed the blinds. He drifted off into dreamland after going over the events of the evening about a thousand times in his head.

XII

Karen's little bungalow

TOMORROW CAME. It always does. But now his former excitement was supplanted by a degree of trepidation. He was going to her house. It was a little scary, depending on whether Bob was right about her.

She wanted him to come around noon. He made himself some breakfast and did other things to cause the fat intervening hours to go away. Finally it was ten and he couldn't stand it any longer. If he was early, he was early.

It turned out she lived in New Canaan. He was going to the Promised Land. There was very little traffic; he had no difficulty finding her street with his Garmin. But for some reason he couldn't figure out where her house was. The nice GPS lady kept saying "you have arrived at your destination," but all he could see was a red brick guardhouse with an iron gate.

Then it dawned on him. This *was* her driveway. Now he almost felt like turning around and going home. Instead he pulled in. There was actually a man sitting in the guard house. A very bored-looking man reading a newspaper. Jim rolled down his window and said "Karen McNamera."

"What about her?" the dour man said.

"I—have an appointment to see her."

"Are you Mr. Wilmot?"

"No—I mean yes."

"You are, or you aren't?"

"I'm Jim Wilmot." He wasn't used to being called "mister."

"Very good. Go on up."

The gate opened and Jim drove in, not knowing what to expect. It was a long driveway lined with huge gorgeous sugar maples, perfectly spaced. A mammoth brick mansion came into view in a slow reveal as he drove around the bend. This was her "house"?

He parked in the circular drive at the front door. Now he wished he had brought along a hostess gift, some flowers, anything to make him feel a little less naked. He got out of his car and went to the massive door and rang the bell. It opened, and a dark, wiry woman puffed up in a starchy uniform looked at him. "Yes?"

"Jim Wilmot to see Karen?" He still wasn't sure he was in the right place. It just didn't seem possible that the girl with the Jeep lived here. Unless...

"Come right in. She be happy to see you," she said through a thick accent.

He be happy to see her too. But where was she? He stepped into a giant foyer with a circular staircase. He looked at the elaborate woodwork and the moldings and the chandelier and his jaw dropped. The closest he had come to anything like this was in the Newport mansions, which he toured with his parents when he was a kid. It wasn't quite as gaudy—but it was close!

Karen came gliding down the staircase in a light-colored blouse and shorts, ready for travel. She walked right up to him and gave him a kiss and a heartfelt squeeze. He squeezed her back. He felt funny squeezing her. He was watching himself squeeze her. It did not seem real in that setting.

"Did you have any trouble finding it?"

"Not at all. But I can't believe you live here."

"Can't you?" she said looking at him with a curious expression.

"This place is stunning. Both the house and the grounds."

"Yes, it is a little stunning. But are you really surprised?"

"Is it your parents' house?" he said, pretending not to know what she meant, which of course he did.

"No, it's all mine. My parents have never been here. And only one of them is welcome. I would show you around but I have to get to Westchester Airport and we don't have much time."

"No need to. You do what you have to do."

"Let's go to the atrium. Maria—can you bring us some coffee?" He noticed a change in her tone. It became mirthless, businesslike, not at all like the night before, in spite of the passionate hug—and it *was* passionate. It was more like they were on the beach again and yesterday had never happened.

She led him to the back of the house and a beautiful two-story open atrium full of all kinds of exotic plants and flowers. They sat down at a glass table on a sort of indoor patio.

"This is gorgeous," he gushed. He wasn't exaggerating. It really was, lush greenery and white marble and polished brass, everything so perfectly in its place.

"I guess so. It doesn't seem all that gorgeous to me right now."

"Really? Most people would kill to have a place like this to sit and have their morning coffee."

"I didn't have to kill for it, fortunately. At least not yet. But this is very difficult for me."

"What is? I don't understand."

She looked at him. So long it became uncomfortable. "So you know I'm going away."

"Yes. You told me."

"For a long time."

"So you said."

"You don't seem very surprised."

"People have to travel for work these days. I understand that."

"But is that the only reason you weren't surprised? Because people have to travel for work?"

"I was surprised by the fact that you didn't know how long. But I guess these things happen."

She shook her head. "I see you're going to make this difficult." She was about to say something and then stopped. "Come."

They went to a part of the house that was like an annex. She took him to the smallest room he had seen so far, which made him feel strangely comfortable. This comfort wasn't going to last long, however. She pointed to a framed poster on the wall for a movie called *Wishing You Were Here*.

"Do you know who that is?" she said.

Now this was a question. First of all, the person on the poster was plainly she. There could be no doubt about it. He didn't even try to resist the obvious conclusion. And the name on the poster, in giant letters, was Kerry Morgan. So Bob was right after all. She really was the famous actress.

"It looks just like you"

"Yes, it does, doesn't it. Do you see the name?"

"Kerry Morgan."

"Do you know who she is?"

"She's a movie actress."

"And?"

"So you are—Kerry Morgan?" It was the question he had been dying to ask for a month, although not under these circumstances.

She laughed, almost scornfully. "You're saying you had no idea it was me all this time?"

"You told me your name was Karen McNamera."

"That is my name. Kerry Morgan is my stage name."

Duh! Why didn't he think of that before? It wasn't a *choice* between Karen and Kerry. They were one and the same.

"I see. So then I take it you're making a movie. That's why you have to go away."

"Yes. I'm making a movie. It could be two weeks. It could be a month. It could even be six months. I doubt it, but you never know with these things."

"That must be hard."

"It can be, but not as hard as you. You know who Kerry Morgan is, but you didn't know it was me. Is that really possible?"

"It's entirely possible," he replied, *sort of* telling the truth. "I do know who she is—I mean who you are. Everybody does. But I've never seen one of her—your—movies."

"What?" she said, now laughing. "That's not very flattering."

"I don't really go to the movies. Or rather, I'm sort of into old movies, as I told you. I know every leading lady up until about 1958. After that it gets kind of fuzzy."

"So you're saying you're a snob."

"I don't know. I hope not. I'm just saying I love old movies, especially in black and white. But that has nothing to do with you. I think you are an incredible actress."

"How would you know if you've never seen me?"

"Are you kidding? I've heard you play Rosalind and Hermia, remember? You are amazing, as I told you at the time. And I wasn't exaggerating one bit. Nobody can play those roles like that."

"I did enjoy that," she said softening a bit. "It was the only time I really felt close to you. Don't misunderstand. I wanted to be close to you. You just don't know what it's like to be in my position."

"You didn't know if you could trust me."

"I guess you could put it that way. You seemed a little too good to be true. Saving me from the parking lot. Driving me around. Rushing home to find my ring. It was unbelievable."

"And that was the problem."

"Yes."

Jim did not know what to say. He couldn't bring himself to do any more pretending. He *had* known who she was, sort of, for over a month now; although he could not be certain. But the things she was talking about happened *before* he had any inkling. So in a sense he was telling the truth. At that point he literally had not known she was anyone other than who she told him she was.

She took him back to the atrium, and the dark maid brought them their coffee along with warm scones and butter and jam.

"Help yourself," she said. "I had Maria make them for you this morning."

"Thank you very much," he said reaching for one and forgoing the butter, which seemed too complicated a maneuver under her inquisitive eyes. He took a bite. It was delicious.

"So, we established that I'm going away," she said with a certain coolness, or so it seemed to him.

"Yes," he replied, caught with his mouth full.

"And how do you feel about that, now that you know—well—everything?"

He finished chewing the dry scone and swallowed, a process that seemed to take forever, and then had to wash it down with coffee because a crumb became lodged in his throat. He felt highly self-conscious, but at least this ridiculous little pantomime was giving him time to think about his reply.

"I'm not exactly sure what you mean about 'how do I feel.' My *feelings* haven't changed. You are the same person, whether you are Karen or Kerry. I feel the same way about you either way. Probably the bigger question is how you feel about *me*."

"And why is that?"

"I'm not exactly a movie star. I'm just a lowly copywriter."

"A lowly copywriter from Yale. A lowly copywriter who loves Shakespeare. But I'm glad you're not a movie star. Believe me. I've had enough of that particular gene pool."

This was not something he wanted to press. In some cases it's better not to know too much. He tried to change gears. "So tell me about the shoot. May I ask again where you are going?"

"Of course! We are headed off to Scotland. It's a period drama. Not quite sure how I feel about it at this point. A lot has happened since I agreed to sign on."

"I've heard Scotland is beautiful."

"It is. But I've seen it before. Also I've never worked with this particular director. I've heard different things about him, not all good. Plus my co-star can be rather annoying."

"Sorry to hear that. The things we don't know about the lives of famous movie stars."

"Believe me, there are times when I would rather be anything other than a 'famous movie star.'" She stopped and looked at him. "Like right now."

"Right now?"

"Yes. I feel terrible. It seems like we finally get together, and now I have to go away."

Jim was flabbergasted by this comment. It was virtually the last thing he was expecting to come out of her mouth. "You'll be back. Lord knows, I'll still be here."

"Will you really?"

"I believe so. No one's told me otherwise. Besides, I don't have anywhere to go. I'm just a wage slave."

She smiled kindly at his bumbling attempt at humor. "I'm going to tell you something, and maybe I probably shouldn't. I really, really don't want to go. Do you understand?" She had her hands in her lap, fingers folded in a stress position, and she was looking down at the table and almost seemed like she was going to cry!

"Would it be impertinent if I said I don't want you to go either?"

She looked up at him. She tried to smile. She looked so sad. "You really don't get it, do you?"

"I'm not sure what it is you want me to get."

"I think I may be falling in love with you. I didn't plan it this way, but there it is. Funny how things happen."

Oh, how he longed to reach out at that moment and put his hand on her hands, just like they do in the movies. Instead he just sat there frozen in his chair with a little smile on his face.

"You're not going to say anything?"

"I'm too stunned," Jim replied quite truthfully.

"So let me ask you something before I go and may never have a chance to say this again. Do you have any feelings for me? It was hard to tell, with the way you acted on the beach."

"Of course I have feelings for you. More than I dare say."

"You never let me know. I didn't know what to think."

"Honestly, I didn't know what to do. I didn't think you were interested in me in that way."

"Even after I kept inviting you?"

"I thought maybe you just thought of me as a friend."

She paused. Then she unclenched and put her left hand on top of his. "You *are* my friend. I was hoping you maybe wanted to be something more than that."

Jim gulped. "I was hoping the same thing. Believe me."

"The whole time?"

"Yes, the whole time."

She looked at him and shook her head. Then she smiled. "I really don't want to go."

"You wouldn't want to deprive all your fans of a new movie."

She laughed a little. "You should try watching one of those while I'm away. You might be surprised."

"Nothing about you would surprise me."

There was some more of this sweet and sorrowful talk, but she was up against a hard deadline, and soon it was time to go, go, go. That was the impression he had of her from that point on, the impression he retained while she was away—a perpetual motion machine. They parted very cordially in the driveway. Very cordially indeed. There was a hug that went on for quite a long time and even for a moment or two after that. There was a definite tear in her eye and a deep kiss when she finally had to say goodbye.

"In case you were wondering, I love you too," Jim said.

"Thank you for saying that. Although it took you long enough."

They both laughed a little. And then another kiss.

Karen/Kerry drove off in the back of her white limousine leaving Jim standing there all by himself. The man from the guardhouse was driving. When she was gone he looked around at the big house and the grounds and suddenly felt quite exposed. He got out of there as fast as he could.

XIII

The oracle

SO THE GLORY DEPARTED, and Jim was left feeling amazed, as well as somewhat dazed. Apparently there had been a whirlwind romance between him and Kerry Morgan.

Yes—*that* Kerry Morgan. He couldn't believe it. The idea took some getting used to. "Did he have feelings for her?" He certainly did. He just couldn't believe that she had feelings for him. She said he hadn't given her any signs. Well, she hadn't given him any signs either. And now he not only had a sign. He had her own words to convince him that the impossible was possible.

He sat down on the same couch where she had massaged him to try to take it all in. He was calm for a moment, and then he was delirious. He jumped up and danced around the room and lurched out onto the deck for a gulp of fresh air and back into the living room, where, not having had much sleep the night before, he promptly collapsed again on the couch.

His spirits sank with him into the soft leather. He zoomed out of his body and saw himself lying there all alone in his cottage on the lake. The object of adoration was likely to be gone for some time. She did not know how long. He wasn't even allowed to call. She said she couldn't afford the distraction on the set. But she promised she would call him when she could.

This injunction didn't actually change anything, since he was not the one who had been doing the calling in the first place. He had always been at *her* beck and call. Still, it stung a bit. It made him conscious of the huge gulf between them, which now had grown into an ocean.

He never felt he was in her league when she was Karen, but now his unworthiness seemed overwhelming. He knew he had no business pretending to be the paramour of Kerry Morgan. That would be like Anchises trying to husband up with Aphrodite. A goddess may descend when someone or something catches her bright eye, for whatever unknown purposes goddesses have, but mortals cannot ascend. They have their place and clay feet.

It seemed they were in a fledgling relationship. But he did not know if such a relationship could survive a long separation. They were not really bonded, at least not to his way of thinking. They had spent several evenings on the beach together—but not *together* in the other sense of the word. She was pretending not to be Kerry Morgan while he was pretending not to have his suspicions. It was impossible to form a lasting bond under those circumstances.

But then again she seemed very eager to have him wait for her. *Very* eager. She even invited him to her house. Mortals do not get invited to Mt. Olympus. She certainly seemed to be thinking of him as something more than a fling, according to her own words. In fact she said she loved him. But he was not sure if he could trust himself to believe it. He pictured himself in her ridiculous mansion and felt awkward all over again.

Jim had certain ideas about these things—for instance, that money can't afford to be in love. But was he just prejudiced? Was he a "snob," as she said? He closed his eyes and pictured her in his arms on that very couch, and hope returned. The visitation was real; he didn't imagine it. He remembered the tenderness in her eyes. He remembered all her sweet nothings. True, he could not forget the strange nights at the beach and her seeming aloofness. But she had been guarding a tremendous secret, as he now knew.

Her caution was at least partly justified. He did in fact have a notion about who she really was, at least after the first trip to the beach, although he could not be sure. But the very fact that he'd had this notion at all made it impossible for him to condemn her for being suspicious of him. That would be like a thief condemning a storekeeper for watching his shelves.

As it happened, she had nothing to fear from him. He was not trying to insinuate himself into her good graces. He did not have any selfish objective in view. He was not angling, even though they were by the Sound. He was simply assenting to her invitations. But then again, he might not have been so willing to assent if she did not strongly resemble Kerry Morgan. He was not completely pure, especially after feigning surprise at her disclosure.

These thoughts tended to exonerate her. Maybe she really did want to have a relationship with him but was afraid to make herself available. He could imagine why—but his reservations did not go completely away. The bottom line was there was no real bond to keep them together while she was away on her shoot. Would he ever see her again, or was the whole thing just a glorious dream?

Sleep eventually overcame him while he was wearing himself out with these perplexing thoughts. Then the phone rang. He jumped at it, thinking it might be Kerry. It was Bob.

"What are you doing tonight?"

"I have no idea. Why?"

"How about Beethoven's Seventh at Carnegie Hall? I happen to have an extra ticket. It was for a pretty lunatic I work with, but she's going to Cleveland for an emergency meeting or something. I'm being stood up for Cleveland. Can you believe it?"

"You're just bitter. Unfortunately I have to side with the pretty lunatic. I have a long day tomorrow and don't want to be spending the night on the Saw Mill."

"Come on! It's the Vienna Philharmonic. Your favorite band."

"To tell you the truth I'm kind of stuck here waiting for a call."

"A call? What kind of call?"

Jim couldn't help himself. "From the parking lot girl, if you really want to know."

"You mean Kerry Morgan? I didn't know you were seeing her."

"Actually I've been seeing her all summer; sort of."

"So it really was Kerry Morgan. I was right all along."

"Yes, you were. Although I didn't find out for sure until today."

"I'd love to hear *that* story. I hear she's going off on a shoot."

"Oh really? How did you know that?"

"Page Six. They've been on it all week. Big drama in star land. I was kind of wondering if that was you, the 'unknown suitor.' I almost feel famous myself. After all, I was there at the beginning."

"Okay, please tell me what is going on."

"Well, apparently she had a big breakup with that nitwit Brick Dancy—I assume you know who he is."

"Is that his actual name?"

"That's what he calls himself, anyway. Seems they were a red-hot item for a while and then something happened. Brick ran off with a voluptuous country songbird and Kerry was left consoling herself with—well—a mysterious stranger."

"You make it sound like I'm getting her on the rebound."

"Wow, what a genius. Did you forget about the ring? 'Celebrity marriages. They never last.'"

Jim did remember the ring. His hair stood on end.

"Anyway, that's why I'm waiting for a call. She's supposed to check in when she gets to her hotel."

"Why don't you just call *her*? Then you can go."

"I'm not supposed to do that."

"What? You're kidding," Bob said laughing.

"It's a stress thing."

"Sounds like you're the one with the stress. But what about poor me? I've got an extra ticket."

Jim had an inspiration. "You could try Grace. She's down in the city. She just started at Columbia."

"Gracie? Really? I did not know that. Excellent idea. Maybe I'll give her a call."

Jim gave him her number, but he could not go back to sleep after this mind-blowing call. The sun was shining, and it was a beautiful summer day, but that wasn't why he was wide awake. He was thinking about Kerry and what Bob said.

First he tried to discount it. He couldn't be the 'unknown suitor.' They'd spent the entire summer at arm's length. There was nothing romantic about it—until last night. So that part was wrong. Unfortunately the part about the breakup rang true. It would explain so many things, starting with the way they found her. And yes, there was a ring. He had held it in his own hands.

A long, lonely Sunday stretched itself out in front of him like a desert. Was he making a fool of himself after all? With someone like Kerry Morgan, pretending to be her paramour, as if he deserved such an honor? She belonged with her own kind. This was a girl whose idea of a picnic was lobster salad and Dom Perignon. There was no way he could keep up with that.

He did not want to be a boy toy. That was not how he pictured himself. And now he had to deal with the "rebound" scenario. It was the perfect explanation for her apparent interest in him. It was why she had kept him at arm's length all summer. She was trying to convince herself that she really did want to descend to his level. She had to talk herself into finding him worthy of her interest.

He thought of the tenderness he had witnessed just last night and that morning. He thought of the stunning thing she said to him. It did not seem feigned. But the rebound syndrome was not based on feigning per se. Rebound love seems quite real to the rebounders. They just don't realize their emotional attachments are being driven by something other than love.

Jim felt kind of lousy after the call from Bob. He wanted to do something to get it out of his mind. Then he had a great idea. Karen/Kerry told him to watch her movies. He *wanted* to watch them. He wanted to see her face. Plus he was curious. He already knew what she could do with Shakespeare. He wanted to see how her talent translated onto the screen.

He ran out to Blockbuster and bought three of them. He came back home and popped one in called *Every Little Bit*, a romantic comedy, and sat back to enjoy it. The film opened by panning a tidy Cape somewhere in a green idyllic setting, the front door framed in a long shot that took in a straight cobblestone walkway and cottage garden. The camera slowly zoomed in as the score snake-charmed the audience.

Then the door flung open and there she was, in living color. It reminded Jim of how John Ford introduced his most famous star in *Stagecoach*—I'm here! He instantly realized something that had not been clear to him from simply seeing her in person. She was not just a movie star. She was a megastar. Like Ingrid Bergman. The zoom was slow, but it did not fall flat. *She* held it up. She was completely riveting. Jim saw right away what all the fuss was about.

There are wonderful actors that we are happy to see on screen, great character actors who give pleasure in many ways, like Barry Fitzgerald or Jessica Tandy. Then there are the actors we literally can't take our eyes off of, even when someone else is talking. They seem destined to dominate the frame. Kerry was definitely one of those. The camera absolutely loved her. Jim suddenly felt very proud just looking at her.

The story was nothing to write home about. Everyone was doing their best to make it work, but there is just so much you can do to overcome a middling, predictable script. Jim started playing his favorite parlor game of trying to guess what the next line would be. He was doing pretty well and enjoying himself. That is, until the handsome lead and Kerry managed to find their way into a scene with ominous overtones.

They were in his apartment and it seemed inevitable that they were headed to the bedroom. Just as Jim knew the lines before they spoke them, so he knew this most-unwelcome plot development before it developed. The scene unfolded in all of its predictability right in front of his horrified eyes on his oversized TV. The woman he thought he might be in love with was clearly on her way to some sort of encounter with the leading man, and there was nothing he could do about it. The leading man was not as riveting as Kerry, but it didn't matter. He was riveting enough to be revolting.

At first they were relatively kind. There was a touch, a glance, a kiss—and a long pause. Toward the end of the pause Jim started to feel that the camera could not help cutting away. Some unforeseen modesty, it seemed, was about to descend upon Hollywood, perhaps in an attempt to avoid seeming too "formulaic." But that was not what happened. Just when Jim thought he might escape unscathed, they tore into each other like, well, wild animals.

He watched in dread fascination. He did not seem to be able to tear himself away. At first he thought he might be stimulated; then he felt like he was going to be sick. The spell was broken. He switched off the video player and sat there in a cold sweat, wishing it were possible to erase one's memory banks. But what had been seen could not be unseen.

It was a long, dreary day for Jim, although it was also a perfectly beautiful summer day in late August. He went for a bike ride and he went for a swim. The Open was on, so he switched on the TV and watched as much of it as he could stand. He was too distracted to really get into it.

Finally the phone rang—it was Kerry.

"Hey! I'm glad I caught you."

"Me too. I was waiting for your call. How was the flight?"

"Fine. Smooth sailing all the way. I'm in a hotel in London."

"That sounds nice. I'm in a lake cabin in Connecticut."

"That sounds nice too." The way she said this made him melt. "I miss you!"

"I miss you, too," he said. And suddenly he really meant it. The horrifying movie went out of his mind and he meant it.

They had a wonderful talk, sweet and tender. It was the first time she had ever talked to him like that, not about love per se, but so full of the ambience of love. After they hung up he sat there for a long time trying to sort through his feelings. On the one hand he thought he was almost sick with love. On the other hand he couldn't trust himself to believe it really was real. And on the other, other hand he strongly suspected he was making a fool of himself.

He wanted to do something—resolve the situation—answer his own questions—but there was nothing he could do from four thousand miles away. He was here and she was "over there." He had to accept it. She was in the movie star wars and he was the object of affection that had been left behind to wait in suspense for a Dear John letter.

He almost wanted such a letter. Only double misery could cure the misery he was feeling now. This adorable girl had made love to him. Unfortunately she also made love to other men, and in a very public way. They were movie stars like herself. It seemed crazy to think he could ever really earn her affections, win her heart, make her want to stay with him, have the domestic happiness he longed for, with that level of competition. He dilated when he saw himself lying next to her on that very couch. He shrank back to nothing when he remembered her tangled up with her fellow luminary, an image which he now could not get out of his head.

And yet she had called him. There really was a call from Kerry Morgan; he had not dreamed it. What if she really was in love with him, as she said? It was not impossible. He had heard of unequal Hollywood marriages that seemed to have staying power. Love is greater than place or station. He really believed this. Or tried to. True, he could not give her gigantic diamond rings, but he had other things to offer. He could love and support her in a way her fellow stars perhaps couldn't or wouldn't. He could make himself her safe haven. He could appreciate her art.

There was so much tenderness in her voice. It gave him feelings he could not begin to understand.

XIV

Signs and wonders

THE NEXT WEEK brought an exciting new development on the work front. It was Wednesday morning and Jim was sitting in his office knocking off tasks one by one when a call came in from Dave, asking him to come up to Davidson's office, the new VP of marketing.

Up he went and found the two of them chatting amiably. Davidson was a middle-aged man, silver-haired, sleek, and a little scary; handsome in a rugged way but above handsomeness; in other words not visibly conscious of it, as men in his position try to pretend to be.

"So, Jim (said Dave in a teasing tone). How's your workload?"

"Not bad. Lots to do for the convention, but otherwise manageable. What's up?"

"You think you have time to do a little copywriting?"

"Sure. What did you have in mind?"

"New ad campaign. Give us a few concepts from scratch. We want to throw a rock through a window."

"Okay. Which product?"

"Starlan."

Jim was pleasantly surprised but careful not to show it.

"What's the angle?"

"Simple. Starlan's the best in the business. The one you depend on to get business done."

Actually this was a pretty good copy line in itself, but Jim refrained from pointing it out. They talked some more about the positioning. Jim nodded and smiled and walked briskly out of the room when dismissed, like a man who knew what he was doing, or at least knew not to outstay his welcome.

So Dave was right—there was a revolution going on. In the past, the in-house creative team had *never* been allowed to touch Starlan ads. Collateral materials sometimes, but not actual ads. They were always alchemized by mysterious means, presumably between Henry Booth and the "agency of record," Westbrook. No one knew where they came from. They just appeared.

Dave thought this was a dreadfully old-fashioned way to do business, not to mention autocratic. He wanted to implement scientific marketing practices—testing and focus groups and all that. He had been talking about this ever since arriving at Prometheus Corporation, but Henry simply ignored him. Dave had nominal control of the budget—he was the one writing the job orders—but Henry never even brought him into the loop for the company's premier target. He treated it like his little fiefdom.

Naturally Dave didn't like that. He was the Starlan product manager and had his own ideas about how the advertising budget should be used. Henry had the ear of Clay Rivers, the CEO, but with Davidson on board Dave sensed an opportunity to inject some common sense into the ad development process. Starlan was still going strong but seemed to be showing signs of plateauing. It was time to kick things into a higher gear.

Jim did not know where he stood in this titanic struggle. Henry had hired him and he was loyal to Henry. He also looked up to him. Henry was no fool, as Dave liked to make him out to be. He was creative in his own way and knew what he was doing. His advertising may not have been the cleverest in the software industry, but it was sensible and workmanlike. Most of all it seemed to sell product. Everyone knew what Starlan was. It had practically taken over the market.

On the other hand it was nice to be smiled on by a rising star like Dave and nice to find himself in the VP's office and called upon to do creative work. Henry never let him do any of the real creative stuff. He kept all the creative projects for himself and his agency and left the trimmings to Jim, the spin-offs, the tech writing, the convention signage, etc. Jim was doing well and was known to be doing well, but he felt he could do better. He felt he had a lot of potential that was not being tapped.

He went straight to his office and started pounding out copy. Sloganeering came easily to him. In a couple of hours he had five concepts that he liked; by the end of the day he had ten. He printed them out and zipped down to Dave's office.

"Yo!" Dave said, almost laughing when he saw him. "You got something for me already?"

Jim smiled and handed over the concepts. Dave sat down and began to page through them. There were some "uh-huhs," and a couple of "goods," but then he got to the last concept. "'We know our way around.' Nice!"

"Yeah, I like that one too," Jim agreed. "I was thinking of a man in a suit and a bowler hat with umbrella, sort of a Magritte thing, with the tip of his umbrella poised on a miniature maze. But of course the line lends itself to a lot of different treatments."

"Great stuff. Let's take some of these and send them down to the agency and have them comped up. I don't want to show them to Davidson until we really have something to show him."

"You mean Westbrook? Henry will never allow that," Jim said, his spirits sinking.

"No, I'm talking about Triton. That's a new agency Davidson has us working with. Cheryl can give you the contact info." Cheryl was Dave's admin.

Uh-HUH. Things really were getting interesting. Jim emailed the concepts Dave had chosen. A week later they came back in comps. In general the agency stayed faithful to Jim's intentions, which was surprising. Agencies never did that. At least not Westbrook.

And they looked pretty good! This new agency apparently had a top designer on board. Jim was impressed. So was Dave. "This stuff is fantastic. It'll knock their socks off."

They called Davidson's admin and got an appointment. Jim was kind of nervous about it, but Davidson was just as impressed as Dave. He didn't like some of the concepts—a few he nixed on the spot—but there were three that "had legs." And the one he really liked was "We know our way around."

"Let's get these tested," he said in his inexorable way.

"Should we bring Henry in?"

"Why? He doesn't believe in testing. Let's get them out there and throw in one of his own ads and see what happens. If the results are good, he won't care one way or the other. It doesn't matter where the ads come from, as long as they work."

Jim didn't think this was quite right, but he didn't say anything. He had gone behind Henry's back not just by writing copy for Starlan but by sending it to an agency without his involvement. This was a glaring violation of the usual protocol. He wondered how Henry would react when he found out about it. Henry was very protective when it came to Starlan.

Meanwhile something unsettling happened on the home front. It started when his mother decided to have an impromptu "harvest dinner party," as she called it. As it happened, Bob called later that same week and invited himself up—seems he had scored a couple of tickets to a game at West Point. Jim told him about the party. He said he'd love to go, so Jim made sure he was included too.

It was a perfect fall day in October, the colors breaking through the morning mist. They enjoyed the drive to West Point and they enjoyed the game and pageantry, with the help of an occasional trip to the Yukon. Then they headed over to the party. They were both surprised to see the blue Jetta in the driveway.

"What's Arthur doing here?" Jim said. Bob didn't have a clue.

Pretty soon they found out. Jim's mother and Arthur happened to be standing by the door when they walked in. She greeted them with a big hug; then, gesturing to Arthur, she said (a little saucily), "And this is Erin's date, whom I believe you know."

They looked at each other. They looked at Arthur. Jim followed his mother into the kitchen.

"Her 'date'? What are you talking about?"

"You know, dear; that thing where you go out with someone, do something nice, have a good time."

"I know what a date is. What is Arthur doing with Erin?"

"Well, obviously, he's going out with her. Has been since August, from what I understand."

"You're kidding me. He can't go out with her. He lives three hours away. He's Catholic. Besides, it's just wrong."

"'Wrong'? In what way? I thought he was your friend."

"That's not the point. It's just wrong."

"You're not usually at such a loss for words. But I don't see anything wrong with it. Arthur is a very nice young man. I've always liked Arthur. So respectful and considerate. I can't think of anyone better for her. And she seems happy."

"I wish you had warned me."

"Why?"

"Because this is really weird."

"It is? I thought you weren't interested in Erin."

"Are you trying to punish me for that?"

"'My object all sublime, I shall achieve in time,'" she sang in a smiling small voice as she turned away to the oven.

Jim stomped out. Carolyn had a good laugh. She adored Erin O'Connell and had had high hopes for her and Jim. In her opinion, it was not possible for him to find a better wife. They thought things were all set between them, she and Bill and the O'Connells. After all, they had been together for three years. They were just waiting for Erin to graduate.

Well, now Erin *had* graduated—and apparently they broke up! Amy indicated that Jim was the reluctant party. Carolyn was mad at him for being so foolish and embarrassed by his behavior. How could he not see how wonderful Erin was and how much she adored him? More to the point, why had he wasted three years of the dear girl's life if he never intended to marry her?

She suffered for about a month. Then she decided to think it was funny. Not ha-ha funny, but ridiculous. She could not control her son. She could not make him love Erin, even though Erin was perfectly lovable and would make him very happy. Rather than make herself miserable over his stupidity, or willful blindness, or whatever it was, she made up her mind to laugh at him. Even if he was her own son.

It was his punishment for making Erin unhappy. Things had not been the same between the two families since the breakup. Nothing was said openly—the O'Connells would never do that—but there was a noticeable cooling on their side, as seemed perfectly natural, since their daughter was the aggrieved party. The very fact that they didn't feel comfortable talking about it was probably the cause of the cooling.

This cooling, in turn, was the main impetus of the party. They had hardly seen the O'Connells over the summer, except at church. Carolyn was very sad about that. They had become so close. She wanted to mend bridges. She also wanted them to know she was not taking her son's side in the debacle. Quite the opposite. If anything, she sided with Erin. It was even better when Amy told her Erin was dating Arthur, who would be down for the weekend. She absolutely insisted on them coming.

"Won't that be a little awkward?" Amy said.

"Awkward? For whom?"

"Well—I guess for Jim."

"Oh, who cares! He deserves it. Let him see how happy she is."

Carolyn wanted to make it *very clear* to the O'Connells that she heartily embraced the idea of a new beau for Erin and was not clinging to the fact that she and Jim had spent so much time together. Was it "awkward" for her poor son to see Erin with his friend? Too bad. He deserved it. What she really wanted to do was take him over her knee and give him a good spanking, but this was almost as satisfying in its own way, and, she was thinking in the back of her mind, perhaps more efficacious.

Actually her plan was working better than intended. Jim was in agony. He was not expecting to see Erin with Arthur. It was the last thing he was expecting to see. He could not get it to sink in. He kept looking at them as if they were some apparition he could blink away, a hallucination brought on by sitting in the fall sun at West Point for three hours, shaded only occasionally by a tilted flask. But every time he looked at them they were still there.

He wanted to run away. He was feeling things that were a little beyond his control and did not want to expose himself. He wanted to go to his own house and lie on his bed and think about this for an hour or two. He considered going up to his old room but didn't want to give his mother the satisfaction. This was war. She had ambushed him. He had to carry on and not let her know he was suffering. Plus he didn't want to be rude to the other guests.

He'd never had a rival with Erin because she had always been unreservedly attached to him almost from the first time they met. And now that he did have a rival the effect was shocking. He felt it both physically and emotionally. He could not believe how pretty she looked sitting by the fireside in the soft light surrounded by friends. Her cheeks were rosy. She was laughing. She was drinking a Coke, not getting bombed like some others. He liked that about her. But then why did he feel so bad?

It was as if he had never seen her before. For three years he had not really looked at her because he was holding her off at arm's length. But now he realized how pretty she was. He was jealous of Arthur. His mother's triumph was complete. He kept glancing at Erin surreptitiously. Sometimes it was more than just a glance. He had scorned her, cast her off, and she was there with someone else—his close friend, in fact. But he could not help himself. His eyes had a mind of their own

He longed to touch her, hold her. It was a surprising revelation for someone who was supposed to be in love with someone else; and not just anyone, but Kerry Morgan. He longed to be able to go to her like he always had and talk with her or even just sit with her and say nothing at all. He was so overwhelmed by these feelings that he tried to catch her eyes at one point. But Erin was too good for him. She refused to play along.

Ouch, ouch, ouch, ouch, and ouch! Her goodness was a double rebuke. He tried to tell himself Arthur wasn't right for her, but he knew this was just sour grapes. No fair-minded person could say anything against Arthur. He was idealistic. He was kind and generous. He could be a little dull, perhaps, when compared with Bob; a little pedantic on the immortal subjects of art and culture. But he had certain sterling qualities that Bob might be suspected of lacking. He was noble. He believed in the Golden Rule and aspired to a higher way of being. His treatment of women was impeccable.

Jim definitely would not have wanted to see Erin paired up with someone like Bob. That would be disturbing. Of course it also would never happen. Erin's antipathy to Bob was pretty strong. When he thought about his friends, and for that matter everyone he knew, there was no one who seemed more worthy of her than Arthur. But these thoughts did not console him. Not at all. Maybe Arthur *was* good enough for her—but he wanted her for himself.

There it was. It came to him. It surprised him, unnerved him, but any attempt to unthink it was impossible. He wanted her for himself. But he was the one who had broken up with her! He was the one who had pushed her away—and directly into Arthur's arms, or so it seemed. He was ashamed of doting on her with Arthur right there in the room with them. Like the monks of old he took up the barbed whip of self-recrimination. He (Jim) did not deserve her! He had given her up! Any suffering he incurred now was entirely of his own making.

This fervid repentance made it possible for him to resist most of the temptations that came his way to glance at her. But Erin was completely forgotten when Grace came downstairs, fashionably late. She too was radiant. Jim followed her gladly with his eyes until she planted herself next to Bob. Then his gladness went away. Erin might not have had any interest in his playboy friend, but this did not seem to be the case with his own sister. There was a self-consciousness between them that was highly disconcerting.

A cold knife inserted itself into Jim's nervous system. He remembered recommending her as a concert companion. Did they get together that night for Beethoven after all? Worse, did it lead to something more? Because good Lord, the one thing he did not want to see was Grace with Bob. He never would have mentioned her if he had any idea. Bob was his friend, maybe his best friend, but he did not want him dating his sister. In fact now that he thought about it he did not want him anywhere near her. It suddenly occurred to him that Bob's apparent whim to come up for the weekend may not have been entirely spontaneous. And this thought inflamed him even more. He was being used.

He wanted to go and part them. No, seriously, this is what he wanted to do, like a hero in an Italian opera, because he was the one who had brought them together. But that would never happen. He realized there was nothing he could do but stand there and stare. In short order they crossed over to open flirtation. She was leaning toward him. She smiled on him. She laughed at his jokes even when they weren't funny and gave every appearance of considering him the most brilliant individual ever to have walked the face of the earth.

Bob was eight years older than Grace and even older in ways that Jim did not want to contemplate. She was beautiful and brilliant, but she was also headstrong and did not always show the best judgment. Their mother had hovered over her when she lived at home and generally managed to keep her Wagnerian self-immolating tendencies in check, but there was no one to hover over her in Morningside Heights. She was on her own, and this thought was suddenly scary to Jim.

Bob was making a crazy amount of money and living in a nice apartment in Brooklyn and driving around in a Porsche. All right, so it was "pre-owned," but *she* didn't know that. Also she had always looked up to Jim's friends. The age difference made it inevitable. But she didn't know Bob the way he knew Bob. Let's just say she did not have a realistic view of his shortcomings as a potential paramour. And Jim could not see himself trying to warn her about his friend, no matter how much he loved her.

It was not his role to try to educate his sister on the potential pitfalls of the mating game. He also knew no such talk could be expected from their father, who worshipped her and was one of the most indulgent fathers on the face of the earth. But *someone* had to warn her. Who? Should he try to talk to his mother about it? He was still too mad at her for that. Also, what was he going to say? That his good friend could not be trusted? He could not say any such thing, even if it happened to be true.

Of course he could always try to confront Bob directly. No he couldn't. Bob would just laugh at him. He deserved to be laughed at. He was the one who brought them together. And Bob knew about Kerry. Who was he to be casting aspersions on anyone else's love life? But the words "love life" made him pause. He really didn't want his sister to have a love life, at least not with Bob.

Erin and Arthur and Bob and Grace. It was a very strange and mixed-up night. The whole world seemed out of joint—although everyone else was having a jolly good time. He could barely bring himself to talk to Bob afterward, when they were alone. Bob had his own reasons for not wanting to talk, having a secret to conceal. The next day was not much better. Jim made them breakfast and they wolfed it down with barely a word, and then Bob immediately took off with a somewhat forced goodbye.

That sealed it in Jim's mind. The reason he had come up was to see Grace. The whole thing about the game was just a ruse, just as Tanglewood had been a ruse to placate Erin. But what was this particular ruse about? Was Bob serious about his sister? He did not seem very serious about her the night before. She was the one doing the chasing.

Jim did not know what to think. He made up his mind to talk to Grace about it. But with everything going on at work he forgot.

XV

Convulsions

SO BOB LEFT. Jim was glad at first, until he realized he was alone. It was a rainy October day and it was raining in his soul. He did not want to be alone, but he had nowhere to go. He could not go home again, as the sage predicted. He did not want to see his mother after what happened last night. He knew she would gloat. He especially did not want to see Grace, knowing what she was concealing.

Was he the only one who saw what was going on? It seemed impossible. But then he realized he had a vital piece of information that others were lacking. Also Grace and Bob were not overt. They did not actually touch each other, for example. They clung to each other in a different way, or perhaps it would be more accurate to say she clung to him and he seemed content to let her. To Jim it was all too clear, but he could imagine others *not* seeing it, especially since they had other things on their minds.

What the merry prankster Carolyn had on her mind, apparently, was revenge. She wanted to make him look at Erin and Arthur all night long. He wasn't sure how he felt about that. Under normal circumstances he would have been annoyed with her, but the circumstances were far from normal. Her machinations had revealed to him that he still had strong feelings for Erin, feelings he did not even know he had. He tended to agree with the message she was sending. He had been a fool.

Meanwhile it was beginning to look like he was making an even bigger fool of himself with Karen/Kerry, who had not called in over a month. He thought about Erin's sincere heart and warm attachments, and then he thought about everything that had happened with Kerry, starting with the parking lot. As fascinating and desirable as she was, he had not seen much indication of a warm heart. There was beauty and talent galore, but he wondered if there was any tenderness. He was not sure what place he had, if any, in her affections, in spite of her proclamations.

He knew he did not deserve any. She was famous and he was nobody. She lived in an almost unbelievable mansion and he lived in a lowly lake shack. She was over in Scotland working with other glamorous and famously talented people while he would be heading back to Prometheus Corporation on Monday to write daft prose about moderately well-designed software. They were from two different worlds. Did he belong in hers? He could not bring himself to believe he did.

And yet *she* seemed to think he did. She did not reveal any such misgivings. She treated him, on the whole, as an equal. She was a little bossy at times, but not domineering or scornful. She did not seem to look down on him or be disappointed in the connection. They had spent some very pleasant moments together. When she was in his arms she seemed entirely human. He had gazed into her eyes and they seemed like human eyes. Her skin was soft like any other. If you pricked it, would it not bleed?

On the other hand, he was sitting there all alone in his house while she was off with her kind. He hated being alone. What he wanted more than anything was to call her and try to glean some happiness from the dustbin of his existence; but that was the very thing he could not do. She had enjoined it, and he felt bound to obey. There was no joy in this enjoining, however. It was not like the knight who gladly does his lady's bidding. It was more like the little kid who is told to stay in his room until called.

These thoughts made him mindful of the quality of resistance that came from Kerry. He could not pretend it wasn't there. In a sense it was justified. She was different from other mortals. This was a simple fact. She was a superstar in an unbelievably competitive business where differentiation is everything. It was not just her stunning beauty, this differentiation force; it was something he could not quite put his finger on.

Arrogance? No, that wasn't the right word. He would not call her arrogant. Ambitious? Perhaps. He knew it was impossible to get to where she was without ambition. Maybe ambitious people have this air of difference by nature. Maybe it *was* the difference between them and other people. He'd known professors who were like that. Davidson and Rivers were like that. When you were with Kerry, you knew she was different. Even when you were holding her in your arms. It was not because they were necessarily cultured or wise. The difference did not seem to be specifically qualitative. No, it was somehow innate, which made it seem impossible to overcome. Or at least that was the case for Jim. He did not feel confident that he could ever overcome this difference and become one with Kerry in his own mind.

But then again, did it matter? Do two people really become one when they are in love, or was this just a quaint poeticism? To tell the truth, he did not aspire to oneness with her. He didn't think highly enough of himself for any such thing. But he did want to love and be loved in return. He wanted to feel he was somehow dear to her and not just a funny guy to meet at the beach. She had indicated something of that nature, but could she really *love* him? Was it possible for her to submit to the leveling power of love and still maintain the differentiation that made her unique? He did not know. He was inclined to doubt it.

He longed to call her. He could think of nothing else, sitting there alone in his house at the breakfast table, watching the rain come drizzling down. She had not called for so long it dismayed him. It made him even more aware of his insignificance. If nothing else he wanted to put an end to all this uncertainty and get on with his life. Maybe she really *wanted* him to call! Maybe her prohibition was just a test to see how devoted he was. He picked up the phone and held it in his hand. He put his finger on her number and almost pressed it. But no; the directions were clear.

Which was worse—to look needy or seem indifferent? There might be some respect for him in the latter; there was none in the former. Then again, what if she *didn't* call? Was he just going to let it end like that? "Faint heart never won fair lady." But life was not an operetta. If he was bold and called her she might cut him off. If he was faint and waited she still might cut him off. The only thing he knew for certain was she had told him to wait. "Will you wait for me?" Yes, he would wait. That was one thing he could do to show his worth. He could wait, even if he was being a fool.

And then, miraculously, the phone rang. He saw the familiar "Karen" and rushed to answer it; and, yes, it really was her voice on the other end, as tender as the day she left.

"Oh my gosh you probably want to kill me," she said.

"Kill you! Why?"

"I know I promised to call. It's just been so crazy here. They told me this guy was nuts. That doesn't even begin to describe it. Thirty-seven takes just so someone could say 'today?' Everyone on the set was ready to kill him."

"I would be happy to call. But you asked me not to."

"No, I know. Thank you so much for that and for being patient. I am *so* grateful. You must have wondered what in the world was going on."

"I just missed you, that's all. I wasn't wondering."

"That is so sweet of you. I missed you too. I just feel terrible. I really should have called. I had every intention of calling. It's just unbelievable how fast that month went by."

"Time flies when you're having fun," he said—and then regretted it, not because it was a cliché but because it brought certain unwanted images from the movie into his head.

They talked for quite a long time. Jim was surprised. She did not seem to want to go. It was the first time she had ever opened up to him. She talked about the shoot and her fellow actors and their various idiosyncrasies with almost boundless energy. He was worn out just listening to her and was almost glad when she decided it was time to hang up. He needed to rest and sit and think.

Afterwards, he felt flattered and amazed. He was starting to think she wouldn't call but she did. She called at the same exact time that he was sitting there thinking about how much he wanted her to call. Could it be a coincidence? Or was there something in the stars? It did not feel like a coincidence. It felt like the most amazing thing that had ever happened to him in his life.

She was surprisingly frank in her comments on the cast. Naturally she had never talked to him about those things before, when she was pretending not to be Kerry Morgan, but after two months of secretiveness and caution it was a little overwhelming to be bombarded with so much information all at once, some of it quite salacious. He found out things about a couple of actors that absolutely floored him. He felt grateful that she trusted him enough to share such things. It seemed like she trusted him completely.

She acted like they were on the most intimate terms and had been doing this forever. She even talked about her own struggles and insecurities. She told him about having some trouble with the role and connecting with her character, which she blamed on the script. She told him about an iconic older actress whom she found intimidating. She could not do a scene with her without "screwing up." And naturally the more it happened the more she stumbled.

Before she signed off she told him again how very, very sorry she was about not calling earlier. Could he ever forgive her? Of course he could. She sounded so contrite. He melted. You could see a puddle of him on the floor. She also reiterated her deep gratitude for his patience. She knew it had to be hard for him not to call, not to know what was going on. She just needed him to hang on a little longer. She only had to get through a couple more weeks, and then they could spend all the time together they wanted.

At first he couldn't believe he heard her right. Then he felt a little faint. Did she really want to "spend time" with him? It sounded like she had something more in mind than the biweekly appointment to which he had become accustomed. It was more than he had allowed himself to hope for. He sat there for an hour just doting on this unbelievably sweet phrase.

Then he started thinking about other things. She seemed very eager for him to know how grateful she was for his "patience"; that is, grateful he hadn't called. She said it several times and in several ways. At some point it began to sound like sounding other than gratitude. It almost seemed like she wanted to make sure he got the message that the way to make her happy was not to call her, to wait for her to call.

Which put him right back where he started. He was overjoyed to hear from her, he was thrilled by the promises she made, but he still had his place, and his place was not to call. She wasn't nasty about it by any means, but the message seemed clear. And to tell the truth it was no less difficult for him to hear this message now than it had been the first time. It wasn't that he didn't understand. He did. She needed to focus on her performance and could not afford any distractions.

But it was not pleasant to think of himself as a distraction. The sweetness of her promises made him more determined than ever to comply, but compliance was a bitter pill to swallow because it made him feel he was not as important to her as he wanted to be. Would she think of him as a distraction if she really loved him? For that matter, don't lovers want to be distracted by each other? Isn't that what love is all about? To find an attachment that distracts you from the horror of the world?

Jim did not necessarily sense such an attachment in Kerry. There was more tenderness in the call than there had ever been with her before, and he was grateful for that, but he did not receive the reassurance he was seeking. She seemed to think of him as part of her world, but what part? Was he the guy she read Shakespeare with? The guy who was patiently waiting by the phone? In other words, a bit player on her stage? He knew it would be insanely egotistical to think otherwise. This was Kerry Morgan, after all.

He told himself he could make peace with such an arrangement, if that was what she wanted. She was so amazing that maybe just having a place in her heart, and not actually having her heart, was enough for him. He would be her house husband, if things ever got that far. Just as top executives have many lives of which their wives and children are just a part, so he would be just a part of Kerry's life. It was natural and necessary. It could not be otherwise.

He told himself it was not a bad bargain. The price he had to pay for her love was to accept a certain role and a certain way of looking at reality. It did not mean he was nothing, as he normally felt when he thought about himself and Kerry. It meant he was something—to her. He had an important role to play. He was the person she came home to, her Penelope, fending off all suitors.

He pictured himself as her port in the storm. She was the star, but he would be the person behind the scenes who helped make stardom possible; the wind beneath her wings, and all that. Besides, having proximity to a star meant being raised into starry regions. With Kerry he would find himself in very elevated company. He pictured himself at parties. He saw himself talking to Harrison Ford. He thought maybe he could get someone to look at that play he had been working on.

Then he snapped back to reality. It almost seemed like she found value in him because he did *not* attempt to insinuate himself into her space. He did not cling to her or pretend to have any special right to her company. A large part of his appeal appeared to be his willingness to stay away. But this willingness was an illusion. In reality he wanted to hold her in his arms and never let her go.

It sounded like she appreciated him because he showed restraint. He could see where she might have gotten this idea. There were those picnics at the beach. He had not tried to initiate anything; he always waited for her to call. There was the Westport adventure. What was amazing to her, he now deduced, was that he did not attempt to take advantage of the situation in any way, considering who she was.

But this restraint was not really what it seemed. It was mostly a sign of fear, not independence. He was very much attracted to her but not at all certain of his standing. He did not want to be rejected, and this fear was multiplied many times over when Bob made him aware of her possible identity. *Of course* he was not going to call her if she really was Kerry Morgan. He could not imagine himself doing any such thing.

In sum, he had lucked into the image of strength and steely independence that he seemed to have acquired in her mind. He was not staying away from her because he felt no need or longing to be with her; he was staying away because he did not know if she wanted him to come. In this case she had specifically told him *not* to come—or rather not to call, which amounted to the same thing.

The thing she seemed to love about him was not real. And now it might become the script for their whole relationship. He had seen her infrequently in short bursts. Was this what he could expect in the future, if indeed they had any future together? Could he look forward to many lonely afternoons like the one through which he was now suffering, if he had the temerity to attempt to launch himself into her exalted orbit?

On the other hand there was this: "Then we can spend all the time together we want." Yes, she had actually said these sweet words. It was the way she said them, with such tenderness in her voice. And of course she had also told him once that she loved him, or thought she did. He had not forgotten. Far from it. Maybe he had her all wrong. Maybe she wanted the same thing he wanted. The only way to find out was to stay the course. A little suffering now could lead to great reward.

Fortunately there were some exciting things going on in his professional life just then which tended to relieve the pain of her absence. The market research results started coming in from his ad concepts. They looked good, according to Dave, who knew a lot more about these things than he did. It seems the favorite ad scored very well on recall, messaging, and all the usual stuff they purport to measure. The results from the other ads weren't too shabby, either, but the umbrella ad really stood out.

Dave's palace coup seemed to be succeeding. It sounded like they were actually planning to run the ad Jim had created. Dave already had his minions working on the media buy. Comparisons were made to the witty Apple campaigns that helped turn Macs into a must-have brand, in spite of the fact that they cost more than twice as much as the competition. It was a heady time at Prometheus Corporation.

Jim was flattered by all the attention. He couldn't help it. The praise went straight to his head like a drug. Still, all along there was the shadowy figure of Henry Booth, forgotten but not quite gone, lurking in the corridors and staying out of everybody's way, slipping in and out of Clay River's office. It hurt Jim to see him this way. He felt like he had betrayed him. He felt like he should go to him and have a little heart-to-heart talk.

One day he saw Henry in the cafeteria having lunch with Philip Laundergan, CEO of Westbrook. It was sad. He knew they couldn't have any real business to talk about. Starlan was being handled by the new agency, and the rest of the product line would be moved over as well in time. At least that's what Dave said. They were trying to recapture a moment that had passed—their moment, when they ruled the roost with imperious certainty. They looked old and gray. They had never looked that way to him before.

Jim was very busy that fall making trips down to the city, usually with Dave, to visit the agency and update collaterals and convention materials with the new ad content—*his* content, the concept that had flowed from his fingers to the keyboard and out into the public square. He never enjoyed his job so much. People listened to him. He was singled out in meetings. The agency treated him with a level of respect to which he was by no means accustomed, including fabulous meals at ritzy restaurants.

The rest of the time he was working hard, which he enjoyed doing. He liked being productive. The days seemed to fly by as one brilliant document after another flew out of his laptop. Comps were coming in and going back out all the time. He made comments on them and people actually listened. It was all so new and exciting that he didn't have time to think too much about Kerry and her continued absence, which now extended itself into the second week of November.

Then all of a sudden she was home. She just appeared one Saturday on his doorstep. She wanted to surprise him! He was enchanted. He looked at her and she looked at him and there was a little shyness at first, quite natural, after two months of separation, especially since they didn't really know each other very well. But then she fell into his arms. Literally. The scene was perfect. No one could have scripted it any better.

They had a wonderful week. They were together almost all of the time, either at his house or at hers, to which he was gradually becoming accustomed. He told Maria to call him Jim. It came out

"Jeem." But then Kerry was gone again. She was on her way to Iowa to spend Thanksgiving with her family. She was so sorry. The plans had been made long ago. The thought flickered in Jim's mind—why not take me along? But it was presumptuous. Like he was part of her family!

XVI

Home for the holidays

THANKSGIVING CAME AND was the usual cheerful event at the Wilmot household with grandparents and aunts and uncles and cousins and tag football between courses. It was all very nice, and Jim enjoyed it, but he was a little sad when he thought of Kerry being so far away. He wished she were there with him. He wished he could share her with his family. Would he ever be able to share her with his family? Still, he knew he was going to have to get used to it. She had already informed him about a new movie that would take her out of circulation for the winter months.

The turkey and pies came out and were eaten and then everyone went home and took all the fun with them. Jim was alone on the couch with a glass of port in his hands that he didn't really want, trying to force himself to watch a dreadfully lopsided football game that he didn't feel like watching. He would have loved a card game or Scrabble, but his siblings were not available. Grace was nowhere to be seen. He had not talked to her all day. He did not know what to say to her. He was afraid to ask her about Bob because he was afraid of the answer.

Their brother Eric was hard to talk to under any circumstances. He was the middle child but appeared to have come from a different blood line, or solar system. An aspiring stock broker, he exhibited all the seriousness of their father without the general benevolence. He liked to expiate upon things like derivatives, in which Jim had no interest, while heaping scorn on frivolous topics like literature, music and art. At that very moment he was in the living room working on his laptop; Jim decided to leave him alone.

He went home to an empty house and felt like the loneliest man on the face of the earth. The rest of the weekend was not much better. He didn't want to call Bob because of the thing with Grace. He didn't want to call Arthur because of the thing with Erin. He couldn't call Kerry because he did not know if she wanted him to call, even if she was no longer on a shoot. He had no interest in Black Friday or trying to mix with the masses at the mall. That was only fun if you had someone to laugh about it with.

Unfortunately he didn't. Kerry was off in Iowa having a good time with her family and without him. The feelings of separation and longing were almost unbearable. He broke up the monotony by devoting way too much time to conquering a new video game, until it lost its fascination and he couldn't make himself go on. It was taking up his time but it wasn't what he really wanted to do with his time. Man cannot mate with machines. At least not yet.

On Sunday afternoon the goddess returned. Once again she flattered him by coming to his house and flinging herself tenderly into his arms. It turned out Thanksgiving hadn't gone quite the way she planned. Jim caught his first glimpse of the true state of her family and its relations. Gathered at the feast were her mother and older sister; that was all. Her father was not present and had not been present since she was a little girl, when he and her mother were divorced. No other family members were there. It sounded like they all hated each other.

Apparently Kerry had not seen her family in some time; years, in fact. She described her mother as a classic stage mother. As a young girl Karen/Kerry had shown unusual talent in the key areas of singing, dancing and acting, and had become a celebrity in their windswept prairie town. She also had the drive without which the means mean nothing. Her mother had micromanaged her budding career through middle school and high school and summer stock and anything else on which she could get her grasping fingers.

Eventually Karen began to resent being told what to do. There was a big blow-out one day, and she ran off to Iowa State to do Women's Studies or some such thing and get away from the crazy theater world. But she couldn't help herself. It was in her blood. She tried out for Portia her second semester and got the part. Then she played Rosalind the following fall, to acclaim. Her director, who was very taken with her, in every way, invited a friend of his who had Hollywood connections to come out and see this young phenom—and the rest is history.

Kerry had already cut ties with her mother and did not deem it necessary to restore them when she found herself starring in her first movie at the age of nineteen. After all, she was doing pretty well on her own. She had her own manager and her own agent, professionals, top people in the business. She didn't need her mother giving her advice or attempting to shepherd her career.

Unfortunately this message did not reach Francine McNamara,

who still saw herself in the symbiotic relationship she had forged with her daughter over so many years of successful collaboration. She felt she had played an important role in Karen's success, and now Karen needed her more than ever. She needed guidance from someone who really cared about her and didn't just tell her what she wanted to hear.

With these explosive dynamics, the Thanksgiving excursion was doomed from the start. Kerry had been on her own for nine years and did not agree with her mother about needing to be mothered. In fact to her home was impossibly parochial, having seen what she had seen and done what she had done. A girl who has stood on the stage at the Oscars and held a statuette in her hand is not likely to feel the need to endure lectures in a drab four-room ranch on a cul-de-sac in a drab development.

And then there was her sister, Jen, with whom she had never really been close, and who seemed determined to be helped along in her nascent musical career. She was really quite pushy about it, perhaps feeling, at age thirty, and not without justification, that the time for going long was running short. In her case her mother had gone way off the tracks. She was just as determined to make her a star as Kerry without realizing she lacked the talent.

The only one in her family who did not disappoint her was her father, who continued to ignore them. She almost admired him for this. He was off working on his carpentry just as he always had and never tried to capitalize on her success. In fact he never bothered to contact her at all. This left a big hole in her life as a child, but now she had almost come to depend on it. At least one parent was not determined to pester her.

Kerry had insisted on having a big traditional Thanksgiving dinner with all the trimmings. Her mother pointed out that this did not seem very practical for three dieting females, but she was determined. She knew no one wanted to cook, and she herself did not know how to make such a dinner, so she had it catered. By the time the food arrived they had been together for two long days, much of it spent bickering, and were in no mood to give thanks. They tried to make a go of sitting around the table, but her mother couldn't wait to turn on the TV and watch the Cowboys.

Kerry had planned to stay the weekend but wound up leaving the next day. She made a stopover in Hollywood to catch up on her new movie and give holiday greetings to a few friends. Jim didn't ask who they were and she didn't say. In any case she was home now, and she seemed very happy to see him. She fit nicely in his arms, but she also let him know that she was very, very busy. She had a lot of work to do to get ready for the upcoming shoot.

They were together for about a week and a half, and then she was gone again. She wasn't really gone—she was down in her apartment in the city, "taking care of business"—but she might as well have been. She was too busy to call, apparently, and he was not stupid enough to try to call without a clear invitation.

XVII

In which there are elves and gnomes

OH WELL. There was always work to console him. The first Starlan ad appeared during NFL games in targeted areas the following week. The reaction in the office was ecstatic. No one had seen anything like this in their rather staid marketplace and certainly not from Prometheus. It was like they had all turned into celebrities.

The ad looked great. Jim smiled when he saw it. He watched the whole game from beginning to end just to make sure he didn't miss it. He was busier than ever. All of the products were moving to the new agency, just as predicted, which meant he had a lot of work to do. He enjoyed it. He had never experienced work as a pleasure before. There was usually so much back and forth, so much give and take, and he had always been relegated to such dull stuff, that it had generally been a chore, a place to earn a paycheck.

Everything seemed to have changed, however. He was doing real creative work and had developed something of a Midas touch. Oh, there were compromises to be made and minor changes to his precious copy to be endured; but what went out over the airwaves and into the journals was very much like what he had developed. He was an up-and-coming star in his little sphere of existence, or at least that's what Dave told him.

One radiating effect of his newfound *virtus* was he started to feel slightly less unequal to Kerry. He began to feel like he might actually have something to bring to the relationship other than the jokes she seemed to like so much. But this fledgling confidence was soon tested by the coming holiday.

Kerry was still down in New York, but she started calling several times a day, which was a pleasant surprise. She was acting like they were, well, lovers. It was hard for Jim to take this in, but the evidence was there. Then there was an even bigger surprise. She invited him to her house for Christmas to "spend the holiday with her alone." She actually used the word *alone*. It was quite affecting.

Of course he accepted. Then he realized what he had done. He was supposed to be home for Christmas. How was he going to explain the change in plans? He couldn't invoke Kerry. He did not want to betray her confidence. What was he going to do, call his mother and tell her he had a date with Kerry Morgan? She would laugh him to scorn. He was inclined to laugh at himself.

Jim had not yet reached the point where he really felt like Kerry Morgan's paramour. He had not spent enough time with her to gain any sense of assurance. He never had a moment with her, even their most intimate moments, where the Essex analogy was not present to his mind. He could not try to fob himself off to his family as Kerry's lover when he did not really believe it himself.

He had to come up with a plausible excuse for skipping Christmas dinner, but no such excuse came to mind. Then he found himself confronted with an even more perplexing challenge. If he was Kerry's special friend, then shouldn't he be thinking about something special for a Christmas gift? He was going to her house for Christmas. He knew he had to bring a gift. But what?

His feelings about Kerry were complicated. There was nothing he wanted more than to spend time in her adorable arms, but was it love? He was not sure. For one thing, she never seemed to be around, even when she was home. He supposed it had to be so, but it was frustrating. Then there was the sense of entitlement. He often found himself biting his tongue when he was in her presence. He did not know how well this yoke would wear over time.

But perhaps worst of all there was the mind-boggling diamond ring he had held in his hands. What could he give her, "poor as I am," to compete with something like that? What could he possibly afford to give Kerry Morgan that was in any sense commensurate with her worth and standing? Gifts between lovers are intended to show appreciation. He knew it very well. But how could he afford to show her the appreciation she was due?

The only kind of gift that seemed to make sense was jewelry. Such is the poverty of the male imagination. Jim's poverty ran deeper, however. When a man is in love, he wants to make a bold statement. But he was not one of her fellow movie stars with unlimited resources. He actually had to try to figure out what he was doing. Just how bold could he afford to be?

There is nothing more ridiculous than trying to calibrate boldness. He set out for the mall one snowy Saturday. It was mobbed. He wound up parking at the back of the lot and couldn't believe his eyes when he stepped inside. There was a huge throng of people moving inexorably like lava. He inserted himself into the flow and was swept along by unconscious forces.

He stopped at every jewelry store he saw. It was a challenge to wedge his way up to the crowded counters with his fellow clueless males. This was not conducive to doing what he needed to do. He needed space to think about things and make his calculations. He gazed down in growing bewilderment at the cliché designs mixed in with the gauche and the drab. Nothing really stood out.

He went all the way around the mall twice, upstairs and downstairs, with no luck. He noticed a pretty diamond pendant in one store. The clerk came over. Only ten thousand dollars! Ha, ha—just kidding. In the end he went back to the first store he tried, fully determined to find something credible. There was a diamond bracelet he liked. It was $5000. He stood there pondering it for quite a long time. Then he came to his senses.

He went to another counter. Hanging from its little pedestal was a ruby bracelet that was relatively unique for a corporate jewelry store. Only $3100! It seemed like a bargain, although of course he had no way of knowing. A pretty clerk appeared and informed him that it was on sale for one day only for twenty-five percent off. He did not want to disappoint her, either Kerry or the clerk. Out came the plastic. After taxes it came to only $2500. Not much more than a mortgage payment!

Jim was pleased with himself. The perilous mission had been accomplished. He had done what he set out to do, and done it rather well. This sense of self-satisfaction did not last long, however. It was a long walk to the car in the bracing north wind. The cold blast on his face made him wonder if he had been stupid. He had too much debt on his credit card as it was, and $2,500 seemed like a lot to spend on someone with whom his relationship status could best be described as uncertain.

Besides, he knew it was a drop in the bucket. Starlets get trinkets all the time. They don't even have to pay for them. They just show up at a midtown store and agree to be photographed with the owner. Suddenly he felt foolish. The bracelet was a meaningless gesture. It did not show how he felt about her because he did not know exactly how he felt. Worse, it would not impress her because she could not be impressed.

He was trying to do something that could not be done—raise himself up to her level. The more he tried, the more he realized how impossible it was. This depressed him. He wanted to be her equal, but the humiliating experience of trying to buy her a Christmas present made him more aware than ever that he was not her equal in any sense of the word. There was nothing he could do to pretend otherwise.

She had to stoop to accept his humble oblation. This was a very difficult position to find himself in. He would always be nothing more than a supplicant. He would always have to depend on her smile and being in the sunlight of her mind—which meant he had to be willing to do whatever was necessary to keep the sun shining and stay clear of any stray clouds that might want to blow in. Was he ready for such an arrangement?

Plus—he had just spent $2,500 on a Christmas present! Was he out of his mind? He did not have that kind of money. He also did not have that kind of relationship with Kerry. If they were truly in love—if he felt secure in her affections and worthy of her, as well as certain of his own feelings—then perhaps $2,500 would be nothing. But under the circumstances it seemed like sheer madness.

These gloomy thoughts continued to oppress him at his mother's open house for friends, family and neighbors. He invited Kerry, but she could not come. It seems she had something "important" to do. This something was a little vague, but he did not have the courage to push for details. The fact that he lacked this courage did not make him feel very good about himself.

He was standing alone in the candlelit dining room with a glass of punch in his hand. There wasn't anybody nearby to talk to; he didn't feel like talking to anybody. He was feeling sorry for himself. He could have had a date, but she refused to come. Was it always going to be like this? Was she always going to be too busy to see his family, to stoop to his level, as he saw it? He tried not to think such enervating thoughts but was not entirely successful because of his feelings of resentment.

Erin and Arthur came into the room. He could not take his eyes off them. All of a sudden he was surprised by the descent of an unexpected longing, a longing he had never known before, at least not in a conscious way. It wasn't just the punch or the sentiment of the season. It was the ancient stirring of hearth and home. He could feel it in his bones. He could visualize the hearth, a fieldstone fireplace and heavy mantle adorned with bittersweet and mistletoe. It was momentarily overpowering.

Jim wanted the same thing most men want—a sweet wife and a place to call home. He looked at Erin standing there with smiling Arthur and felt a little ill. He knew he could have had these things with her. She believed in the same things he believed in, wanted the same things. They had talked about it many times. She was one of the best people he knew; maybe *the* best. He did not compare his goodness with hers. As far as he was concerned, she was way above him in that regard.

But something had kept him away from Erin. Something had made him want to separate himself from her. What was it? Pride? Conceit? At the time he thought he could do better. She wasn't witty or brilliant, like Grace. She didn't know enough about books and didn't seem to care. She wanted to be a nurse, for God's sake. Could he see himself marrying a nurse?

Well, as a matter of fact he could, looking at her pretty face in the candlelight. But it was madness to think such things. She was there with his good friend Arthur. This was the second time he had seen them together at his house; they must be serious. He did not allow himself to wish that it might be otherwise. He could not do such a thing to his friend. For that matter, he could not do it to Kerry, even though he wasn't sure if she would care.

He wished he was free to go off with Erin as they had so many times before at parties to chat or simply to be together. But she was not free. Not anymore. She had been free last spring, but he had failed to do anything about it. He could easily have been the one standing there with her by his side, but for some reason he had pushed her away. And now he had to accept the consequences. She and Arthur were very much together, and he was very much alone.

There was more pain for him to get through. Christmas was the following Wednesday, which meant this was probably his best opportunity to try to break the bad news to his mother about his change in plans. He waited for an opportunity. Finally he found her alone in the kitchen. She was not happy.

"What do you mean you're not coming? Since when?"

"I'm so sorry. Something just came up."

"*Something?* Like what?"

"A friend in need called and invited me. I don't know what I was thinking. I guess I wasn't thinking."

"What 'friend' is this?"

"Someone from college. You don't know him."

"Okay, but I don't understand why you have to see him on Christmas Day. There are 364 other days in the year. What about the day after Christmas Day?"

"It was the only time we could get together. He's been—depressed. Clinically depressed. I said yes without thinking and then it was too late to take it back. I'm so sorry."

"You should be sorry. Your sister is going to be furious. You better go tell her right now."

Grace *was* furious. She tried to talk him out of it, and when it became clear that he wasn't going to budge she ran away crying and left him feeling miserable. Jim wanted to make Grace happy. He wanted to make all of them happy. He was sorry to have told a bald-faced lie to his mother, but he had gotten himself into a dilemma and didn't know how to get out of it. He was too afraid of Kerry to try.

All right, it was a little more complicated than that. Part of him did want to go to her and spend the day with her. Who wouldn't? You would have to be crazy not to want to be alone with Kerry Morgan. And he had not seen her for some time—a couple of weeks. He missed her. He wanted to see her. He wanted to bring her his extravagant little gift, even if it was a drop in the ocean.

Three days later it was Christmas, a beautiful sunny day, unseasonably warm, and he was on his way to New Canaan. He buzzed himself in at the gate. No guard this time; the staff had been given the day off. Kerry greeted him at the door. She looked typically adorable in jeans and a white blouse, her luxurious mane tied back but not tamed. She clung to him with all her might and everything else was forgotten.

She took him to the atrium with great delight to show off her Christmas display. He was impressed. It practically filled the room, and included exquisite full-gage Lionel trains and the usual quaint little houses and even various elves and gnomes tucked ingeniously among the shrubs. It reminded him of the holiday train exhibit at the Botanical Gardens. Not as grand, of course, but very pleasing to the senses.

"Did you do this yourself?" he said, knowing the answer in

advance.

"Not exactly," she said with a laugh and shining eyes as she worked the controls and made strange and wonderful things pop their heads out of the shrubbery. "The gardening crew did it for me. But of course I picked out all the trains and everything. And I did contribute some finishing touches here and there."

"It's amazing. Your team is very good."

"Yes, they are. Here—do you want to try this?"

Actually he did. He played with some of the controls and had fun making trains whistle and gnomes appear and disappear. He loved it. "You must be a Christmas nut like me."

"Oh, I'm very much a Christmas nut. I just love Christmas—although it was not always the hap, hap, happiest time of the year at our house growing up. But I love everything about it. And I love Christmas movies, especially *It's a Wonderful Life*."

"I'm a bit of a Capra fan myself. Those are truly wonderful old movies in glorious black and white."

"Not like the crappy movies they make these days," she teased.

"I didn't say that. I would never even think that," he lied. "But I do admit having a special love of old movies. 'Think I'll go see what the wife is doing.' Those movies have such soul. I guess they seem corny to some people today."

"They're not corny at all—not to me. But you really should spend some time looking at new movies, too. Like my movies. Did you ever get around to watching any of them?"

"I did! I watched *Every Little Bit*. You were amazing."

This was "amazing" in two very different senses of the word.

"Really? You liked it?"

"I thought you were wonderful. I literally couldn't take my eyes off you. Of course I could be a little prejudiced."

"That was a hard one for me. I was going through a rough time. I managed to survive it, but I can tell you it wasn't easy."

She wanted to go to the beach before they ate, since it was so nice out, so mild; a nostalgia trip. She drove them in the yellow Jeep, not to the usual spot but to the house of a friend up the road, who wasn't home. They had a nice walk on the gray sand and breathed in the salt air and enjoyed the sounds of the gulls and waves. There was a kiss on the beach, sweet and tender.

Back home they got down to holiday business. She had dinner all ready (from Maria) and just had to heat it up. He helped carry it out to the atrium. They sat down in the middle of the Christmas village and ate with trains chugging by and dainty lights blinking on and off and Bing and Frank and other standards on the stereo. The food was absolutely delicious, the wine was the best he ever tasted (red for him and champagne for her), the setting was perfect, and the company was divine. She was back in her talkative mode. She told him about all the things she had been doing since she last saw him. She had so many things to do before the next shoot.

She seemed to be apologizing to him. No, she *was* apologizing. He could not help being affected by this. Whatever feelings of resentment he might have been harboring regarding her prolonged absences were washed away by her soft voice and sweet smile and the intoxication of the moment. He had been uncharitable. Of course she couldn't be with him all the time. Of course she had a lot of things to do and not enough time to do them.

They had dessert—a divine confection from Make My Cake—and then came the business end of the afternoon: opening the presents. They went into the living room where the Christmas tree was. With a strike of a match she lit the fire that someone had undoubtedly set up for her. It burst into bright flame. Then she reached under the tree and pulled out a box.

"This is from Santa," she said, handing it to him.

It was large, but quite light. It turned out to be a picnic basket she had found in Scotland, a nod to their first dates on the beach. Jim began to wonder if he had overspent.

"And this one's from me," she said, handing him another large carton. "Hope you like it." He opened it and pulled out a leather bombardier's jacket. He found himself in bit of a spot. The name of the designer was not familiar to him. Also he tended to associate leather jackets with large, humorless men on motorcycles. But he was able to rise to the occasion, smiling broadly, exclaiming eloquently, and of course trying it on.

"That looks very good on you," she with a certain kind of smile.

"Grrrr," he replied, although he wasn't sure why.

In any case he was now beginning to feel better about his own gift. As lowly as it was, it was no lowlier than the two gifts from her. Christmas wasn't supposed to be about gifts anyway, except for the greatest gift of all, represented on a nearby table. He did not feel quite so small and ridiculous. He reached into his pocket and pulled out the little box that he had wrapped himself in a less than expert way.

She opened the card and read:

> When there is movement between two hearts,
> There is movement in all things;
> For love is the power that moves all things
> Bringing them willingly under its heel,
> Not to their detriment but to glory.

"Wow! Did you write that? It's beautiful."

"Yes, unfortunately that is my handwriting."

"What do you mean? You have very nice handwriting."

"Thank you. It was forged in the fires of Mordor."

"But what do we have here?" She pulled off the wrapping paper and opened the box. "Oh my gosh—it's so cute. What a nice little bracelet!"

"Rubies. You know—Dorothy."

"Yes, Dorothy. I get it. Tap my heels. I'm going to put it on right now. See? What do you think?"

"It looks wonderful. Because of the wearer, not the bracelet." This was not empty flattery. It did look nice on her exquisite little wrist. But then so would a rubber band.

Anyway, it seemed he had managed to get through the gift exchange without embarrassing himself. After that there was a private screening of the aforesaid Christmas classic in her theater. They spoiled the lines by reciting along. They laughed and they cried and held hands affectionately. Then they became very affectionate indeed. She invited him to stay, but Jim felt he had to get home. He left before he turned into a pumpkin.

XVIII

The fault is not in our stars

THE NEXT DAY she called early and invited him to come down to the city with her to skate and shop. In fact she got him out of bed. Jim, dazed, could not say no, although he really felt he should spend time with his family after yesterday's desertion.

They used her Pullman. It was pleasant but strange, sitting in the back seat with her for the long drive. She was wearing his bracelet. This made him feel better. He was wearing her jacket. She stroked the sleeve suggestively. She kissed him more than once. The kisses became passionate. It was awkward with the driver visible in his rear-view mirror; who, as it turned out, had a name—Chuck. And no, his job wasn't to man the guardhouse. He just did that for fun when he was bored. Otherwise he was the chauffer and all-around good guy.

The skating was fun. They went to Bryant Park on the theory that it would be less crowded than Rockefeller Center. It was still crowded, but at least the line wasn't too long. He had not told her he was a prep hockey star (one of the reasons he got into Yale, along with the legacy thing and the fact that he could play double bass). She was impressed. Her skating skills were not so good, but this gave him a golden opportunity to be the hero and give her someone to lean on.

He felt a little less heroic later on when she was taking off her skates and her scarf slipped. She was recognized immediately and drew a small fawning crowd. This was a new experience for Jim, to see her approached by starstruck fans. He wasn't sure whether he was proud or embarrassed to be at her side. At first the adulation was fun; then it made him mindful of his nothingness.

They went to a high-end restaurant for lunch where she was recognized again but the patrons were too, well, dignified to let on. She insisted on paying. Jim resisted. She wagged her finger. ("Paying" appeared to consist of a nod to the fawning manager who came to the table to offer his compliments. Jim did not see any other sign of a transaction. But maybe Chuck was taking care of things behind the scenes.)

Then there was the shopping. Jim was not much of a shopper and was soon overwhelmed by her seemingly boundless energy. He was amazed at the things purchased and the amount of money spent. He saw numbers he had never seen in a clothing store before. Fortunately she was not too weighed down with bundles to prevent her from repeating the experience at the next stop. The Chuckster took care of all that, while otherwise managing to stay out of sight.

These were high-end stores, so the patrons did not bother her. Still, it was interesting to see the reactions on their faces. It was how the villagers might have reacted if Artemis suddenly appeared in their midst with her bow—a sense of veneration and even awe. Jim saw this from two perspectives. He wondered at their ability to be amazed by her, a mere mortal after all, and then he wondered about her feelings. Was she embarrassed about being viewed as a goddess? He imagined she was. He would have been. But then he wasn't a goddess, was he?

Just when he reached the point where he didn't think he could endure one more ritzy store with smirking clerks, Kerry decided she was done. They got in the car and headed to her apartment. He longed to ask her about the fan adulation but politely refrained. He was afraid of offending her. There were kisses etc. as the sun went down over the famous Manhattan skyline, but we will leave it to Chuck to provide more detail in his fascinating memoir.

The apartment overlooked Central Park and was amazing. It was almost dark, and the city lights looked beautiful from her aerie—all the energy of the city without the entropy. Jim stood at the huge picture window for a long time in wonder while she changed and did things in the kitchen. He heard Chuck in there with her. It turned out they were conjuring supper.

So they were having supper in the city, too? How long was this visit supposed to last? He wanted to drop in on his family and try to mend things, if at all possible. Apparently filial duty would have to wait. She showed up at his side with champagne. You know the one. He was getting used to it. Romantic jazz materialized from an unseen stereo sounding simply fantastic on high-end speakers.

Kerry made a toast: "To a wonderful day and wonderful night with my especially wonderful guy."

"To the most wonderful snow goddess in the world," he replied in kind with a smile. He almost said "ice goddess" but managed to change it at the last second.

They sipped. They kissed. The champagne mingled on their lips. There was a fire in the fireplace. There were city lights and the stars were out. The apartment was dark but glowing with candles.

In short, Jim never did make it home that night. He wished he had brought his own car. He did not think it prudent to ask for a ride. The following morning was maddeningly languorous. Her utter lack of any sense of urgency might have been enchanting in other circumstances, but Jim had five messages on his phone from his mother and was dying to know what was going on. He was afraid to check them. It felt disrespectful somehow.

He was very glad when she finally decided it was time to go. It was almost noon. The ride home was even stranger than the one in. She was very amorous, and he felt compelled to seem likewise, but all he could think about was his family even whilst engaged in enthusiastic osculation. It was not like his mother to leave so many messages. What was going on?

They got back to New Canaan in very good time with no traffic on the roads, but his ordeal was not over. All the packages had to be brought in, and while he was not expected to be her beast of burden, he did feel obliged to hang around until the process was completed and she was comfortably ensconced. He broached the tricky subject of departure. Kerry was not very happy. She wanted him to stay. But he told her there were things he just had to take care of and promised to make himself available later on.

He was completely exhausted, emotionally speaking, by the time he got in his car and drove out of the estate. Now he had to deal with the messages on his phone. It could not wait until he got home. He was looking for some place to pull over. There didn't seem to be any. Then he came upon a large cemetery. On impulse he pulled in and drove to a quiet spot. (Of which there were many.)

Surrounded by tombstones and sad-looking holiday wreaths, he took his phone out of his pocket and called his mother.

"Where have you been?" she barked.

"I told you—down in the city. With a friend."

"The city! Not with Bob, I hope."

"No, not Bob."

"That's too bad. I'd like to talk to him."

"Really? Why?"

"Well, I hope you're sitting down."

"I am. I'm in my car. No, I'm not driving."

"Good. I don't know how to tell you this. It seems your sister has somehow managed to get herself into an interesting situation."

Jim gulped. "Interesting? In what way?"

"Use your imagination. Apparently it involves your friend Bob."

"No. That's impossible. He would never be that stupid."

"He's rather more capable of being stupid than you realize. Not to mention rude and irresponsible."

"Are your sure it was Bob?"

"That's what she says. She doesn't have any reason to lie. The results came back yesterday. She's been a mess ever since."

"Does he know?"

"Yes, of course he knows! She's been calling him ever since. I guess she has some crazy idea about him coming to her side to save her. Please tell me it's not crazy."

"I don't know. I wouldn't bank on that, I'm afraid."

"I'm beginning to think the same thing. At this point he's not even answering her calls or returning messages."

"So I suppose you want me to try to talk to him."

"It would be kind of nice. He is your friend. She needs to know what's going on, after all. If it turns out to be bad news, she needs to know sooner than later."

"Okay, I see your point. I will call him."

"You promise?"

"I do. I promise."

"Right away?"

"As soon as I can. Right now I'm on my way home."

Jim felt physically ill as he pulled back out onto the road. He had been suppressing his misgivings about Grace and Bob all fall; now his own foolishness was blowing up in his face. Why did he have to tell Bob that Grace was in New York? Why did he suggest her as a date? Was he out of his mind? At the time he *was* sort of out of his mind. He was thinking about Kerry in Scotland. But that was no excuse. He should have been thinking about his sister.

Bob was Jim's friend. But he did not necessarily think of him as a "man of good character where women are concerned." There was a reason why he had resisted Bob's enthusiasm for bringing Kerry home from the parking lot on that fateful night. He was suspicious of his motives. He knew his friend too well to feel comfortable trusting him with the comatose maiden. But then why in the world did he trust him with his sister?

Bob and Grace were the worst combination imaginable—highly combustible and highly improbable. She put Bob on a pedestal, as her brother's friend, which was why she thought he would come to her side in this crisis in her life and rescue her. But Jim did not put Bob on a pedestal. He had no illusions about his views on women and marriage. He could not imagine Bob descending from his lofty bachelor perch to save Grace.

Bob was not interested in starting a family. He was nobly determined not to bring any children onto "this screwed-up planet." Jim had heard him express such sentiments many times. He was never sure if he should take him seriously, but now he was afraid he had to. His mother was right. It seemed highly significant that Bob was not responding to Grace.

His commission was to bring his friend to his senses and get him to communicate. Unfortunately, he had no confidence in his ability to do any such thing. They were great friends but not in any sense intimate friends. They did not, for instance, share any deep thoughts about themselves or their lives, which would seem to be the definition of intimacy. Their connection was culture and a certain shared sense of humor and background and whatever other mysterious elements go into friendship. Jim was not nearly as iconoclastic or cynical as Bob, but he did share these qualities to some degree, which may be why they were drawn together.

But his awareness of those qualities made him dubious about the call he had been commissioned to make. He could not appeal to Bob's better nature because the very idea of a "better nature" was one of the things Bob was cynical about. He believed in enlightened self-interest and nothing more. Jim knew he could not argue him out of this position because frankly Bob was a much better arguer than he was. There was a reason why he was already on his way to becoming a successful lawyer at a young age. Even when he was dead wrong it was impossible to get the best of him.

Jim's heart went out to his sister during the long drive home. He couldn't imagine what she was going through. He remembered how she ran away crying when he told her he would not be there on Christmas Day. Did she have a secret she wanted to share with him or a need to have him in her confidence—a need for him to be there for her while she waited for her news? If so, he had let her down. He had broken his promise to the family so he could go play with Kerry Morgan and make believe he was her lover.

He longed to do something for Grace, but the last thing he wanted to do was call Bob. He could not do anything in any case until he got back to the house. The drive became longer and slower when a heavy snow began to fall, making the roads quite slippery. He managed to arrive home in one piece, but the uncertainty of his sport tires on the slick roads had taken away his nerve.

He kept finding reasons to put off the call. He fed the birds. He did dishes. He rearranged his closet. He even vacuumed. He almost never vacuumed. But he was very meticulous about it. Then he realized what he was doing and felt like an idiot.

Night and Duty were closing in. He could not put off the call forever. He sat in the kitchen and tried to psych himself up, like a medieval knight going into battle. Finally he thought he was ready. He reached for the phone, which was in front of him on the table.

Bob answered almost instantly. "Hi there."

The tone was so neutral that it undid him.

"Hi, it's Jim."

"Yes, I realize that."

"How are you doing?"

"Okay. And you?"

"Well, I thought I was okay until I got a call from my mother."

"Yes, I know all about it. My mother calls me quite often."

"That's not what I mean. I'm talking about Grace."

"Amazing Grace?"

"My sister."

"That's who I meant."

Jim started getting angry. "She doesn't feel too amazing right now. And apparently it has something to do with you."

"Not sure what you mean. I'm down here in New York minding my own business."

"You're not answering her calls."

"Well, actually you're wrong about that. I did answer her call. I offered to help. Did she tell you about that?"

"Help in what way?"

"In the obvious way. I offered to pay for everything."

"*Pay?* What are you talking about?"

"You know exactly what I'm talking about. She's a freshman in college. She needs to get on with her life."

"What if she doesn't want to do that?"

"Well, that's her problem, isn't it? I did offer to help. I don't see what else I can do. She should have told me the truth."

"Now what are you talking about? The truth about what?"

"Hate to break it to you, but this was not my fault. I'm always very careful about these things. Very careful. She told me she had taken 'precautions.' But apparently that was not the case."

Suddenly it occurred to Jim that his friend was way better prepared for this conversation than he was.

"You're saying she lied to you?"

"What do you call it? Look, I've done everything a reasonable person can do. Again, I'm perfectly happy to help. But this is a little too much like entrapment, if you ask me. She seems to think I'm going to marry her or something. I don't have any intention of getting married. And she might as well get over that right now."

Jim completely lost it. "You really are a bastard, you know that?"

"Why am *I* a bastard? She's the one who lied."

"Oh, go ---- yourself." And with that charming signoff he terminated the call.

He was dizzy. The conversation went just as badly as he feared it might and worse, because Bob had a nice little ambush set up for him. His glorious righteous indignation was completely neutralized by the accusation Bob had made, on so many levels it was too hard to count. Did Grace really do what he claimed? Did she lie about taking precautions? Was she in fact hoping to get pregnant, as Bob seemed to think? There was only one way to find out—but he couldn't imagine asking her such a thing.

He sat immobilized for over an hour, staring off into space on a dark December night. He was angry with Bob, but he was not very happy with his sister either. The rage he felt at the end of the call began to funnel off to her. If the accusation was true, then not only was Grace compromised, but he had been compromised as well by her lack of openness. He had ridden into battle without knowing what was hiding in the woods. And as a result he got slaughtered.

Oh, well. He couldn't blame her for that. It was his mother who commissioned him to make the call, not Grace, and she probably didn't know the facts either. But it would have been nice if *he* had known. He did not like making a fool of himself, especially in front of his friends. He felt stupid enough having to call Bob in the first place; to have his amped-up brotherly wrath turned around on him was positively humiliating.

Unfortunately it was all too believable. He could imagine Grace, in a moment of passion, making such a guarantee, not necessarily to entrap Bob—that part of the accusation seemed less and less likely as he calmed down—but out of a reluctance to disappoint him. Jim did not like dwelling on such things, however, for it led him into the fringes of mental imagery that was by no means welcome.

There was no way to make this better, no way to redeem the situation. It was a mess from beginning to end. After all, Bob would not have said such a thing if there were no truth in it. He could check it too easily. And his tone was telling. This was not just something he was throwing out for effect; this was something he firmly believed and was comfortable using as a weapon. In fact he made it sound like *he* was the aggrieved party.

Their parting was not good. Cursing was not something Jim generally did. He never cursed in anger at his friends. He felt terrible. But at the same time he was angry at Bob. He considered Bob the guiltier party of the two. He should not have been fooling around with a teenager, certainly not with his friend's sister. It was a betrayal of both Grace and himself.

He was so embarrassed by his language that he almost wanted to call Bob back to apologize. But no, he could not call. First of all he did not feel like apologizing. He had his pride to consider. Bob's insinuating tone throughout the call was hard to swallow. He did not show any sympathy for Grace—none whatsoever. He was the man of steel from beginning to end. Jim did not want to apologize to a man of steel. It would just bounce right off.

In fact he could not imagine ever calling him again. He couldn't do it for Grace's sake—and he couldn't do it for his own. He was not ready to admit that his anger might have been partly misguided. Nor was he going to give Bob the satisfaction of thinking he had gotten away with it. In Jim's mind, Bob had seduced his sister, even if she happened to be willing.

The phone rang. He braced himself. Then he looked—it was his mother.

"You probably know why I'm calling."

"I believe I do."

"Did you talk to him?"

"I did."

"That doesn't sound good."

"Let's just say this is a little more complicated than you know. He's not too happy with Grace right now."

"I don't care if he's happy with her. He has a responsibility."

"I agree, but he doesn't seem to see it that way."

"So what then? He's not even going to call her? He's not even going to talk to her?"

"Actually it sounds like they did talk. You'd have to ask her about that. But that's what he said."

"What do you mean? Can't you tell me what's going on?"

"It's not my place. This is between them. All I can tell you is they did have a conversation. It was probably not the kind of conversation you would like, but they did have one. It's not like he completely shut her out."

"And that's it? That's all you can do for me?"

"I know you're upset. I am too. But I don't see any way that this is going to work out the way she thinks it is. I hate to say it, but I think she's on her own."

Jim was trying to sound calm and collected. He was anything but. He was just as agitated as his mother—for Grace's sake. He could not imagine the impact on her, not only of the pregnancy but of Bob's refusal to have anything to do with her. Bob's rejection of Grace also felt like a rejection of him. It was raw pain, and there was nothing that could be done to make it go away.

XIX

Fortune's wheel

IT WAS JUST the beginning of his bad news, however. He spent a very pleasant weekend with Kerry. They went down to her apartment for New Year's Eve and ate at another fabulous restaurant. This time she did let him pay, since he kept insisting. He winced when he saw how much it was. Seemed like a lot of money for some soup with weeds in it, a tiny piece of beef, and a soufflé.

Then the holiday was over and he went back to work. Jim did not know it at the time, but it was the beginning of the biggest calamity of his life. How could he know it? He was the toast of the town, or at least of his office building. The ad campaign looked great and was getting positive reviews from the people who review that sort of thing. Everybody at Prometheus Corporation was excited about Starlan and the future.

Kerry had gone off to her shoot in Arizona, which was hard, but in terms of his job he felt he had entered a new realm of existence. The agency laid the world at his feet. He found himself being taken to well-lubricated lunches and offered tickets to games or shows or even the opera, some of which he did not scorn to accept. He was enjoying all the perks that come to those who find themselves in the fortunate position of being romanced by people who have a lot of discretionary cash at their disposal and are determined to be your friend. It didn't take long for the novelty to wear off, however. They weren't really his friends. He was getting tired of the account VP, who was about as superficial as it is possible to be, and his kamikaze assistant, who seemed to think it was her job to watch his deadlines. The copywriter hated him, for obvious reasons, and didn't know how to hide it over lunch.

Also he had mixed feelings about the perks. He knew this was how agencies did business, but he did not necessarily agree with it. He had a natural aversion to stacking the deck. He thought about Henry Booth. Would he have allowed himself to be flattered in this way, with all of this schmoozing? It seemed unlikely. Henry was all business and didn't like wasting the company's money, not even on a Fed Ex. Jim admired him for this.

At least Jim wasn't as blatant about it as Dave, who accepted an invitation to Jackson Hole over the long MLK weekend and wasn't too bashful to brag about it. One day Jim heard him barking out to his admin to "call the agency and see if they have any tickets for the Knicks game tonight." This did not strike him as being very smart. Too many people could have heard him.

Still, January was a pretty good month, even with Kerry gone and Grace's predicament. It was a long month, as January tends to be, especially since he was coping with a lack of companionship. He had made Kerry a promise and was determined to keep it. Why, he didn't know, since he couldn't imagine the relationship going anywhere, now that she was off on her second shoot in five months. Even when she was home he hardly saw her. But he didn't even think about other women.

Okay, he *thought* about them. He was human! One person he found himself thinking about quite often was Erin. He wondered how things were going between her and Arthur. He was almost tempted to call her and find out. But he was ashamed to realize that what he really wanted was for her to be free. She would probably see right through him. She usually did.

One good thing that happened was a skiing foray to Stowe with Eric and Grace. Their father treated them. Seems there was some concern about Grace's state of mind, now that she had decided she was too upset to go back to school. Jim had a surprisingly good time with his siblings. Grace was still teary, but she was her usual maniacal self on the slopes. Eric was almost charming. He didn't make any of the usual rude comments and was a pleasing dinner companion. Maybe he was trying to be nice to Grace.

The real storm clouds did not begin to appear until February, when Jim started hearing rumors about a new product that might give Starlan a run for its money. It wasn't necessarily better, but it was from a well-entrenched company with lots of bundling possibilities. The advance reviews were positive. Some seemed biased, but it didn't matter. People believe what they read.

The competitor debuted with a blizzard—media blizzard, that is. They had deeper pockets than Prometheus and made a strategic decision to buy as much of the market as possible with heavy promotion and cutthroat introductory pricing. March did indeed come in like a lion—for Prometheus Corporation. Sales for the rival product skyrocketed, mostly at the expense of Starlan.

Nobody at the management level was saying a word. Davidson went AWOL, supposedly traveling. Rivers and Booth seemed to be spending a lot of time together behind closed doors. Dave was full of bravado for a while—"this will pass"; "they'll never match our ad campaign"; "it's not Starlan"; etc. Then as sales continued to bleed even *his* confidence was shaken. He almost seemed to be looking to Jim for reassurance.

Jim didn't have any to give. In fact he had a bad feeling. The new product was introduced less than two months after his own celebrated ad campaign went on the air. There was a bounce for Starlan in January, but the bounce had peaked and was now turning into a rout. Dave said not to worry. It was just bad timing. His ad was still better. The testing said so. Besides, it wasn't their fault if the company wouldn't spend enough money to compete.

A sympathetic person in management might have agreed with him. Unfortunately Davidson had made two very potent enemies in both Rivers and Booth. There was a board involved too, since Prometheus had gone public, and it was always possible that the board would side with Davidson and the new direction he had taken. But they would have to do so in the face of falling profits and panicking shareholders. To Jim it did not seem likely.

He found himself in the first existential crisis of his career. The campaign he had practically created single-handed was floundering. Companies measure these things on cold, hard numbers (when they want to), and the cold, hard numbers said his campaign was off the mark. It would be bad enough if he had stayed in the background and resisted all the praise being heaped on him. But he felt very much like a target. He felt even more like a target when he met Henry Booth in the hallway and Henry wouldn't look at him.

Now he began to have doubts about the campaign. Was it too glib? Did it sell Starlan? He thought about Henry's campaigns. They seemed stodgy and unimaginative, but they were successful. In retrospect he could see why. They were direct. They treated advertising like a form of communication instead of entertainment. This may have been appropriate, since most of their customers were large businesses.

Jim's ad was almost the opposite—lots of entertainment with subtle communication. He still felt it was a better ad, but he could not say with confidence that it was more effective. Especially with the horrible sales numbers coming in. Jim's ad was running out there like a throbbing thumb while Starlan was taking a beating. It simply was not possible for him or Dave or Davidson to make the case that the ad was successful or that the coup they had pulled off was good for the company.

By the end of the month Dave had turned into a veritable tower of gloom. He kept talking in hushed tones about how terrible the numbers were and his fears about Davidson and those who supported him. It got to the point where Jim dreaded having him slip into his office with a nervous look up and down the hallway. He didn't need to hear any more bad news. He was apprehensive enough as it was.

Another bad sign was that his workflow slowed down to a trickle—and then stopped. There were no projects coming in, no meetings, either for Starlan or any other product. There was no more contact with the new agency. The status calls were cancelled. He did not know exactly what this meant, but it could not be good. He sat in his office on frigid winter days glaring at his computer screen with a growing sense of desperation.

March was over, and "a host of golden daffodils" sprang up from the frozen earth, but that was when the really jolting thing happened. A brand-new ad campaign for Starlan appeared out of nowhere. Dave came bombing into his office with a trade magazine and stuck it in his face.

"What does it mean?" Jim said, trying to take it all in.

"It means we're out. That's what it means. Your campaign is toast."

"Did you know about this?"

"No, I didn't know about it. Davidson didn't either. He's just as surprised as I was."

"How is that even possible?"

"It's possible because Rivers has taken over. Davidson is just a figurehead now. And probably not for long."

"You think they're going to get rid of him?"

"What do you think?"

Jim decided to keep his thoughts to himself. This development wasn't just troubling; it was terrifying. It made him feel like a *persona non grata*. His own campaign had disappeared without a trace. No one even bothered to say anything to him. But the really spooky thing was no one knew where the new campaign had come from. It was a complete surprise, and that didn't seem good. It seemed they had been cut out of the loop.

It was a very strange time for Jim. He went to work every day and sat in his office, but it was like he didn't work there. He didn't have anything to do. No one talked to him, except Dave, and he didn't really want to talk to Dave or be seen with him. He came in, fiddled his way through the mornings, ate lunch without any pleasure, fiddled his way through the afternoons, and went home. And the next day he did it all over again.

They let him come in, but they were not letting him *in*. He was not included in any of the day-to-day operations. Henry was nowhere to be seen and made no attempt to contact him. This was strange because Henry was technically his boss. He thought about going to see him, but what would he say? Was he going to ask him the obvious question? He was afraid of the answer.

He kept coming to work. Nobody said anything, so he started to think maybe the storm would pass and things would get back to normal. He did not expect to work on Starlan. He would be happy to work on the lesser products again. But please give him some work! He was starving for it.

XX

There she is again

KERRY ANNOUNCED SHE was coming home. For the first time Jim wished the shoot could go on a little longer. He was not sure if he was ready to welcome her back.

They say absence makes the heart grow fonder, but it can also make it grow stranger, especially with the embargo on calling still in effect. A lot of changes can take place in two months. Jim remembered how shy he felt around Kerry the last time she came home. It was "getting to know you" all over again.

This time it was worse because he felt like he had lost his standing. He had begun to feel a little more equal to her when she was home over the holidays. A *little*. He was enjoying success of his own. Dave was talking up his copywriting skills, and he allowed himself to swallow some of the sweet poison. He did not compare himself to her—he wasn't completely crazy—but he did feel a little more comfortable in her presence.

This illusion of comfort had been stripped away by the slow-moving train wreck at work. It made him feel unworthy. It was also embarrassing. He remembered forcing her to suffer through a football game so she could see his famous ad. Now this same ad had been ignominiously yanked off the air and was considered a failure. *He* was a failure, hiding in his office all day with nothing to do. What was he going to say if she asked him about it?

Could he afford to tell her what was going on, talk about his troubles, seek commiseration? He didn't think so. He did not want to look like a failure in her eyes. But this made the prospect of a reunion doubly daunting. His uneasiness about work would always be standing between them every minute they were together, his great secret, adding to the stress he already felt whenever he was around her and the perceived need to be very, very careful.

They spent the weekend in New Canaan. She seemed overjoyed to be back in his arms; he felt compelled to mirror her enthusiasm, in spite of the fact that he was apprehensive about work and even a little depressed. He knew she liked it when he made jokes, but it was a joyless task. It made him feel like Lear's fool when what he really wanted to do was open his heart to her. There was nowhere to hide in New Canaan, no room to call his own, and this was hard.

Kerry was adorable and could often be sweet, but she could also be intimidating. She treated him like a lover, but sometimes she treated him like a member of the entourage. It wasn't overt. It was mostly her knack for deflecting anything that might prevent her from getting her way. Jim had not noticed it so much before. He was very much aware of it now in his tender frame of mind.

It made him even more aware of his dependence upon her good graces than ever. He was not a polished courtier and didn't pretend to be. He felt a need to be careful around Kerry, but carefulness made him awkward. It was causing him to blunder. He felt like he made more missteps in those three days than he had in all the months they had been together.

Fortunately Kerry seemed unaware of all this. She was too busy venting. She had a great deal to say about her co-star and the director, neither one of whom had any idea of what they were doing, apparently. The producers were worried about screen chemistry. Well, how could they expect screen chemistry when they paired her with a freaking buffoon?

This train of thought was painful for Jim. It reminded him of the passionate love scene. He found himself rooting against Screen Chemistry. Maybe it was good for the film, but it was bad for his poor psyche. He felt insecure enough as it was. He didn't need Screen Chemistry to come along and push him over the edge.

This conversation happened late on a cloudy Sunday afternoon and cast him down into a deep funk. He was so low that he could not even pretend not to be low. The best he could do was register medium-high. She started to notice, and he realized it was time to go. He reminded her that he had work the next day and things to do at home, not having been there all weekend.

The other thing dragging him down was the saga of Grace, who was going in and out of crisis like a fishing boat buffeted by thirty-foot waves. Grace was still waiting for Bob to return. Bob was not going to return, as far as Jim was concerned. But that didn't stop her from waiting. She was clinging to false hope. She would have been better off letting go, in his opinion.

The more she clung, the more she reminded Jim of his role in the debacle. It was hard for him to see his sister go through such terrible pain and even harder to feel he was partly responsible. He lived in perpetual dread of her telling their mother about how she and Bob got together. This dread made him reluctant to give her the advice he felt she needed to hear.

Jim wondered if her romantic illusions were preventing her from making a full accounting of the path upon which she seemed to have embarked. Was she ready to be a single mother? Did she realize how it would affect her prospects for happiness?—because there was no chance of her being rescued by Bob, who would never attach himself to someone who came with the baggage of a child, even if it happened to be his own.

Meanwhile a cloud of perpetual gloom had descended on her. She had little interest in food and started to lose weight until her mother gave her a stern lecture about the responsibility of eating for two. Then she ate too much and gained too much weight. She did not seem to be able to stop crying. She cried all winter long until her cheeks were raw. They would be sitting together having a nice conversation and she would suddenly burst into tears and run away. It was scary.

Jim knew this had to be particularly hard on his father. He was not the sort of man who would betray partiality for any of his children, but Grace was his darling. He doted on every stage of her existence from when she was a tiny dark-haired beauty, to when she was a personable little girl who smiled endearingly at visitors, to the obvious verbal skills she exhibited at an early age without much prompting on their part and the scholastic honors that seemed to come so easily to her, culminating in a scholarship to Columbia.

His first reaction to the news was a dreadful rage that he tried to conceal from the world—not at Grace but at the viper they had nurtured in their bosom. His daughter refused to give him Bob's number; she was afraid of what might happen. Eventually he found it necessary to make peace with the change in his existence. After all, it was simply another mental accommodation to life, another reticulation of the self.

Carolyn's feelings were more complex. For one thing, she was not completely surprised by what happened. She was the one who had been the most intimately involved in Grace's upbringing and had dealt with various misadventures in the difficult teenage years, most of which she did not bother to share with her husband, both to preserve his tranquility but also because she did not want to detract from his adoration.

She suspected there was something going on after the fall party. She saw how they looked at each other. She knew Grace was headstrong and occasionally thoughtless, in spite of her academic brilliance. She also knew she tended to romanticize her brother's friends. It seemed all too possible that Bob would be able to make inroads where so many boys her own age had failed.

Grace's situation was almost always weighing on Jim's mind and added to the discomfort he was feeling with Kerry. Her debacle was also his debacle. It was his friend that was involved and he was the one who had brought them together. Kerry knew he had a sister of whom he was very fond. He had often talked about her. He wasn't talking about her now.

Grace's friends were at school. They could not console her, even if they had been so inclined. One person who did not abandon her, however, was Erin. Jim was thrilled to hear from both Grace and their mother that Erin had visited her a few times with her usual kindness and always made her feel better. Grace loved her so much. Jim felt glad when she said this, warm inside. And then he felt self-conscious.

XXI

The winter of our discontent

SPEAKING OF WORK, things just seemed to keep getting curiouser and curiouser at Prometheus Corporation. Jim did not know what was going on, but it did not seem good. There was a disturbing conversation with Dave, now their own Tiresias, in which he revealed that "Westbrook" was not a town in Jersey somewhere, as previously thought, but a clever conflation of West and a little river; to wit, West and Rivers, or "brook."

In other words, there were family ties between Phil Rivers and the agency. His brother-in-law owned it and Rivers himself was, apparently, a silent partner. This was not good. In taking business away from Westbrook, Davidson and Dave had been taking business away from the CEO. Not directly, perhaps, but family ties are important.

In mid-March, layoff rumors began to swirl. The hottest one, courtesy of the evil admin, was that the entire advertising department was going to be outsourced along with its marketing partners. Jim was somewhat inclined to dismiss this due to the source. Besides, the whole department? It seemed highly unlikely.

It wasn't. The bad news came in April, on a cold but sunny Friday. They were marched up to Henry Booth's office one by one and informed that the company had decided to "move in a different direction." For Jim, it was the most difficult conversation he'd ever had in his life. Henry had hired him, mentored him. He longed to say something to him, but what? That he was sorry? It seemed fatuous, under the circumstances. So he said nothing.

Dave called the next day to commiserate. He had a theory. The board had wrested control of marketing from Rivers and Booth when it brought in Davidson. They had no choice but to go along, but they must have known about the new competitor. So they let Starlan take a hit to get rid of Davidson and regain control.

This seemed incredible to Jim. Would they actually imperil their lead product just out of spite? But the ways of the business world were a mystery to him. He did not play office politics and did not even know how. One thing was certain—they had regained control of marketing. Whether it was part of a diabolical plan or kismet or simple blind luck was impossible to say.

For his own part, Jim found himself in a downward spiral. He was a young fellow who'd always had a youthful disregard for the future; now it looked like the future was about to get its revenge. Like much of America, he was living about one mortgage payment away from disaster. Prometheus gave him six weeks, which seemed like a lot at first but vanished into thin air the next time he had to make a mortgage payment.

He found himself in uncharted waters. He could weather one more mortgage payment, and might be able to pay his bills for another couple of months, with the help of unemployment, but that was about it. He had student loans. He had credit card bills he accumulated while furnishing the house. He thought about his last big purchase—Kerry's bracelet—and gulped. At least he hadn't bought the boat he was thinking about last spring!

The economy was sluggish; companies were not hiring. He started looking for a job immediately but did not happen to be gifted at the single most important thing successful job hunters do—networking. He could not bring himself to pretend to be someone's friend simply to enlist him or her in his army of "connections." Pretending was not something he was good at.

Anyone who knows about how things work at companies large and small also knows that this reticence of his did not bode well for his prospects for employment. His fancy degree and three years of experience were not enough on their own to get him what he was looking for. There were a lot of hungry copywriters out there who were willing to settle for a lot less than he needed just to keep up with his bills.

Then there was the psychological burden of having been let go. This was the first time any such thing had ever happened to him in his sheltered life. He found it difficult to tell his family, in spite of how close they were. He couldn't believe how hard it was to go to them and say the simple words "laid off." His tongue felt twisted as they came out of his mouth.

And these were people who would not judge him! He knew even before he walked into his parents' house on a chilly spring evening with his heart in his mouth that they loved him and would continue to love him, no matter what. But frankly he did not know if the same was true of Kerry. Would she be merciful? Would she take his side, as Grace did so fiercely when he broke the news? He liked to think she would.

Telling Kerry scared him more than his precarious financial situation. You can lose a house, but a house cannot dump you. He didn't think Kerry would reject him just because he had lost his job—he didn't want to believe it—but he could not be sure. The very fact that he wasn't sure was what scared him. He did not know her well enough to have any idea of how she would react.

He thought about his poor claims upon her affections. She was impressed by his Yale degree. She was impressed by the fact that he stood on his own two feet and did not cling to her, as she made clear in many ways. But he did not feel like someone who was standing on his own two feet anymore. He felt like his feet had been knocked out from under him.

He did not realize how traumatic it can be to lose a job. All kinds of defense mechanisms go up, but they cannot shield you from the monsters of the id. You can try to make yourself feel better by saying the whole department had been laid off, but the whole department cannot help you shoulder the burden of shame. In the end this terrible burden comes down to you and you alone.

He looked back and realized there were a lot of things he should have done differently. For instance, he should not have betrayed Henry Booth. Dave was dynamic and catered to him, while Henry wasn't around very much and ignored him, but that was no excuse. He had been disloyal to the person who hired him. At the very least he should have given Henry a heads-up that he had been asked to write copy for Starlan.

He also should have stayed far, far away from the new agency. That was a mirage and a trap. He had no way to see it coming, but he should have been smarter about his behavior. He remembered thinking at the time it was all too easy. They were creating ads and buying ad time and Henry never said a word. Now he realized why. Henry didn't have to say a word. He was giving them enough rope to hang themselves.

To some degree Jim felt he was a victim of bad luck. His campaign had been doing fine in terms of ROI until the new product came along. But he contributed to his bad luck by letting himself be spellbound by Dave and not paying enough attention to the signs. At the time it seemed like they—Davidson and Dave—were winning. It seemed like Jim had no choice but to write the copy. After all, Davidson was the vice-president of marketing.

But even then it felt funny to go against Henry. A little voice kept telling him he would be better off talking to him and finding out where he stood on the idea of doing a new campaign with a new agency. For that matter it should have been obvious where he stood. They were taking away his power and position. It was a naked power-grab. Henry couldn't have liked it very much.

Of course if he *had* gone to Henry he might have made enemies on both sides and been caught in a crossfire. He couldn't do what Davidson wanted him to do without betraying Henry, and he couldn't warn Henry without betraying Davidson. It was an impossible position to be in. That's what he told himself, anyway.

But the truth was he had not agonized over this decision very much. He was a little too happy to be enlisted by Davidson in his subversive scheme. He regretted it now, but it was too late. There was no way to undo what had been done, no matter how many times he went over it in his head. He had allowed himself to be coopted into a takedown effort against his own boss, and had lost.

So what did this have to do with Kerry? The feeling of failure, the pain of being repudiated, his growing anxiety about money—all of these things conspired to make him feel even less worthy of her than usual. It was hard to think himself worthy of her under any circumstances. Even in his own mind he didn't feel like he had any business being with her. He never felt truly comfortable around her, not for a minute; not like he was comfortable with Erin.

She smiled on him because he was independent and discreet. As far as he could tell, these were the only footings of the eminence he currently enjoyed. But he couldn't help wondering if he would enjoy it for long. He could still be discreet, but he wasn't sure how long he could be independent, not without a job. What if he lost his house? Would he have to move in with his parents? How would she feel about him then?

He could not go to her house without thinking about his diminished status. He could not welcome her to his cottage, which could almost fit in her living room, without wondering how much longer he was going to be able to keep it. This was his mental climate, and it was not very conducive to playing a role of steely independence, which he thought was what Kerry wanted.

XXII

Coming-out party

AND THEN HE couldn't even be discreet anymore. His sister decided to have a thirtieth anniversary party for their parents at the end of the month. Grace was making a comeback. The tearful phase was pretty much over and she was becoming more like herself, for better or for worse. She offered to do the cleaning and the cooking. All her brothers had to do was help pay for the food.

Grandparents and aunts and uncles and cousins were invited. So too were close friends like the O'Connells—and Arthur for Erin. This was daunting for Jim. He really didn't want to see Arthur and Erin. Not together, anyway; not at that moment in his life. He gulped down one of his father's excellent martinis when he arrived, and another one while he was sitting by the fire, where, frankly, it was difficult or impossible to keep his eyes off Erin, and yet *another* one at dinner. Consequently he was feeling quite anesthetized when the following interesting conversation took place among those who were sitting with the anniversary couple.

"We don't watch movies too much anymore," he heard his mother saying through his fog. "It seems like most of them are R-rated, and we just don't want to see that kind of thing."

"I know exactly what you mean," Amy O'Connell said. "I don't understand why they have to show it. It's so inappropriate. No one needs to see that. It doesn't add anything to the story."

"But it adds to the box office," Grace cracked, flush from the single glass of wine she had allowed herself on the special occasion for which she had worked so hard.

"What I don't get is the actors," Jack O'Connell said. "They don't seem to have any sense of shame. It's not just that they get seen by millions of popcorn-munching fans and their family and friends, including their parents. But the very idea of shooting the scene—under the blaring lights and everything—"

"Like that new movie with Kerry Morgan," his wife agreed. "It was just so unnecessary. She was supposed to be the girl next door. I was disappointed. You have to wonder what she was thinking."

"Why don't you ask *him*?" Grace said, nodding towards her brother with a mischievous smile. "He knows all about Kerry

Morgan. He's gone out with her."

At this point a general silence descended on the table as everyone stopped what they were doing and looked at Jim, causing his face to turn bright red, or even redder than it already was. Bob must have told her. It was the only way she could have found out.

"Is this someone you met at school?" his mother said.

"Not really."

"But you actually *dated* her?"

"Well—I guess. Sort of."

"You dated Kerry Morgan?" Eric said. "You're kidding me. How in God's name did that happen?"

"He did some kind of favor for her. Something about helping her out when she was incapacitated or something. I don't know, I forget. True story, though. Don't know why he's keeping it such a big secret. Unless it's just his natural modesty."

"It was the girl in the parking lot!" Arthur piped up helpfully. "The one Bob was talking about when we went to Tanglewood."

"Did you go out with her more than once?" his mother said, apparently determined to humiliate him.

"A couple of times, I guess."

"And are you *still* seeing her?"

"Not really. I mean, not very often. She's usually off doing a shoot or something. In fact right now."

This caused a buzz as it became evident that he had not only dated the supernova but was still in contact with her. What was she like? Was she as nice as she seemed? Jim answered in as few words as possible, which he hoped were not slurred. Eventually the novelty wore off and the conversation veered off in a different direction. He felt the immediate danger passing, but the damage had been done. His sister and brother seemed delighted by the connection; his mother clearly was not. He could hear the tone of incredulity in her voice. Then he saw her glance at Erin. He knew she had never forgiven him for not following through on three years of an implicit promise, as she saw it.

The thing was he agreed with her. Her obvious consternation embarrassed him because he too suspected that he was making a fool of himself with Kerry—and especially now that he didn't have a job. He could take no pleasure in the stardust evident in the eyes of the other diners. It simply made him feel his perceived lack of standing more acutely.

They weren't thinking like his mother. There was no stardust in her eyes at the idea of him dating someone like Kerry. More likely there was dismay at his presumption and foolishness. She would not want to see him involved with a movie star for one very good reason. She would not want him mixed up in the unhappiness too often on display in that particular dysfunctional community.

The glance told him she thinking about Erin and the impact of this revelation on her. It was one thing to treat her the way he did; it was another entirely to dump her for a pipe dream. A movie star? Really? This was what she seemed to be thinking as she sat there looking at him in dismay. How could he be so shallow and so blind with Erin sitting right there in front of him?

Jim felt he could read her mind because these were things that he himself was thinking. Then he made the mistake of looking at Erin. She was looking right at him. The look on her face was not like anything he had ever seen before—a mixture of bemusement, disgust, perhaps even contempt, all gathered in one perfect storm.

He didn't think the look was about *them*. It wasn't because she had been thrown over. It wasn't a jealous look. No—it was about *him*. It was a look of sound judgment. She was in agreement with his mother. He was overreaching. And unfortunately he was in agreement with both of them. Yes, he probably was acting like a fool with Kerry. It pained him to think that it was so obvious.

He did not want to look like a fool in Erin's eyes. He coveted her good opinion more than any other person he could think of— including probably Kerry. He was terrified that Kerry would not respect him, now that he'd been fired, but it was for an entirely different reason. It wasn't because he felt any kind of connection to her. It was because he did *not* feel such a connection; at least not yet, with her off on another shoot.

He was in a relationship he wasn't completely sure he wanted to be in but was afraid to get out of. He loved being smiled upon by Kerry, in general. And he felt he really did love her in some way. But she was almost never there. She spent a week with him when she came home from her shoot and then she was off to the city to meet with people about publicity for the movie she shot in the fall.

It seemed like she always had more important things to do than to spend time with him. When she *was* with him she often seemed emotionally remote. Or at least that was how he perceived her obsession with her career. He realized, sitting there in his stupor, that he did not really feel very close to Kerry, as was implied in the conversation. He felt satellite-close.

Did he love her? He was not sure. Sometimes when he was home alone and not happy about it he wondered if he had any tender feelings for her at all. He had feelings of awe at her talent, and certain others inspired by hormones, but intimacy? He didn't think of her in those terms. Then again, what is intimacy? Has it ever been quantified? Perhaps they were intimate and he just did not know it. Perhaps he didn't know intimacy at all.

He might have been expecting too much. He knew many men would be thrilled to find themselves in his position. He was the consort of Kerry Morgan. He still could not quite believe it. She treated him well, spoiled him even. There had never been an argument or even a serious disagreement between them. She was very agreeable—most of the time. When she wasn't it was because she was under career pressures of various kinds.

But what was the real significance of this lack of disagreement? Was it because he always agreed with her? Was it because he was in love with her and thus happy to agree? Or was it because he was afraid to disagree? It was not because he always agreed with everything she said. He could definitely rule out this possibility. He always acted like he agreed, which was a different thing altogether.

The second possibility—that he was in love with her—was problematic. *Was* he in love? Yes, Kerry was a star of the highest magnitude, unbelievably desirable, almost to the point of madness, but movie stars look different when they're sitting next to you on the couch. She wasn't really "Kerry" at all. She was Karen. Not that people didn't have a right to change their names. He was all in favor of name-changing, if it came to that!

But Karen/Kerry was a duality of which he could not be unaware. Sometimes he could not help wondering if she was playing a role as Kerry, in her mansion in New Canaan and her astonishing apartment overlooking Central Park. She had not been born to such wealth or such a lifestyle. Why did she seem so natural in those most unnatural settings? Was it because she was acting? Was Kerry perhaps her greatest role?

He was unsettled by the occasional sense of entitlement. It was understandable for someone in her position but not especially attractive. He had been with her in shops and restaurants when she had taken advantage of her position and power, not by demanding special treatment, to be sure, but by allowing it to happen, like Caesar accepting the crown. The proprietors brought their burdens on themselves, but it still seemed unfair to him.

The worst thing by far, though, was his own foolishness. He often felt like a stooge when he was with her. He could not bring himself to believe she really loved him or even could love him. He felt like the affirmative action love interest. He was allowed a place in the sun *because* he was a commoner—because he was not one of her social set, her crowd. She suggested this herself, on more than one occasion, although with a positive spin.

This led to the third possibility—that he was afraid of her. And when he was honest with himself he had to admit that he was a little afraid of Kerry. He had been awestruck by her even when he thought she was just Karen, and of course much more so when he learned her secret identity. The main reason why they never had a disagreement was that he was afraid of alienating her and losing the sunshine of her smile. He could not bring himself to cross her. He did not feel secure enough in her affections to try.

So why was he still holding on to this impossible dream? For one thing, he thought he *might* be in love with her. He wasn't sure. He did not know the positive—but he also did not know the negative. Sometimes he thought he was very much in love with her. Other times he wondered if he loved her at all. But wasn't this normal for lovers? Waxing hot and waxing cold? Human weather?

Then there was the fact that she kept calling him. This was painful in one sense, since it was a constant reminder of her desire to control the flow of communication, and yet it made him feel good to receive a call from Kerry Morgan while she was off on a shoot in some exotic venue. It made his whole day, especially now that he was out of work and did not have much else to look forward to. The calls kept coming. What was he supposed to do? Ignore them? He didn't want to ignore them.

Sometimes there was a two or three-week hiatus in those calls, and then he would almost begin to hope that she *wouldn't* call—that he could drift quietly out of her orbit and be lost in space, as it were. This was especially true after he was laid off and dreading the prospect of having to tell her. But every time he thought it might be over she called him again. And to tell the truth he was always happy when she did.

But now his foolishness had been exposed for all to see. He was shaken by his mother's tone and the look from Erin. He also wondered about Erin's parents. He could imagine what they were thinking. Erin was not good enough for him, but now he was chasing Kerry Morgan, who was far above him—and who was also pretending to fornicate (he hoped she was pretending) in her most recently released movie. He did not want them to think ill of him. He liked Erin's parents and felt linked to them in some way after spending so much time at their house in past years.

Besides, he had gone far beyond thinking Erin was not good enough for him. In fact he was coming around to the view that he was not good enough for Erin. He was Adonis without the beauty. He had spent half a year lolling in the lap of an amorous goddess, which, thanks to Grace, was now common knowledge. He could not present himself as Erin's suitor again. He was not pure enough. Not that he was before, but he felt it more than ever. She would never have him after this, never even want him.

But what was "after this"? Was he already thinking of his relationship with Kerry as doomed? He was certainly not thinking of it as not doomed. It was not doomed *for now*. This was the best he could do for himself. He did not know if there was a wild boar in the bushes ready to puncture his glorious illusion with its merciless horn. Being skeptical by nature, he assumed there must be. He heard hoof steps when the phone did not ring for one or two weeks at a time. Such a relationship could not last.

Jim happened to be in the midst of one of those dry spells right at the time when his sister revealed the irresistible secret to the family and all their friends and relations; but then Kerry did call, and there was so much tenderness in her voice, and she arrived on his doorstep on a mild spring day in April looking just plain fabulous, and he was flattered all over again and sucked right back into his perplexity.

She was home for quite a while this time—over a month, until the trees were clad in green and the azaleas were in bloom. They saw each other often. Very often. They practically lived together. Sad to say, it took him almost all that time to bring himself to tell her about the change in his employment status. Meanwhile he spent a good deal more money than he should have in an attempt to keep up the façade.

Naturally the longer it took him to tell her, the more awkward he felt. By the time he finally managed to open his mouth it looked like he was trying to hide something—which of course he was. The shame of concealment rode piggyback upon unemployment. She did not react openly, but he was sure he had slipped in her estimation. How could he not? He had slipped in his own.

Oh, well. It was inevitable. He knew he would have to slip sometime. He wondered if he could survive such a fall.

XXIII

Independence Day

THEN SHE WAS gone—again—jetting back to her shoot. He sensed something had changed between them. She did not seem to exhibit the usual regret upon parting. She seemed a little preoccupied and a little too eager to get into her friend's private jet. There was no hug on the tarmac; barely even a half-hearted wave. Was he an embarrassment to her now? If so, he couldn't blame her. He embarrassed himself.

Then as the plane zoomed away he thought of Erin. He knew she would not think any less of him because of what happened. No, she would have been all kindness and compassion. But why was he thinking about her? She belonged to someone else. She and Arthur had been dating for almost a year. There was talk of an engagement, not just idle talk from his sister but from his mother, who was not given to tongue-wagging.

Oh yes—he had done a very good job of driving poor Erin away. At the time he thought he *wanted* to drive her away. He thought it would be better for both of them if they parted and she stopped thinking of him as her soul mate. But it had been a long time since he felt that way. He had very warm feelings toward Erin now. She and Arthur seemed to be headed for happiness. He tried to convince himself he was glad for them. Meanwhile, what was the likelihood of finding happiness with Kerry, who was never there?

The month of June dribbled by like blood from a rose prick. Kerry was gone and barely communicating. He was home alone thinking about his financial predicament and knocking himself out to apply for jobs that seemed increasingly impossible to get. Every day was more painful than the last at the same time that nature was garnishing the earth with her most delectable flowers. Was he ever going to find a suitable job in his field?

His resources ran out. There was nothing in the bank. The severance was long gone. He had no income beyond skimpy unemployment. He could not stand to be in his house and he could not stand to be out of it. He was not at home in his own skin, which he managed to burn after falling asleep on the dock with a cheap beer in his hand. He was faithfully sending out resumes, just as he had ever since the Great Disaster, but to no avail. Most of the time he did not receive any response at all. The rest of the time there was form language about "not a good fit right now," etc.

Then there was the Fourth of July party. Apparently it was an annual tradition for Kerry, even though she had only lived in New Canaan for three years. She flew in from her shoot to manage the arrangements and direct the patriotic flower plantings around the faux woodland pool. Jim was actually flattered when she invited him. It was stupid, but he was. It seemed he had not been forgotten, in spite of his deteriorating financial situation, of which she was not aware, fortunately. He was actually going to meet some of her friends for the first time.

But the more he thought about it the less he wanted to go. The idea of a party was fun, but he was feeling so battered after two months of rejection that all he really wanted to do was lie in bed with the covers up over his head. On top of that, he really couldn't afford the gas, not to mention that it might be the last time he could drive his car, since he also couldn't afford the insurance.

Oh, well. The things we do for love. He drove down with very mixed feelings and almost turned around when he saw how many cars were in the driveway and what kind of cars they were. There were no top-list movie stars on display when he arrived, but he did recognize a couple of well-known character actors. It was strange to see them in that context. Later on there was quite a bit of comical behavior involving one of them up at the pool, where the keg and margaritas were. Jim saw things he had never seen before.

Other than that, there were a lot of people whom he did not know, friends and business associates of Kerry, presumably. This made him feel unexpectedly awkward. They looked far more comfortable in that place than he felt. It was almost as if he had not spent any time there at all. Kerry was too busy to follow him around and introduce him. And how would she introduce him if she did follow him around? As her "friend"? Perhaps even her "special friend"?

Alas, he never got the chance to find out. Every time he saw her she was either in a large group, which he did not have the courage to front, especially since he had not had a chance to talk to her and did not feel certain of his status, not having seen her in some time, or she was running off to greet someone or make sure things got done. She was popping in and out of doorways like something out of Escher. Rather than try to keep up with her, which she gave no indication of wanting him to do, he decided to soothe his existential anxieties with cold beer and conversations by the pool.

These conversations were superficial, as they usually are at such affairs, but perhaps particularly this affair, which seemed to sport more than its usual share of superficiality. He had never seen so many people with a high opinion of themselves—and he had gone to Yale! The gentleman's conversational tactic is to encourage others to talk about themselves, but in this instance no such thoughtful expedient seemed necessary. They were very happy to talk about themselves whether you encouraged them or not.

At some point in the meandering afternoon he was cornered in the shrubbery by an earnest young writer of the female variety who apparently mistook him for someone important and insisted on regaling him with tales of all the famous people who had read her latest screenplay and all the famous people who were interested in her screenplay and so forth and so on. If they were so interested, then why was she talking to *him*? He did not know. To make matters worse, he looked up and saw Kerry eyeing the two of them from a nearby porch with a smile that seemed a little too pert.

He walked around with a very red face after that but still managed to have his fair share of lobster tail and tenderloin, which he ate at a table in the garden while listening to the jazz band. There were other people at the table who did not know him or his relationship to Kerry and seemed content to ignore him, and he was content to ignore them as well, as long as he could pretend to be absorbed in the music. He switched to red wine because it was on the table. He did not know how much alcohol he had consumed in the hot summer sun, but it was enough.

Then as evening came he noticed a palpable buzz descending on the crowd. What was going on? People were talking excitedly. It was hard for him to understand what they were saying because of his own buzz. Then he heard the name Kevin James from his tablemates, heartthrob of adolescent females everywhere. Kevin had just arrived and was somewhere inside with Kerry.

This hit Jim hard. On one hand he was curious to see this phenom that everyone was so excited about. Yes, he had heard of Kevin James, although he had no idea about his movies. But the other thing that hit him was the part about him being with Kerry.

All of a sudden he was not sure he wanted Kevin James to be with Kerry. The thought of it made him feel kind of funny.

He went inside. It was not hard to figure out where the two superstars were on account of the large, noisy crowd spilling out of the ballroom. He walked in that direction and stepped into the room. Then he stopped cold. There they were, the two of them, about twenty feet away from him and standing very, very close, hand in hand. This closeness seemed to make the bystanders quite merry, for reasons Jim was unable to discern.

Or unwilling. Take your pick. In any case discernment was not part of the portfolio he had chosen for himself by finishing up that bottle of most excellent Bordeaux. It didn't even taste like wine. It tasted like a cloud. That was why he kept swallowing it. But you cannot consort with Bacchus and expect to be as discerning as Cato. All he saw in the distance was a blur of the two-headed unicorn that was Kerry and Kevin.

Suddenly he had an overwhelming urge to go home and lie down on his own bed and unwashed sheets. He was tired. He had spent the whole afternoon in the sun and was feeling it. There was no reason to linger. He didn't think he would have a chance to see Kerry alone, not with Kevin James there, as well as the rest of the clamoring crowd, which showed no sign of dispersing. Who was this Kevin James, anyway? He looked like he was about eleven. Everybody was fawning over him. It was disgusting.

These impressions flew through his mind in a blur, along with the ballroom lights and the mirrors and the chandelier and all the garish colors of summer. He was dizzy. He was disoriented. He had to go. He went to the kitchen and found Maria and told her he had an important meeting in the morning and asked her if she would please convey his apologies to Miss Morgan. He felt he could trust Maria with this important mission because he knew he was a favorite of hers.

It wasn't until he was in the car and on the road that he remembered it was Saturday. Oops! Oh, well. It didn't matter. He very much doubted Kerry would care. Not after seeing her with the scandalously youthful Kevin James. Not after seeing the way they were intertwined with each other like two strands of ivy.

He was wrong. She did care. The call came early the next morning and woke him out of a sound sleep.

"What happened to you last night?" she said, sounding not very happy. "I was looking forward to finally getting to spend some time together, and then Maria informs me you went home."

"Oh—well—I was just really tired. I was going to say something, but you seemed busy."

"Busy! What do you mean 'busy'?"

"With your friend."

"What friend?"

"Kevin James."

"Oh, really. And what about you and Alex? I noticed the two of you seemed pretty friendly. Is that why you left?"

Alex was the earnest screenwriter.

"Of course not. She was just telling me about some script she's working on. Sounds very interesting."

"But I noticed you disappeared, and then she disappeared."

"It's just a coincidence. Believe me, I have no interest in her. I didn't even talk to her after that."

"But why were you talking to her at all when you wouldn't even talk to me?"

"I wanted to talk to you, but you were busy taking care of your guests and didn't seem to be looking for me."

"That was for your benefit, believe me. You have no idea. I was protecting you. Do you want to have your house mobbed by photographers trying to break down the door? Do you even know what that's like?"

"I am so sorry. I didn't think of that."

"I wanted to see you. It seems like I haven't seen you in forever. Don't you want to be with me anymore?"

"Of course I do. I mean, I was there all day. But then I saw you with Kevin James and just felt like it might be better for me to get out of the way."

"There you go again. There was nothing to get 'out of the way' of. Kevin is like a little brother to me. The first time we acted together he was thirteen. In fact he left right after you saw us. I immediately went to look for you—but Maria informed me you had gone. And by the way, I don't appreciate you making her your go-between. If you have something to say, you should say it directly to me."

"Sorry about that. I didn't realize. There was such a big crowd around you that I didn't think I could get to you."

"Great. You might have tried, at least. And now I'm flying out.

So I don't get to see you at all."

Jim knew he was in the wrong. He never should have left without saying something. What was he thinking? The truth is he wasn't thinking very much at all. He'd had too much to drink. He saw her with Kevin James. He saw all the guests ogling them. Something snapped and made him want to go home.

He offered to come down, but she said she was flying out before noon. She did calm down a bit with all of his apologies. He reemphasized the chance nature of the Alex connection. She laughed when he told her Alex seemed to be trying to sell him her screenplay. The call ended cordially. But this time there were no assurances on her side, as there usually were when she was going away for any period of time. He wondered if he was ever going to hear from her again.

He was kicking himself, lying there on his bed in a summer sweat. He had acted like an ass. His hangover made him feel especially Bottom-like, hairy all over. Yes, it was Kevin James that had driven him away. But he could not tell her the real reason. It was not sexual jealousy, as she seemed to assume. First of all Kevin looked like a high-school choirboy; second, what he saw between them did not seem particularly sexual.

No, what drove him away was a very different kind of jealousy. Seeing them together made him acutely aware of the fact that he had no right to pretend to be at her side. It was like Queen Bess meeting Henry IV. They were Hollywood royalty. The reaction of the crowd said it all. The public *wanted* détente between Kerry Morgan and Kevin James. It appealed to something deep in the human psyche.

He did not know what that something was, but he also knew he could not compete with it. No matter how hard he tried, he could never be Kevin James. He could never bring the oil of gladness to Kerry, certainly not in the same way. He saw how they looked at each other. It was a meeting of the minds. They knew each other in a way that was simply not attainable for people like him who were not in the inner circle, who were not being glorified the way they were glorified or suffering the way they suffered.

Or maybe they were just pretending to know each other in deep ways. Maybe it was all a big show for the many bystanders. He did not know. What he did know was that in either case he could never fill the need that Kevin James filled. He would never be greeted by her in the same way, with mutual respect, star to star, power to power. He could never help her form the centerpiece of a fan adulation orgy.

But there was something else that now started to bother him, a tangent to this train of thought. Running away from the party—because that's what he had done, when you come right down to it—was the first time he had ever shown any independence in their entire relationship. Up to that point he had done exactly what she wanted him to do. He had bowed to the stiff wind of her will in all things big and small and never contrived to make his own desires known. Yes, literally never.

Now wasn't it pathetic? There was no intelligent way to rationalize such behavior. Was he prepared to spend the rest of his life this way—always accommodating her desires and feeling too frightened or intimidated to express his own? He did not want to be afraid of the person he was in love with. Perfect love casts out all fear. Maybe she had a right to be upset with him for leaving, but what about *his* rights? Did he have any?

After all, she had ignored him. He was at the party for eight long hours and she had not talked to him or come to him once, except for greeting him when he arrived. Didn't he deserve at least a soupcon of her time and attention? Or was she embarrassed by him and his hang-dog expression? Maybe she didn't want her high-powered friends to know they were connected. She claimed it was "for his benefit." How could it benefit him for her to ignore him?

All day long, a hot and dreary Sunday, he wondered about these things, hashing and rehashing and overhashing them in his mind. He did not know what to think. He was beginning to think, like the hemlock philosopher, that he did not know anything at all. He was trapped in a relationship that he did not know if he was really even trapped in or was just imagining it. He had no job and no money and no idea of how he was going to get his hands on either.

Independence Day had been one of the strangest days of his life.

XXIV

Dry bones

KERRY DID NOT CALL. In fact weeks of hot sultry summer weather went by with no calls coming in at all—not from Kerry, who was off on a shoot; not from prospective employers, who remained ominously quiet; not from his family, which was occupied with other things, principally Grace's blossoming pregnancy; not from Bob, who was the cause of that pregnancy; or from Arthur, who was dating his ex-girlfriend; or from any of the other friends with whom he had failed to stay in contact over the years and couldn't bring himself to call just because he was desperate.

He had never felt so isolated and alone in his life. Down, down, down he went in those roiling summer months into a slough of anxiety and despair. He had no money. He could not pay his bills. He was finding out how difficult it could be to find a job. His first job had come easily, literally from the first resume he sent out after college; but back then he was living at home and had no specific income needs, and he was willing to take a junior starter position just to get his foot in the door, as his father advised him to do.

Things were different now. He had to make a certain amount of money in order to meet his obligations, which complicated the process considerably. First of all there were not a lot of jobs being advertised at the level he had reached at Prometheus, at least not in the summer months when everyone was on vacation. Not until he had to look for a job did he realize how well he had been treated there and how fortunate he was to have had such a position.

He had been advised to follow up his resumes with a call, but it was impossible to get past the Human Resources department, as they called themselves. The faceless functionaries with whom he spoke were not interested in hearing him make his case and would not put him through to the decision makers. When he finally did manage to get an interview he found out why. They had received over two hundred resumes for the opening.

Two hundred! For a job paying about half what he was making at Prometheus! It was mind-boggling. He knew he had certain limitations when it came to his resume. He was modest, and he was honest. He could not bring himself to do the kind of boasting the experts recommended. It was hard to believe any prospective employer could fall for it. They made small things seem large and treated obvious collective accomplishments like personal triumphs. This was not something he could bring himself to do. He found it too embarrassing.

The biggest accomplishment of Jim's young career had been the Starlan ad campaign. A lot of people were impressed with the campaign at the time, but he could not take refuge in their praises, not after the world had passed judgment on it by yanking it off the air. In fact he was reluctant to put his so-called triumph on his resume at all. He was afraid prospective employers would look into it and find out that it had ended in ignominy.

Still, he did not know how much longer he could afford to be humble. He had missed a mortgage payment in July and was about to miss another one, even with the grace period, of which he had never availed himself in the past. He missed a car payment and had used a credit card to make the previous one. There was the cell phone bill, the electric bill, the Internet bill, the taxes, and all the other nagging little bills that seem inconsequential until you have no money. Needless to say, cable TV was long gone.

He kept lowering his expectations for the type of job he would accept—and still there was a dearth of response from prospective employers. It occurred to him that his resume, while perhaps not beefy enough for the better jobs that were being posted, was probably too beefy for many of the jobs for which he now found himself applying, jobs he didn't even want in the first place.

He thought about putting his house on the market. This was the most painful thought of all because of pride and Kerry, but he finally gave in and called a realtor. Unfortunately he had bought it when the market was hot. The market was not hot now, and the selling price they quoted him would leave him in a considerable hole. He did not know what he was going to do if it did sell. Move in with his parents? This was a bitter pill to swallow. He didn't want to do it to them, and he didn't want to do it to himself.

Meanwhile Kerry was M.I.A. She had not called in almost six

weeks. He was beginning to accommodate himself to the idea that it was finally over. He had been expecting to wake up from his Technicolor dream for some time—pretty much from the moment he began to suspect who she was. But he couldn't make up his mind how he felt about it. In one sense he was relieved; if it was inevitable, then it seemed like a good idea to get it over with as soon as possible. But in another sense he hated it, partly because he thought he did have feelings for her—she certainly could be adorable—and partly because of his ego.

Then at the end of August she shocked him by calling. It was hot summer night, a Tuesday, and he was sitting on the couch in his living room in his underwear, trying to read Tennyson, basically wondering how he was going to go on, when the phone rang and he saw the familiar number with the "best friend" moniker. He had forgotten it said that. It had a strange effect on him.

The conversation was strange as well, because—well—it was not very strange at all. One might expect a degree of strangeness after a long separation, especially considering the way they parted, but this was not the case. Kerry sounded perfectly normal. It was as if everything was just the way it had always been—as if there had been no loss of job, no Fourth of July party with its aftermath, no long wasting period of silence.

There she was on the other end of the line chirping very much like her usual self, very much like she had in the halcyon days of first love. The shoot was over and she was on her way home, probably arriving Friday. The good news was there were no more shoots in the foreseeable future. She was exhausted and looking forward to a nice break and to the fall and doing things she loved to do, like taking foliage drives and going pumpkin-picking. It sounded very much like she wanted to do them with *him*.

When could they get together? She would love to come up and see him on Saturday. Of course Jim wanted to see her, but he was faced with a ludicrous dilemma. He had a large shiny For Sale sign festooned in his front yard. He did not want her to know about his financial challenges and could not see himself removing it for the sake of the day. He also could not think of a plausible way to invite himself to New Canaan or how he could afford to drive there.

Then he had a brilliant idea. He remembered the craft fair at church on Saturday. It was a charming little county fair that spilled over onto the green. Fair weather was forecast. Besides, it was a place where he could take her without spending any money. Kerry seemed delighted with the idea. It was just her sort of thing. She was definitely coming. She couldn't wait to see him!

Jim hung up the phone in a daze. Was she really excited at the prospect of a homely country fair? He hoped she wouldn't be disappointed. She always came to him after a shoot—it was a gesture she seemed to enjoy making for some reason—but this was different. She would be meeting him in a public place where there were likely to be a large number of people wandering around with cheeseburgers and candied apples.

This was surprising for two reasons. First, she did not like to be exposed to crowds. She did not like people pressing on her, partly because she didn't like the invasion of privacy but also because she had an inordinate fear of germs. Second, he made it plain that his family was involved in the fair and likely to be gathered there at any given time (with the exception of Eric). She did not seem to be troubled by this. In fact she welcomed it. She seemed almost… excited. She wanted to meet them, especially Grace.

He was surprised. In the past she had always brushed off any invitations to family events. Her manner of brushing them off was so high-handed that he had given up making them. It seemed they were about to move on to a new phase in their relationship—but did that mean their relationship was moving in a forward direction? Jim did not know. In any case the call had been the only sweet spot in the entire month of August.

He was charmed by her interest in Grace. He thought about Mr. Darcy and how eager he was to have Elizabeth meet his sister. It seemed he wanted her to see that some of what the world perceived to be cold pride in him was actually something very different. Jim was similarly proud of Grace, but in this instance there was one little detail he had neglected to share with Kerry. And this particular detail seemed unlikely to go unnoticed.

Then he thought about his mother and how she would react to the vertical interruption. They were quiet country people and content with their quiet country fair; they did not need the presence of a movie star in order to feel validated. It was likely to be seen as an intrusion. Also he knew she was skeptical about the liaison. He couldn't blame her; he tended to be skeptical himself.

He was stressed about trying to hide his financial difficulties from Kerry. He had to be careful to arrange things so that he did not find himself in a situation where money was called for. And what if she wanted to go to his house? He went out the next morning to see if anything could be done about the sign, but a tentative nudge revealed it wasn't going to come out easily. Besides, what if the realtor came by and saw it was gone? It seemed like more trouble than it was worth.

There was quite a long span between Tuesday and Saturday and too much time to think for someone who had too little to do. He worried about how he was going to greet her after such a long absence and especially in his diminished state. He tried to picture what he would say to her and how he would act. She had agreed to meet him at the church, but this was likely to be awkward. People would see her, people he knew. There would be the usual reaction. How was he going to handle it?

He thought about her holiday party and its sumptuous trappings. He had no such trappings. He had nothing to offer her except his poor jokes. He never did, but now he did not see how he could hide his nakedness. He was in a position of complete supplication, and yet he felt compelled to pretend this was not the case. He had seen her with Kevin James. She was not looking for a supplicant. Would he be able to look her in the eye after such a long separation and the way they parted? Or was he back to where they began—a befuddled observer of his own very strange story?

Saturday rolled around and Jim went to the church early and waited for her on the steps. At some point he realized he needed to make a visit to the little men's room but was afraid to desert his post. She drove up an hour late looking simply irresistible. She hopped out of the Jeep and seemed genuinely happy to see him. He couldn't quite believe he was standing there with her on the green. The full impact of it was not evident until it happened. He was terribly proud of her, of course, but he was also humbled and highly self-conscious. He saw all the people scattered on the green and going in and out of the church. Would they recognize her? How would they react? The whole thing was a bit overwhelming.

She had concealed herself under a large floppy summer hat with a tied sun scarf, in addition to her usual sunglasses. Thus screened from prying eyes, she plunged into the scattered crowd with him. They strolled around the craft booths and stopped occasionally to check out the wares. She pointed out some things that caught her fancy. He longed to buy them for her but had no money. They went to the gazebo and listened to the fiddlers. A young girl stopped dead in her tracks, but Kerry waved at her with an Obi Kenobi smile, and she ran away to scream with her friends.

"So where is your family?" she asked him at this point.

"Oh, they're probably around here somewhere. I know my mother is in the church hosting the art exhibit."

"What are we waiting for? Let's go see her."

Jim was amazed. They went in. The crowd was absorbed in the paintings and did not notice their illustrious guest. Jim spotted his mother sitting in the corner with the cash box. Carolyn saw them coming and rose to greet them.

"Hi, there," he said, more embarrassed than ever. "This is my mother. This is—"

"I know who this is," Carolyn interrupted with a calm smile. "Of course I know. So happy to meet you at last. Thank you for coming to our humble little fair."

"Thank you. Very nice to meet you, too—at last. I think your son has been keeping us apart."

"I believe he has. He's highly ashamed of his family. Not philosophical enough for him, I'm afraid."

"I am not ashamed of you. And I never said anything like that."

"You're ashamed in the way any normal child is of his parents. After all, they're embarrassing and say stupid things. We haven't heard from him in over a month, by the way. We were starting to wonder if he still existed."

"That's funny. I haven't heard from him in over a month either, although I was on a shoot."

"He doesn't call you?"

"No, he's very bad that way."

"Well, that makes me feel better. If he can't motivate himself to call *you*, then there's no reason to expect him to call his mother."

Jim could see from Kerry's face and smile that the implied compliment was felt. This was not about her stardom. His mother was impressed by her and she wanted her to know it. Of course he wasn't sure if it was necessary for them to make him the object of their pleasantry. In his mind they were misrepresenting him. The most outrageous misrepresentation was Kerry's. She knew perfectly well why he did not call.

"Your father is over there checking out a picture for the den, if you want to introduce your friend. New artist called Jill Campbell.

Very nice painting. Don't think he can afford her."

"No, he looks happy. We can catch up with him later."

"Why don't you come over after the fair? We're having some people for an informal little cookout. I need to decompress after the week I just had."

"I would love that," Kerry said, answering for him. "I've been in your house before, you know."

"You have? I did not know that," Carolyn replied, looking at her son in wonder.

"Oh yes. It was quite an experience. I'm looking forward to seeing it again, seeing if it really was real. Also I would love to spend some time with all of you. I've heard so much about you."

"We would love to spend some time with you, too. Although to tell you the truth we haven't heard anything about you. Keeping you all to himself, I guess."

"Yes, he does things like that. Always keeping things to himself."

Jim was unnerved by this comment. What was she implying? What "things" was he keeping to himself? Had she somehow found out about his desperate situation from her multitudinous sources? Or was he just being paranoid? In this case paranoia seemed justified. He was terrified at the thought of her finding out just how bad things really were and how far he had gone down into the rabbit hole.

On the other hand, she was coming to the Bridgewater house for supper. It sounded like she *wanted* to come, like she wanted to get to know them. This was hard to digest with everything else that was going on, but it made him feel good. It seemed to indicate that she valued the connection—and presumably him. He had never been so grateful to his mother in his life. Apparently she made a good impression. Also a major problem had been solved. He did not have to worry about Kerry seeing the For Sale sign after all.

They were walking out of the church in a good mood when Jim spotted someone literally running toward them with a large camera in his hands. He froze. He did not know what to do or how Kerry would react. The photographer rushed right up to the bottom of the steps and started to shoot, all in one motion, like an Apache warrior shooting an arrow from his horse. Kerry shrunk back and slipped her hand through Jim's arm.

"Time to go to your house," she whispered.

"You mean my parents' house?"

"Sure. Doesn't matter. We can take the Jeep."

This was uttered in the familiar tone of command. They went straight to the Jeep. Kerry jumped in and placed the key in the ignition with preternatural calm. Apparently she was used to this sort of thing. Jim also jumped in and was barely able to get his seatbelt on before she pulled out and zoomed away. By this time they were causing quite a commotion. The photographer was still snapping pictures like a man possessed and quite a few people were standing around with puzzled expressions.

"Stupid paparazzi," she said. "I was afraid this would happen."

"I'm surprised it didn't happen earlier," he said. "I didn't know how long we could go without people realizing you were here."

"It was worth it. I got to meet your mother. I have an invitation to your house. I'm so excited. I can't wait to see it again."

"I'm glad it's still there for you to see," Jim quipped, or attempted to quip, being completely surprised by what she said. He directed, she flew, and soon they were pulling into the driveway.

"I remember this. What a nice old house! Classic. We don't have anything like it in Iowa. Out there a hundred years is considered old."

"This one is considerably older than that. About 1725, in fact."

"It really is a Colonial, then. So charming, with all the plantings and those old trees. You just can't get this kind of country charm where I come from."

Jim pondered these words and treasured them. At least he still had something of value to offer the goddess, even if it wasn't his own house. He took her inside.

"Oh, yes. It's all coming back to me now. The kitchen's over there, right? I remember how awkward you looked. I can still picture it. You didn't know what to say."

"It was a very strange situation."

"It certainly was. I can laugh at it now. I wasn't laughing then. I wasn't sure what was going on."

"What were you thinking as you came down the stairs?"

"I didn't know what to think. All I knew was I was in a strange house and there was a strange man in the kitchen making breakfast. A nice house, though. And a cute man."

"Oh, thanks."

"But what were *you* thinking?"

"Well, I guess it's safe to confess this now. I was terrified. I didn't know how you were going to react."

"Terrified? Really? Why?"

"It was such a crazy story. I didn't know if you would believe it. I was afraid you would suspect me of something."

"I really didn't suspect you of anything. I wasn't sure if you knew who I was, so that always makes things kind of interesting. But I wasn't afraid of anything like *that*, if that's what you're thinking. Maybe I was too hung over."

"Glad to hear it. And no, I had absolutely no idea of who you were. That didn't come until later."

"I remember you making me breakfast. That was very sweet. I was impressed. And I was not able to eat it, which made me feel bad. I also remember that you wouldn't look at me. Was there a reason for that?"

"There was," he confessed. "You were too beautiful. It was like looking directly into the sun."

This was said in complete sincerity. There was not a molecule of flattery in it. She seemed to realize this because a smile came over her that indicated pleasure. "Say, do you mind showing me your sister's room again? I'm kind of curious about the ring."

"Not at all." He led her upstairs. "That's my brother's room, by the way," he said as they passed by the shrine. "And here's Grace's room. Do you remember it?"

"Of course. Where was the ring?"

"Right over there by the window, under the register."

"So that's the famous register," she said shaking her head. "I still don't get it."

"Maybe you were hoping it would hatch."

She laughed. "My nest egg. So this is Grace's room. And where is your room, exactly?"

"Oh—right over here."

They walked across the hall. She seemed delighted with it. She saw his hockey trophy from prep school and was impressed. She looked out the window at the driveway.

"I just realized we're all alone," she whispered with a smile.

"That's true; we are."

"It's been such a long time," she said, pulling him onto the bed. Indeed, it had been. He agreed. Inspired by the moment, they did everything in their power to make up for it.

Later they showered (together, in fact) and Jim straightened up the bed. Then the rest of the family arrived. It wasn't just the family—the Wilmots were in tow, including Erin and Arthur. He saw the look Erin gave him when they found them there alone.

He introduced Kerry to Grace. To her credit, Kerry gave no sign of noticing anything untoward, although Grace was very toward at that point in her pregnancy. She looked her straight in the eyes as she took her hand and shook it warmly. "You are just as beautiful as your brother said you were."

"You too!" Grace blurted. "More, actually."

He introduced her to Erin and Arthur. It was strange to see Erin and Kerry together. Arthur complimented her on a couple of her films, quietly, as was his usual manner. Jim was proud of his family and friends. They were not overwhelmed by her presence. But then Megan came in, Erin's younger sister, and was obviously smitten. Kerry just smiled. She had seen it many times before.

Kerry seemed eager to fit in. She attached herself to Grace, and before long they were on their way to becoming great friends. Everyone went out to the patio for a drink. It was a beautiful summer evening, mellow and sweet, and the mood was cheerful, especially among the older couples, who were worn out after a week of prep and happy about the results, which were for charity.

Kerry was full of nice things to say about the fair. Jim had never seen her like this before. Her actual physical appearance changed. She was still ravishingly beautiful, of course, but softer somehow. He could not help wishing she had accepted some of those other invitations to spend time with his family. Maybe she would have surprised herself and enjoyed them.

The hors d'oeuvres came out—cucumber sandwiches and cheeses—and the first drinks were consumed, and soon it was time to start making dinner. Kerry surprised him by following his mother and Mrs. O'Connell out to the kitchen and insisting on being given things to do. Really—she insisted. She knew how to insist. And she dispatched her tasks very efficiently. She was by no means the incompetent in the kitchen that she claimed to be. Jim listened to the three of them chatting gaily while they made salads and prepared meat for the barbecue. He was amazed. He hoped that the general impression of Kerry was improving.

The men did the barbequing—or rather Jim's father did, while the others stood around with beer bottles in their hands and cracked jokes. Jim sensed that Mr. O'Connell was a little cool toward him, but this had been the case ever since his falling out with Erin. The topic of Kerry came up. His father said she seemed "surprisingly normal." Arthur of course thought she was great. Mr. O'Connell remained silent and grave.

Grace set the outdoor table, and they all had a very pleasant dinner together on a perfect summer evening under a peach sky. The barbequed chops were fat and juicy, the salads from Carolyn's garden and fresh-picked corn on the cob from the local farm stand were delicious, the conversation was animated and non-stop. Kerry sat next to Grace and paid particular attention to her. Jim noticed his mother watching them. He wondered what she was thinking.

The main meal was over, and it was time to clean up and serve dessert. Kerry helped carry dishes to the kitchen and stayed to fill the dishwasher. Erin and Arthur were talking to Megan about college, and Jim's father and Jack O'Connell were talking about the stock market. Since Jim was not involved in any of these conversations, he decided to take a walk and see how the gardens were doing. They were all in splendid order, of course, although most of the summer perennials were past their peak—coneflowers, daisies, lilies, phlox, achillea—and the fall flowers were just getting started—asters, Montauk daisies, aconitum.

Jim meandered around the yard a couple of times enjoying his mother's handiwork and then sat down on the double Adirondack chair near the annual beds in the shade of the spruces. His sister came waddling in his direction and sat down beside him.

"Hello there, brother mine."

"Hello. Welcome."

"How are you doing?"

"As well as could be expected. How about you?"

"Good, good. I'm getting to know your friend."

"I see that. What do you think?"

"I like her. She certainly seems eager to fit in."

"I noticed that. And she seems to be succeeding."

"Are you surprised?"

"I don't know. To tell you the truth, I didn't know what to expect. I've hardly ever spent any time with her in company—and the last time was a disaster. She's actually sort of uptight about public gatherings. But everyone's making it so easy for her. Everyone except Megan."

"You can't really blame her for that. She didn't know Kerry Morgan was going to be here."

"She recovered nicely, in any case. I think I saw them talking at some point."

"Yes, as I said: your friend is trying very hard to be agreeable. She talked to me nonstop through dinner."

"Did you mind?"

"Not at all. She didn't ask any embarrassing questions. She could be quite funny on the subject of you."

"Oh, thanks. That's just what I needed for my self-esteem."

"Speaking of which, how is your self-esteem doing these days?"

"Not quite sure. It's been a long, hot summer. But at least I didn't have to pay for any heating oil."

"How are things going on the job front?"

"I've fired a lot of missiles, let's just put it that way. I can't say the response has been overwhelming."

"What about money? Are you okay?"

He tried to say something glib about that too, but it wouldn't come out. "I'm okay—I guess. I'm surviving, anyway."

"Can you pay your bills?"

"I'm trying. In a couple of days I'll be three months behind on the mortgage. I am paying the electric bill with unemployment, no matter what. It would not be good to have that shut off."

"Are you going to say something to Mom and Dad?"

"Like what? It's not their fault I stupidly lost my job. I can't expect them to do anything about it."

"What if they *want* to do something?"

"That's just it. I don't want to be a burden."

"That's a funny way of looking at it." She saw Kerry walking toward the table with a platter of watermelon slices. "What about her? Can't she help you?"

"She probably could, but I'm certainly not going to ask. I feel stupid enough as it is."

"Why not? She probably spends more money on clothes every month than your three mortgage payments combined."

This stopped him, since he knew it was true. "I would never ask her," he said, recovering. "I do have some self-respect left. Not much, but I don't want to squander it on that."

"What nonsense," she replied. She looked at Kerry again and shook her head. "I know one thing. Erin would never hesitate to help you. If she didn't have the money, she would do whatever she had to do to get it. And you know it too."

"What does this have to do with Erin? She's with Arthur."

"'She's with Arthur.' Right. You keep telling yourself that. Don't get me wrong. I like Kerry. I really do. But she's a movie star. Do you really think that's likely to go anywhere?"

"I have no idea what you mean. Okay, so she's a movie star. She can't help it. But you've seen her yourself. You've seen how normal she is and how wonderful she can be."

"Anyone can be anything for a dinner party. I'm talking about the rest of your life. Have you ever heard of screen chemistry?"

Jim blinked. "Yes, I've heard of it."

"What exactly do you think screen chemistry consists of?"

"A screen and some chemistry?"

"That's right, joke about it, but you know very well what I'm talking about. These actors and actresses are famous for falling in love with each other at the drop of a hat for the sake of screen chemistry. They know that's what the public wants to see. But the thing about screen chemistry is it can't really be faked. It's not really acting. Are you sure you're comfortable with that sort of thing going on? Every time she does a movie?"

"I didn't know you were so knowledgeable about these things. Yes, I've thought about screen chemistry. And I have seen some of her movies. It's no big deal."

"Oh, really. Did you see the one with Brick Dancy? Because that's the one you really should see. It might take you a year or two to recover, but you really should see it. Very enlightening. Also did you know they used to be a thing?"

"I believe I did hear something about that." He refrained from saying he heard it from Bob.

"You're killing me. I mean, I don't have anything against her. I think she's charming. I just don't see how you can compare her to Erin. She's nothing to Erin, as far as I'm concerned."

Jim was shocked into silence. Grace waddled off and left him in befuddlement. He thought they were getting along so well. Besides, he knew how much Grace loved movie stars. It surprised him to discover her that attitude toward them was decidedly nuanced. But the thing about "screen chemistry" was devastating. Of course he knew what it was all about. And no, he wasn't going to watch the movie with Brick Dancy. There was just so much a man could take.

His heart and mind were in turmoil after this sneak attack. He wanted to go running after her and tell her how wrong she was, how very, very wrong; but was she? Instead he walked down the road to the pond. Grace's mocking tone hurt, but he knew she was right—including the part about Erin. She wasn't telling him anything he didn't already know. It was foolish to expect happiness with someone like Kerry when the unhappiness of movie stars was on full display every time you stood in line in the grocery store.

He walked around the pond slowly, admiring the waterlilies and the swans, thinking about Thoreau. Then back to the house. He stopped at the end of the driveway. For a moment he felt like running away. Grace had exposed him and shattered the illusion of normalcy everyone had been working so hard to create with a goddess in their midst. It was an illusion, and that was all it was. They were all busy pretending that the impossible was possible. Which left him where? He was the unmoved mover of the illusion. They were doing it for him. But this did not make him happy. No, it made him feel terrible. He could not enjoy the illusion once he knew what it was.

He knew what Grace was thinking, and he assumed everyone else was thinking the same thing. He knew Mr. O'Connell was; he wasn't even trying to pretend. He suspected Erin was. He was afraid to look at her and find out. He had brought on this double-mindedness by foisting Kerry on them. This could not be *their* party, as they had planned, their time to have fun and enjoy each other's company. It had to be about him and his "friend."

He wandered back onto the property and turned into the rose garden and was surprised to find himself coming upon Grace and Arthur sitting together on the carved stone bench. It was surprising because Arthur had never really cared for Grace. A little too high-spirited for him. They were engaged in a good-humored debate about the use of color in painting. Grace appealed to her brother.

"So what is your opinion, oh Dour One? Do painters do better when they try to imitate the splendid colors of nature or when they set nature aside and work from the imagination and the archetypes of the mind?"

"I don't know that I have an opinion on that particular subject."

"There, you see?" she said laughing. "It's two against one."

"How do you figure? He said he didn't have an opinion."

"But he's my brother. So obviously you lose."

Arthur accepted his defeat gracefully.

Jim moved on, but the scene stuck in his head, the two of them sitting there together in the evening light. There was something sweet about it. He hoped his sister could find someone like Arthur, someone kind and caring to love her and her, well, love child.

XXV

A pleasant surprise and some confusion

SEPTEMBER CAME AND, yes, Jim missed another mortgage payment. Things were getting a little hairy. There were calls coming in from creditors and impertinent collection agencies. Eventually he stopped answering the phone. What was he going to say? He was giving them all the money that was coming in from unemployment. He wasn't spending any on himself. Then one of the denizens of said institutions actually made a site visit. It was the most humiliating conversation he'd ever had in his life. So he stopped answering his doorbell as well.

One sunny Saturday, two weeks after the fair, he had just finished boiling his daily plate of generic spaghetti and was carrying it out to the deck when the aforesaid doorbell happened to ring. At first he ignored it, but then it rang again, and then someone started pounding on the door and calling his name in a friendly manner. He put down his plate and went to the window to sneak a look. He was shocked. It was Bob. He opened the door.

"Hello! How are you?" Bob boomed like someone who was unsure of his reception.

"I'm—fine. How about you?" Jim mumbled, dazed by this sudden apparition. There had been no contact between him and Bob since the ill-fated conversation about his sister.

"I come bearing breakfast," Bob replied, brandishing a sizeable Duncan Donuts carton and coffee tumbler.

Jim's mouth immediately began to water. He hadn't been able to afford quality coffee for some time and the box of donuts almost made him emotional. They sat down at the breakfast table. There was the usual small talk about the Red Sox and the weather and a vintage recording of the Brahms piano concertos that had recently been reissued, awkward at first but better as they went along. Then Bob meandered around to the point.

"So how have things been going? I heard you lost your job."

"How did you know about that?"

"A little bird told me."

"No. She called you? What did she say?"

"Just that the 'mortgage thing' may be getting a little dicey. Is that true? Is the mortgage thing getting a little dicey?"

"I guess you could say that. I haven't paid it in three months."

"You're not the only one. The economy is terrible. Half of America is in the same boat. And the boat is sinking. But I brought something that might help. I hope you don't mind." He fished a padded manila envelope out of his leather satchel, placed it on the table between them, and nudged it gently in Jim's direction.

"What is that?" Jim said skeptically.

"That, my friend, is an envelope."

"I can see it's an envelope. What's in it?"

"Why don't you open it and find out?"

Jim contemplated him for a moment with his best poker face. Then he reached over and picked up the envelope and peeked inside. There were four thick stacks of what looked like hundred-dollar bills. A *lot* of money.

"What is this?"

"I believe they call those 'Benjamins.'"

"No—I mean why are you showing it to me?"

"That's for you. A little loan."

"I can't accept this. Are you crazy?"

"Probably. But do me a favor and take it anyway. Think of it as an investment. This way I still have the famous lake cottage to go to when I feel like getting away from the madness."

"I'm afraid I'm not a very good investment right now. The job hunt isn't going very well."

"Do I look worried? Listen, this is money I literally don't need. It's a bonus I got for some case I worked on. To tell you the truth I threw it in the bank and forgot about it. Then I got a call from—well, anyway, I realized I was in a position to help. Look, this is what friends do. You would do the same for me."

"Maybe. I hope so. But I feel foolish."

"Okay, so you feel foolish. People go through rough spots sometimes. That's the way it is. We get by with a little help from our friends. And now I'm out of clichés. Anyway, it's not a big deal. I won't miss it. Honestly. You might as well take it."

"But if anyone knew about this…"

Bob laughed. "You don't get it. This was her idea. I didn't even know you were out of a job until she called me."

"I still can't believe she actually called you. How did that go?"

"It went fine. But this isn't because of her, if that's what you are thinking. So don't go all Raskolnikov on me. I really want to do this. I would have done it on my own if I had known."

They sparred some more, but in the end Jim gave in and allowed himself to accept the cash infusion that he really did want and desperately needed. Bob said he had to get back to the city for a big case he was working on.

"Oh! I almost forgot. I have something for you." He reached into his bag and pulled out a recent issue of *Star*. "Thought you might like to have this, since you happen to be in it."

Jim went pale. He took it but was afraid to look at it. Then he couldn't help himself. Right there on page one was a photo of Kerry and him in front of the church.

"Oh my God. I don't believe this."

"Must be serious if you're taking her to church."

"Not really. She just came up for the fair. But is this real?"

"Of course it's real! I saw it in a gas station on the way up and couldn't resist, although I hate buying these things in public. Very nice photo of you, by the way. You look dashing."

"We *were* dashing—to the car to get the hell out of there. The guy was a lunatic. I never saw anything like it. No wonder the stars are so afraid of them."

"Don't kid yourself. They love it, no matter what they say. By the way, check out the headline."

Jim looked down again. The words were dancing on the page. The first thing he saw was "Kerry's Mystery Man." He paused over that for a moment. Then his eyes drifted down to the subhead: "Is this the lucky guy who's driving Brick crazy?"

"I don't get it," he said. "What does 'Brick' have to do with it?"

"I don't know. That's where it gets kind of interesting. Have you been seeing her all this time?"

"Well, yes. Pretty much. I wouldn't necessarily say 'seeing her.' I don't see too much of her these days. Usually she's off on a shoot."

"So you're not actually romantically involved with her?"

"I'm not sure how to answer that, to be honest. I certainly wouldn't describe it as a traditional relationship. More like a series of random encounters held together by—I'm not quite sure what."

"Well, I don't know what to tell you. The tabloids seem to think they're doing the on-again off-again thing, like Taylor and Burton."

"It wasn't 'the tabloids.' It was just one photographer. She warned me what it's like when they all come after you."

"Just one?" Bob said, wheels turning.

"Right. Just one. Why?"

"Well, don't you think that's a little suspicious?"

"I'm not sure what you mean."

"They usually travel in packs. So why would there be just one?"

"Tell me what you're thinking. The suspense is killing me."

"I'm not really thinking anything. It just occurs to me that it could have been a set-up, if there was only one photographer."

"A 'set-up'! What are you talking about?"

"To get a picture of you two on the front cover. It's just interesting that they have this picture. Read what it says. It's almost like she wanted it to be there so someone would see it."

"Whoa. Wait a minute. Are you saying she set the whole thing up to make this Brick person jealous?"

"I don't know. I'm just putting two and two together. I mean, think about it. What was a photographer from the *Star* doing at a country fair in upstate Connecticut? Those people don't even know where Connecticut is. I mean, it could just be a coincidence. But you have to admit it's a little weird."

"You certainly have a jaundiced way of looking at things," Jim said, but inside he was collapsing. The shock of seeing himself on the cover of a high-circulation scandal sheet robbed him of his certainty. Could Kerry really do such a thing? No—he refused to believe it. There was her sweetness at the fair. There was the thing that happened in his room after the fair. There was the way she interacted with his family and friends.

Then again, Saturday was already two weeks ago and he had not heard from her since. She warned him she had things to do in the city, but he wasn't expecting it to take this long. Jim did not know what to think. He looked at the tabloid and read the headline over and over again, as if he could make it say something other than what it actually said. He was unsuccessful in this effort. The comment about Brick definitely seemed to imply what Bob was saying; not necessarily that she had arranged the whole thing, but that he (Jim) might be an unwitting pawn.

"Driving Brick crazy." What did it mean? Why would Brick be going crazy if he did not have an active interest in Kerry? And why "driving," specifically? Why the present tense? Were they implying that Kerry was doing the driving? That it was all quite deliberate? Now he turned the page and actually forced himself to read the story. It did not contain the specific answers he was looking for. It did not reassure him, but at the same time it did not confirm Bob's hair-raising scenario, or anything like it.

Actually it was kind of matter-of-fact. The prose was a little lurid, but there were no lurid details in the prose. All it said was that she had been seen with a "mystery friend" at a country fair in Connecticut. Jim was not identified. There was no reference to anything else. In fact the article—if you could call it that—was reassuringly bland. No one had attempted to look into the connection more deeply. Not yet, anyway.

But how long would it take before that happened? He was out in the open. They had a picture of him. It was just a matter of time before one of his friends or acquaintances saw the newspaper and identified him. And then what would happen? Would they show up in a mob on his doorstep? If so, he was doomed. There would be no way to conceal his interesting housing situation from Kerry.

Jim thought about the behavior of the photographer. The guy was like a ravenous beast. If they were all like that, then what chance did he have in preserving his privacy and peace of mind? They would trample on him and there was nothing he could do about it. They had the First Amendment on their side. He considered the Second Amendment, but he couldn't literally shoot them while they were shooting him. Or not all of them. Could he?

He wanted to. The zombie photographer scared him. The whole idea scared him. It was one thing to be Kerry's sometime consort in private and quite another to try to pretend he belonged with her on the public stage. He was not good enough for Kerry; he knew it perfectly well. It was hard to think that the world would know it too. And his family! He thought about his mother looking at the picture he was holding in his hands and felt ill. He had allowed the Kerry circus to invade their (mostly) tranquil lives.

Bob's interpretation filled in certain blanks in the narrative. Jim had not heard from Kerry for almost two months after the Fourth of July debacle—and then she called him out of the blue. The call surprised him. He thought it was over. Then there was her strange willingness to meet him at the fair. She did not have to be talked into it. She did not insist on coming to his house first. She was perfectly happy to go directly to the church, even though it was a public place and she knew there would be lots of people there.

This was surprising, but then again maybe it wasn't. Maybe she called him because she had a specific plan in mind. Maybe she was willing to meet him in a public place because she wanted to give the photographer an opportunity to catch them together. On the other hand, she would have had to tip him off in advance. This seemed a little too conspiratorial. He did not think of Kerry as a conniver, as someone who was underhanded, a Vivian Rutledge. But it was not impossible. Especially if Brick was still in the picture.

But then what about the little interlude in Bridgewater? What about pulling him onto the bed? Why would she do something like that if the person she was really interested in was Brick? It wasn't necessary. No one saw it or knew anything about it. She had nothing to gain from it if her plan was to get Brick back again. Or maybe that wasn't her plan? Maybe she was just trying to drive Brick crazy, as the headline writers would have it.

He did not know what to think. He started to throw the newspaper away but wound up tossing it into the bottom drawer of the living room side table. Then he went to the kitchen and picked up the envelope Bob had left behind. He shook out its contents and counted one of the stacks. Fifty bills; times four, that would add up to $20,000. Jim was stunned. He wasn't expecting anything of that magnitude.

The first thing he thought of was his sister. How would she feel about him taking so much money from Bob? He called her.

"I just had a very interesting little visit from a friend of ours."

"Kerry?"

"No, someone even more interesting than that. And I think you know who I mean."

"I could probably guess. Was it worthwhile?"

"I'm not sure how to answer that. I have more money than I need to cover my debts and September too, if that's what you mean. But I want to make sure you're all right with this first."

"I'm the one who called him. Of course I'm all right with it. He has plenty of money. And you'll pay him back."

"That isn't what I mean. I don't want it to be a payoff."

"Oh, for heaven's sake. That has nothing to do with it. He's your friend. That's all the reason he needs."

"But he hasn't really been my friend for some time now. We haven't talked since—"

"I know. He told me. It's all right. You need to get over yourself. You insist on having scruples, but I don't want your scruples. Believe me, I'm perfectly fine with it. In fact I'm glad."

"Okay. If you say so. To tell the truth I really do need it. Getting a little desperate over here. But how did it go? I mean the conversation."

"It wasn't like that. It was fine. It was almost like a business call, nothing personal. I simply told him about your situation. Said I thought he would like to know."

"Did he—"

"What? Apologize? He doesn't need to. That wasn't what this is about. Stop worrying about my feelings. I'm over it. It was just a schoolgirl crush anyway. I realized it from talking to him again. He's not really my type."

"No, I never thought he was. I feel so bad about telling him to call you."

"Don't. It's over. That happened a long time ago, and now it's time to move on to something new."

She seemed unusually chipper. He was surprised. Maybe it was because of the pending parturition. In any case he felt much better after this call. Much, much better. He went to work on repairing his financial situation. As it turned out, he was able to get himself caught up with less than half of what Bob had given him. This left plenty of wiggle room for future contingencies, if, God forbid, they should arise. It would get him to the end of the year, anyway, even after unemployment ran out, which was soon. And if he didn't have a job by then—well, he didn't know what he was going to do.

He was done with all that and feeling extremely relieved. Then he couldn't help himself. He went to the living room and looked at the newspaper again. He read the story several times. It remained opaque. They were trying to draw a very large inference from a minuscule amount of data. They didn't have any concrete evidence or they would have used it. The story wasn't impactful. It was more of a non-story. He was relieved about that.

But what if Bob was right? Two weeks had gone by without a word from Kerry. Bob's scenario provided a tailor-made explanation. Perhaps she did not want to contact him. Perhaps she had no intention of ever contacting him again. After all, the story was out. The point had been made. If it was all a plot to drive Brick crazy or get him back again, then presumably she would have no further use for him.

Jim forced himself to Google "kerry brick" and was astounded at how many hits there were and the tone of them. It did not take him long to see where Bob was getting his information. There was speculation going all the way back to the spring about the two of them getting back together. It could all be made up, of course, wishful thinking on the part of the rumor mill; but where there's smoke there's fire. It seemed *something* was going on between them.

Jim died inside reading these articles. He disappeared into pure nothingness next to Brick, even in his own mind. This was not like Marc Anthony and Caesar; this was more like Caesar and the cup bearer's slave. If Kerry still had any interest in Brick at all, then Jim was doomed. He could not compete with Brick if he decided to come to her, and he could not displace Brick from her heart if he did not come. He could not afford a giant diamond or treat her in the way she was used to being treated. It seemed hopeless.

Of course he had been suspecting for a long time that it was hopeless. But now he tried to make peace with the possibility that Kerry had what she wanted and might never call him again. It was painful to go through this thought process, but he tried to tell himself that he was not all that upset about losing her. He never felt he really had her, and in that sense he could not lose her. She had come to him on loan; that was all.

True, it was embarrassing to lose her, having just introduced her to his family and friends, but they would understand. In fact his sister and probably his mother would be glad about it. Then he had a painful thought. He remembered the look on Erin's face when she saw them together. His little dalliance with Kerry had put an impossible barrier between them. But then again, what difference did it make? Erin and Arthur were engaged. It was not like there was any chance of him ever getting back together with her.

The news of the engagement surprised him. He knew there were rumors, but he never believed it would actually happen. He never really felt they were right for each other. In a sense they were too much alike, both so easygoing and accommodating. There was something almost incestuous about it, like Fanny and Edmund. Well, okay, that wasn't the right word, but he did not know what the right word was. They were not the opposites that attract; let's just put it that way.

He could not quite see Erin being in love with Arthur, even

though he held him in the highest esteem. For one thing, Arthur, lapsed Catholic, could be an outspoken agnostic, and he knew Erin had strong feelings on that subject. He was also given to making lengthy dissertations on various topics in his self-perceived role of public intellectual. Jim was happy to tolerate these dissertations because Arthur was his friend and frankly he didn't see him all that often. But it was hard to imagine listening to them day after day. Not exactly Casaubon and Dorothea, of course, but similar.

And then there was the matter of the feet. We are tempted to say the "little matter," but in one sense Arthur's feet were not little at all, *viz*, the olfactory sense. Jim wasn't sure whether he was ambivalent about changing his socks or there were other more sinister causes afoot, but they generally gave off a scent that one might call "ripe." Many were the occasions in days of yore when they would be sitting in front of the fire at his parents' house and Jim would be thinking to himself, "Dear God, please do not let him take off his shoes"—which was exactly what Arthur did, since he loved nothing more than to liberate his "puppies," as he called them, from their leathery confines, or even their Nikes.

Now these were not nice thoughts, and Jim was thoroughly ashamed of himself for having them, but he also knew *why* he was having them. It was because of his feelings for Erin. He now realized that he was in love with her and always had been. Every time he saw her he became more convinced of it. He tried not to feel that way, for Arthur's sake and for many reasons. He tried to tell himself he did not love her, but love does not like to be argued with, as many have found to their chagrin. The more he tried to talk these warm feelings away, the more they made him their slave.

For what was the point of having such feelings? There was no point. She was engaged to Arthur. That was the end of it. He could have whatever opinion he wanted on Arthur's feet, but it did not change the fact that they were planning to get married. But even if they weren't, he had no chance with her, not anymore. It was not just the dreadful way he had treated her, for which he never apologized. That was bad enough. No, it was the whole thing with Kerry, which had compromised him permanently in her eyes.

He saw her expression when she looked at them. He knew how to interpret the look because he knew her so well. They had found him and Kerry alone in his parents' house, which might lead to suspicions, and those suspicions were true. He could not pretend to be worthy of someone like Erin after cavorting with Kerry for the past year or more. He knew exactly how she felt about the whole sleep-around Hollywood scene. He could imagine what she was thinking of him now.

He knew what *all* of them were probably thinking after the barbeque—not just Erin but his family and also hers—that he was with Kerry Morgan, with all of the things that "with" implies. Now in his mind he was not really with Kerry at all and never had been. He had been with her in the physical sense, to be sure, from time to time, but spiritually? No. He kept hoping this blessed assurance would develop, this veil would descend, but it never did. He had been with her for over a year and still did not feel like he was with her at all, not really.

No one else knew this, however. They did not know how he was feeling. They had no idea about his ambivalence or how much he had agonized over the exact nature of his attachment to Kerry, or hers to him. Even he thought he was overreaching and making a fool of himself. Kerry's occasional kindness had not ever deluded him into believing that the relationship could come to a successful conclusion. He had been expecting it to end ever since it began.

But did this make things better or worse? Would Erin forgive him for wasting a year of his life with Kerry if she knew he never thought it could amount to anything? Or would she despise him even more? After all, what was the real reason for hanging around if the relationship seemed doomed? Was it just for snuggles? Was it the brush with fame? What was it? He did not know the answer to these difficult questions. But if he could not justify his behavior to himself, then he knew he could never justify it to Erin.

XXVI

In the fall of the year

JIM DID NOT know it yet, but the visit from Bob was a sign that things were looking up.

First Grace had her baby, a pink little girl, dubbed Anna Waldstein Wilmot, for her beloved grandmother and also—wait for it—the famous Beethoven sonata. Jim was glad she didn't name her "Moonlight." AWW! weighed in at seven pounds two ounces and seemed suitably adorable when held by her uncle in the hospital. Grace glowed and was happy, and Jim was happy for her, although he could not help wondering what the future would bring.

Then in the middle of a sunny and beautiful September day he had an unexpected call from former coworker Dave Rodriguez. Seems he had landed an account management job at a start-up agency in Stamford, which just happened to have an immediate opening for a copywriter. It wasn't much, but the upside was potentially tremendous (according to Dave), depending on how things panned out.

Jim had no trouble getting the job, with his inside connection. He swallowed hard when he heard the starting salary, but the enthusiasm of the young principals was infectious. They already had one large account on the hook and were angling for another. Jim had the impression they knew what they were doing and were likely to be successful, but it wouldn't have mattered even if they didn't. He was glad to have a job, any job, and to be out of the house and headed off to an office in the morning.

Turned out they were better than he expected. They knew exactly what had to be done to succeed in the advertising business. That is, they were fantastic salesmen. Although Jim's title was "copywriter," the agency was so small that he became the de facto creative director, a role at which he soon proved to be quite adept. He had a knack for sloganeering as well as the versatility to be able to see a successful ad campaign in his head. He was also able to take customers by the hand and lead them to a smart solution—which, he discovered, was basically the key to success, since they themselves were often clueless.

Jim was well on his way to making himself indispensable at Cooper Hartmann Ltd., having been scared out of his wits by five months of unemployment. Was there some problem that needed solving? He was the first one on the scene. Was there a project that needed late night or weekend attention? He jumped at the opportunity to help. He did everything and anything, which is sometimes necessary in a small agency, and thus gained a lot of traction in a relatively short time.

Jim did so well that Fenton Cooper invited him into his office in late October when the leaves were changing and gave him a raise. He was impressed with him and wanted to make sure he stayed around. Jim took a hard look at his expenses when he got home and decided he could make a go of things with the new salary. It would be tight. The heat would have to be turned down, the cable would remain off, the naked spaghetti might have to stay on the menu for a while. But he thought he could do it.

So it was that he felt emboldened, with great pleasure, to write a check to Bob for the $10,000 he hadn't used yet and drop it in the mail with a letter expressing effusive thanks and reiterating his promise to settle the rest as soon as humanly possible. This helped to restore some of the self-confidence that had dwindled away almost to nothing. He also went out in the yard and yanked up the For Sale sign. It came out more easily than he thought it would.

Then in early November they landed their biggest account yet. Jim led the creative efforts on this one from the start and was rewarded with a surprisingly large bonus. He couldn't believe it when he saw the check, but maybe they realized they had gotten him cheap and wanted to do something to make up for it. Whatever the reason, it gave him more breathing room in the budget. He put it in the bank and used it very sparingly as a lever for unplanned expenses.

So there was definite, marked improvement on the career and financial side of things. His personal life was a different story, however. Kerry never did call after the tabloid bomb. It seemed his year-long adventure in romancing a screen goddess had ended without even a whimper. He was surfing the Net one day and saw that she and Brick had "reunited." Apparently he was so low on the totem pole that he didn't even merit a notification. Then again, she probably figured he could read.

It was certainly a novel way to be dumped. For a while he felt offended, angry even, but then he felt like laughing. He was glad to be free, glad the long ordeal was finally over. It came as a relief. It was going to end anyway—they both knew it. Her very telling lack of thoughtfulness spared him a superfluous conversation. He was glad he didn't have to be told something humiliating that he already knew. He was glad not to have to endure the breakup in person and swallow his pride one more time, which he knew he would feel obliged to do, since he could not see himself remonstrating with her and making things worse.

It was a fitting ending. She was unconscious when she came into his life and unconscious upon exit. Besides, no explanation was needed. She preferred Brick Dancy. The discomfiture was painful at first, but he recovered. It hurt less than he thought it would, and then he realized that perhaps this was because he did not love her and had never really loved her. Or if that didn't pan, then it was probably because he had seen so little of her. In any case he told himself he was happy to have Brick take her off his hands. If Brick could tame this sweet Kate, then God bless him. Jim knew *he* couldn't. He didn't even know where to begin.

All in all, he was not overly disappointed to be dismissed from the glittering orbit of Kerry Morgan and to shrink back into blessed anonymity. He just wished he had not brought her to the fair. Losing her would have been easier if he had not allowed his family and friends to think he had her. Fortunately the only one who seemed to know about the *Star* photo and embarrassing headline was Grace. She teased him a little but stopped when he told her it was over. She was glad. She assured him he could do better. She said it more than once, as if she knew something he didn't know. He assumed she was probably thinking about his new job.

His mother, whose tongue he feared the most, never said a word to him about it. She never asked about Kerry after the party or showed any further interest in the connection. There could be many explanations for this, but he decided to accept it with gratitude and not kill the cat through undue curiosity. He did not expect to hear anything from his father, who was not the sort of person who tried to insert himself into other people's business.

All in all, he convinced himself he was getting off easy. He was tired of the connection. It was starting to seem like an obligation; maybe it always had. He didn't have to sit around waiting for her to call or suffer the perpetual humiliation of not being allowed to call her himself. He didn't have to be afraid of making a mistake every time he opened his mouth around her. He didn't have to be sick with loneliness while she was off on one of her shoots. His heart did not seem to be terribly broken. The only thing broken was his pride. And he had just enough sense to be grateful for that.

There was psychological fallout, however, and it was significant. The unceremonious manner in which he was dumped made him feel like he had played the house boy to a star. His encounter with the enchanting deity had shattered all pretense of innocence, like Odysseus and Circe. Lounging around with her in her house or his own did not ennoble him, as he was inclined to think at the time. It did not make him feel special or unique; or at least not anymore. No, it made him feel unfit for polite society. It was a smudge.

Especially when he thought of Erin. Oh yes, he was still thinking of Erin. Even though she was engaged. He was thinking about *how* he thought about her, and then how he thought about Kerry, and it made him sick in his soul. He did not feel worthy of Erin now. He had never felt worthy of Kerry either, but this was different. Erin was too good for him. He realized how much he loved her. It was not the kind of love he thought he was looking for. It was not romantic love, per se, although it was romantic in a way that perhaps has never been told. It did not have a category; it had no philosopher. It was not like the poetic idea of love that had intoxicated him from the first time he read Mallory as a teenager. It was far more, well, mundane.

But he realized that this was not necessarily a bad thing. Being mundane made it suited for everyday life, which was not really the case with Kerry. He realized something else that seemed important. Erin had loved him for himself. There are people who love you for who they think you are, or the way you look, or how much money or power they think you have, or talent. This was like Kerry loving him because of Yale. Then there are people who love you in a way that has no reasons. The love Erin had for him was not based on *appearances*, and thus it was neither a delusion nor subject to change. At the time he was too stupid to see how precious this kind of love was. He was now inclined to think of it as the key to happiness.

When men are alone and not otherwise occupied, like Jim in his small house on long fall nights, their minds turn naturally to the opposite sex. And the only person his mind ever seemed to turn to was Erin. At this point he was not thinking about Kerry anymore. It was as if she had been some sort of wraith that passed through consciousness without leaving any distinct impression. But he was thinking about Erin pretty much all the time, at least when he was not otherwise occupied, and even then. Sometimes he would call out her name, as if summoning her from the mists. She did not come. And then he would laugh at himself.

But wait a minute. Wasn't she engaged? Indeed she was, and to his close friend. And this was another reason for despising himself. He was thinking about Erin when he should have been thinking about Arthur. He would never do anything to hurt either one of them, but the fact was that he missed her terribly, especially now that he wasn't wasting his time dreaming the impossible dream. He had not seen her since summer. He wanted to see her so much. It was wrong, and he knew it was wrong; but still he longed to see her. Of course he had no way of seeing her without calling her, which he would never dream of doing under the circumstances.

Thus he was delighted, to his shame, to receive an invitation from his mother to an Octoberfest party. The O'Connells were on the invitation list, including Erin, who was rumored to be coming. Then he found out from his sister that Arthur probably would *not* be coming. Seems he was stuck up in Boston at a conference or something. Grace seemed very intent on making this known. He knew why. She still had ideas about him and Erin. She was wrong to be thinking such things when Erin was engaged, and he was wrong to be thinking them as well. But somehow it encouraged him that they were both thinking the same wrong things together.

It would be the first time he had seen Erin alone in more than a year. He found himself unexpectedly filled with emotion. Again, he knew it was wrong to feel this way, but he could not help it. He also knew it was foolish to feel this way. Arthur would be there in spirit if not body. If he were not such a good friend, then perhaps Jim would not feel barred from trying to reconnect with her. After all, what if it was their destiny to be together, as his sister seemed to think? Did it make sense to let a little thing like an engagement stand in their way? Well, as a matter of fact it did. It did not matter whom she was engaged to—Arthur or Genghis Khan. It was wrong to try to claim his old privilege when she was involved with someone else and presumptuous to set himself up as an arbiter of whom she should or should not marry, having declined to marry her himself.

But then could he talk to her as a friend? Was it possible for them to *be* friends after all that had happened? For that matter, how could they *not* be friends, if she was going to be married to Arthur? Hadn't they asked him to be their best man? They would have to get past the awkwardness at some point. But could he rise to such heights of disinterested behavior? Could he talk to her as a friend when what he really wanted to do was take her in his arms and tell her he loved her? When that was what he really, really, really wanted to do?

It cannot be said, and it also cannot be unsaid, how mixed up Jim felt going to this party. So what if it was at his own old home? He felt like a stranger there now because of Kerry, because of bringing her there. Fortunately there were no O'Connell cars in the driveway when he arrived. This was good; he felt a need to establish a beachhead. He went inside and was greeted with warm hugs but found himself feeling very anxious. He went to the bar. There was a pitcher of frozen margaritas that Grace had made up. He poured himself one. It did not provide any comfort.

He went to the kitchen to see if he could help, but his sister and mother laughed at him. He wanted to stay, he wanted to visit; but he was too anxious about Erin. He went back out into the living room and sat down with his father and talked to him about the economy for a while, but his attempt at making conversation was awkward, especially since he didn't know anything about the economy and his father was a verified expert. He found himself doing a lot of half-hearted listening and sage nodding of the head.

Then the O'Connells arrived, and he had an unexpected attack of shyness. It was all very strange. Mr. O'Connell seemed bemused. Was he thinking about Kerry? Mrs. O'Connell pulled him to her and gave him a heartfelt hug. This surprised him. Then Erin. He did not know how to greet her. He certainly didn't try to hug her. They just sort of stood there nodding at each other, in her case very slightly. He had a nervous smile on his face. She was not smiling at all, and that was not characteristic.

He was in the same room with Erin, but it was heaven and it was hell. He did not know what to do with himself. Should he try to talk to her? He wanted so much to talk to her, to make contact with her, not to feel like such a stranger to her. It seemed rude not to try, at least. But at the same time he was not happy with his own motives. Was it true graciousness or was it something else? And if it was something else, would she see through him?

In one sense he *wanted* her to see through him—now that he'd had a radical change of heart towards her—but in another sense he definitely didn't. He wanted her to know how much he loved her and appreciated her but did not want to sabotage Arthur. He also did not want to sabotage himself. He was assuming a great deal. What if she no longer had any of the old feelings for him? What if she had no desire to reciprocate his belatedly manifest love? The possibility of rejection is a stark barrier at any time, but especially after what had happened with Kerry.

Now he thought about Kerry. He pictured her in scenes around the house and yard the last time they were all together. One scene in particular came to mind, and then he knew for sure he could not approach Erin. There were too many feelings and they were too complicated—but the most complicated feeling of all was one of shame, both at having neglected her in the past, and at having been unfaithful to her with Kerry, unfaithful in a most public way.

She and her mother followed Grace and his mother to the kitchen. Erin was last in line. He saw her coming from his corner and heaved a misfired "hi" in her direction. She seemed surprised. They had already said hi, sort of, at the front door. Why was he hi-ing her again? She stopped and looked at him. She returned the greeting, but her tone was guarded, perplexed, perhaps even a little scornful. Or was he reading too much into things?

In any case she did not linger. She continued on into the kitchen without looking back. He was momentarily upset with her for her lack of responsiveness, and then he was not upset. What did he expect? That she would come to him and smile on him and suddenly it would be as if they had not been separated by a year and a half of silence? As if nothing had ever happened? As if there had been no Kerry coming between them and making Jim look like a fool or worse? As if she were not engaged? She *was* engaged.

He had been looking forward to this moment all week, and now he felt ashamed of himself and depressed. He was doting on someone who was engaged and should have been off-limits to his overactive imagination. It was foolish and terribly selfish to expect or even hope for anything other than what had actually happened. Her behavior was appropriate and reasonable. It was natural for her to be puzzled by his awkward second greeting. It was natural for her to seem a little cool toward him and his shenanigans. He realized he would have been disappointed in her if she weren't.

He wanted her to come to him and throw herself in his arms.

But he also *didn't* want her to come to him—for Arthur's sake. Her faithfulness was one of the things he admired most about her; the strong attachments she formed and her unwillingness to bring pain to the people she loved, or in fact to anyone. Did he want her to forsake the very qualities he admired? Would he continue to admire her if she responded in an unadmirable way to his awkward flirting? This awkwardness was very evident to him. He was acting like a cad. He had a burden of love that was improper, and its very impropriety was shining through in his comportment.

She was in the kitchen with his mother, having an animated conversation. He could hear them. They all seemed so cheerful. He longed to go in there and be cheerful too, but he didn't dare. Then she was sitting in the living room on the loveseat, her cheeks red in the glow of firelight. There was a place next to her and he saw himself in that place; but Grace came and sat down beside her with the baby, and the temptation passed.

Grace passed little Anna to Erin. Jim watched in fascination as a look of joy came over Erin's face and as his sister reacted to her joy with a smile that was overcoming sadness. The dynamic seemed perfectly clear to him. Erin saw this as an opportunity to bring grace to Grace. He marveled at her kindness. He also marveled at the expert way that she handled the baby, so unlike his own bumbling. Anna seemed very content with "Aunt Erin," as Grace kept calling her. The reason for this was not clear. She seemed to be trying to send Erin a message of some kind. For a moment he wondered if it had something to do with him.

Eventually they found their way to the dining room for the feast his mother had prepared: Sauerbraten with Franconia potatoes and baked squash and buttered beets and roasted Brussel sprouts with bacon and kielbasa and homemade rolls. It all looked incredible. He knew it was not about the show with his mother; it was about the love. People were milling about, chairs had not yet been chosen. There was one next to Erin; Jim looked at it but decided to stay where he was. Still, he managed to wind up across from her—well, not directly across, to be sure—he wasn't *that* cheeky—but in a good place for observation.

Observe her he did, every chance he got, and sometimes when he shouldn't have; he knew it. She seemed to notice, but she also seemed to be ignoring him, which he decided was a good thing. In fact, she seemed rather grave. It was not the usual smiling Erin to which he was accustomed. But wasn't this perfectly natural? Arthur was not there. It probably felt a little strange to her to be out in company without her fiancée.

Jim felt no need to talk. He was too absorbed in his thoughts, especially with the pleasant view. No one asked him about Kerry, which was the thing he had been dreading. It was as if she had been collectively forgotten. He was relieved in one sense, but in another sense it was somewhat deflating. It seemed to indicate a silent unity on the impossibility of such a connection, and thus his inadequacy. He wanted everyone to think he was perfectly capable of cavorting with Kerry Morgan, but at the same time he wanted them all to forget he'd ever had anything to do with her. Similarly he wanted Erin to notice his renewed interest in her, but he did not *really* want her to notice because he knew it was very, very wrong. So he hid it with considerable pain to himself.

Grace tried to engage him on the hot topic of texting and the addictive nature of Blackberries, newly arrived on the scene. He gave a polite answer but was otherwise content to stay self-contained, since he was not addicted. He tried to focus on listening to the conversation around the table, which was lively, as it always was with the O'Connells. But no matter where his eyes went, his attention was focused entirely on Erin, studying her discreetly, trying to understand her. This was enough to keep him occupied through the two hours of dinner.

There was a loop running in his head, and it went something like this:

She looks fantastic—I never realized how pretty she was before—will she look at me?—no, I don't want her to look at me—I should not be looking at her at all—oh Lord, I'm making a fool of myself!—why can't I give her up and leave her alone?—she doesn't need a monster like me in her life—Arthur is a much better person than I am—he's the one person I would choose for her myself, if it were up to me to choose, which it isn't, so don't be silly—I wish he were here to take the edge off this ambivalence—I'm so glad he isn't...

And so on. No wonder he seemed self-absorbed. He was hot and he was cold. He was ecstatic and he was miserable. He was full of hope and he was in despair. With all of this tumult, it was all he could do to remain calm and in his chair. The food helped. He felt better when he was eating and concentrating on the good things on his plate. But the periods between courses seemed long. There was that noise in his head. He hoped no one else could hear it.

After dinner Grace came to him while he was moping by the fire. They were alone.

"What do you think of Erin?" she said in a low tone. "Doesn't she look fantastic?"

"She does. Her engagement becomes her."

"And what if she were *not* engaged? Would you still be interested after all this time?"

"She *is* engaged. She's getting married in couple of months. I'm in the wedding party, remember? Besides, she doesn't want to have anything to do with me."

"Why do you say that?"

"Because I'm not good enough for her. She would never want me now, especially when she has someone better."

"I don't know. You might be surprised."

They were interrupted by the returning fathers, but this conversation left Jim in a tizzy. His sister was literally playing the Devil's advocate. The one thing he did not want to do was to indulge in speculation about how Erin would feel about him if she were free. This was too much like wanting her to be free when she wasn't, too much like rooting against the engagement.

The party was sheer pleasure and sheer torture, but Jim would not have traded it for anything in the world because *she* was there. The suffering was worth it if he could see Erin and be in the same room with her. As difficult as it was to know how to act or what to say, given the broken state of their relationship, and of course the engagement, which overrode everything, still there was no place he would rather be. On the whole, he left feeling fairly content.

Except of course that he was not content. He had seen her, but to what end? It seemed hopeless. There was going to be a wedding. Even if there wasn't, there were his manifold deficiencies. Erin's coolness toward him spoke volumes. Things had changed between them. She was not the same Erin anymore, the Erin he could count on to smile on him no matter what he did and how much he neglected her. He had ruined this connection between them.

The next day his mother called.

"You seemed a little quiet last night."

"Oh, you know, thinking about work. Pretty busy right now."

"I see. Was it my imagination, or were you looking at Erin?"

"Well, she looked great. Who wouldn't want to look at her?"

"I don't know. I was wondering if you had changed your mind

about her."

"No, I haven't changed my mind at all."

This was his clever reply. After all, what did she want him to say? That he was in love with her? He was very much in love with Erin—besotted, almost—but he should not have been; not with his friend in the picture.

XXVII

A strange disclosure

JIM WAS WORKING very hard and trying not to think about Erin while also thinking about her all the time. Then two days before Thanksgiving he received a dramatic message from Arthur. It seems he had to talk to him "as soon as possible."

If there was anything Jim hated it was drama, but he managed to suppress these feelings for the sake of his sensitive friend. He called him right away.

"Will you be home tonight?" Arthur said in a tone that can only be described as overwrought.

"I'm at work, but I can probably get there around nine," Jim said, wondering what in the world this was about.

"Would it be all right for me to come over? We need to talk."

"We're talking right now."

"No—I need to see you in person. It won't do any other way."

It won't do what any other way? Jim had no idea. He wished Arthur had chosen something other than a work night to insist on seeing him. He was busy with the new client and did not want to get locked into having to leave at a set time. Besides, why the urgency? Then he had a dreadful thought. Had Erin told Arthur about Jim ogling her at the party? Had his perfidy been exposed? But he calmed down. It didn't seem likely. He was pretty sure his ogling had not been detected. At least not by Erin.

But what then? He simply couldn't imagine. Then he realized what it was. Arthur wanted to wiggle out of having him be his best man. It was the only possible explanation this close to the wedding.

Jim wasn't surprised. The only surprising thing was that he had asked him in the first place. Erin must have realized it wouldn't work after seeing him at the dinner party. It would be way too awkward, and she was right. In any case he wasn't upset about it. He really didn't want to be the best man at Erin and Arthur's wedding. He was happy to be released from the responsibility and was not in any sense offended. He even got a good laugh out of it.

Jim tore himself away from the office at 7:15. Dave gave him one of his looks, but it didn't matter. He had already agreed to see Arthur. He had to push things on the highway in order to get home on time but managed to get into the house and turn on a couple of lights before Arthur arrived. His dapper friend came in with a hang-dog expression. Jim offered him a drink, which he gladly accepted. Then he asked for another one, which was surprising since Arthur didn't really drink. His hand seemed to be shaking a bit as he raised it to his lips. What the heck was going on?

"So I guess you're probably wondering what this is all about," Arthur said with a nervous little laugh, in his somewhat formal way.

"Not at all," Jim said. "It's about the wedding."

Arthur stared at him blankly. "You know?"

"Of course I know. And I understand perfectly. Believe me, it's no big deal. I'm already over it."

His friend looked even more stunned at this pronouncement. Then he smiled knowingly. "*She* told you," he said with a nod.

"Now why would she tell me anything about it?"

"Well, she is your sister, and you have such a great rapport."

His *sister*? What did Grace have to do with it? "Yes, I guess we do," Jim said reeling.

"I'm surprised she didn't tell me she told you. But I guess that's the way it is with brothers and sisters. I wouldn't know, not having one myself."

"It is a special relationship," Jim averred.

"Apparently so. But then you don't mind? Really?"

"Mind? Why would I mind?"

"On account of Erin. I mean the engagement and everything."

Jim was still struggling to catch up. "Is there a problem with the engagement?"

"Well, duh!" Arthur said, now looking at him strangely. "I mean, obviously. I have to call it off. And I don't know how I'm going to do it. Erin is such a wonderful person. It's not her fault, what happened."

"What did happen, exactly?"

"You know, I don't really know what happened. I wasn't even thinking about Grace. Then we ran into each other at your mother's house—the time you were there with Kerry Morgan. It was like magic. It was as if we had never seen each other before. We started talking and just couldn't stop."

Arthur's meaning now began to break through the fog in full scorching glory. He was in love with Grace? Was it possible? It seemed to be the import of his words. But it was very surprising.

Arthur had never been able to stand being in the same room with Grace when she was a little girl. She was too precocious for him. Then again, she wasn't a little girl anymore. No, she had definitely grown up.

"So you're saying Erin doesn't know about all this."

"No way. She has no idea. That's what's so terrible about it. I definitely don't want to hurt Erin."

"But of course you're going to tell her."

"Of course! But I'm dreading it. That's why I wanted to talk to you first. You know her better than anybody, probably even better than I do. What do I say? What do I do?"

"You're just going to have to tell her the truth. And under the circumstances she should probably know as soon as possible." No, he wasn't thinking about himself here. He was thinking about the impact on Erin and the onrushing March wedding.

"I know I have to tell her. You don't have to say it again. But I'm just sick about it. I've never done anything like this in my life. I mean, it wasn't like I chose this thing with Grace. It just happened. I didn't have any control over it. Do you think it's all right?"

"Good heavens—who am I to say?"

"But am I making any sense? I'm so confused. I feel like I almost owe it to Erin to go through with it at this point. But that doesn't make any sense either, does it? I mean, if I'm in love with someone else?"

"Are you sure you're in love with Grace?"

"Oh, am I ever. I just want to be with her all the time. I mean *all* the time. I've never felt like this in my life. It kills me every time I have to leave her and go back up to Boston."

"You mean you've had actual dates with her?" Jim said, his astonishment growing by leaps and bounds.

"Of course! A concert and a movie, a couple of other things. Your mother's been watching the baby."

"My mother!"

"Well, she doesn't know it's me. She just knows Grace is dating somebody, which of course she is happy about. So what do you think? Is it all right? I feel like I've made a terrible mess of things."

Jim stood there looking at him for a moment in shock. He was having a hard time processing what he'd just heard. Arthur had been having dates with Grace while he was engaged to Erin? What?

"I guess there isn't anything you can do about it, if you really do love her," he managed to say. "But Erin—"

"Yes, I know. You don't have to keep harping on it. It's bad. It's really bad. I guess the best thing is just to go and tell her and be honest with her, as you say. There isn't any way around it. Right? I mean, I never really felt like I deserved her anyway."

But he felt like he deserved Grace? "So that's why you just had to come see me tonight."

Arthur nodded. "We're supposed to go shopping for wedding rings this weekend. Obviously we're not doing that."

"I don't know what to tell you. Clearly you can't go shopping for wedding rings if you are thinking about breaking up with her. You have no choice but to tell her."

"No, I know. I agree. I know I have to. Thanks for being such a great friend."

Arthur left looking very abashed. Jim could not believe what had just happened. He had so many feelings all at once that he didn't even know what he was feeling. Was he shocked? Was he sad? Was he, well, happy? Was he angry? Was he sympathetic? Was he censorious? He was all of those things at the same time in a big mash-up. One snarky thought did occur to him, however—so much for the high-minded King Arthur. It seemed he was just as human as anyone else.

But *Grace*? Who could have seen that one coming? Now Jim remembered something—seeing them together on the bench at his mother's party. He remembered thinking they seemed rather cozy. At the time he attributed it to her interesting condition. Arthur was playing the role of the gallant knight who took pity on people in distress. But apparently not! Arthur was being gallant in an entirely different way. Or maybe it was a little of both.

What was the reason for this sudden passion? Grace was attractive, to be sure, but she had also been very much pregnant at the time. This would tend to detract from her attractiveness. But in Arthur's case it might have worked in her favor. Compassion made her an object of special interest. Arthur was not just her lover but her rescuer. Jim could see him being enthused about that.

On one hand, he felt relief. He had been very worried about Grace and her situation. He was worried she would not go back to school. He was worried she would not be able to find someone to love her. It seemed this was not the case. She found Arthur. He was the perfect person for her in many ways. Arthur was too cosmopolitan to concern himself with trivial matters like patrimony and social convention. He would make a wonderful husband for Grace and was better equipped than anyone Jim knew to take on the mantle of father to a child who belonged to someone else.

But that was not enough to account for the *passion* the poor smitten fellow expressed, the kind of passion he usually reserved for music and art. Jim thought of Arthur's former resistance to Grace. What could possibly have changed it into love? Maybe the resistance was *rooted* in love. Maybe it was his way of fighting an attraction that he thought was inappropriate, because of her age or because she was Jim's sister or for some other unknown reason—who can fathom the mind of someone like Arthur?

It hardly seemed to matter. The surprising facts on the ground were that Arthur was in love with Grace and Grace, presumably, seconded that emotion. But where did that leave Erin? It left her in a terrible place. Broken engagements are ugly things, but especially when there is another party involved. Erin would be humiliated—at the hands of Grace! This was a dreadful thought.

Jim had never seen Arthur so discombobulated in all the years he had known him. It was not his style to be discombobulated. He was always cool, calm and collected. He was the one who stood off to the side, quietly observing the human comedy with philosophical detachment, perhaps some disdain. But disdain did not become him when he had fallen in love with someone else and was about to break Erin's heart. No, the feelings Jim sensed in him were genuine terror and remorse.

He doubted that Arthur would be able to approach Erin with his usual grandiloquence. A simple style was what was needed for the news he had to communicate, and empathy. Jim longed for simplicity and empathy for her. He did not want her to be hurt. He did not want her to be unhappy. He especially did not want his sister to be the cause of her unhappiness.

At the same time he was not entirely able to resist certain other thoughts that seemed to want to force themselves into his empty head. In short, Arthur's dreadful news meant that Erin would be free. And what exactly did that mean for him? For one thing, it meant he was no longer inhibited by scruples regarding the engagement. If she was free, then he was free as well.

He could not help it; this thought gave him joy. He did not know if it was possible for her to love him again, after everything that had happened, but at least he was not prohibited from trying to find out. At least she was not going to be married, which was the thing he had been trying to steel himself to ever since he heard about the engagement.

But good Lord—what about Grace? What in the world was she thinking? She was supposed to be Erin's friend. Every time the families were together she attached herself to Erin like a barnacle. And now this? Really? What about the late, lamented dinner party? She knew—and still she sat there talking to Erin as if nothing were out of the ordinary? He could not believe it.

Had this really been going on since summer? Arthur indicated there had been dates; how did that come about? Jim couldn't imagine him calling Grace out of the blue, especially when he was engaged to Erin. But then did she call him? Or maybe email? And had she really deceived their mother about the nature of these dates? Maybe she didn't have to deceive her; maybe she just withheld information.

One thing was certain—her mother was not going to be happy when she found out. They had been carrying on while he was still very much engaged to Erin. She had a soft spot for Erin. She was angry with Jim when he let her go and still could not help needling him about it whenever she had the chance. She would be furious with Grace for stealing her fiancée. Had Grace told her yet? She had to tell her soon. There was a plan for the two families to go to Westport on Black Friday.

Wednesday was like a disconnected dream. Jim went to work, but all he could think about was the conversation with Arthur and the changes taking place in his little world. Arthur must have broken the news to Erin by now. How did she react? Was she crushed? It seemed likely. Jim knew her tender heart. He did not want her to be crushed. She did not deserve it.

Thanksgiving came, and it was all very weird. The sweetness of the holiday was overthrown. He felt self-conscious walking into the familiar old house on a gray November day, knowing his sister would be there, wondering how the subject was going to be broached, if it at all, and how he would comport himself if it was; in short, knowing what no one else at home seemed to know—or perhaps they did know it by now.

After greeting his parents, and fetching firewood and starting a fire, he sat down in the sun porch with a cup of hot chocolate—it was a mild day—with his Wordsworth collection and started to read while he waited for guests to arrive. He had not been there long when Grace appeared and closed the door behind her.

"I'm glad I found you alone. I need to talk to you."

"I already know. He told me."

"No, I know that. The thing is *they* don't know."

"You must be joking. What about tomorrow?"

"I know! Don't lecture me. I'm stressed out enough as it is. I just don't know how to tell them. I mean Mom. Dad won't care."

"I can imagine it will be a little tricky, considering."

"You're not kidding. She's going to kill me. But please don't say anything until I have a chance to work it out with her."

"Does Eric know?"

"No. Why would I tell him if I haven't told them?"

"So I'm the only family member who has been honored with this knowledge."

"Don't be sarcastic. He just felt he had to talk to you. Actually it was kind of sweet. He seemed to think he needed your approval or something."

"It's not that I don't approve. It's just that—"

"I know—Erin. Believe me, I feel terrible."

"Has he managed to tell her yet?"

"Yes. I know that for a fact. He did tell her last night."

"Well, that's good anyway. I guess. Is she all right?"

"Apparently yes. He said she was a little upset at first, but she seemed to be okay in the end."

"I doubt that. But I assume you're not going to Westport."

"What? Why not? I'm going. I have to go. I owe it to her. But I'm dreading it. I don't know what I'm going to say."

"Just tell her the truth. That's what she wants to hear."

"In this case I don't think the truth is going to make her very happy. But this is good for you, eh?"

"What do you mean?" he said, as if he didn't know.

"It means she's free. It means she's not engaged anymore. You two belong together anyway."

"Don't try to console yourself with that. This is going to hurt her very much."

"I know. I feel absolutely sick about it. I don't know what I was thinking. I guess I wasn't thinking at all."

XXVIII

Black Friday

THANKSGIVING WAS AS PLEASANT as people of good will sharing a good meal, if strange on account of the unseen dynamics. What happened the day after, however, was one of those ridiculous things that sometimes occur in human affairs, like the Friar not getting the message to Romeo.

Jim was a little surprised that Grace was determined to go to Westport with Erin and the O'Connells. She said it again as he left the house. In her view, it was absolutely necessary. What she had done to Erin was terrible, but she felt she should have the common decency to show up and face her and not act like a coward.

In his view, it was not so necessary. He did not know quite what to make of this show of moral courage, or whatever it was. She said she "owed it to Erin," but why would Erin want to see her after she had stolen her fiancée? How could this in any sense be beneficial to Erin? It might have been braver to stay home and not rub salt in the wound. Also he knew she did not want to miss the excursion, which made her heroism seem a little self-serving.

He could not picture them together in those circumstances. It would be terribly awkward, not just for Erin but for everyone. On the other hand, it was possible Erin would show more common sense than his sister and stay home. No one, absolutely no one, would blame her if she did; although for selfish reasons he sort of hoped she would come.

In any case it turned out he was wrong. The five Wilmots, with little Anna in a bundle, drove down to Westport together early Friday afternoon—Eric had returned to Poughkeepsie—and went to the appointed rendezvous. The O'Connells arrived a little later and parked opposite. Jim hopped out of the 4Runner and looked in their direction. Then *she* stepped out of their car. Uh-oh!

He saw her but he couldn't believe he was seeing her. To face his family after what had happened—it occurred to him that she had all the courage Grace was only pretending to have. He loved her more than ever. She looked wonderful. Her color was good; no signs of distress. She was wearing a blue corduroy shirt and twill pants and quilted vest. She looked feminine and adorable and surprisingly at peace with herself and the world.

The thing he was dreading most was the meeting between her and his sister, but he was pleasantly surprised. It was entirely amicable. Erin seemed like her usual self. She hugged Grace warmly and tickled little Anna's nose and smiled. Grace seemed self-conscious, but Erin was too kind to notice. She put her hand through her arm as they walked. She really was amazing.

One of the things he had always appreciated about Erin was how she treated Grace. She was several years older than Grace, and yet she had acted like her equal and friend from the beginning. This was wonderful to a girl of fourteen who was very sensitive. It created a strong bond between them in Grace's mind and was the source of her high estimation of Erin.

For these very reasons, what Grace had done to Erin seemed unforgivable. It was not just selfish; it was betrayal of the worst kind. Falling in love was one thing, but carrying on behind her back seemed almost brutal. Erin's kindness went above and beyond. No one could have known there was any friction between them. They seemed happy with each other's company and inseparable.

Erin seemed remarkably unaffected by what had been done to her by her young friend. It was one thing to make an appearance under such circumstances but another to refrain from showing any kind of anger or pique toward Grace. None whatsoever. But then he reflected that perhaps she didn't *feel* any anger. Perhaps she was not terribly unhappy about the engagement coming to an end.

This was a matter of interest to him because he did not want her to be in love with Arthur. He was just as selfish as his sister in one sense—he wanted her to love him. He also did not want her to be angry with Grace, or their family. He needed all the credit he could get with her if he had any chance of regaining her affections. More than anything, he wanted her to be indifferent to the change.

From observing her, he convinced himself she was. She and Grace and Megan headed off on their own to the type of stores in which their parents were unlikely to have any interest. His heart jumped every time he saw them popping in and out of various establishments, talking and laughing and having a good time.

They shopped for a couple of hours—or, in the case of the men, they sat on frosty city benches with a steaming cup of coffee in their hands and made trenchant observations regarding the differences between the sexes. Then the sun started to go down and they decided to look for a place to eat. Mr. O'Connell found a table in a nearby restaurant that looked cozy. They went in chatting happily and enjoying themselves.

Jim was pleased to find himself in Erin's proximity at the end of the table—right across from her, as a matter of fact. Grace was next to him, baby in papoose, and the indomitable Megan was at the end. Jim could not take his eyes off Erin. She was not engaged; the former impediment to admiration had been removed. The cold air made her cheeks pink and blended in with the cream of her soft complexion. Was it possible to love someone so much? He was sick with love.

His mother was sitting on her left. From time to time she would look at Erin in wonder or bewilderment. Finally she couldn't help herself. "I'm kind of surprised to see you," she said confidentially when an opportunity presented itself.

"Oh—I'm fine," Erin said blushing. "I've had a couple of days to recover."

"Two days isn't very long. I guess you must have had some idea."

"Not at all. It was a complete surprise. Although maybe there were a couple of things—. Well, anyway, I think I'm getting past that. Besides, I wanted to come. I didn't want to be alone. I wanted to be with all of you having fun and not just moping around the house feeling sorry for myself. As if I have any right to do that."

"I still think it's very brave of you. In fact I can't quite believe how brave."

"Not really," Erin said with a little laugh. "I'm not as upset as you think I am. We probably weren't meant to be engaged, to be honest with you. Well—obviously."

"Maybe got into it a little too hastily."

"No, it's not that. We're just not right for each other. I think we both sort of thought it was the thing to do. You know how Arthur is. I think he thought he had to propose to me because we had been seeing each other for so long, or other reasons, and I thought I had to say yes because—well, I guess for the same reason."

"So that was his explanation?"

"Basically, yes. And...other things."

"He made her give the ring back," Megan piped up indignantly in her bright teenager's voice. "I would've sold it and kept the money. He was the one who broke off the engagement."

"I wasn't going to do that. It wasn't his fault. We just weren't right for each other. I guess I already said that."

Carolyn looked at her for a long time. Then she looked at her daughter. She seemed to be on the verge of saying something but thought better of it. She turned her attention to the conversation of the older crowd.

"So when you say it wasn't his fault, you mean you're okay with this?" said Grace, who had been paying very close attention while pretending not to for her mother's sake.

"I don't know about 'okay.' I just don't think he did anything wrong. It was better to break off the engagement if he didn't think we were right for each other than to go through with it and make us both unhappy. Not that I would have been unhappy—oh! you know what I mean."

"I think I do. Not sure. To tell you the truth, I didn't know how you would feel about seeing me."

"I love seeing you. That's why I'm here."

Grace looked amazed. Jim felt the same way. It certainly was remarkable. Just at that point little Anna began to make a racket. "I think that's the diaper," Grace said, quickly excusing herself. Jim saw her pull out her cell phone as she headed to the bathroom and wondered if she was checking messages from Arthur.

An awkward silence ensued. He didn't want to lose the interesting thread. "I have to say, I find Arthur rather amazing," he commented, nodding towards Grace's departing posterior. "Not every guy would be willing to take on a ready-made family."

"Take on—what do you mean?"

"Well, the baby. I don't know if I could do it. I just think it's a very noble gesture on his part."

"What does that have to do with Arthur?" she said, looking, he thought, a bit stunned.

"Well—you know—I mean the two of them—" he stammered.

"The two of them what?"

"Just that he doesn't mind. That's all I'm saying."

He could tell from the look creeping over her face that he had made some sort of dreadful blunder.

"Arthur doesn't mind what?" Megan said loudly.

Jim froze. Erin also was frozen and simply sat there staring at him. The older crowd had grown quiet and was looking in their direction—apparently they heard the outburst.

At that point Grace promptly reappeared, heading toward the table in a hurry. She stood there looking at Erin, who was still looking at Jim. "I'm so sorry," she said in an under voice. "I'm so sorry. Please don't be angry with me." Erin reached furiously for her purse and knocked over her glass of water in the process. Then she ran out of the restaurant.

"What just happened?" Jim implored his sister.

"He didn't tell her," Grace replied as she sat down with the baby in her lap.

"I thought you said he did," he replied in shock.

"About me," she said through her teeth.

Jim sat there staring at her with his mouth open, trying to take it all in.

"What's wrong with Erin?" their mother said.

Grace took a breath. "She just found out something."

"She didn't know? I thought he was supposed to tell her."

"I guess he didn't tell her *everything*."

Carolyn looked at her friend Amy. "You didn't know?"

"About what?"

"About Arthur and...Grace."

"Arthur and Grace? I don't know anything about it. What am I missing?"

"Seems they're seeing each other."

"What! Did Erin know that?"

"Apparently not," Grace said in her misery.

"Where did she go? I'm worried about her."

"I'll go," her husband replied, and promptly bolted from the table, perhaps feeling he'd had enough of the Wilmot siblings for one day.

That was pretty much the end of the excursion. Mr. O'Connell found his daughter standing by the car. She refused to go back into the restaurant. He hugged her and she hugged him back. She was crying. She was very angry. And to tell the truth, so was he.

It came out in the Wilmot car on the way home.

"What was that all about?" Carolyn said to Grace as soon as they were by themselves.

"It's not my fault. He was supposed to tell her," Grace said defensively.

"How could he not tell her? Didn't he know we were getting

together today?"

"I thought he did. I don't know."

"I'm starting to wonder about that young man."

"Don't blame him. It's my fault. The whole stupid thing is my fault."

"I'm not even going to ask what that means. Do you realize what just happened? She was humiliated in front of everyone."

"I know. I feel terrible. What am I supposed to do?"

"The first thing you're going to do is call her the minute you get home and apologize profusely. She has been a great friend to you all these years. This is no way to repay her. After that, your father and I will decide whether it's the stocks or dunking."

"I know what I have to do. I'll take care of it."

"Let's see if we can forego the attitude, missy. You have no right, not after this. I can imagine what the O'Connells are thinking and saying about us right now."

"She's not the only one who's ever been hurt. Besides, it wasn't supposed to be like this."

"Oh for heaven's sake, don't play that card. Don't you dare compare yourself to her. Not after what you did to her. Not after what just happened."

"I'm not! I get it. What I did was unforgivable. But you don't understand."

"I understand enough. The O'Connells are our friends and we just gave them the shock of their lives. Let's just hope they're still talking to us when this is all over. By the way, when *will* this be over?"

"I told you, I will take care of it. I'll call her tonight."

Carolyn forced herself to stop. This was the outflow of feelings that had been building up inside her all day. She was amazed to see Erin and doubly amazed at how she was getting along with Grace. It never occurred to her that Erin didn't know the whole story.

The rest of the ride went by in a dreadful silence. When they reached their destination Jim hopped into his car and drove straight home. He barely even said goodbye. He wanted to get away from them as soon as possible in the fall evening gloom. The day that started out so pleasantly had turned into a complete disaster. To have the whole saga come out in front of the O'Connells! His mother was right. It was mortifying.

He poured himself a glass of cheap booze and sat down on the couch and stared off into the distance, or at least at the wall. He felt sick, unsettled. There had never been any friction between the two families or any kind of argument. They were close friends. But what happened at the restaurant was just raw. There was no way around it. He felt too fidgety to sit there by himself, for many reasons. He had to know what was going on. He tried to resist but wound up calling his mother.

"Is she all right?" he said.

"Who—Grace? She'll be fine. I guess you probably think I was too hard on her."

"Not at all. I was referring to what happened at the restaurant."

"Oh, that. She deserved it. She left us all exposed. And anyway, she wasn't the one who was hurt. I feel so badly for Erin."

"I know. Me too. Do you think they'll ever forgive us? Mr. O'Connell looked like he was ready to kill somebody."

"Can you blame him? She's his daughter. But no, I think they'll recover. I already called Amy and talked to her about it. And your sister is supposed to call Erin one of these days."

"That should be interesting. She doesn't really have an explanation. Or not a good one, anyway."

"Her explanation is going to be that they fell in love. There is no other explanation. And then she's going to have to apologize like mad and beg for forgiveness. Otherwise I'll kill her myself. The good news is Erin will probably get over it, in five or ten years."

"I hope so. Faster than that."

"Say—is this about your sister, or you?"

"No, I mean they were such good friends—"

"I don't know if you can expect them to be good friends again. That may be a bit of a stretch. I'm just saying Erin will probably forgive her because that's Erin's nature. I can't see her holding a grudge for very long. Now if it were me…"

"Ha! You're funny. But I guess my point is that Erin probably won't want to have anything to do with our family."

"There you go again. Are you sure you know your own mind? Because you certainly seemed mixed-up about this Erin thing."

This conversation did not provide the reassurance he was looking for. Yes, he was concerned about Erin and Grace and their relationship. Their friendship was a source of joy to him; he hated to see it ruined by his sister's stupidity, or whatever it was. But even more he was seeking reassurance regarding Erin and himself. He could not come right out and say this, of course, but it was probably the main motive for the call. And his mother saw right through him.

The inevitable estrangement between Erin and Grace would also mean estrangement between Erin and himself. There was already a barrier between them of his own glorious making, but now it had just become that much more formidable. Erin would not want to have anything to do with the Wilmot family after this, not with Grace and not with him either.

But then he had to laugh at himself. He was just as bad as Grace. He was trying to turn Erin's disaster into his own. He wasn't the one who had been humiliated in front of everyone. He wasn't the one whose close friend had been carrying on with her fiancée behind her back. Besides, if there was estrangement between Erin and himself, then whose fault was that? He couldn't blame Grace. He had done it all on his own.

In fact if he had done what he was supposed to do there never would have been an Erin and Arthur in the first place. She was in love with him once (Jim). He knew it. She would have been happy to marry him. And she would have made him happy. But he did not want to be happy at the time. He wanted something else. Lord knows what, but he certainly got his wish. He was unhappy and foresaw no change in the forecast.

Now his mind turned to Arthur. He was just as annoyed with him as his mother was. In fact he was more annoyed because Arthur's behavior reflected on him as his friend. So much for those high moral principles he was always preaching about. What Grace had done to Erin was bad enough, but Arthur was even worse. After all, he was the one who was engaged to her.

What were they thinking, sneaking around behind her back? How did they think it would end? She was going to have to find out eventually. There was no way around it, if they really were in love and determined to get together, which seemed to be the case. Maybe they were trying to protect her. Maybe they were trying to spare her feelings. He couldn't believe they would do it maliciously. Grace's remorse said otherwise.

Arthur was remorseful too. Jim had seen it. Besides, he wasn't one to judge. His own feelings were not pure. Yes, he was upset for Erin's sake—but he was also upset for himself. He was thinking of the impact of their betrayal on his chances with Erin. He was just as guilty as they were of selfishness. Still, he couldn't help being angry with them. What they did—the way they handled it—was not only wrong but downright stupid.

Arthur hadn't told her the truth about breaking the engagement. Apparently his excuse was they were not right for each other. Jim happened to believe this was the case and was gratified to find that Erin seemed to feel the same way, but it was shameful to conceal the real reason for the change. It was pure cowardice. Arthur was afraid to tell her about Grace because it would make him look bad. There was no other reason for it. But then he wound up causing her twice as much pain in the end.

Would the two families ever get past this unfortunate series of events? Jim wanted to share his mother's optimism. But it wasn't going to be easy, especially if Grace and Arthur really were serious about each other. It seemed the Wilmots were determined to make Erin miserable. First there was Jim and the engagement that never happened; then there was Grace and the engagement annihilated.

The inevitable tension between the two families put another barrier between him and Erin just at the time when the barrier of the engagement had been removed—by his sister. All he could think about was the expression on her face as he was rhapsodizing about Arthur and the baby. She must absolutely hate him.

XXIX

Regrets

BLACK FRIDAY WAS certainly memorable. But now it was Saturday, and he was alone in his house with nothing to do but think. Of course he was mostly thinking about Erin. Grace was supposed to call her. Did she? He obsessed over this all morning. Finally he couldn't help himself. He called her.

"How did it go with Erin?"

"It went. That's about all I can say. I did tell her everything. I figured she deserved to know, especially after what happened."

"You told her about the party after the fair?"

"Yes. She was a little surprised. She didn't realize it had been going on that long. But it hasn't—not really. It was just recently that we started actually seeing each other."

"But you must have been in contact with each other."

"Yes. You are right. Who am I kidding? Stupid email."

"How did she seem? Was she still upset?"

"She seemed cold, which is perfectly understandable. She wasn't rude or anything. She didn't yell at me. Not that I was expecting her to. But she was definitely rather chilly."

"She didn't warm up at all?"

"Not really. And I was very apologetic. I don't know how many times I said I was sorry. But maybe this isn't the kind of thing you can apologize for."

"No, I'm pretty sure she was glad to have an apology. And it was the right thing to do. But it's probably too soon after the fact. She will need some time to process things."

"The thing is I don't think she was ever in love with him. Not really. I just don't believe it. I never believed it. And I'm not saying that as an excuse. I know I don't have any excuses. It's just an observation."

"I don't know. You could be right. You mean from the way she acted around him?"

"Yes. Not that she was ever mean or disrespectful or anything. She would never do that. But it wasn't like they were *together*. I have an eye for these things. And anyway, she had a very good reason not to love him. She was in love with someone else."

Jim had to pause for a moment while he recovered. "Do you

think she'll ever want to see us again after that? I mean, I can't believe how obnoxious I was. I wasn't trying to be. But I can imagine what she thinks of me."

"I hope so. I hope I didn't ruin everything. I really do love her, and the O'Connells too. It would be terrible for this hideous mess to drive the two families apart. I would never forgive myself."

There was a lot to mull over after this call, and Jim had plenty of time on his hands for mulling while he waited for the college basketball games to start. The first thing was that there had been no reconciliation, apparently. This was what he wanted to know most of all. It sounded like Erin was still angry with Grace—and for good reason. But he had been hoping against hope that Grace might be soften the anger with her communication skills.

Then again, communication skills were not something you could use to sway Erin. She was so direct in her feelings that she did not respond to misdirection. It was as if she had an invisible shield. It was not possible to argue her into complaisance. All Grace could do was throw herself on her mercy. To her credit, that's exactly what she did, apparently—but Erin did not relent in her coolness, which was the thing he was afraid of.

At that time in his life he did not want Erin to be cool toward Grace—or toward the Wilmot family in general. But what did he expect? How could she not be cool after what happened? It would take a superhuman effort to rise above such open humiliation. He knew he couldn't do it. He was surprised she talked to Grace at all. If he had been in her shoes he would not have even taken the call.

But of course she did. She was willing to suffer for the sake of courtesy. No matter how painful it was to talk to the erstwhile friend who had betrayed her, she would take the call because she was a nice person who wanted to be forgiving. Now Jim thought about the call in a different way. Of course it was painful and difficult for Grace—but it had to be much more painful for Erin.

So what did it mean, the fact that she took it? Did it indicate a *willingness* to be reconciled, at least, if not reconciliation itself? Did it mean Erin still had feelings for Grace even after what happened? Or did she take it out of duty? He did not know. But he longed to know. He longed to call her himself but did not want to inflict any more suffering than had already been inflicted.

Then he thought about what Grace said about her and Arthur. It could be that this was just a self-serving rationalization, or maybe she really did think it, independent of her own feelings. In any case it was an interesting observation, especially since it reflected his own thoughts on the subject. He had seen Erin and Arthur together many times over the past year without ever thinking they were violently in love. Or at least Erin didn't seem to be.

If that was the case—and it was a big "if"—then perhaps Erin would come around in time. If she was not in love with Arthur, then she might not feel the need to cling to any bitterness toward Grace and, by extension, Grace's entire family. Not that Erin was a bitter person; not by any means. But it was only natural to feel some resentment. If Grace was right, however, the resentment might not run very deep.

It was then, and only then, that he allowed himself to think about the *other* thing Grace said. He knew what she meant. She didn't have to spell it out for him. In her view, Erin was never in love with Arthur because she was in love with him. This thought made him happy. But was Grace right? Was it possible for Erin to love him now, especially after what happened the day before? Here's where the coolness became crucial. If Grace was unable to mitigate it with her considerable powers, then it must run deep.

Jim was the one who had revealed the truth to her. He was the messenger. It wasn't his fault that Grace and Arthur had fallen in love, but she could easily blame it on him, especially considering their past history. She could blame it on the family as a whole, which was enough to negate any tenuous claim he might have on her affections. He wanted so much to call her. He really, really wanted to call her and apologize. He even picked up his phone several times with that very intention. But he couldn't bring himself to do it. He had no right to invade her privacy. Besides, Grace had stolen his thunder.

What he thought he could do, however, was send her an email. He was comfortable in prose. He could edit himself. He pulled out his MacBook and started typing:

> Dear Erin,

No, that wasn't going to work. He had no right to dearness.

> Hi, there.

No—too flip. He wasn't trying to be cute. He wanted to be the opposite of cute (without being ugly).

> Hi, Erin. It was wonderful to see you yesterday. I just want you to know that I feel terrible about being the bearer of bad news.

Uh-oh. Now what? Several self-justifying statements were typed and deleted. He wanted to stay away from anything that smacked of angling. He wanted his apology to be spare, pure, and sincere. His desire for purity made him chaste. He almost couldn't think of anything to say. Then he settled on this:

> I know I don't deserve to ask for forgiveness, but I did want you to know that I am very sorry about what happened and very sorry for the pain it obviously caused you.
>
> Sincerely,
> Jim

He wanted to say so much more. For instance, he longed to tell her how much both he and Grace loved her. The problem was they had not *shown* they loved her, and therefore he was not entitled to indulge in such blandishment. He thought about just saying *Grace* loved her, which would have been a noble thing to do, but he was afraid of leaving himself out. He didn't want to give the impression that he did not love her when at this point he loved her more than anything in the world, including himself.

He sat there looking at the draft for several minutes. Then he got bold and pushed "send." He was on pins and needles waiting for a reply. He was on pins and needles for a long time. A week went by without any missive from Erin appearing in his in-box. Finally the following Saturday there was an email. He couldn't believe it when he saw it. By that point he had figured she was too angry to reply. And of course he couldn't blame her.

So much depends upon an email in your in-box. He was thrilled by it and terrified at the same time. He almost didn't want to open it. What did it say? He was afraid to find out. He put it off. He went out and picked up yesterday's mail. He came back and looked at the email again and still couldn't open it. He decided to make himself some lunch, even though it was only ten o'clock. A tuna melt was dutifully prepared and consumed. It was quite delicious, if he might say so himself. But the email was still unopened.

He went back to the Mac and dragged his cursor over with a mighty effort. Then he clicked. He blinked. There did not seem to be much on the screen. Then he saw the single word:

> thanks

Humph. Not exactly what he was hoping for. But he consoled himself with the thought that it could have been worse. It could have been a tongue-lashing. He knew he deserved one. And after all, it was a good word. There are few words in the world more gracious than *thanks*. That's why one of the pleasantest words in the whole American lexicon is Thanksgiving.

But this naked little "thanks" did not seem like much of a feast. It was a lean goose of gratitude. He stared at it for a long time, perhaps hoping it would dilate, but it seemed determined to remain unchanged. And the more it tarried in that unadorned state, the more he felt his enthusiasm waning. This was thanks with no stuffing and no gravy. It was the very least that someone with Erin's warm temperament could do.

Something else occurred to him. Maybe it was the only thing she could say without saying something negative. He was grateful she didn't say anything negative, but it pained him to think that she couldn't say anything positive, not even some tiny little thing of interest. His own message was warm and full of feeling. Or he thought it was. Didn't she see it? Didn't he make it plain enough?

Should he try again? Good Lord, no. Let it be. The effort had been made. Her feelings were now known. It was enough. He did not want to tempt her to go negative. The more he thought about it, the more he felt inclined to be grateful for the very restraint of "thanks." It didn't say anything, so it left him free to imagine something. Of course what he liked to imagine was it showed a thaw and a willingness not to hate him, at least.

On the other hand, it had taken her a whole week to produce this parsimonious reply. He could not bring himself to put a positive spin on the delay, no matter how much he tried. It suggested a strong reluctance to respond. In all likelihood the only reason she replied at all was that she felt obligated. She had to say something, and the safest thing to say was "thanks."

Suddenly Jim felt depressed. The word "thanks" dropped in from another galaxy. His thoughts and feelings were one way, but hers were something very different. For Erin to be unable to muster up more than a single uncapitalized word was remarkable. It suggested strong feelings, but not the kind he wanted. It suggested she could barely bring herself to speak to him.

XXX

Erin is very confused

JIM WAS RIGHT and wrong about Erin. After what happened in the restaurant she never wanted to see him again. She was so angry she thought she was going to explode. She didn't know who was worse—the "friend" who had cheated with her fiancée or the laughing brother with his taunt about Arthur and Anna.

The more she thought about it, the more she realized the brunt of her anger fell on Jim. This was remarkable for many reasons, but mostly because it made her realize something. The fact that she was angrier with Jim than Grace confirmed that she was not really that upset about losing Arthur. She was *conventionally* upset. After all, when your fiancée dumps you you're supposed to be upset. And it is not pleasant to have it happen in front of the whole world. Vanity was offended.

But she—Erin—was not particularly offended, now that she thought about it. She was not happy about Arthur cheating on her, of course, or about Grace betraying her, but her lack of outrage made it plain to her that she did not love Arthur, not in the way she wanted to love him. In fact she was glad for the catastrophic event that ended the engagement. Otherwise she might have wound up marrying Arthur even though they didn't love each other. After all, they never *said* they didn't love each other. And both of them were willing to go through with it just to spare each other's feelings.

But the bottom line was she was glad the engagement was over. It was a relief. She wasn't glad about the way it ended, but the more she thought about it the more she realized she wasn't terribly upset about it either. Without a catastrophe it might never have ever ended at all, which was much worse, because she could not picture herself going through life yoked to someone she did not love.

At one time she had convinced herself that it was likely to be her only option. She was in love with someone who did not love her back. There was no remedy for that. But no one else came along that she could love, at least not the way she loved Jim, and this put her in a bind. She very much wanted love and marriage.

She wanted a family. But she thought she might have to ratchet down her expectations somewhat when it came to a mate.

It wasn't that she didn't love Arthur *at all*. Of course she loved him, just in the way she loved many people, either for their good qualities or for the sake of love itself. She admired many things about him, including his politeness, his thoughtfulness, his sincerity, his sentiments, his manners, his eagerness to please. She did not like the fact that he did not share her faith, but this was something she thought she could make peace with over time. She knew a lot of couples in the same boat.

One thing she could not get past, however—she simply did not love him the way she loved Jim. She did not feel a strong force attraction to him. She did not have the feeling that they were in any sense meant for each other, as she did with Jim. It was almost like an arranged marriage—and she herself was the one doing the arranging! She knew the difference because she had something to compare it with. She had been in love once, really in love, and this was not the same thing at all.

To be blunt, she did not want to marry him. That's why she was grateful for the breakup, in spite of the short-term pain it caused her, which was considerable. All the pain was hers; he did not seem to be feeling any pain. Therefore she felt justified in bring grateful. Even her raw feelings toward Grace began to moderate as she admitted this fact to herself. The phone call helped. Grace seemed sincerely apologetic. She cried, and Erin was touched by that, truly touched. She had never seen Grace cry. She wasn't sure it was even possible. Beauty and brilliance Grace had in abundance, but she did not often exhibit tenderness.

Then Erin started thinking about Grace and Arthur. It was a surprising match, but she acknowledged the benefits. Grace needed a helpmate who would love her and take care of her and the baby. Arthur was perfect for that particular role. Nor was it a one-sided arrangement by any means. Grace was quite a catch. She was both stunning and gifted. And Arthur wanted intellectual conversation, which was something Erin had neither the inclination nor frankly the ability to provide him. Grace could repay his sacrificial attitude toward Anna, if any repaying was needed, with more intellectual conversation than he ever dreamed of.

There was the strange matter of paternity. Grace told her who the father was. She was not surprised. She would not have put anything past Bob, who was not her cup of tea. But what about Arthur? It was one thing to take on the child of some anonymous past husband or lover and quite another when that child was the offspring of one of your closest friends. He had to know. She assumed Grace must have told him. This made his willingness to acquire an instant family seem even more remarkable.

For these and other reasons, Erin gradually came around to the realization that she was *glad* they had found each other, genuinely glad for both of them, in spite of her fresh wound. It was right and propitious in so many ways. She didn't come to this conclusion immediately. She lay awake all night thinking about it. But when she did, she was rewarded with a feeling of peace. Not just peace, but relief! She was glad she didn't have to worry about making Arthur happy anymore. It was not a good sign if it's something you have to worry about.

The next morning, at breakfast, she decided to put her parents' apprehensions to rest. No, she was not broken-hearted over the surprise break-up. She even hinted that she was glad about it to some degree, without being too specific. They were surprised but did not say anything—at least not in front of her. Neither one of them had ever felt Arthur was right for her. He was a little too stiff and full of himself for their taste, a little too self-consciously cultured and aware of his superiority, a little too condescending at times to their daughter; and there were other reasons, too, of a more practical nature. They were almost as relieved as she was by the break-up, although they would never show it.

So the morning was going well. Erin realized she was feeling better. The shame of being dumped was being pushed back by the relief of being free from an entanglement she didn't want, like a Canadian high pushing a stranglehold of clouds out to sea. Then she got the email from Jim. She was shocked. She had not heard from him in a year and a half. It was strange to see his email address. She looked at it and shook her head in dismay. She almost deleted it. She did not need any more aggravation just when she was starting to feel a little better about things. She could still see the weird smile on his face when he was telling her about Arthur and the baby. She hated him.

Well, maybe not "hate." No, that definitely was not the right word. But she was upset with him. She had been for a long time. She was upset because of what he'd said to her after graduation, and because of the three years she had wasted doting on him. She was upset about the thing with Kerry Morgan. It was ridiculous. He was embarrassing himself and didn't even seem to realize it. Yes, she knew about the tabloid article. Megan showed it to her. Megan thought it was hilarious. Erin did not share in her elation. She read it over and over again when her sister wasn't looking in an attempt to make it say something other than what it said. Jim was the dupe in a love triangle between Kerry Morgan and Brick Dancy. There was no other way to interpret the words.

This gave her feelings that are impossible to describe; but we'll give it a go. She was ashamed of him and she was ashamed for him. She thought about his mother and his family and how hard it had to be for them to see him exposed to public scrutiny and comment. She thought about the day of the fair, the only time she had seen Jim and Kerry together. Did he really have to bring her to a charity event? Didn't he realize how disrespectful that was to the people who had worked so hard on it? Besides, what was he thinking? She would never marry someone like him, neither rich nor remotely famous. That wasn't the way it worked. He was just being used.

Or at least that's the way it seemed to her. She wasn't sure whether it made her madder at Kerry or at him. Let's just say there was plenty of anger to go around. She did not hear anything more about the scandal. She had no idea how it all turned out and told herself she didn't care. Then she saw him at the dinner party. Apparently he and Kerry were no longer an item. He barked out a weird "hi" to her at one point and she didn't know what to make of it. Had he been drinking? Was he making fun of her? What exactly was he doing? She didn't know.

She'd had a nice (if strange) Thanksgiving. Her family had been especially good to her because of what happened, going out of their way to show love and compassion. She was feeling relatively tranquil when she hopped in the car for the drive to Westport. She was looking forward to getting outdoors and walking and doing some shopping and having fun with the Wilmots, even if Jim was going to be there. He *was* going to be there, wasn't he? She couldn't make up her mind whether she wanted him to be.

At that point Erin had no idea—none—about Arthur's real reason for breaking off the engagement. He did not say anything about it. He said they were not "right for each other," and therefore it might be better for both of them if they didn't get married. He said it exactly in those dry analytical terms. They had entered into it lightly, and he thought much too highly of her to let her do that, etc., etc. Arthur certainly could talk!

She was glad when he finally stopped. She agreed with the first thing that came out of his mouth and did not feel any need for the subsequent litany of impeccable self-serving rationalizations. But among the many reasons proffered for breaking up there was nothing at all about Grace. She remembered feeling he had something else to tell her, but he had already said too much. A fraction of the verbiage with which he had favored her was sufficient to cause her to give him up forever, since it was what she wanted anyway.

But as it turned out, the little reason he left out was the most important one of all. He was in love with someone else! Erin had no idea of this when she arrived in Westport with her family and was greeted warmly by the Wilmots and especially Grace. She very much enjoyed the little shopping spree and taking her mind off things. The weather was perfect for the season. There were even occasional snow flurries to make the Christmas shopping more fun.

She did think that Grace seemed unusually solicitous and eager to please. But she assumed it was because she felt badly for her and was trying to cheer her up. She had no idea about the ulterior motive. Then they got to the restaurant. First Mrs. Wilmot—whom she loved dearly—started asking her strange questions. The questions did not comport exactly with the facts as she knew them. She sensed something was not right. She did not know what.

And then she found out. First Grace ran away from the table, and then Jim started in with that stupid grin of his. He was full of praise and fulsome words about Arthur and the baby. What in the world did Arthur have to do with Grace's baby? She was confused. She sat there staring at him. Then all of a sudden she realized what was going on. Grace returned and started babbling. *He* was still looking at her with that supercilious grin. She had to get out of there. She had to get away from Grace and her brother. It felt like they were ganging up on her.

These were the still-raw feelings that came back and washed over her as she sat there staring at his unopened email. In a sort of dream, she opened it. Her emotions were in such violent upheaval that she could hardly focus on it. The words were like little stones on the page. She understood them but could not digest them. Their meaning never quite made it in, certainly nowhere near her heart, which is where they were intended to go.

He seemed to be apologizing, but it did not feel like an apology to her. All she could see as she read this "apology" was the grin on his face the night before. It made it seem insincere. Why did he write at all if he couldn't say more than this? The email was almost cold, it was so brief. No explanation. No inquiries about her. No indication that they had ever meant anything to each other.

"I know I don't deserve to ask for forgiveness." What was that supposed to mean? Was he taunting her? She couldn't make sense of the pose he was striking. If he was so sincere, then why was he asking for the forgiveness he knew he didn't deserve? Or was he really asking for forgiveness at all? Maybe Grace had put him up to it, or his mother. The paucity of words made it seem likely.

Oh sure, she forgave him. But she could not forgive him. Whatever it was that he was trying to engineer through this email—and she honestly did not know what—she was not interested in being a part of it. She deleted it. She was agitated. She was angry. She did not want to have anything to do with him and did not want him sitting in her in-box, taunting her. She did not want to give him the power to hurt her. She had already been hurt too much.

This was her stance for a week. She was not angry with Grace anymore. She got over that. No, all of her anger was redirected to her brother. He had ignored her all day when they were in Westport, had not said a word to her, not even hello. And then there was that smirk when he finally did condescend to talk to her. He was making fun of her. That was the reason for the smirk. There could be no other reason.

But Erin could not stay angry for a whole week. She did not have it in her. Also as time went by there was some erosion in her certainty. She knew she had been very angry with him, even agitated, when she read the email, which may have affected her ability to understand it. Now she wanted to read it again. She remembered some things that were not necessarily repugnant. Maybe she overreacted. She knew she was defensive.

Just one problem—she had deleted it. She could not revisit it to see if it really was as bad as she thought. She tried to remember the exact words, but the only thing that came back to her was the part about not deserving forgiveness. At the time she was inclined to see this as posturing, but now she was not so sure. She wished she could have it back again so she could check herself.

She was not an email expert. She did not think to look in the trash. So she was stuck. But she knew she had to respond. She couldn't just pretend she had not received it. Now that she was feeling a good deal less angry, she was inclined to respond in a positive way and say something nice. But she could not let go of the idea—or the fear—that he was making fun of her; still making fun of her the way he did their last night together.

She opened a new message and typed the first letters of his address, which automatically populated. She couldn't make up her mind whether she was happy or annoyed about this. Besides, what in the world was she going to say? She had too many thoughts—too many feelings—to sort through. She did not know what to say, but she knew she had to say something. Finally in a rush she typed the word "thanks" without even bothering to capitalize, and all in one motion pushed Send, her fingers trembling.

She breathed a sigh of relief. She had done her duty. She had responded. Let him make of it what he will. She almost convinced herself she didn't care.

XXXI

The holly and the ivy

JIM WAS EXTREMELY BUSY at work. The year was rolling up with a bang with new clients and new campaigns and things that absolutely, positively had to be done no later than EOD. The partners were reluctant to add help until they felt a little more secure in their cash flow, so there were lots of fourteen-hour days, which, with two hours of commuting, were all-consuming. There were Saturdays and even a few Sundays.

He didn't mind, however. He was enjoying it, the simple fact of having work at all and being productive, as well as the excitement of doing new things. He was also enjoying the void of himself that this busyness created. The frantic pace tended to put his loneliness out of mind. After all, he wasn't lonely at work! He was surrounded by like-minded people, and they were on a Mission.

But in the back of his mind he knew the bonds he was forging at work were not real bonds. Their only attractive power was mammon. Jim was a young man with the world at his fingertips, but he did not have the one thing he wanted most. He did not have the love of a good woman. And the only woman he had in mind was Erin. When he was home and had nothing to distract him— "that's the time he missed her most of all."

Jim's feelings about Erin had completely turned around for two reasons. One was seeing her with Arthur for over a year. He tried to deflect the shock this continually caused him by telling himself that Arthur was good for her, but the old truths held true. Jealousy is a great provoker of love. And it was because of his jealousy of Arthur and his happiness that Jim began to see the truth about himself. There was light in his pain. The other reason was Kerry. He had fallen out of love with the idea of the goddess. He had seen the difference between the Real and the Ideal. Imaginary love can't be compared with the type of love he felt for Erin. They were two entirely different things and led to two entirely different ends.

And then too there was love talking to him. He felt a deepening in his understanding of love; of its true nature and its importance to his otherwise meaningless existence. He was spending so much time by himself (when he was not at work) that he actually began thinking seriously about such things; tentatively at first, but then more and more. He began to see that love is not an endorphin high. There were highs and there were lows, but endorphins were not the essence of love. No, love was the thing Erin had. It was a steady thing. It was a steady light. It was solid in a storm. It was deeply rooted. It could last a lifetime. As shallow as he admitted himself to be, he began to thirst for this kind of love. It was love without the toxic word 'love' thrown in. It was love based not on selfishness or self-gratification but on sacrifice and yes, sometimes pain, like what he was feeling right now. These were the only things that could purify the word 'love' and give it the value everyone heaped upon it in novels and movies and social media.

He wanted to respond to her email in the worst way, but his newfound respect for love prevented him. After all, what do you say to "thanks"? The normal response, of course, would be "you're welcome"; but it seemed foolish and awkward to send an email just to say that, especially if she was being sarcastic, which he strongly suspected. And if not, what exactly would she be thanking him for? His plea for forgiveness? Again, "you're welcome" did not seem like a sensible response from someone who was in need of it.

He wasn't sure that it was even possible for her to forgive him after everything that had happened. The past spied on him like an avenging tiger, waiting for an opportunity to tear him to pieces. Pictures would wander into his head of himself and her on the swing and the horrible things he said to her. Or of himself and Kerry at the Bridgewater house and the look on her face when she saw them together. Or of the scene at the restaurant and the fresh wound he had just inflicted by embarrassing her in front of her family and friends. He almost wished he could die.

These were pictures that were permanently impressed upon his neurological cells. They were never going to go away. They seemed to have a mind of their own, unconnected from his conscious mind and its self-preserving rationalizations. They came to him whenever they felt like it, had their way with him, tormenting him in the deepest way when he was alone and defenseless. They deprived him of standing in Erin's world. What right did he have to be thinking of her and wanting to send her emails after everything that had happened? There was a chasm between them of his own making. It would take a miracle to bring them together.

He cheered up when Grace called him with an invitation to an informal eggnog get-together on Christmas Eve.

"Who's coming?"

"Oh, the usual suspects. Some family, people from church."

"Arthur?"

"No, he'll be up in Braintree with his family, unfortunately."

"So I guess it's safe for the O'Connells, then."

"Yes, I believe they are coming. I know they were invited."

"Have you heard anything from Erin?"

"Nope. I hope she comes. I really do love her. I never meant to hurt her, believe me. But I can perfectly understand if she doesn't want to. I've been a complete jerk."

"Does she know Arthur won't be there?"

"How would she know that?"

"I don't know. I just thought it might make a difference."

"I'm sure it would. You should definitely call her and tell her."

That shut him up. But this conversation made him hopeful. It sounded like there was a chance, at least, of Erin being there. Then he had another one of his brilliant ideas. He decided to go to church on Christmas Eve. That would double his chance of seeing her. He was vaguely aware that it was not the best reason for going to church, but all he could think about was Erin. He wanted to see her more than anything in the world.

The longed-for day finally came. It was slow at work, since most of the customers were on vacation. In the afternoon the bosses brought in some champagne for a holiday toast and handed everyone an envelope (more on that later) and told them to "take the rest of the afternoon off," which was a gesture Scrooge himself might have admired, since it was already four.

By this point Jim was going out of his mind. He had been hoping to sneak out early so he could avoid traffic and be sure to make the service. That didn't happen. He didn't actually manage to disentangle himself until almost five. He practically ran to his car and went a hundred miles an hour, but that was just in the parking lot. By the time he got out on the road, it was a parking lot too.

Never had the commuter slowdowns seemed more exasperating as the minutes ticked by right in front of him on the dashboard, taunting him, as it were. It took over an hour just to get out of Stamford. The ordeal shriveled his insides like a prune. He stuck to country roads from then on and managed to get home by six-thirty while terrorizing several unsuspecting deer. He jumped in the shower and ran out to church without even thinking about supper.

Jim was nervous as he climbed out of the car and into the cold night air. He had not seen Erin since Thanksgiving. He sent up a little prayer. It was very little. It was "Dear God." He stopped there because he didn't know what else to say. Then he felt foolish. He had not done a great deal of praying in the past, for world peace or the relief of human suffering or anything at all, which made it seem a little self-serving. He got to the church early. It was empty, except for the choir. He saw some who knew him looking at him curiously and felt awkward, so he slunk back to his car.

Pretty soon more cars started to arrive. He saw his family talking and joshing as they walked in. Then he saw the O'Connells. Erin was with them. Honestly, he thought he was going to cry.

He took a deep breath and followed them in at a discreet distance. There were lots and lots of people, which made the expedition more challenging. He spotted his family on the left side, about half way down, their usual place. The O'Connells were settling in a little ahead of them on the right.

He stepped into the aisle, waving to old friends along the way but feeling extremely self-conscious, since he was not often seen in that particular institution. His mother emitted an audible "Oh!" when he touched her shoulder, setting off a good deal of tittering in the neighboring pews. She made room for him to squeeze in. He immediately commenced reconnoitering.

He had a side view of Erin, partially obstructed, but almost full if he shifted a certain way and no one else moved. She looked absolutely adorable. He couldn't believe how adorable she looked. He thought of the charming song by Brahms:

> This whole week, I have not
> Seen my delicate sweetheart.
> I saw her on Sunday,
> Standing in front of the door:
> That thousand-times beautiful girl,
> That thousand-times beautiful heart,
> Would to God I were with her today!

Then he remembered that Brahms was not one to darken the door of a church. And that was the problem. The church offered a sweet blessing to love and marriage, but the poet was admiring his sweetheart from *outside* the church. Her mind was on spiritual things while his was on, well, other things; on the love between a man and a woman. The poet saw her in front of the door and loved her but could not follow her in for this very reason.

The girl in the song was Erin. Her heart was in the church and the pure notion of love that it alone afforded; love that is sacrificial. He could not pretend to follow her into this inner sanctum without being a rank hypocrite, since it was not pure love that brought him there. It was the first time he had been in church since Easter, and even then he went under compulsion. Physically he was closer to her than he had been in a month, but the distance between them seemed wider than ever. "Would to God I were with her today!" This is the plea of someone who knows he cannot "be" with her and also knows why. The very purity he finds so adorable in her prevents him, because to be with her was to make her impure.

Jim became aware of the fact that he was fully absorbed in his mission of gazing at Erin while *she* was fully absorbed in another mission entirely, singing the beloved carols with all her heart and listening intently to the ancient readings with a calm smile. This made him admire her even more, if possible, but it also made him more aware of his unworthiness. The more he loved her, the more he realized he had no right to love her; that a love like his was the despoiling of her love; that he really should just leave her alone and not act in the selfish ways he was trying to repudiate, apparently without much success.

Did he really "belong" with her, as Grace seemed to believe; Grace who was sitting on the other side of his mother and father and fussing with Anna? It certainly did not seem that way to him at that humbling moment. For that matter, why would she even want him? He longed to be sitting beside her—there was a little space—he thirsted for this divine water—but his own thirst disgusted him. It was not worthy of her and her pleasure. She looked like an angel, with her blond hair braided and tied back. She was good, he knew it; but he was—well, what? A little bit of a mess, to be honest.

He thought of himself in his bachelor bungalow, who he really was and what he was really like, and then he looked at her with a hymnal in her hands and candlelight shining in her eyes and felt depressed. He was damaged goods, a lover in soiled weeds, a wolf among the worshipers, a fool fully conscious of his foolishness. What did she have to gain from such a connection?

She was a perfect picture, sitting there smiling in her pew. Did it make sense to spoil this picture by mingling it with his tawdriness, his year-long dalliance with debauchery (as he was now inclined to see it)? Wasn't it a "far better thing" for him to go away quietly and never sully her angelic existence again? Better for her, and therefore better for him, since all he wanted was her happiness; truly, even more than his own, as he thought at that moment.

There was nothing he could do to redeem himself or prove his devotion. The days of the quest were long gone, if they ever existed; gone even as Cervantes had demolished them five hundred years ago. There were no malevolent knights lurking in the woods for him to thrash. That was just a lovely—if somewhat violent—old dream. He was not sure he could conquer them even if there were. He could not prove himself to the fair maiden because he was not a noble knight. He was just a copywriter wearing a suit.

All of his reading had turned him into a hopeless dreamer. It did not prepare him for a separation that could not be overcome by conquering, the type he was experiencing now, a separation in his own mind. He could see his beloved—he was looking at her when he should have been listening to the sermon, which was no doubt very interesting—but he could not see any path to the happiness he desired. He could not even be sure if it *was* happiness, because he did not know if he was capable of making her happy. He knew he could not be happy unless she was. But he did not know if she could be happy with him.

Now he almost wished he had not come at all. The more he looked at her, the more she acquired a circumscribing halo in his eyes that made her seem unattainable. The service was over and there was the awkwardness of how he would greet her. Sorry to say, he punted. He gave his mom a hug, wondering why she ever felt the need to bring him into the world, and squeezed down the crowded aisle with a fake Christmas smile on his face.

He went to the Bridgewater house and resuscitated the fire. Then he went to the kitchen to look for other things to keep him occupied and quiet his brain. The sink was full of dishes; he rolled up his sleeves and dove right in. He managed to break a delicate wine glass in his agitation and cut his finger. The blood oozed out, but he kept right on washing. It seemed fitting somehow.

He heard the front door open; his family was arriving. The noise level went up as Grace entered the premises in full fettle. He smiled and shook his head. Then other people were arriving, but Jim remained glued to the kitchen sink. He was afraid to see who it was. He was afraid it would be the O'Connells with Erin—and he was afraid it would be them without her.

He bandaged his finger and started helping his mother with cheeses, sausages, crackers, etc. Grace came in and joined them. She was in high spirits and teased him mercilessly for his inartistic food presentation. He smiled wanly at her good-natured abuse. He didn't pretend to have talent of that nature. And at least she wasn't teasing him about Erin.

Then Mrs. O'Connell came into the kitchen. They had arrived! He greeted her but had a hard time looking her in the eye. Too much history. He was interested to see how she would interact with Grace. There did not seem to be anything unusual in her behavior. She chatted much as she always did, with lots of joyful laughter.

What did it mean? Had the O'Connells gotten past the Thanksgiving disaster? This hopeful thought made him happy. He did not want the friendship between the two families to be damaged by his stupidity. He cherished it, and not just because of Erin. It probably helped that Arthur was not there. There was nothing to remind anyone of painful memories. It was much as it had been before any of the last year's drama had ever happened.

The kitchen became crowded, as it does on such occasions, and the Ghost of Christmas Present sprinkled his magic dust on all assembled. Jim was feeling a little glum, to be sure, due to his painful feelings about Erin, but he was determined not to show it. He smiled and laughed right along with everyone else. Come to think of it, how did he know that they were not smiling and laughing along with him? He didn't.

He started cutting up vegetables for crudité. He was taking his time because he was hoping that Erin would come into the kitchen. She always did. He was laboriously producing carrot strips, but then he was done, and he felt awkward. There was plenty of help. He was not needed. It was time to move on.

He headed out into the dining room. He couldn't decide whether he wanted to see Erin or dreaded it. In truth it was a little of both. He was afraid of how she would react to him. Her terse "thanks" was still reverberating in his hollow being. He was also oppressed by the dark thoughts he'd had in church. For a moment he almost wished he wasn't there.

Then he saw her. She was in the living room, talking with Eric, which surprised him, and a couple of his cousins. They looked up as he came in the room but he turned away. He felt embarrassed and did not know what to do with himself. Seeing her there was disorienting. He was in the same room with her, but all he could feel were the barriers between them.

He went into the den and found his father and Mr. O'Connell and some of the older men watching a tedious football game. He did not feel comfortable there either, but he made himself stay. Where else was he going to go? Every room had something to dismay him. He gazed at the TV, although he had no interest in what was going on. It was just moving shadows on a screen and undifferentiated noise to him.

All he could think about was Erin. What was she talking to Eric about? He burned with curiosity. She was smiling and seemed to be enjoying herself. He wished he had the courage to join them but was afraid he would chase her fair smile away. She looked happy without him.

Grace came in and announced that the food was on and the appetizers were hot and anyone who didn't come had only himself to blame. Some of the men lumbered out to the dining room. In fact only Jim, his father, and Mr. O'Connell were left. Jim looked at their guest and caught him looking at him. The expression of his face was not cordial. He could not sit there any longer. He got up and joined the migration.

He went to the living room and did not see Erin. But then he found her in the crowded dining room still talking to Eric. He turned around and walked out. What was wrong with him? The living room had emptied out, so he went to the bow window and sat down by himself. Then suddenly he felt very conspicuous. He didn't want to be seen sitting by himself. He didn't want anyone to think he couldn't fit in, was a rebel without a cause, whatever.

He was in despair. He longed to see Erin, but it was almost like he could not stand to be in the same room with her. He was too emotional or too mixed up about what he should do. At the same time he could not stand to be alone in a crowd. So he went back to the den and sat down and forced himself to watch the game.

In the room people come and people go, including cousins he was close to, and he had some surfacy conversations, although not about Michelangelo. Erin did not come, however, and he did not know how he felt about that. Was he disappointed or relieved? In either case he could not blame her. He wanted her to come, to magically appear, to walk over and sit down by his side, but it was not her duty to circulate among the guests. She was probably near the fire, which he knew she loved. If he wanted to see her so much, all he had to do was get up and walk in there. But he felt paralyzed. He didn't know if she wanted him to. He didn't know if he should.

People started leaving. Jim stayed stuck to his seat. The house grew quieter and still he did not move. He sat there with his eyes fixed on the TV, which he was not really watching. He had not had any interaction with Erin all night; it seemed pointless to try to correct the deficiency now. Soon the last guests had gone on their merry way. Eric wandered into the den and sat down next to him.

"What's up with you and Erin?" he said in his usual subtle way.

"I'm not sure anything's 'up' with us," Jim replied defensively.

"She wasn't very kind to you. She said you were acting like a jerk."

"She said that?"

"She sure did. I said it looked like you were trying to avoid her, and she said she was glad. That kind of surprised me. I never heard Erin say anything like that before."

"I'm sure I deserved it," was all Jim could bring himself to say. This conversation flattened him. A little while later he said goodnight to his parents and headed for the door. Grace was nowhere to be seen; he didn't bother looking for her. He felt exhausted and needed to get out of there. He went home.

All he could think about was what Eric told him. Did Erin really say he acted like a "jerk"? He had never heard such language come out of her mouth in three years together. The sentiment was just, however. He had indeed acted like a jerk. He *had* gone out of his way to avoid her. The reason was not what she thought it was; quite the opposite. But the appearance of it was certainly jerky.

How to feel about this? Should he try to convince himself he was glad if she thought he was a jerk? It was an effective way to let her go, which he almost thought he wanted to do, not because he didn't love her, but because he loved her too much. Or was it in fact the most painful thing he had ever heard in his life? The last thing he wanted was for Erin to think of him as a "jerk."

Wait a minute—it was the last thing he wanted but it was also what he thought he wanted? Yes, because he had practically talked himself into thinking that Erin would be better off without him and his dark shadow. In short, he didn't think he was worthy of her after Kerry. Still, he was having a hard time letting her go.

XXXII

Happy holidays

TIM DROVE TO HIS dark, lonely house on the dark frozen lake and went in and tossed his keys on the kitchen counter a little more vigorously than was necessary and plopped down on the couch in a funk. He went there because he craved being alone after his devastating conversation with his brother, but of course as soon as he got there he did not want to be alone.

Ironically, he put on *Home Alone*. He felt he needed something funny to distract him, and he was, well, home alone. Of course he had seen it about five times, so the pleasure it was capable of giving him was limited. He wasn't laughing at the hilarious pranks as he lay there with a wandering mind. It was almost as if he were watching it for the memory of how much it used to make him laugh.

Grace called.

"So did you talk to Erin?"

"No. I didn't see her."

"What! You were in the same house together. How could you not see her?"

"Okay, I saw her but I didn't see her."

"You really need to come with some new material, Mr. Bones. But why didn't you talk to her? I'm sure she wanted you to."

"Not according to Eric. Apparently she thinks I'm a jerk."

"I did see him talking to her. That was weird. But you know she would never say anything like that about you. You really should have talked to her. I'm sure the reason she came was to see you."

"You don't know any such thing. Anyway, maybe it's better if I don't talk to her."

"So, what? You don't like her now?"

"I mean better for *her*. She doesn't need someone like me. She needs someone who's good and can go to church with her."

"What's so bad about going to church?"

"Nothing. That isn't what I mean. I'm not making fun of her. I just don't think I'm good enough for her," he said, and then realized this was the second time he had said this to his sister.

"Boy, that is lame. She has always loved you. She's unattached. You're stupid if you don't do something about it."

This was one time when he didn't mind being bawled out by his sister. It was the perfect counterweight to Eric's devastating news. Of course she had no way of actually knowing if Erin still loved him unless Erin told her so herself, which he knew was never going to happen after the disaster with Arthur. There were not going to be any more heartfelt tete-a-tetes between Grace and Erin.

Which was unfortunate, because Jim really wanted to know what Erin was thinking. Was he a jerk, as Eric claimed, or was there a possibility that she still had feelings for him, as Grace believed? He knew there might be some self-interest in Grace's certainty. It could be that she wanted to bring them together to make up for what she had done. Her belief in Erin's affection might be wishful thinking for many reasons.

But he did not discount it. He was trapped somewhere between the "jerk" and the beloved. Should he embrace the jerk and leave poor Erin alone? It seemed like the decent thing to do. He had inflicted enough pain on her for one lifetime. But what if he was the beloved? Could he give her up in that case? He tended to agree with Grace. It would be stupid, especially considering his feelings.

The only way to find out was to call her. But he could not bring himself to do it. If there was any chance that she thought he was a jerk—and there was no reason for Eric to lie—then his pride would not let him call. He was beginning to think he was a jerk too, deep down in his innermost being. He did not see himself as the suitor in any of the old books he loved, except perhaps Hamlet.

The bottom line was he believed what he said to Grace. She deserved someone better. And this in itself was enough to prevent him from trying to call. He decided to put it in God's hands. No, seriously—this thought actually did occur to him in his chastened state, in the penumbra of the word "jerk." If it was part of the plan—that is, if there was such a thing as a plan—and Someone for some reason decided to have mercy on him and considered him even remotely good enough for Erin—then it would happen.

He was not sure how he felt about this course of action, or why God, if he existed, would have any interest in the lives of foolish mortals like himself, but he did know he could not make it happen on his own power. He was not like Hamlet in one sense—he had no desire to direct the play. It seemed entirely possible that he would lose Erin through inaction, but he tried to make peace with this idea. He was going to lose her anyway if it was true that she thought he was a jerk.

He sat there for quite some time absorbed by his thoughts and not paying attention to the movie. Then he noticed the envelope from work. It was on the coffee table where he had tossed it. He picked it up and pulled out the card. There was a picture of a sleigh and an anodyne "Season's Greetings." Oh, and a more personal message inside: "Jim—Thanks for all the hard work! You are doing a fantastic job. We appreciate it. Fenton & Chris."

Jim unfolded the check and just sat there staring at it for a long time. $5,000. He couldn't believe it. The prideful thought came into his head—So I'm a *jerk*, am I? But then he felt foolish. As if Erin would be impressed. A $5000 check was not going to change her mind about him. In fact it might have the opposite effect, since the last thing she was interested in was money.

He loved her so much. He had to admit it. He'd been holding off this thought with the word *jerk* but now it simply overwhelmed his defenses. The fact that she could not be swayed by money made him love her even more. And he knew it was true. He knew her well enough to know that. They had talked about it many times. She had not been shy about making her feelings known.

Pop stars say "money can't buy me love" from the cocoon of fabulous wealth, but Erin actually believed it. She did not love the glittering world. Her heart was pure. Meanwhile he was sitting there gloating over his check. He had been working seventy or eighty hours a week, but it was not because he had a pure heart. It was because he did not want to think about what was in his heart.

It was another sleepless night, like Chaucer's poor dreamer, with similar feelings and thoughts, and Jim equally dismayed by the upheaval of unanswered love. The moon was bright and beautiful on the snow, but it made him feel cold inside as he lay there thinking about the party and about Erin and Grace and Eric, but mostly about Erin. He pictured her in his mind, sitting by the fire. He loved her so much. What was he going to do?

The next morning he headed back to Bridgewater for the obligatory present-opening and Christmas dinner. He remembered where he was the year before, in Kerry Morgan's mansion. He remembered how strange it was and how he made a fool of himself with that stupid bracelet, which was still on his credit card. Something occurred to him. She was "Kerry Morgan" now in his mind, just as she was for everyone else. It was almost as if it had never happened.

But it did happen, and it left scars. Grace still had not forgiven him for deserting them on Christmas Day. She made it very plain that this year he was expected to be where he was supposed to be. He didn't mind. He wanted to be with his family. He certainly didn't want to be with Kerry Morgan—not that she would have him. He couldn't believe he had ever been with her at all.

It was like a weird dream. But in other ways it was not like a dream. Kerry had used him up and stolen his soul. He took no pride in the connection. Just the opposite. He wished it had never happened. He could not be just Jim anymore. He could not go to his family on Christmas and enjoy the rituals in innocence. He could not sit there watching them without remembering what happened with Kerry and knowing that they too had Kerry on their minds—every time they looked at him in that setting.

The same was true when he thought of Erin. Kerry stood between them in too many ways. It wasn't just the mark of sensuality that she had left on him, the "expense of spirit in a waist of shame," the emptiness of long afternoons, etc. It was how foolish the whole thing had to make him look in Erin's eyes. She didn't have to say it. He could see it.

Erin saw through him and his pretensions. Everyone did, but Erin was the one who counted the most. He never liked to make a fool of himself, but he wished he had not done it in front of her, and in such a spectacular fashion. It could not be undone. He could not go to her and pretend it never happened. Things could never be the same between them as they were before the ice maiden came into his life.

He remembered how much he had wanted to keep the liaison secret. Even he knew he was playing the part of the fool. He remembered being outed by Grace at the anniversary party. He was abashed, but unfortunately he also kind of liked the attention. Then he remembered the fair. God forgive him, he felt proud standing there on the green with Kerry Morgan. He did not know it was the last time he would ever see her.

He was *glad* he did not see her. He told himself did not want to see her. He felt like he had been let out of jail. He wasn't in love with her. He didn't even think he liked her very much. But he'd had to pretend to. He had to laugh at all her jokes and take her frequent social and political commentaries seriously, which was not always easy. He had to jump when she commanded and put his own needs and desires aside. It was exhausting!

No, he never loved her. That's what he told himself, anyway, hindsight being 20/20. He just wished he had been the one who broke it off. It would have been nice if he had the courage. Then again, the way it ended was fitting somehow. She humiliated him one last time by dumping him without even telling him about it. In fact he didn't know for sure that he *had* been dumped. All this time he had been half expecting her to come back from a shoot and give him a call as if nothing happened, since that's exactly what she had done in the past, many times.

He did not want her to call, or at least he was pretty sure he didn't, but the open end was like a bracket. It continued to hold him in her ghostly clutches even while he was no longer in her arms. He was still her houseboy even though he was no longer in the house. He could not look at Erin without being conscious of Kerry. He felt like he and Kerry were joined in Erin's mind, although they were not joined in his own, and never had been, as he now tried to convince himself, with varying degrees of success.

He tried to put aside these gloomy thoughts as he went into the house and greeted his mother in the kitchen. No one else was up, not even little Anna. He poured himself a cup of coffee and made a fire and sat down to wait. He was entranced by the flames. Then he found himself going up the chimney like smoke.

There was some stirring upstairs and a baby's cry. Pretty soon Grace arrived with Anna in her arms and promptly plopped herself down for a feed. Jim was embarrassed by this all too-public show of maternal affection and ran off to the kitchen where their mother was making breakfast.

"By the way, what happened to you last night?" she said.

"What do you mean?" he said, knowing perfectly well.

"You just sort of ran off. We were looking forward to relaxing together after the party. Having an eggnog."

"Oh, I was just tired. Been working long hours."

"Tired! That explains it then. I thought maybe it had something to do with Erin. Guess I must have been mistaken."

She gave him one of her looks. He poured a cup of coffee for

Grace and returned to the living room. He did not particularly want to be in the room with THAT going on—the slurping sounds were a bit much—but before long they were joined by the rest of the family and the presents were pulled out, with Grace playing Santa, and opened one by one. It was all very relaxed and wonderful. There was genuine joy and surprise and love in the exchange.

By contrast, Jim could not help remembering the somewhat contrived look of merry surprise on Kerry's face when she opened the bracelet. She was a world-class actress and she was faking it. She had to be. He wasn't blaming her. Not at all. It wasn't her fault that there was nothing he could afford to give her that she could cherish as much as she was pretending to cherish his little bauble. She was pretending for his sake; he appreciated that. But he simply was not capable of giving her the kind of quiet joy that he saw around his family circle.

Christmas Day was the highlight of the holidays. The office was closed through New Year's. He was looking forward to having some time off, since he had been just about killing himself at work, but now he almost wished he were headed back to the office. It was better than being home alone and thinking about Erin.

He drove up to Okemo with Eric for some skiing. It was a bright, sunny day, cold enough for the snow to be pretty good, and they had a good time. The "jerk" thing did not come up again, to Jim's relief. But he wasn't going to do that every day of the week. For one thing, he didn't feel he could afford it. He was being very careful about money now, having experienced disaster.

Anyway the next day was not so bright and sunny. The clouds rolled in and the temperature rose and it started to rain. He could not go outside. He could not stay inside, not with the great restlessness he was feeling. He could not do anything but prowl around the house and try to distract himself with books, video games, music, etc.

Then the next day came and it was still raining, with splats of wet snow mixed in, and now he really was going stir crazy. Instead of enjoying his vacation, he was looking forward to it being over. He even pulled out his laptop and did some administrative stuff and answered emails. It made him feel better. It also made him feel worse, since he realized how pathetic he was.

The next couple of days were better. The sun came out. He went for a long walk and he went to the mall. On Thursday night he went to a bar with some friends from prep school. They had a good time. Maybe too good. He did not have any clear recollection of getting home.

Then New Year's Eve came and he had no date and no invitations to parties. It was too late to think about trying to get a party together himself, so he spent the night at home feeling completely bored and isolated. He was glad when Monday came and he was on his way into work. At that strange moment in his life the only place he felt at home was work, and the only time he felt at home at work was when he had ten tasks lined up on his pad and was mowing them down one by one with relentless precision.

But wait, you say—what about the endless round of parties, bar-hopping, concerts and general mayhem that makes up the life of the typical young professional? He did some of that. He was not the least popular person on the planet. Not by a long shot. He even went out for a drink with his new work friends one night when they managed to cut the day down to ten hours in the doldrums of January. He went down to the city to go to a concert with Bob, the first time he had seen him since the loan. It was awkward—he still owed him a considerable sum of money, although he had been steadily paying it down. But Bob was good about it. He didn't say a word. They managed to have fun and made a pact not to be such strangers, in spite of their very busy professional lives.

So yes, Jim had his share of *that*, but it wasn't what he wanted. You can have fun sitting in a bar drinking craft beer and yakking about Dostoyevsky, but it's not going to make up for the way you feel when you wake up alone on Saturday morning, completely alone, and you should be happy but you're not because you don't know what to do with yourself and you're feeling like a loser.

They say men don't want to get married because of the fear of commitment, but what they don't say is that most men also don't want to stay single because of the fear of going insane. Or at least Jim didn't. Winter is nervous season in New England. The sun comes up way too late and goes down early with a pathetic little whimper. There are beautiful days to be sure, but they are cold and vast. If they are not white, they can be demanding.

Jim squeezed in as much skiing and home-improvement as he thought he could afford. He also did a lot of reading. His love of the sublimely ridiculous *Tristram Shandy* led him on an unexpected journey. Somehow in the course of his education at the storied university he had missed out on eighteenth century prose, except for the usual suspects like Johnson and Swift and Fielding. Now he found himself astonished by the sweetness and depth of such writers as Burke and Smith and Boswell.

Still, he was alone. He did not picture himself as C.S. Lewis, sitting in his library and reading himself into old age with his brother moldering in the next room. He loved books but he didn't want to marry them. He wanted to marry Erin, even if she did not quite share his love of books. Erin! This name had become so sweet to him—and his own shortcomings so bitter.

Waking or sleeping, working or playing, Erin always came back to him and the ache he had in his heart. January went by, and then February, and now it was two months since he had seen her. He longed to call, he longed to write, but he had no reason to think she wanted him to. There were many times when he picked up the phone and started to call. He even let it ring once. But in the end he always shut himself down.

Then at the beginning of March his mother (and sister) decided to have a "winter blues" party. The purpose of such parties is to drive the cold winter away and form a bridge in the mind, however tenuous, to April and fresh breezes. This wasn't what the party meant to Jim at all, however. Erin would be there. He could not wait for the day to come.

He decided to be fashionably late. He wasn't really trying to be fashionable; he was seeking refuge in the crowd. He was pleased to see that there was quite a mob when he arrived, maybe fifty people. He spotted Mr. O'Connell right away, who frowned, and Erin soon after, sitting in her favorite place by the fire and chatting happily with church friends. He froze. He couldn't stop looking at her. She did not know he was there.

It was almost full moon and the crowd was uproarious and there was a certain madness in Jim's soul. There was laughing and joshing and high spirits and old friends and quite a punch that his sister had made—red, sparkly, and sweet. He had a cup and then another. Come on, Grandma's punch cups were small! People were little back then! He was trying to stiffen himself to talk to Erin. Gen. Washington said it is necessary that there should always be a sufficient quantity of spirits for the army, and Jim was no braver than your average foot soldier.

He started to feel a little better—less nervous. He meandered around for a half hour or so, pretending to be dropping in on various conversations with people he had known all or most of his life, but in fact not really listening; thinking about Erin. He went into the kitchen and helped his mother for a while. It felt good to make himself useful. It also helped him to gather his wits.

He wandered back into the living room. Erin was talking to Grace. He was surprised. They seemed deep in conversation. Apparently all was forgiven. Grace saw him and waved. Erin looked up but did not wave. To wave or not to wave? He could not answer the question. He retreated from the field.

Back to the punchbowl. A refill and then another. Apparently a good deal more fortitude was required than he realized. He was definitely beginning to feel it. The telltale sign was when the crowd noise crossed over to buzz mode. He tried to have a conversation with a couple of people in the dining room. He pulled it off, on the whole, but his mind was elsewhere. He would be standing there talking to someone and looking them right in the eyes, but what he was thinking about was Erin talking to his sister.

His sister! She would talk to her but not him? It was outrageous. Grace had stolen her fiancée. He had never done anything quite that gauche. But then he remembered he didn't actually know if she would talk to him. He hadn't tried. That was why he was drinking all the punch.

He found a spot where he could talk to people and still see Erin and Grace. He was waiting for an opportunity. He had to catch her alone. Well, not alone alone. Not with fifty people in the house. But at least not with someone else. The trouble was she and Grace were having a wonderful time together. Erin was laughing and talking and seemed very much like her old self.

He burned with curiosity. What were they talking about? Him? There was nothing he wanted more than to go over there and join them. Then Erin stood up. He went on full alert. She started heading in his direction, probably looking for something to eat. He was in a group. He excused himself and stepped out to greet her.

She seemed surprised when she saw him standing there in front of her. He did not know whether this was a good thing or a bad thing. He could not read her anymore, although she was not the sort of person who tried to hide anything. He hoped it wasn't an unpleasant surprise. He stumbled on the uneven oak floor and almost dropped his punch glass.

"Hi," he croaked, and as the word came out of his mouth it was like someone else talking. He heard it coming back to him on a nanosecond delay. Now he wished he hadn't drunk so much.

"Hi," she said. No expression. Maybe a little puzzled.

All of a sudden he felt like a stranger. He did not feel like they had ever known each other at all. His mind went completely blank. She looked so beautiful. He longed to take her hand in the old familiar way. But they weren't really familiar anymore, were they? It had always been so easy to talk to her and now he couldn't think of a single thing to say.

"I saw you talking to Grace."

"Yes, she was telling me about going back to school."

"Everything okay there?" he said, attempting a confidential smile.

"Okay? What do you mean?"

"I mean—you've forgiven her. Obviously," he babbled.

"There's nothing to forgive *her* for." She gave him a look and continued on into the dining room.

What did she mean? Was she talking about him—or Arthur? The arch look made him think it wasn't Arthur. He was the one who needed forgiveness. But it was ambiguous. It *could* have been Arthur. Maybe he was overreacting. Maybe she wasn't referring to him at all. But the thing was he wasn't sure. And he didn't have any way of making himself sure. He wasn't going to go to her and ask her what she meant, not in his impaired state. He had too much sense to try to charge up that hill again.

Besides, she did not seem interested in talking to him. It felt like she was sending out barbs. He was full of love and she was full of something else. Actually he was full of punch, which may have been the problem. He knew she didn't think very highly of people who drank too much. Maybe she was unhappy with him for that.

But who was she to be unhappy? This was his life. He was going to indulge in a little punch if he wanted to. He was going to stick his whole head in the punch bowl, if the spirit moved him. After all, it was his house. He didn't like it when people tried to tell him what to do. His mother was like that sometimes, and it simply made him want to do the opposite.

He was angry. She had no right to judge him. He loved her so much; why couldn't she love him back? Then suddenly he wasn't angry anymore. The word "love" carried off his anger. He did not know if she was judging him. And if she was, he deserved it. He'd had too much to drink and was acting like an ass.

He could not believe what he'd said. "You've forgiven her." What was he thinking? He wasn't thinking at all. He was just trying to come up with something to say. It wasn't any of his business whether she had forgiven Grace—except in the sense that it was. He wanted her to forgive Grace, but not just for Grace's sake. He wanted to remove any impediments between her and himself.

But this was not something you could possibly say. You could not inflict pain on Erin in an attempt to reassure yourself. It wasn't up to him to be glad if she had forgiven Grace. Only Grace had the right to be glad about that. Worse, it sounded like he thought she *hadn't* forgiven her. This was the furthest thing from his mind. If anyone on this crazy orb was capable of forgiving from her heart he knew it was Erin, no matter how much she had been offended.

He'd had his chance. He was bold. He blew it. He drank the punch to make him brave, but it also made him foolish. He said something he never would have dreamed of saying if he was sober. He was terrified of what she was thinking about him, actually terrified. His only consolation was that she probably was not thinking about him at all. She certainly didn't seem to be thinking about him. She had returned to her seat and was talking to Grace again. They were laughing. Were they laughing at him?

A few more agonizing minutes went by and then she got up to greet a girlfriend who had just arrived. She walked right by him but all she said was "Rachel!" as if he wasn't there. He felt crushed all over again.

He grabbed his sister.

"What were you and Erin talking about?"

"Girl things. Why do you want to know?"

"You seem awfully chummy."

"We were having fun. It's good to laugh with her again. It's been a long time."

"You weren't by any chance talking about me, were you?"

"Don't we have a high opinion of ourselves. No, the fascinating topic of you did not come up at all. We were talking about Arthur and why he isn't here, to tell you the truth."

"Why isn't he here?"

"Because he's afraid of seeing Erin," she said laughing. "Not just Erin but the whole O'Connell family. But you would know something about that, wouldn't you?"

Grace headed for their aunt, who was holding Anna, and left him there to deal with his confusion on his own. He was agitated. He thought very hard about walking out. He wanted to make a statement of some kind, but to whom? Erin didn't seem to care if he left. His mother would guess the cause and have a good laugh at his expense. Walking out was a stupid statement.

He started mingling again. He wasn't really interested in what anyone was saying. All he was thinking about was Erin. He knew there was an excellent chance to change the dynamic. Dinner was coming. They would get their buffet plates and find a place to sit and maybe he could maneuver himself into her proximity. But she wound up back in the living room in the same place by the fire, surrounded by friends.

In fact all the good places seemed taken. He made himself a plate and went out to the kitchen to eat. Then he helped fill the dishwasher and do the leftover dishes, of which there were many. He did not stop indulging in punch. After dessert he went back to the living room and saw Erin and Grace sitting on the piano bench. Grace was playing Broadway tunes and Erin was singing along in her sweet voice.

They were surrounded by a gaggle of onlookers. It was impossible. He decided it was time to check out. The good thing was he could do it unobserved with such a large crowd. He sneaked out to the porch and literally out the back door when he was sure no one was watching.

The temperature had plunged to below freezing after being in the low forties during the day, thus creating the dreaded black ice. He slipped a couple of times on his way to his car but was saved by his skating skills. He thought about putting salt down for the guests but felt too annoyed and agitated to stop. He climbed into his car and took off without waiting for the defroster to do its good work, peering out from a small clear space he'd made in the fresh ice.

This is probably why he never saw the icy patch on the road, although how you would see it at night is hard to say. When he hit it he lost all control. The car spun once, twice, and then he was headed straight for a tree. There was a long moment of terror. Somehow he missed it and wound up in a meadow. He sat there trying to gather his wits and calm his nerves. He had spun to the uphill side of the road and was able to pretty much roll back down through the crunchy snow, which was not deep.

He managed to make it home without further incident, going about twenty miles an hour. He sat in his favorite chair still in a state of shock. He was not sober enough to be thinking clearly, but he could see the large tree coming at him and feel the car bouncing in the meadow. He had been very lucky. The car was operational. He was still in one piece. There were no police and no DUI or loss of license, which he could not afford with his long commute.

After half an hour his heart rate and respiration returned to normal. But then he began to think about the party and Erin. It was definitely a mixed bag. There was a lot to cherish. He had seen her. He had seen a lot of her, in fact. He had spoken to her. He had gone to see Erin and succeeded. Then again he had not seen her, not really, not the way he wanted. Plus he felt he had made a fool of himself with his stupid comment.

Grace said they were laughing at Arthur for being a coward. First of all it was amazing that the two of them could be laughing together at all after everything that had happened. It said a lot about Erin and her forgiving nature that she would even talk to Grace. But a happy thought occurred to him. If she could laugh about Arthur, then maybe Grace was right. Maybe she had never really been in love with Arthur.

Why did this make Jim happy? Because it suggested there might still be some room in her heart for him. Now, based on his exchange with her, he could not be comfortable that there was a great deal of room. But at that point he was willing to settle for any room at all, or even the faint possibility of it.

Now he almost wished he hadn't left the party. At least while he was there he could still see Erin and there was still a chance of something good happening. Now all he could do was brood.

XXXIII

Intermezzo

ERIN WAS QUIET in the car on the way home.
"Boy, Jim was really bombed," Megan observed out of the blue.
"No he wasn't. What makes you say that?" their mother said.
"Every time I saw him he was at the punch bowl. Ask Erin. I saw him talking to her. His face was all red."
"I don't know anything about it," Erin said. "We don't have anything to say to each other."

Their parents glanced at each other in the faint dashboard light. Jack was glad. He believed Megan and didn't want Jim Wilmot to have anything to do with his daughter, or his weirdo prep-school friends either.

Amy's feelings were a little more complicated.

XXXIV

The Ides of March

THE NEXT MORNING Jim woke up with a wicked hangover. The punch was too sweet and now lingered malevolently in every pore of his body. He lay there for a long time trying to come into focus. Okay, so it was probably only ten minutes, but it seemed like a long time in his miserable state. An image was forming in his mind. A tree was coming at him at warp speed. He chased it away and it would come again.

Gradually it began to dawn on him that this tree was part of his personal history. It was not from a movie; it was not a lingering dream. From far-off places of mist and cobwebs he was slowly returning to himself and the remembrance of a little mishap on the way home. Bits and pieces of the incident were coming back to him, like the sensation of his poor car bouncing violently on the rough meadow. His teeth still hurt from that.

He dragged himself out of bed feeling very apprehensive. Was the car all right? He threw on some jeans and a sweatshirt and ran out to look. It was cold but he did not notice. He was too worried about what he was going to find. Fortunately it looked fine. There were a couple of scratches he didn't remember having, and there was some grass and mud stuck to the front bumper, which seemed to be drooping a bit.

Other than that, everything else was intact, at least in a cosmetic sense. He went back in the house and made himself some pancakes and wolfed them down in an attempt to absorb some of whatever venomous substances were still sloshing around in his stomach. He felt slightly better. Then he felt worse. He lay down. He couldn't lie down. He also couldn't stand or sit up. He felt too awful.

He started to become very curious about the accident. He wanted to see the place where it happened. He grabbed his keys and headed for the car. He still didn't put on a jacket; the bracing cold felt good. He did not remember exactly where to go, but he knew it was not far from his parents' house. So he drove over there, keeping his eyes peeled to the side of the road.

He found it. There was the tree, and there were crazy tracks in the snow. He parked and got out of the car to take a look. The tree was huge. A stout oak. He had missed it by maybe six inches. Worse—and he had been completely unaware of this the night before—he missed a boulder on the other side by no more than a foot. He was literally between a rock and a hard place. It was like threading a needle. There did not appear to be any damage to the property, which was a relief.

He drove home feeling considerably chastened. Just a few inches either way and there could have been a complete disaster. As it was it was just a little disaster. The car was making odd noises, although everything seemed to be running fine. There were no warning lights. He was thankful for that.

As he drove home he remembered something about the party. He remembered trying to talk to Erin. Was he coherent at that point? He certainly hoped so. He didn't want to give her any more reasons to despise him. What did he say to her? He could picture her, and himself talking, but he could not remember. Uh oh. He remembered. He said something about forgiving Grace.

He was trying to pay her a compliment, but it came out horribly wrong. Now he felt as sick in his soul as he felt in his body. What other stupid things did he say or do? He could not remember and this scared him. He remembered helping in the kitchen. He remembered louring over the punch bowl. There was something about Grace and Erin at the piano. Everything else was pretty much a blank.

All day long he dreaded a scorching phone call from his sister or mother. No such phone call came. It was ominously quiet on the home front. Then as his fear of being yelled at began to wane he found himself *wishing* someone would call. He wanted to be told that he had not done anything outrageous or made a complete ass of himself. He wished he could say he didn't. He wasn't at all sure.

The next day he stumbled into work still feeling punky and thought of Groucho's joke about being blind for three days. It didn't seem so funny now. Finally he couldn't stand it. He went out to his car at lunch and called his sister.

"Just wondering if anything exciting happened after I left," he fished, shivering in the cold.

"I don't know. When did you leave? Don't bother answering that. No, nothing exciting happened. At least not at the party."

"Was Erin all right? I tried to talk to her, like you said, but she didn't seem very willing."

"What did you say?"

He was trapped. "I was just asking her about you. You two seemed very friendly."

"I believe we were. We may have gotten past our little disaster. Although she may not be happy with the latest news. Arthur and I are engaged."

"You are? Really?"

"Is that all you can say?" she said laughing.

"No, I'm sorry. Congratulations. That's really wonderful."

"He came over last night. He had the ring. No, not that ring. This one was for me. In fact we designed it together."

"So Erin doesn't know."

"No, but she will. Our mother wants to have an engagement party. I'm all for a party, but I almost wish she wouldn't invite the O'Connells."

"Tell her not to. She'll understand."

"I don't know. It's more complicated than that. She'll be inviting other people from church. I think it would be too strange not to invite them, since they are basically our closest friends."

So now Jim had another thing to worry about or look forward to—he wasn't sure which. He shared his sister's reservations, but he couldn't help wanting another opportunity to see Erin. If she was there—and he hoped she was—he was determined to talk to her. He was going to make the effort, at least. Completely sober. She could laugh at him. She could brush him off. But he was going to try. It was all he could think about.

But no invitations were forthcoming. Two long weeks went by without an invitation. Then he had a visit from Arthur.

"So I guess you know about the engagement."

"Of course."

"What do you think?"

"I think it's great."

"Do you? Because I was kind of wondering. I know I might have been a little hard on your sister in the past."

"No one can blame you for not being attracted to a prepubescent girl. In fact if I'm not mistaken it's against the law."

"I just didn't know her very well. I didn't know what she was really like. But now I'm kind of nervous. Do you think I'm good enough for her?"

"Good enough! What in the world are you talking about? As far as I'm concerned you're a saint."

"I won't insult your intelligence by pretending not to know what you mean. Believe me, it's no big deal. I'm ready to be a father. But no—I mean she really is incredible. Don't you think? She's so beautiful. I still can't get over the fact that she's interested in me. You know me. I never really dated or anything like that. I was always too awkward around girls. My thing is arts and culture. This is all new to me. I guess I'm still in shock."

"But you do want to go through with it, right?" Jim said, feeling some alarm as he recalled a similar conversation with Arthur in the past, in fact the last time they were in his house together.

"Definitely! Oh, more than anything in the world. I just don't know if she can really love me."

"Grace is the last person who would agree to marry someone she didn't love. That's just not who she is."

"Well, you know, it's not always what it seems when people do that. Sometimes there are mitigating circumstances."

Jim realized what he had said. "I'm sorry. I didn't mean it like that. I'm just trying to reassure you. She would not agree to an engagement unless she really loved you. That is a fact."

Now Arthur looked glum. Jim hated it when he did that. "Would you mind if I asked you an awkward question? You know about this engagement party, right? They're talking about the invitation list. Maybe you already know what I'm thinking. I don't know what to do. I know the O'Connells should be there. Your families are so close. It's just—strange."

"Maybe, but they should be invited at least. They can always choose not to come."

"Again, I don't know. This is going to be hard for me. I haven't seen her since—well, since it ended. And I guess you know it didn't go as smoothly as I intended."

He was thinking about himself! Jim almost laughed. "You can take it. You're tough. I saw you sit through the entire *Ring* once. This should be a breeze."

Apparently the point of the visit was to enlist his support in getting the O'Connells disinvited. Jim wasn't going to let Arthur derail him just because he felt uncomfortable. He wanted Erin to be invited. He was hoping she would come. She didn't seem to love Arthur. It shouldn't matter to her if he was engaged to Grace. Or so he told himself, anyway.

Arthur's blather about how this "was all new to him" seemed a little too obviously like a false-flag operation, considering his engagement to Erin. He was pretending to be surprised at having a pretty girl be in love with him when what he was really doing was trying to warm Jim up for his main attack. Jim was a little annoyed with him for that, since in his view Erin was at least as lovable as Grace, if not more. It seemed like Arthur was devaluing Erin, but of course he was just trying to flatter Grace's brother.

In any case, talking about these things with Arthur raised certain questions in his mind and made him want to see Bob again. He invited him up for the weekend. Saturday was sunny and mild for the end of winter, so they drove up to Kent Falls. They were standing on an observation deck half way up, admiring the magnificent ice-laden cascade, when the following interesting conversation took place.

"So I guess you heard about the engagement."

"You're engaged? I didn't know that."

"No, not me. I'm talking about Arthur and Grace."

Bob stared at him blankly for a moment. "You've got to be kidding me."

"No, I'm dead serious. In fact there's an engagement party in a couple of weeks."

"Well! Didn't see that one coming. I haven't heard from Arthur since we saw him at your mother's party."

"That was a long time ago."

"I know. I feel bad. With him up in Boston and me in New York, we just never seem to have any time to get together. And as you know, I'm not the greatest when it comes to communicating."

"A lot has happened since then, believe me. The thing with Grace started at the end of the summer. I was as surprised as you are. But they seem very happy together."

"Grace and Arthur. I wouldn't have put those two together in a million years."

"I know what you mean. But he seems to be madly in love with her. And she is very fortunate to have someone who—that is—."

"No, I agree. Completely. But I still can't get over it. I mean, he must know—right? I'm assuming she told him."

"I don't know what he knows, to be honest."

"Hmm. That could be awkward. In more ways than one."

"Yes, it could. Her name is Anna, by the way."

"Anna. I like that. But she *must* have told him."

"I assume so. It would be crazy not to."

"And he still wants to marry her?"

"Apparently."

Bob shook his head in dismay. "Well, I hope she did. She doesn't always tell you everything, I can tell you that much. It could come as a rude surprise if she didn't."

"I agree. That's why I was kind of curious about whether you had heard from him."

"Again, not for a long time. And I can't even imagine trying to call him now. Any more than I can imagine him marrying her if he knew about me and the baby, to be blunt about it."

This conversation stirred up strange emotions in Jim. He too was amazed by Arthur and his willingness to become involved in such a messy situation. Arthur was never one for messes. He went out of his way to avoid them. And this seemed like a mess of the colossal kind. So Jim could not help wondering the same thing as Bob. Had she told him? Did Arthur know that Bob had an affair with Grace and the baby was his?

If he didn't, then *someone* had to tell him. And if Grace refused to do it, then Jim would have to tell him himself. He wasn't going to do unto Arthur what Arthur had done unto him. He owed him that much as a friend and concerned party.

XXXV

Disaster

THE LONG-AWAITED invitation finally showed up in his in-box. The party was scheduled for April 10. It was still almost four weeks away, but Jim thought he could stand it. He had waited this long; he could wait a little longer.

The following day his phone rang. He pulled it out and was shocked when he saw the name "Karen."

"Hello?" he said uncertainly.

"Hi there," she purred.

"How are you?"

"I'm fine. The question is, how are you? I haven't heard from you in a while."

"Been pretty busy. Got a new job. Long hours."

"That's great! Of course I knew you would. So what have you been up to, other than working yourself to the bone?"

"Oh, just the usual. Seeing friends and some other things. How about you?"

"Same here. Looks like I'm going to have a break until summer. I was wondering if you wanted to get together."

Jim was scrambling. "That probably wouldn't be a good idea."

"Really? Why not?"

"Well, I guess I should tell you. I'm—engaged."

"Engaged! Well. Who's the lucky girl? Do I know her? Wait a minute. Is it that pretty girl I met at your parents' house?"

"Well, actually—yes."

"That's so funny. I sensed there was something between you two, although as I remember she was there with someone else. Well, congratulations. She seems like a very nice girl."

"I'm a little surprised to hear from you," he admitted. "I thought you were getting back together with your ring friend."

"Oh, those stupid tabloids! Everything is always so exaggerated. We did a movie together in the fall, but that's about it. Unless you can call that being 'back together.'"

Jim became very bold. "About that, would you mind if I asked you something?"

"Sure. What?"

"Did you ever feel anything for me?"

"Oh, that's so funny," she said. "I suppose you don't remember me saying the same exact thing to you."

Now he did. "But at least I answered the question."

"I'm happy to answer it, too. Yes, of course I felt something for you. I still do. Very much so. What would make you even say something like that, after everything we've been through?"

"I've been thinking about the photographer at the fair. There was only one. It was almost like the whole thing was a set-up."

"A 'set-up'! What are you talking about?"

"Like it was staged to make it seem we were together. Not because we really were together, but to make someone jealous."

"You mean Brick? Did you read that in the tabloids too? No, of course it wasn't a set-up," she said scornfully. "I can't help it if those people follow me around."

"No, of course not. I was just wondering."

"But I don't understand why you would ask me something like that. I thought it was pretty clear that I have feelings for you."

"To be honest, I guess I never quite believed it. I didn't see any reason why you would."

"Interesting. Is that why you never came to me for help?"

"Help? What do you mean?"

"When you were out of work and going through a rough time."

"I don't know. I didn't feel it was appropriate."

"Not appropriate! Why not? I would have been glad to help. That's what you do for the people you care about."

"I had the impression you weren't too happy with me and the bottomless pit into which I had descended."

She sighed. "One thing I know without going to Yale, and that's that relationships can be complicated. But yes, I would have been happy to help you. Absolutely."

"Why?" Jim blurted.

"Why? Because you were the first man in my life who ever made me feel safe."

He was stunned by this comment. She had never said anything like that to him while they were seeing each other. Did she really mean it? There was no reason to think she didn't. He chatted a little longer for the sake of politeness, but all he could think about was getting off the phone so he could recover. It was weird enough to have her drop back into his life, but he was not expecting his assumptions to be challenged—the assumptions he had gotten from Bob, now that he thought about it. Maybe things weren't as simple as his friend had made them out to be. Maybe Jim wasn't just a tool in Kerry's expansive toolbox.

To say that this call had no impact on him—that he was able simply to brush it off—laugh about it and forget it—would be false. He felt himself falling into the same snare as before. Did she really care for him after all? Was it possible that Kerry Morgan had loved him in some way, as she suggested? Would she really have been happy to help him out, if he had asked? Had he stressed out all those months over nothing? But then the very fact that he called her "Kerry Morgan" as he was thinking these things snapped him back to reality. As seductive as the siren call from New Canaan was, he was too anchored to be drawn in; too anchored by the love he had for Erin and his determination to see if there was any chance of her ever loving him again.

He was surprised that Kerry "sensed" something between him and Erin. Was it that obvious? Okay, so he lied to her when he said they were engaged, but in his mind he wasn't really lying at all. He felt like they *were* engaged, based on past history and his present feelings, even if Erin didn't know it yet. They were "engaged" in the sense that he was completely pledged to her in his mind, at least. The disconcerting phone call did not de-pledge him. It made him want to see Erin even more. He did not want to think about calling Kerry back and taking her up on her invitation. He let his new devotion to Erin put temptation out of mind.

Plus he knew he would be out of his mind if he said yes to Kerry. The call made him rethink the bitterness he'd been fostering toward her ever since being dumped, as he saw it. She may not be the monster he was so busy making her out to be, but it had been a long time since she deigned to call. A long, long time. Regardless of whether she really did feel anything for him, her idea of a relationship was very different from his. Besides, she had spent the fall making a movie with (former?) flame Brick Dancy. This was a movie that Jim had no desire to see. He did not want to be reminded of the foolishness he had felt for so long.

Spring arrived, a hard season for the lovelorn. Crocuses and daffodils and forsythias and hyacinths were blooming and finches were singing lustily on bright mornings. It was chilly on the day of the engagement party, in the high forties, but sunny. There was a freshness to the April breezes that promised new beginnings. Jim wanted so much to believe in that promise.

The day dragged on forever, and then it was time to go. He was filled with all kinds of emotions as he drove over in the twilight. First there was the engagement itself. He was grateful and amazed at the same time. A terrible burden had been lifted. Grace was not going to have to face the future alone. There was someone for her; and not just anyone, but a person of substance with whom she could have intelligent conversations and fulfill her dream of touring Europe, which Arthur wanted almost as much as she did.

At the same time it was all so odd. First of all his baby sister was getting married. This in itself was hard to grasp. Life really was happening. They were not children anymore. The match seemed a little surprising as well. Arthur could be stiff and formal at times, while Grace was a militant subverter of all that was ceremonious or potentially artificial. There was also the unresolved issue of Anna and how much Arthur knew about her paternity. He still had not talked to her about that.

He felt he needed to. As soon as he got there he took her out to the porch.

"I have something to ask you. I saw Bob a while back, and it's been on my mind ever since."

"Bob! I don't want to hear about it. This is my engagement party."

"I know. That's what I want to talk to you about. I'm sorry if this sounds stupid, but does Arthur know?"

"Does Arthur know what?"

"You know. About you and Bob."

A shocked look came over her face. Then she started laughing. "Of course. I would never try to keep something like that a secret."

"And Anna, too?"

"What's wrong with you? You think I wouldn't tell him?"

"So he's okay with it, then."

"Apparently. We're engaged."

"Wow. I was just wondering. I mean, it seems like it would be a difficult thing to accept. Bob being his friend."

"He's perfectly comfortable with it. He was a little surprised at first. Okay, shocked maybe. But he got over it. Not right away, to be honest. Otherwise we would have been engaged earlier."

"I'm not surprised. We were thinking it would have to make things a little awkward."

"'*We?*' You mean you and Bob?"

"Well—yes."

"I think maybe you two should mind your own business."

She waltzed out leaving him standing there with a red face. He felt badly. He didn't want to upset her. On the other hand he felt relieved. In his mind it was a conversation he could not avoid having. He didn't want another disaster like Black Friday. Or at least he felt like he had to have it. Did he really have to have it? Now that he thought about it he wasn't sure.

It sounded like he didn't trust her. That was why she was mad at him. He had doubts about her being completely forthcoming with Arthur. Why did he have doubts? And what made him think he had a right to plague her with such doubts at her engagement party? It was *because* it was an engagement party. The occasion seemed to beg the question.

But now he realized how completely inappropriate it was. This was her party. It wasn't up to him to try to commandeer it for his own questionable purposes. He felt terrible. He had made a fool of himself again and managed to upset Grace on what should have been her happy day. The party had already started on a sour note.

Things were about to get worse. Erin arrived with her family. He was determined to talk to her this time, determined not to squander the opportunity, which, for all he knew, was the last one he might ever have. He walked right up to her in the crowd, but she would not even look at him. She turned away and began talking to the Maxwells, who had also just arrived.

It was a crushing blow. He had been looking forward to this moment for weeks. But what did he expect? There was no reason to think she had been looking forward to it as well. There was no reason to think she wanted to see him like he wanted to see her; that she was in love with him the way he was in love with her. In fact there was every reason to think otherwise.

Arthur's parents arrived. Jim had not seen them in a long time. He felt obliged to catch up when what he really wanted to do was make another attempt at talking to Erin. When he managed to tear himself away and did find Erin, she did not seem approachable. This was not the usual sunny Erin. There was an edge to her he was not accustomed to seeing.

He was waiting for his opportunity. It occurred to him that he had been doing a lot of this lately at his parents' house. He watched her greet old friends. He saw her put a cucumber sandwich and some cheddar cheese on a plate and head for her usual place by the fire. He had to stop her before she got there. As it happened, he met her in almost the same place as the last time they had talked.

"Hi, Erin!" he said in a way that forced her to stop.

She looked at him. It seemed like kind of a cross look.

"Hi," she said. "How are you?"

"I'm well. And yourself?"

"Fine, thanks."

"Beautiful day today."

"It is. A little cold, but sunny."

"I remember how you used to love April days like this. We used to go for walks."

She seemed puzzled. "I did go for a walk today. With Tucker. At White Memorial."

"That sounds like fun. How is Tucker doing?"

"The arthritis is worse, but other than that he's his usual boisterous self."

"I miss him. Tell him I said hi. I remember going there with you once, and him. It was in the fall."

"Yes, it was fall. It's a nice place to walk at that time of year."

She sort of smiled at him, although she still looked puzzled, and continued on her way to the fire, which was taking the April chill out of the room. He stood there and watched her go. He wanted to go with her. He wished he had the courage to go with her. But he felt he had done enough for the time being. In fact he had done more than he expected.

It was the first time he had talked to her, really, since the night he broke up with her. He felt all tingly inside. She acted cold at first but warmed up a little when she realized he was determined to talk. She recognized his fond tone when he was talking about the walks. She did not reject it, as he was afraid she would. She smiled at him.

There was the buffet and there was dessert and coffee, and then there was the thing Jim was dreading the most—the toast. His normally staid and somewhat abstracted father shocked them with quite the emotional stemwinder, causing just about everyone in the room to cry, including Gammy, who was deaf.

There was a great hurrah when he was done and raising of glasses, and Jim glanced over in the direction of Erin just in time to see her ducking out the doorway. He wasn't surprised; he thought all the celebrating might be hard on her. Naturally he was worried. The chivalry genes were activated.

He stood there waiting and hoping for her to reappear. He stayed in that pose for about ten minutes. Then he decided to look for her. The crowd was pretty thick, which slowed him down, but he made it to the foyer. No sign of her. He went around to all the usual rooms—same thing.

He went to the kitchen, where he found his mother and Erin's mother and some other ladies gaily chatting. He tried to get his mother's attention by making faces at her over Mrs. Maxwell's voluminous shoulder, with no success. They were totally absorbed in one of Amy's comic tales. Finally in desperation he waved. She looked at him. He mouthed the word "Erin." She of course had no idea what it was. He tried again. She shook her head.

He couldn't wait any longer. "Erin! Have you seen Erin?" he whispered impatiently.

"She left."

"When?"

"I don't know—maybe ten minutes ago. Said she was meeting someone."

Jim turned and promptly left the kitchen. Carolyn and Amy exchanged glances. They all went right back to talking as if nothing had happened.

Where was he going? He didn't have any idea. But he felt he had to go somewhere. He wanted to see Erin. The thing about meeting someone, he was sure, was a ruse. He had seen the expression on her face when the cheer went up for Grace. He thought he knew why she left. She was running away. He wanted to run after her, even though he had no idea what he would do if he caught her.

It didn't matter. He felt he had made a little progress with her that evening. He opened the front door and discovered a nasty thunderstorm rolling in. He was parked about thirty yards away—he had gallantly left room for other guests—and had no umbrella, so he stood there in the doorway in agony as rain came down in sheets and lightening flashed in the dark hills.

At one point the storm turned entirely to hail, leaving a white dusting on the lawn. Normally he loved a good thunderstorm, a good toss of the sensibilities, but the timing could not have been worse. Ten agonizing minutes went by before the rain let up enough for him to feel comfortable making a break for the car; and even then he managed to get soaked.

He wanted to hurry but couldn't. It was still raining and the road was slick from hail and spring debris. He found himself heading instinctively in the direction of her house. He drove and the wipers thumped at high speed as the rain picked up again and thunder rumbled in the hills.

Then in the distance he thought he saw some flashing lights. It was hard to tell with the rain splashing against the windshield; but yes, there were definitely lights up ahead, and emergency vehicles. The red and blue lights formed smears in the channels of rain on the glass. He strained but could not see distinctly. There seemed to be something going on at the next bend. He slowed down.

The weird thing was he felt those lights had something to do with him. They weren't just emergency lights on a rainy spring evening; they were a message. He felt himself becoming fluttery. The emergency vehicles were blocking the road at that point. He could not get by. But instead of doing the sensible thing and turning around, he pulled into a driveway and got out of the car.

Jim was not exactly an ambulance chaser. He did not have the macabre curiosity that causes rubbernecking on the highway; besides, he couldn't stand the sight of blood. But in spite of this, and the light rain that continued to fall, he found himself walking—or stumbling—in the direction of the commotion.

Radios crackled and there were people walking around, looking very official and grimly efficient. Even in the falling darkness, Jim could see what the fuss was about. A small car had hit a large tree broadside. It was a truly ghastly-looking wreck. As he drew closer he felt his heart leap into his mouth. It looked like Erin's Civic.

He kept stumbling forward as if in a trance. A state trooper approached him.

"Sir! Can I help you?" he said, with the tone of someone who was not quite sure what he was dealing with.

"Oh my God, oh my God," Jim mumbled.

"Sir! You need to get out of the road."

Jim didn't even realize he was in the road. He didn't have the slightest idea where he was.

"Do you know who was in that car?" he said in shock.
"A young lady."
"Oh my God—it can't be."
"Do you know her?"
"I think so. I think it's Erin. My friend."
"Can you help us get in touch with someone from her family?"
"Is she all right?"
"All I can tell you is they took her to the hospital. Is there someone we can call?"
"Yes. Her parents are at my house. I'll give you the number."

This took some time, but to tell the truth Jim needed it before he was ready to get back into his car and attempt to do any driving. The rain started to let up; the storm was passing; sun broke through the clouds in shafts. He finished his business with the trooper. The last thing he heard him saying into his phone was, "Yes, this is the state police. I need to get in touch with Mr. or Mrs. O'Connell."

The trooper looked at him and nodded, and Jim waved and began wandering back to his car. Then this struggling walk turned into a jog and finally a gallop. It was hard to run on the hail-slickened road in his loafers, but he didn't care. He had to get to Erin as quickly as possible.

He was almost physically ill by the time he reached the hospital. They informed him at the desk that she was about to go into surgery. He sat down in the lobby in agony. In about fifteen minutes Erin's family arrived with his mother. They went upstairs and Carolyn came directly to him.

"What are you doing here?"
"I saw the wreck."
"Oh, my. That must have been hard for you."
"It was the worst thing I've ever seen in my life."
She looked at him. "Have you heard anything?"
"Just that they were taking her to surgery."
"That's what we heard, too. I guess at this point all we can do is wait. And pray."

The waiting went on for quite a long time. It was difficult, hoping for the best, expecting the worst, not knowing what to think. About two hours later Jack O'Connell came to them.

"How is she?" Carolyn said anxiously, giving him a little hug.
"Not good. There are some broken bones and a collapsed lung.

They knew that much before they brought her in. Could be other internal injuries, too."

"Oh, Jack. I'm so sorry. Did you get to see her?"

"No, she was already in surgery when we arrived. We're doing the same thing you are. Waiting."

She gave his hand a squeeze. He tried to smile but was not entirely successful. Then he went back upstairs.

They didn't ask him about the prognosis. They were afraid to. They sat and waited some more. She asked Jim about the accident. He told her again in hushed tones that it was the worst wreck he had ever seen. It looked like she hadn't negotiated the corner and had skidded sideways into the tree. The only good thing was the impact was on the passenger side. If it had been the other…

This was pretty much the sum of their conversation for the next few hours. It was not a situation where talking seemed desirable or appropriate. Finally Megan came down at about three in the morning and told them she was out of surgery. She didn't have any other news, except that there was a broken arm, a broken hip and leg, and several broken ribs.

"Well, I think I'll go home and say hello to your father," Carolyn said to Jim. "I'll come back in the morning."

"I think I'll stay," he replied simply.

She looked at him for a moment, gave Megan a heartfelt hug, and was off.

So now he was there with Megan, and this was a good deal more awkward than being there with his mother, which was awkward enough.

"Do you think she's going to be all right?" she said to him in a dread low tone when they were alone.

"She'll be fine," he said reassuringly through the grogginess of lack of sleep. "She's in good hands."

"But the doctor—I don't know. It was weird. He seemed worried about her."

"Well, you know, they have to seem that way. They don't want to give any false hope."

"I'm so scared."

"I know. She'll be fine."

He said this to soothe her, but he could not soothe himself. He was just as scared as she was. No, he may have been more scared. He had seen the wreck. He could not get the ghastly image out of his head. Every time he closed his eyes it was there in front of him.

They sat in gloomy silence, just as he had with his mother. In about half an hour Megan fell asleep. He felt sleepy too and gradually allowed himself to succumb. It was a restless, feverish sleep. At one point he was at a soccer game in prep school, in street clothes, and Erin was there with him on the sidelines, which didn't make any sense because they had not known each other then; and suddenly they were on the hill overlooking the field, talking to the headmaster, and he was asking Jim if he was ready to play—Jim had been a fairly successful forward—and then he wasn't the headmaster anymore, or he was some kind of mutant hybrid with a bald head and earrings, and there was a cemetery behind where they were standing, and Erin was there on his right, but when he looked he couldn't find her. Then they were at the O'Connell house. Tucker was showing bad manners by jumping up on Jim with his big paws, and then they were out by the pool and Erin was on the diving board, and she went into her dive, but just before she hit the water the scene changed and she wasn't there and someone said "where's Erin?" whereupon Jim's blood ran cold and he started awake—he was in fact chilled—only to see Mrs. O'Connell standing over him.

"You're still here?"

He stared at her befuddled for a moment—still half in the dream. "Guess I fell asleep. How is she?"

"She's out of surgery. Resting comfortably. There were a lot of injuries, but other than that we don't know too much."

"Is there anything I can do?"

"Actually there is, if you don't mind. You can take Megan home. She needs to study for a chemistry test."

He realized this was her kind way of killing two birds with one stone, but he was glad to take her up on her offer. He wanted to go home and shower and regain his bearings. Amy gently awakened her daughter, caressing her feelingly, and told her the plan. Megan was amenable, so Jim took her home and tried to reassure her again, with not much more success, and then he headed for his own house on the lake, shrouded in early morning mists.

He went into his room and fell on his bed and was soon fast asleep. There were more weird dreams, even scarier than the one in the hospital. The sun was shining brightly and his biological clock started switching over to sympathetic mode. And then he knew it was impossible to sleep. He was too worried about Erin. There was only one thing he wanted to do: go back to the hospital.

So back he went. The only news was that Erin "had not woken up yet," from which he gathered she must be in a coma. His parents showed up around noon, after church, and went right up to see her, but Jim did not go up. It seemed presumptuous. What right did he have to pretend there was some sort of special relationship between them? For that matter, how did he know she would even *want* to see him?

No, his act of willing service was to be where he was for her sake. To tell the truth there was no other place he could be in his highly anxious state. It was almost physically impossible to be anywhere else. Now this is a queer thing, you may say to yourself, to be at the hospital and literally doing nothing and think you are doing something. But the nothing he was doing was not just for Erin's sake. True, for Erin it was nothing, since she had no idea he was there. But it was something for him.

Sunday was a long and desolate spring day, stormy outside and stormy in his soul. He managed to read some of *Anna Karenina*, but it was not for pleasure; it was to pass the time. The day dragged on and one or the other of the O'Connells appeared from time to time to say hello and give a progress report, which always consisted of the same thing—"She's still sleeping." He felt for them more than he could say. They were both clearly in torment.

Sunday night came and there was still no change. He managed to drag himself away at eleven and went home to get some sleep but returned first thing Monday morning, six o'clock in fact, and took up his old post. He called Dave and told him there was an emergency and he wasn't coming in, but he did have his laptop with him and was able to answer emails. This was quite soothing, doing something, anything.

Dave sounded a bit skeptical on the phone, but Jim didn't care. He had given his life to these people for eight months; surely they could get by without him for a day or two. Yes, there was a big campaign on the docket, and yes, they were at a critical moment, but Jim, in his usual thorough way, had built a solid foundation. All they had to do was show enough imagination to follow through.

Besides, he was on his laptop if they needed him. For heaven's sake it was like hand-holding. It was ridiculous that they didn't seem to think they could do anything without him. On the other hand, it was sort of flattering. Jim liked the feeling of being needed and wanted. So he kept his laptop open and was quick to jump in when any queries came his way.

Late Monday afternoon Erin "woke up." Jim was in his usual spot and Mrs. O'Connell came down smiling like mad and motioned to him excitedly with her hand. At first he did not know what she meant—or rather, he did but he could not allow himself to believe it. He jumped up and grabbed his things and walked briskly in her direction.

"She wants to see you," Amy said.

These simple words caused Jim to experience an emotion that is difficult to describe. "How is she doing?" he managed to say, when the elevator door closed behind them.

"She's okay," she said, with the kind of emphasis on "okay" that suggested not so much. "Very sore, of course, but okay. She is alert. She's been talking to us. Sort of."

"That's great news," was all he could say, although he found himself wanting to say many things, some of them quite gushy.

They reached their floor and Jim followed her to the room. She went in first and stood next to her husband; Jim hung back a bit, feeling embarrassed and—he didn't know what.

Mrs. O'Connell noticed. "Jim's here, honey. I told you he's been downstairs this whole time. Come on in!"

She beckoned him. He started moving forward, as if in a dream. He passed the bathroom and now saw her in her gadgety hospital bed, this girl who had become the most precious thing in the world to him. It was a bit of a shock. Her right leg was in a cast and in traction. There was an IV. Her head was bandaged, and he could see that the area around her eyes was deeply bruised. Her right arm, the one closest to him, was in a cast as well.

He did not know what to do with himself. He kept walking. He saw her other hand, and it was free, and seemed like the only part of her body that was not bandaged or constrained in some way, so he stumbled past her parents and around the bed and came closer. Then without really knowing what he was doing he reached out and touched that hand, ever so gently.

Which he had done many times before, of course. But this time something embarrassing happened. He became choked up and hot tears literally jumped out of his eyes. The O'Connells looked at each other and immediately scooted out of the room. He didn't notice. All of his being was concentrated on Erin.

She closed her eyes and gave his hand a gentle squeeze. She grimaced with this effort. When Jim realized just how much pain she was in, he had to choke back his emotions. His body was shaking now. He leaned over and started talking in a low voice without knowing what he was saying.

"I'm so glad you're okay. I love you so much. Please don't be angry with me anymore. I'm here for you now and I will always be here for you. Always. I promise."

What?! Did he really say that? Well, yes; yes he did. The force of emotion was so strong at the moment, having seen the car wreck and spent two days wondering if she would live, that he could not do anything else.

He looked down at her through the tears clinging to his eyelashes, turning cold and stinging. She was a little blurry, but he could see what happened next. She looked up at him and there was a faint smile on her face. She made a slight nod, which, he realized, again with a flood of emotion, was all she could do.

XXXVI

Refuge in a hand

THERE WAS A LONG road ahead for Erin to recovery. Jim continued to cling to the one good hand in the weeks and months that followed. When she went home from the hospital he would sit next to her on the screened-in porch, her favorite place in the house, and cling to it literally for hours. He held it very gently, as if afraid of hurting her.

He held onto it all through the month of May, a time of pain and many setbacks. True, he couldn't hold onto it when she was using her walker to navigate to the bathroom or around the house, but he was holding onto it when she tried taking her first steps *without* the walker, and he held onto it many times more when she was forcing herself to walk and trying so hard to get better.

To tell the truth, she was trying to get better for him. She did not want to be this broken person. She was amazed by the change in him, amazed to find him by her side, and hated her brokenness for his sake. She wished she could hurry up, but it was a long and tedious process, and thinking like a nurse, she knew she had to be patient. For weeks she was forced simply to lie there and accept his kindness. She could not do anything else.

One Saturday in the middle of May they were sitting on the porch together. Tucker was lying on the rug in front of them; he had been on guard there ever since she came home from the hospital. Jim was holding her hand as usual and gazing at her. She was starting to feel a little better, emerging from the fog of the concussion and the weakness caused by the body's self-repair.

She was looking at him sideways with her uncovered eye. He could tell there was a question.

"What?"

"So what happened exactly? I don't understand," she said in a voice that was still somewhat weak from headaches.

"You mean the accident?"

She smiled politely at this evasion. "No, I mean *this*. How did we get here? I thought you weren't interested in me."

"That's not true. I was always interested in you. I just didn't realize how I really felt about you."

"I just want to understand. Is it because of the accident? Are you taking pity on me?"

"No—not at all. The change came long before the accident, believe me."

"Really? How long?"

"You remember all those parties at my mother's house where I used to follow you around?"

"I remember the parties. I don't remember you following me around."

"Okay, so I *wanted* to follow you around. I was too scared."

"Scared! Of what?"

"I thought you hated me. I thought you didn't want to see me after everything that happened."

"Well, first of all, I was engaged to someone else at some of those parties. So if you were following me around—shame on you. But after that I didn't know what to think. It seemed like you were avoiding me. You wouldn't talk to me."

"But you didn't hate me?"

"No, of course I didn't hate you. Why would you say that?"

"I was acting like a complete jackass. I think I may have been overreacting because I loved you so much."

"Wow. Did you really just say that?"

"Why? Is it wrong?"

"No, not wrong. Just surprising."

"I want to apologize again for Black Friday. I had no idea you didn't know about Arthur and Grace."

"I know. I figured it out. I was just caught by surprise. I felt like everyone was making fun of me."

"That was not the case at all. Absolutely no one was making fun of you. I was just trying to make conversation in my idiot way. It never occurred to me that I was springing something new on you. Of course it might have been nice if someone had filled me in."

"Imagine how I felt. I was the last one to know. But I got over it. The bottom line is we weren't right for each other. If he wasn't going to marry me, then he might as well marry Grace. I was happy about it, when I managed to recover from the shock. I think they'll be good for each other. But I noticed you changed the subject. You still didn't tell me what happened. When you started to change."

"I don't know. I think it might have been when I saw you and Arthur together for the first time. That was quite a shock. It was also the first time I began to understand what a fool I had been."

"Oh, come on. You were going with the famous Kerry Morgan, if I remember correctly."

"I don't know if I would call that 'going.' I only saw her every three months. She was never really interested in me. Or at least I don't think she was. I don't know why she would be."

"Are you sure you weren't in love with her?" she teased.

"I never saw her. That wasn't love, at least not as I understand it. But what about you? You must have been in love with Arthur if you agreed to marry him."

"I was never in love with him, not really. Don't tell him I said that. I thought it was what I wanted at the time. Hard to explain."

"You seemed pretty happy together."

She smiled. "There's only one person who could make me happy. But is that why you wouldn't talk to me after we broke up? You thought I was in love with him?"

"Well, no; that was different," he said with a bit of a blush. "I didn't think I was good enough for you."

"What! Be serious."

"I am being serious. I saw you at church on Christmas Eve. You looked like an angel. Actually I was spying on you the whole time. Are you really sure you can put up with someone like me?"

"Is that a proposal?" she said, caressing his hand.

"It will be, when I can afford it. But are you sure you want to marry me? Don't you want someone better?"

"There isn't anyone better. This is what I always wanted."

Motivated by this conversation, Erin continued working hard. And she worked harder. She was still in recovery mode well into June but getting a little stronger every day. Jim went there as often as he could. He became something of a fixture at the O'Connell household, going every night after work and every weekend. It got to the point where Amy simply figured on him for dinner, although he often arrived quite late. He won them over with his clear sense of purpose and unflagging devotion to their daughter, as well as his deference toward them.

"I heard you talking to Jim. You seem to be softening on him," Amy said to her husband one day after he left.

"He's been awfully good to her. I didn't think he had it in him."

"That's the difference between you and me. I did. I just didn't think he knew what he really wanted."

"I guess this means they're going to get married."

"It certainly looks like it. How do you feel about that?"

"I'm fine with it. People can change. All I ever wanted was for him to realize how special she is."

"I know. And I think he does. Also I think he's afraid of you."

"Afraid! Nonsense. Prep school wiseguys."

"No, really. You don't realize how you come across sometimes. And you haven't always been happy with him."

"I had my reasons."

"But not anymore?"

"All right, I got the message, loud and clear. He's shown me something. He isn't what I thought he was at all."

XXXVII

Nothing is ever easy

SOMETHING CHANGED FOR JIM in those precious weeks at Erin's bruised and bandaged side. It wasn't just that he grew in devotion to her. It wasn't just that he discovered his true self, to the extent that such a thing is even possible in a young man. But he was also on his way to becoming a recovering workaholic.

They say the first step is to admit you have a problem. Jim realized he had a problem when work conflicted with holding that delicate hand. He still felt driven to succeed and prove his value, but it was not his whole life anymore. He managed to set those limits they keep talking about in the business world with a wink and a nod. Now he wanted to succeed for Erin's sake, for their future happiness, not for the sake of success itself or proving his worth. This produced many salutary changes in his attitude and approach to work.

As for the Wilmots, they found out about his attentions a little belatedly.

"I understand my son is spending quite a bit of time at your house," Carolyn said to Amy during a routine phone call.

"Boy, is he ever. Almost every day."

"Not eating you out of house and home, I hope."

"Oh no, don't be silly. He's too thoughtful for that. He always brings me something, even if it's just flowers, which he knows I love. And he doesn't eat much. Most of the time we hardly even know he's there—they're always out on the porch together."

"So when you say 'together,' do you mean—?"

"I guess. Who knows? But I wish you could see them. It really is quite amazing."

"Well, thank goodness for that. But it's too bad that *she* had to get a concussion in order to knock a little sense into *his* head."

Fortunately Jim and Erin were oblivious to what people were saying about them. They were completely absorbed in each other. Jim was there every day, sitting by her side. They would talk quietly. Sometimes he would read to her, usually Romantic poetry, Keats or Wordsworth, his faves, or they would watch the TV her father had set up on the porch specifically for their entertainment.

Every day there was exercise. Jim saw himself as her personal trainer. Not that he ever tried to tell her what to do—he knew his limitations—but he wanted to be there supporting her and helping her along the way. They would step out into the yard and just walk around and listen to the birds and soak up sunlight. The summer sun felt so good. They soaked it up.

One day, after exercise, they were sitting quietly in the cedar chairs under the maple tree, when Erin said, "Thank you so much for being my nurse all this time."

"I don't mind. I enjoy it."

"Really? I thought nursing was degrading."

"Still storing up that old canard, I see. I do hate myself sometimes. But there was a part of it I didn't understand."

"And what part would that be?"

"I didn't realize about the love."

This made her pause. "So it's *not* degrading, then?"

"Go ahead, rub it in! But I definitely do see it a little differently now. I don't know whether I should thank you for that or scold you for being such a bad driver."

"I am not a bad driver! I guess it's safe to tell you how much that hurt me. I mean what you said. I never wanted to see you again. But I didn't have to worry about that. You never called."

"I know. I'm terrible. Beat me. I deserve it."

"But *why* didn't you call? Was that when you met Kerry?"

"Not exactly. I don't know why I didn't call. Oh, that isn't true. I do know. Everybody was expecting us to get married. I think deep inside I knew we *should* get married. That's the very reason I didn't call. I guess that doesn't make much sense."

"I'm trying to understand. I guess men are different from women. But when you say you thought we 'should' get married, what exactly does that mean? Because people were expecting it?"

"No. That isn't what I mean. I knew somehow you were the one for me from the very first time I saw you. There—is that what you were fishing for? Somehow I knew we were going to be together. Although of course I didn't have any idea how."

"Really? You thought that? That's so funny, because I thought the same thing. At the pizza restaurant, before I even knew you."

"Well, I don't know what to say about that. One of us acted like a fool; the other one didn't. I'll leave it up to you to decide which is which. In any case I know I'm a 'jerk.' At least according to Eric."

"Now what are you talking about?"

"That's what you told him on Christmas Eve. Or are you going to pretend you don't remember, now that you've had a knock on the head?"

"I remember the conversation perfectly. I did not call you a 'jerk.' I've never used that word in my life. I might have said I was upset with you for ignoring me, but he exaggerates everything."

"Well, that's true. He does tend to do that. But I agree with you, even if you didn't say it. I am a jerk, for many reasons. I've certainly acted like one. Are you sure you can forgive me?"

"We are way past that now. I promise I'll never talk about it again. I'm sorry, I just needed to clear the air."

"You were right to. We never talked about it. We needed to talk about it. I guess."

"So you're not upset with me for bringing it up?"

"I can't say it feels good. But no; I'm not 'upset.' I don't want there to be anything standing between us. Talk away! Bring up all the horrifying stuff you want to! I don't have anywhere to go."

There were many tender talks like this during the hours they spent together, although fortunately most in a happier vein. Except for this one time, Erin never brought up painful things from the past. Mostly they would just reminisce. It was fun for them. It was putting the pieces of their lives together and giving them meaning.

In the middle of June she wanted to try going to church to say thank-you to everyone for their prayers and all the meals they had brought. He sensed she wanted him to go with her. He was proud of her progress and glad to go. It was hard for her to stand through the hymns, but she sang out in her sweet voice. Jim looked at her and wished he could be half as good as she was. The pastor made quite a fuss over her. There were a lot of tears.

Sitting there with her in church planted an idea in Jim's head. Well, actually the idea had been there for a long time, but he was too cash-poor to do anything about it. He had just received a bonus at work, so he decided to drop by a jewelry store, just to see what they had. He flashed back on his previous experience with jewelry shopping at the mall. This was far more pleasant. No matter what he got for Erin, he knew she would be thrilled.

He saw a ring he liked very much. He had $5,000 in his bank account. He bought it. He invited her to a picnic at White Memorial and feted her with fried chicken and bean salad and cheddar cheese and iced cappuccinos. It was muggy, sunny and calm. Jim parceled out an oversized brownie and then he couldn't wait anymore—he got down on his knee and proposed.

Erin was not terribly surprised. But she was very, very happy. She was touched by his gallantry, which was sincere, as he had proven. The only thing she wasn't happy about was the ring. He had spent way too much. Erin was not interested in material things. She would be the money manager in their marriage. Jim smiled and shook his head. "Not too much. Not enough." She put it on—it was a perfect fit. Well, of course it was. He had conspired.

So they were going to get married. Now they started to think about setting a date for the wedding. They wanted it to be as soon as possible. They had waited a long time, way too long. Erin was all for "eloping," but their respective families would not hear of it. They both liked the idea of getting married in the fall. Erin knew of a hall that would be perfect for the kind of simple country wedding she had in mind.

But of course there was a complication. When Grace heard about it, she declared that she and Arthur also wanted to be married in the fall, although this was the first time anyone had heard of it. They were engaged first, which gave them precedence in Grace's mind. It seemed suspicious. Usually people took a year or two to plan a wedding, or at least people like Grace. She was adamant, however, and there was nothing her mother or brother could do to dissuade her.

The idea of trying to put on two weddings in the onrushing months was daunting. Impossible, in fact, both logistically and in terms of finding two dates that were viable and didn't crowd together. Everybody was in a tizzy. Erin was upset. Grace decided she was upset, too. Both mothers were upset because they were upset, and both fathers suffered accordingly.

But then the author of all this chaos came up with a brilliant compromise. What about a double wedding? It was unique. It was literary, the conclusion of their midsummer night's dream. It would be fun. Grace became very excited about this idea. It seemed like the perfect solution to all their problems. Jim thought she was crazy, but he broached it with Erin.

"So I don't know if you've heard, but my sister thinks we should have a double wedding," Jim said to her on a hot laconic June afternoon on the porch.

At that very moment Tucker raised his head and looked up at

them with his lugubrious Labrador eyes as if to say "you've got to be kidding."

"That wouldn't work," Erin protested. "First of all, what is a double wedding? I never heard of that before. Second, you can't have a double wedding with someone who used to be your fiancée. Arthur would never go along with something like that."

"He's already gone along with it. You don't understand. They love the idea. You see it in old plays and novels. Plus it's anti-bourgeois, which appeals to them. They think of it as a big joke."

"But it's not a big joke to me. Besides, the hall is too small. I wanted a nice, little wedding."

"I know. I agree with you. But it sounds like they're thinking of an outdoor wedding in Bridgewater, in which case size doesn't matter. They think it would be fun with the foliage and all."

"You sound like you're thinking the same thing."

"I do kind of like that part. Not the double wedding so much, but fall and outdoors. Everybody loves the fall. And everyone else gets married in the spring. Also I don't see how we can both get married this fall in any other way. You can't have two weddings."

"It's so like her to think she has to have a wedding just because we're having one."

"Well, they were engaged first, and she says she was always thinking of a fall wedding."

"So why didn't she mention it until now?"

"I don't know. Draw your own conclusions. Still, it might be a good idea. Just think of how much money my parents and your parents would save. It would keep the peace with my sister. And that way we could get married and not have to wait."

"But what about Arthur? You really want to have a double wedding with someone who was actually engaged to me?"

"I don't mind, if you don't. I never really thought of him as your fiancée anyway."

"Oh, that's nice."

"I think it's more awkward for you than it is for me, to tell you the truth. It's not like I'm jealous of Arthur. Not at all. Or not anymore. But I'll be happy to tell her no, if you want me to."

"No, don't do that," Erin said with a sigh. "You are right. There can't be two weddings. We could never pull it off, and it's not fair to our families and friends. Let me think about it."

Erin was dubious for many reasons. For one thing, this was her wedding. She didn't particularly want it to share it with anyone, but especially with Grace, who could be a prima donna at times. This was unkind, but facts were facts. Grace would try to take over and run things and insist on being the center of attention.

Erin was ashamed of having such thoughts, but Jim agreed with her. She had the most to lose in such an arrangement. She was not forceful, except in the most important things. She would not speak up for what she wanted. Grace would walk all over her—unless he stepped in, which he promised to do. He would be her advocate. He would insist on her rights.

This reassured her a little. Grace had stolen her fiancée; she didn't want her stealing her wedding too. But it was Grace herself who won her over in the end. Jim told her Erin was reluctant and hinted at the reason. She understood. She still felt very guilty about everything that had happened. She wanted to make it up to her. She wasn't trying to be selfish by suggesting a double wedding. She was trying to come up with a solution.

So she went to see her. She began by apologizing profusely once again for the past and begging her forgiveness as if it had not already been given. She told her that she loved her and cherished her and wanted to be her friend. Erin was happy to assure her that she had already been forgiven, although she was embarrassed to be asked. There were tears. There was some laughter. It was quite a scene out there on the porch.

Grace promised—she swore with all her heart—to defer to Erin in all things. Erin had wonderful taste and she was sure she would be happy with whatever her new sister decided. She also told her how happy she was that she was marrying Jim. Everybody in the family felt the same way, even Eric. They were all crazy about Erin. They didn't understand why it had taken him so long.

It was impossible for someone with Erin's modesty and warm heart not to be won over by such a determined assault. She was happy to hear that Grace wanted her to take the lead. Not that she had any desire to lead, but she also didn't feel comfortable being forced to follow. She was impressed by the fact that Grace came to her in person. She could not be indifferent to the gesture. She was grateful for the open discussion.

She came around to the double wedding idea reluctantly. She talked to her mother about it. Amy saw the practical advantages, although she shared the same reservations. Neither she nor Jack had gotten over what happened with Arthur. They were still angry with him. Erin managed to soften her anger by assuring her that she never loved him and was glad when the engagement ended.

She told her mother something else. After the accident, her view of things had changed. Yes, the idea of a double wedding with Arthur and Grace was strange, impossible, but she felt calm about it. Things did not seem to trouble her as much anymore. In fact since her conversation with Grace she was beginning to see it in a positive light—maybe as an opportunity for healing.

Acceptance was what was needed at that point in their lives. She was marrying Jim; Grace was marrying Arthur. There was no point in resisting. It was better by far to accept the awkward reality and learn to live with it; or better yet, to embrace it, if at all possible. If her accident had taught her anything, it was that the hurts we cling to in this world are not important. No happiness can be found in the past. It can be found only in the pliable present.

Amy was amazed to hear such wisdom from her daughter. Not that she didn't think she was capable of it—she adored her daughter—but Erin's words were convicting. It may be hard to be corrected by one's offspring in matters of great importance, but in this case she was glad to embrace the good advice. She agreed with her completely. Both couples had a chance for happiness. It was time to do everything in their power to help them.

Besides, the idea of a double wedding with the Wilmots was kind of intriguing. Erin was right. It would save money and it could also be fun for the very reason that it was so unique. There was no one she would rather plan a double wedding with than her close friend Carolyn. She loved her and was sure the two families could overcome any differences that would inevitably throw themselves in the way.

Her husband was a little harder to convince. "She wants to have a double wedding with that creep?"

"He's not a creep. She explained everything to me. It was just not meant to be. She never loved him."

"I don't care. You don't do that unless you're a creep. If you don't love somebody, you man up and break off the engagement. You don't go running off with someone else without telling anybody. I mean he was right here in this very house acting like everything was normal while carrying on with the other one. That's just unbelievable to me."

"It's a little unbelievable to me, too. But we are talking about your daughter. This is what she wants. She seems to have made peace with it; I think we should try to as well."

"Still, it's weird. Only Grace would come up with a crazy idea like that."

He was not happy, but he was swayable. He knew Erin wanted to get married. He understood the thing with the other two being engaged first. Like everyone else, he was attracted by the economy. He did not relish the idea of shelling out $30,000 for a wedding, which his workmates told him was the minimum going rate. According to early reports, with two families pitching in and an outdoor venue it probably wasn't going to be more than $10,000 each. But most of all he wanted Erin to be happy. Those days in the hospital were the worst in his life. He would do anything for her. Even if it meant accommodating the two goofballs.

Grace *promised* to defer to Erin completely. She meant it with all her heart—at the time. Of course that wasn't quite the way it worked out. She had her own opinions about things. She didn't realize it until she started to focus on the details, which seemed innumerable. She was surprised to find that she had strong feelings about almost every one. There was the tent and the décor; there was the food; there was the wine and other drinks; there was the question of buffet or waiters; there was the band or DJ; there were truly weighty considerations, like the order of worship and number of attendants and flowers and photography and everything else. Erin didn't seem to be doing anything. She was focused on rehab. Grace had to resist the temptation to jump in and do it all herself.

Or rather, she *tried* to resist. She called Erin every time she had an idea, which was almost every day. The conversations went something like this: "What do you think about having the bridesmaids all wear different-colored gowns? I don't want it to be too much like a corporate wedding and everybody having to look alike and conform. I hate that, so homogenized. I want people to be able to express themselves. That way they'll feel more invested."

How was Erin supposed to respond to such a proposal? As framed, it was not just about mere color; it was about freedom and personal expression and who knows what else. It all sounded so very grand. But she was happy to have multicolored bridesmaids. She did not necessarily favor a more traditional approach, although she also did not share Grace's strong feelings about it.

This was the way it went with most of the decisions they made together. Grace had an "idea," and Erin was generally happy to go along with it. There were a few instances where she dug in—like when Grace wanted to have a sonnet read at the ceremony by her maid of honor; 116, as a matter of fact. Erin wanted to have the readings she loved, the traditional readings, and stood her ground. Grace caved, although she wasn't happy about it.

There were some rough spots and tense moments. There are likely to be in any wedding, and twice as likely in a double wedding. The ridiculously overblown American wedding culture made it impossible to avoid them. Jim was beginning to think Erin was right. They should have eloped. It would have been much easier. But in the end everything seemed to come together. Grace toned herself down. Perhaps she no longer felt anxious about her place.

One thing they had to work through was the question of Bob. He seemed like the obvious choice to be Jim's best man. Even Erin agreed, and she could barely stand him. But she did not see how it was possible because of Grace—and frankly, because of Arthur, although she was very delicate on this point. Grace's despoiler could not be in the wedding party. That seemed self-evident.

Jim agreed, but when he mentioned it to his sister she went ballistic. "Are you kidding me? You have to ask him. Did you forget about all the money he loaned you? You would have lost your house without that."

"And subsequently my shirt. But it just doesn't seem right. I don't want you to be unhappy at your own wedding."

"I won't be. I promise. I don't love him anymore. Far from it. I think I'm grown-up enough to see him again without losing my composure. And don't forget, I have talked to him since then. We managed to have a civil conversation."

"Are you sure? That whole thing was pretty rough."

"I am sure. I sort of see it from his side now. I'm not assigning blame anymore. It was just a crazy thing that happened. And I'm glad it happened. Otherwise I wouldn't have Anna."

"But to actually have him at the wedding. It seems a bit much."

"Why? It doesn't bother me. It shouldn't bother anyone else. The only people who know are our parents. What other people don't know won't hurt them."

"But Arthur…"

"I already talked to him. He agrees that Bob should be there."

"As my best man?"

"He might think *he* should be your best man. But he already has a job."

"So you're telling me he really doesn't mind, I mean with Anna there and everything."

"He doesn't. This is the twenty-first century. People don't get all hung up over things like that anymore."

Jim was amazed. Not about it being the twenty-first century; he was pretty sure he knew about that. He was amazed that Grace seemed to embrace the idea of Bob as best man. And Arthur too! He also couldn't believe they had talked about it. They must talk about everything. He was not as enlightened as they were, but there was no reason to object, especially against his own interests.

Erin was not surprised. She knew Arthur had very liberal ideas about such things. It was partly why she was glad she wasn't marrying him. She wondered if he could be as happy as Grace claimed. After all, there was the little matter of human nature. She had known Arthur to express very tolerant opinions about certain things that were not necessarily reflected in his behavior when the question became personal.

Still, she had no reason to doubt him, or Grace either. She did not have any objection to Bob being the best man, if it was not offensive to them. She did not like Bob, but Jim had certain ties and obligations that pre-existed their relationship. She felt fortunate that he liked her maid of honor, Christine. She had been involved in a wedding where this had not been the case, and it had caused problems, since the M.O.H. is deeply involved in arrangements.

There was no danger of Bob trying to insert himself into the arrangements, so she thought she was safe. She knew he liked her, which softened her resistance. On the whole, she agreed with Grace, especially when Jim told her about what Bob had done for him and the fact that he still owed him money. This information almost changed her opinion of him.

Jim called Bob the same day. "Hey! I've got a strange proposition for you. I'm wondering if you would be willing to be my best man. Oh, by the way—I'm getting married."

"What! I thought Arthur was the one getting married."

"He was having so much fun I decided to jump in. You can probably guess who it is."

"If it isn't Erin, I'm going to be pissed."

"Well, then, it seems this is your lucky day. We've been engaged for a couple of months."

"In that case I guess I don't have any choice. I'll have to be the best man. Someone has to protect her."

"But here's the strange part. It's going to be a double wedding. With Grace and Arthur."

"A double wedding! Cue the Mendelssohn. I'm not surprised. It's exactly the sort of thing Grace and Arthur would do."

"But I guess the question is how you feel about that. I mean, Arthur will be in the extended wedding party, as well as Grace, and then there's little Anna."

"Hail, hail, the gang's all here! Buttercup will have to sort it all out."

"No, but seriously—can you live with that?"

"If they can live with it, I guess I can. I'm not embarrassed about anything. I don't know how Arthur's going to feel about seeing me there."

"Apparently he doesn't have any problem with it. At least according to Grace."

"Well, there you go. It's just like him."

Jim told him about the accident. Bob was shocked. He couldn't believe they had come so close to losing Erin. He was happy Jim was marrying her. He didn't want him to marry anyone else. He was especially happy about the Kerry Morgan thing being over. He couldn't believe Jim didn't know what was going on between her and Brick. It was the first time he had doubted his intelligence. And the first time he was embarrassed to be his friend.

He asked what Jim had in mind for a bachelor party. Jim didn't have anything in mind. He suggested a music-listening party with Arthur and a couple of other old friends at the lake house. He had no interest in anything more elaborate or the kind of party Bob probably had in mind. He didn't want Bob to spend any money, especially when he still owed him money.

So that's exactly what they did. They had pizza. They had beer. They had fun. This was one area where Grace had no control over what they did, although she did seem to feel the need to express an opinion. She thought Bob could afford something more than a couple of cases of beer. Jim assured her he was happy with that.

XXXVIII

Wedding bells

ANYWAY THE DAY finally rolled around and it was a clear fall day, warmish for the season, and everyone was in a pretty good mood. Grace drove her brother crazy by arriving at the church half an hour late with her giggling bridesmaids while poor Erin wilted in the parlor. He managed to swallow his anger even after hearing the pre-wedding music for the third time. But then before he knew it the men were at their stations and the processional had begun; yes, the very one to which Bob had alluded.

Erin's modest little group of three bridesmaids, Megan plus two close friends, came up first, followed by Grace's flock of seven. It was quite a spectacle, all ten of them bunched up on the left side of the chancel and inclined to smile at the uniqueness of the double wedding. Then Erin came in. She was perfectly willing to go first and concede the spotlight to Grace. She did not want to be in the spotlight anyway. She was trying hard not to limp as she walked down the aisle, which suddenly seemed very long to her, packed with observers watching her uncertain gait.

At first Jim did not have the reaction he thought he was going to have when she started her long walk. In his mind he had pictured himself being overwhelmed with emotion and shedding a heartfelt tear to show what a great guy he was, etc. Nothing of the sort happened. He felt love, but there were no spontaneous tears. Maybe he prevented them by thinking about it too much.

But then she reached the chancel and paused for a moment. He realized what was going on—she was deliberating the safest way to negotiate the first step—with her good leg or the bad one. That was when he started to lose it. The pause did not last long. She bravely kept going. He was the only one who understood what was going through her mind. And this made it more poignant to him.

He did not know how he wound up being so fortunate. He knew he didn't deserve her. He knew he was unbelievably lucky to have her. He saw the future and the happiness that was possible with Erin. There was nothing he wanted more. The ceremony started, and then came the vows. His were not as polished or pretty as Arthur's, but they were heartfelt. He said some things he had not planned on saying, tender things. Erin looked surprised. Then she started to cry.

The double wedding was actually quite merry. The sheer novelty of it seemed to tickle the wedding party, the onlookers, and even the pastor, who could not help smiling broadly all the way through the service. Jim had feelings he didn't know he was going to have when his sister and Arthur exchanged vows. Grace looked radiant. He had been so worried about her. He loved her so much.

The ceremony was the highlight of the day, as far as he was concerned. Next came the interminable picture-taking. Jim hated having his picture taken. Unfortunately his sister didn't. The photo session went on and on while Grace and her entourage tried to outdo each other in contriving immortal Facebook poses. He was happy for them to have fun, but she was not thinking about Erin or the discomfort she was experiencing as she stood there patiently waiting her turn. Jim was aware, and it was difficult to keep his mouth shut.

After what seemed like forever they piled into the limousines and were on their way to the reception, where everyone had already arrived and had been waiting for over an hour. The warm fall morning turned into afternoon and there were clouds and the wind changed to the northwest and suddenly it wasn't so warm anymore. Carolyn had warned them about this. It can be rather chilly in the Litchfield Hills in October when the sun goes away.

Fortunately everyone was armed with jackets and sweaters and other things to stay warm. The rapidly dropping temperatures had one happy effect, as far as Jim was concerned—they led to an increase in the tempo of the festivities. Things that sometimes take forever at weddings didn't seem to take very long at all. It was all very crisp and efficient. Many of the standard features had been left out. For instance, there was no grand introduction. Grace and Erin figured everyone knew who they were.

The wedding parties sat down. It was like student body left— Grace's hearty horde was massed on one side of the head table, next to the band, which pushed Erin's modest retinue into the margins, in fact almost out of the tent. Jim did not realize how annoying this would be until it actually happened. His sister was literally hogging the stage.

Then another Grace-inspired oddity made itself evident. She insisted on having Anna's crib and a changing table set up behind them. Jim was aghast. It was one thing not to be cowed by public opinion; it was another thing to flaunt it openly. Grace seemed to be making a statement, but what kind of statement was she trying to make? That she was a good mother? Then why expose poor little Anna to the roar of the band? That she was a liberated female? Then why chain herself to the crib and changing table? Or maybe she wasn't making a statement at all.

Anna had not been fed in quite some time, so the first thing Grace did was to sit down in her place of honor with the baby on her lap and unbosom herself to the assembled revelers. Jim saw the expression on Mr. O'Connell's face and thought he was going to die. The feeding led to the predictable result. Anna began to vocalize. Grace jumped up and proceeded to change her on the spot. The crowd roared. Jim felt like crawling under the table.

He was dreading Bob's speech. Actually it was fine. Perhaps Bob realized it was not necessary to entertain the crowd with Grace doing her thing, or perhaps he felt subdued by having Grace and Anna and Arthur nearby. In any case he spoke without notes and kept his closing arguments delightfully short, expressing affection for the groom but especially for the bride, who he thought was the best person in the whole world. Then he remembered something and amended it to "one of the best people in the world."

It was very well done. Jim was relieved. The hardest thing about the whole wedding for him was Bob. If there was any awkwardness between him and Grace, they did not show it. They greeted each other cordially. Grace showed him Anna. He very sensibly declined an offer to hold her, claiming he had a little cold. Arthur smiled like a madman through the whole thing. Jim was amazed.

The only people who did not pretend to be happy about seeing Bob were his parents. Carolyn greeted him but not with her usual smiling face. Bill did not know what to do with himself. He could not believe Bob had even been invited to the wedding, let alone as best man. The ways of youth were unfathomable to him. At first he hung back and was disinclined to acknowledge his existence. But then his beloved daughter came to him with a smiling face.

"You're not going to be cross now, are you?"

"If you only knew how I'm feeling."

"I have a pretty good idea. But be kind and forgiving for my sake. It can be your wedding gift to me. I'll return the other one."

"You can't. It's cash." But he did soften. All he wanted that day was to make his children happy. He greeted Bob and managed to muster a crooked smile, although small talk was beyond him.

After that, Jim was able to relax and enjoy himself a little. The food was great, the band was fun, and everyone seemed to be having a good time in spite of the dropping temperatures. He did his duty and danced with his mother and Erin, although Erin's tolerance for dancing was limited. He was glad. That was enough dancing for him. Bob was a dancing fool. He even danced with Grace, briefly. Jim held his breath the whole time.

By mid-afternoon the sun was scraping the tops of the trees. The bonfire was lit and then was gone too soon. A chill was settling in; there would be a frost that night. People were starting to go home. Grace and Arthur and the attendants were still dancing, but Jim looked at Erin and they both agreed without having to say anything. They made one last circuit of the tables. They gave their parents a big hug. Mr. O'Connell shook Jim's hand and grunted "Welcome." It surprised him. It meant a lot.

An hour later they were changed and on their way to Bar Harbor. Seven hours on the road after an exhausting day! It was a bit much, but they wanted to spend the first morning of married life on Cadillac Mountain. That was the plan. They didn't mind the drive, not really. They were glad to be on the road. They hit a traffic jam in Massachusetts on 495, but other than that they reached their destination in good time. They went directly to the hotel and checked in.

In their room, Jim suddenly felt abashed. He had not thought too much about this part of the adventure. He had not thought about being alone in the bridal suite with Erin and all it implied. There had not been a great deal of physical contact between them during Erin's recovery. At first there couldn't be, and later on he was still afraid of hurting her. There were soft kisses, of course, soft and delicious, but that was about the extent of it.

Erin went into the bathroom. She wanted to shower after the long exhausting day. Jim wandered around the spacious room not knowing what to do with himself. Finally he flicked on the TV. It was a stupid thing to do on their wedding night, but he felt even stupider just sitting there. He couldn't find anything to watch. He felt funny watching sports. He wasn't going to watch CNN. He wound up watching *Raymond*—or rather looking at it, since he wasn't really paying attention to what was going on.

Erin emerged from the bathroom with pink skin, wearing a simple white cotton chemise. She put their things in the bureau and put the suitcases in the closet. He lost track of what she was doing. The next thing he knew she was coming to him. She smiled. It was a sort of a shy smile. He felt shy too.

She surprised him by turning and sitting on his lap. As she did he tried to shift to make a better landing place but wound up jostling her sore leg. He saw her conceal a grimace. The fact that she tried to conceal it filled him with emotion.

"Are you all right?"

"I'm fine. Don't worry about me. I want to tell you something. It used to bother me that you never kissed me."

"I think there's a possibility that I may kiss you now."

"All those years I used to think about it and wonder why you didn't."

"I was stupid. It's the only possible explanation."

"Were you not attracted to me?"

"Anyone would be attracted to you. I certainly was. So were all my friends. I wanted to kiss you. I just never tried because I didn't know where it was all going."

"You were holding out for something better."

"There isn't anything better. I don't want anyone but you."

She smiled at this. "Are you afraid of hurting me?"

"I guess I am. How did you know?"

"I can tell. Don't be afraid. I want you to hurt me."

"That sounds kinky."

"You know what I mean. I want you to love me. I don't want you to be afraid."

She kissed him. He kissed her back. This time he really meant it.

XXXIX

So happy together

AND...THEY LIVED happily ever after! Well, sort of. They went through the typical stuff all couples go through as they adjusted to each other. There may have been times when neither one of them ever wanted to see the other one again—we're just assuming, we don't know this for a fact—but they managed to sail right past those times without losing respect for each other, as all couples must do if they want to survive.

Jim did quite well at the agency, soon acquiring the lofty title of Creative Director, which, as anyone who has ever worked at a small agency knows, does not compensate for the lack of income and horrendous hours that go along with it. Later on he landed a job in an in-house agency for a company that couldn't afford Madison Avenue and knew how to be smart about advertising. Basically he became Henry Booth with a sense of humor.

Erin went back to work after they were married, until the first baby came, a girl, and then they figured out a way for her to stay home, since they were still living in Jim's modest cottage and he was doing pretty well. To tell the truth she did not mind staying home. She was a home manager and a mother, and that was a lot. It was enough for her, at least for now, although eventually she wanted to get back into nursing.

Grace and Arthur also did well. She went to Wellesley, which was close enough to Arthur's townhouse for commuting, and then to Harvard to study philosophy, where she wound up accumulating a Ph.D. along with some "very strange ideas," as her mother put it. They moved to New York when she received a teaching offer based on a paper she had published. Arthur gallantly followed her, since there happened to be a curator opening for him in the city that never sleeps. Little Anna grew up very pretty like her mother and headstrong too. She was not happy when her brother arrived.

As for her other headstrong parent—Bob—he worked hard and made a lot of money, which was a good thing because he definitely needed it. First he married a fellow lawyer, with whom he had a daughter. It didn't work out; they saw so little of each other that the marriage didn't so much break up as sublimate. Then there was the pretty ballerina who, to tell the truth, he started to see some time before the breakup with the other one.

She brought him two more children and wrecked her career in the process, which made her bitter. She turned elsewhere, possibly because Bob was never home, or because of the wildness of the world she inhabited, or both. Then there was the fascinating woman he met working with one of his clients who brought along three kids from a previous marriage and managed to hide her alcoholism and basic insanity until they were married. In the end he wound up with three families and a whole lot of alimony.

And Kerry? Jim made no effort to follow the exciting story of her life, but she did marry Brick Dancy and was wildly happy—the ideal Hollywood couple—nonstop tabloid candids—always smiling as children came along—until she wasn't. Somebody cheated on somebody else or vice-versa and there was a $150 million dollar breakup and she wound up with the heartthrob Kevin James. Naturally the press loved this marriage too, but it headed down the same unhappy road when Kevin was caught with some college girl or girls and Kerry threw him out. Jim lost track of her after that.

Meanwhile Jim and Erin were happily accumulating a family of their own. She wanted six and he wanted two; they compromised and had three. (Jim was never good at math.) They stayed in the cottage for a long time, five years, before finding something that was more suited to their growing family. They were sad to lose the lake but glad to lose the high taxes that went along with it.

They went to church together. Or she went and he followed. She even managed to recruit him into the choir. He had a pretty nice baritone and was flattered shamelessly by the female director, whose other two basses were, well, let's just say somewhat past their prime. Jim could read music, which was a big plus in a small choir. He even got nominated to sing a solo now and then.

It took Erin a long time before she started to feel like herself again. Years, as a matter of fact. And even then she had all sorts of lingering aches and pains that she never told Jim about. She became a fan of naproxen. Fortunately it never hurt her stomach. She never stopped rehabbing, never stopped doing the exercises, and eventually returned to something closer to full strength.

Walking was too difficult for her to become a pastime. She

could not ski with her bad leg, and was afraid to try skating again, although she had been pretty good at it at one time. She could swim, though, so Jim bought them a little motorboat that they took out on the lake. Erin discovered that she enjoyed fishing on beautiful summer days. Jim had to bait the hook, however.

Their kids, of course, were outstanding. So were everybody else's, and that was all right with them. The important thing was they had each other. It had been touch-and-go there for a while, but somehow everything worked out. They could not have been happier that it did.

THE END

ABOUT THE AUTHOR

Jay Trott is an author of essays and fiction who lives in the New Hampshire woods with his lovely wife Beth. They have four children and five grandchildren and enjoy long walks and good company, but don't like it when the bears molest their bird feeders.

www.ingramcontent.com/pod-product-compliance
Lightning Source LLC
LaVergne TN
LVHW041657060526
838201LV00043B/467